The story of Joseph[...] [...]ything in her novels. Born in a c[...] [...]e was one of ten children. Her pa[...] [...] worst in each other, and life was full of tragedy and hardship – but not without love and laughter. At the age of sixteen, Josephine met and married 'a caring and wonderful man', and had two sons. When the boys started school, she decided to go to college and eventually gained a place at Cambridge University, though was unable to take this up as it would have meant living away from home. However, she did go into teaching, while at the same time helping to renovate the derelict council house that was their home, coping with the problems caused by her mother's unhappy home life – and writing her first full-length novel. Not surprisingly, she then won the 'Superwoman of Great Britain' Award, for which her family had secretly entered her, and this coincided with the acceptance of her novel for publication.

Josephine gave up teaching in order to write full time. She says, 'I love writing, both recreating scenes and characters from my past, together with new storylines which mingle naturally with the old. I could never imagine a single day without writing, and it's been that way since as far back as I can remember.' Her previous novels of North Country life are all available from Headline and are immensely popular.

'Josephine Cox brings so much freshness to the plot, and the characters . . . Her fans will love this coming-of-age novel. So will many of the devotees of Cathering Cookson, desperate for a replacement' *Birmingham Post*

'Guaranteed to tug at the heartstrings of all hopeless romantics' *Sunday Post*

'Hailed quite rightly as a gifted writer in the tradition of Catherine Cookson . . .' *Manchester Evening News*

*By Josephine Cox*

# THE EMMA GRADY TRILOGY
Outcast
Alley Urchin
Vagabonds

## QUEENIE'S STORY
Her Father's Sins
Let Loose the Tigers

Angels Cry Sometimes
Whistledown Woman
Don't Cry Alone
Jessica's Girl
Nobody's Darling
Born to Serve
More Than Riches
A Little Badness
Living A Lie
The Devil You Know
A Time for Us
Cradle of Thorns
Miss You Forever
Love Me Or Leave Me
Tomorrow The World
The Gilded Cage
Somewhere, Someday
Rainbow Days
Looking Back
Let It Shine
The Woman Who Left
Jinnie
Bad Boy Jack

# JOSEPHINE COX

## Born to Serve

**headline**

First published in 1994 by
HEADLINE PUBLISHING GROUP

First published in paperback in 1994 by
HEADLINE PUBLISHING GROUP

This edition published in paperback in 2015 by
HEADLINE PUBLISHING GROUP

5

Cataloguing in Publication Data is available from the British Library

ISBN 978 1 4722 3066 9

Typeset in Times by Avon DataSet Ltd, Bidford-on-Avon, Warwickshire

Printed and bound in the UK by Clays Ltd, St Ives plc

HEADLINE PUBLISHING GROUP
An Hachette UK Company
Carmelite House
50 Victoria Embankment
London EC4Y 0DZ

www.headline.co.uk
www.hachette.co.uk

For the darling ladies in the tea-rooms at Hyde market place.

I won't forget the lovely things you said. And I wish you good health and happiness for many, many years to come.

God bless.

# *Contents*

# Contents

# Part One

## 1918

## SINS

# Chapter One

'*I could take him away from you any time I wanted!*' Claudia Marshall slithered out of her undergarment and unashamedly regarded herself in the mirror. What she saw was a vision of beauty; a tall perfectly proportioned figure, with pert white breasts and long slender legs. Her straight brown hair flowed over her shoulders and her pale grey eyes glinted with malice as they stared beyond her own reflection to that of the maid.

Jenny Dickens boldly met the other young woman's taunting gaze. She was a pretty young thing, with short fair hair and soft blue eyes that were easily given to smiling. But she wasn't smiling now. In fact, her cheeks were pink with anger and her fists were clenched by her sides.

Seeing the effect her cruel words were having, Claudia swung round and laughed aloud. 'Poor Jenny,' she cooed sweetly. 'So pleased with herself because at last she's got a man who's promised to marry her. And not before time, is it? I mean, you're five years older than me, aren't you? And at twenty-three you're almost left on the shelf.'

With her hands on her hips, she came across the room to stand before the other young woman. 'Look at me,' she invited, brazenly twirling about to display her magnificent nakedness. 'Ask yourself how any man could possibly resist me.'

When Jenny remained still and silent, Claudia was enraged. 'He might be *your* sweetheart, you little fool!' she said in a cutting voice, 'but he's *mine* for the taking. All I have to do is crook my little finger and he'll come running. I've seen him watching me. And if you weren't so stupid, you'd know he can't wait to bed me.'

In fact, the opposite was true. Claudia had tried everything she could think of to make Frank Winfield notice her but he was irritatingly aloof. Now, thinking of his strong broad shoulders and earthy good looks, she purred with pleasure at the idea. 'That ring on your finger won't mean anything if I decide to have him,' she threatened with a wicked smile. 'And I'm bored. There's no telling *what* I'll do when I'm bored!'

She enjoyed being cruel. It gave her a sense of power. Besides, she had a deep down yearning for Jenny's young man, and it would be so good to humble this proud creature who had the nerve to look at her as though she was something that had just crawled out from under a stone. 'Don't stare at me like that,' she warned, 'or I'll have you dismissed.' After all, Jenny Dickens was only a servant in her father's house.

Knowing that she was out of her depth, and aware that to antagonise this arrogant young woman was to jeopardise her position in this household, Jenny lowered her gaze.

'That's better. Now you can apologise.' With obvious relish, she waited for Jenny to speak.

It took an effort of will for Jenny not to say exactly what was on her mind or she might have told the arrogant Claudia what a cheap and nasty trollop she was, and that Frank himself had said with disgust how there were few male visitors to this house whom she hadn't enticed into her bed. 'It's her poor mother I feel sorry for,' he'd said. 'Elizabeth Marshall is a fine lady and shouldn't be cursed with a daughter who's no better than a whore on the streets.'

'Well, I'm waiting!' Claudia's icy voice cut through Jenny's thoughts. 'An apology, I said.'

Taking a deep breath, Jenny raised her clear blue eyes and looked the young woman in the face. In a firm voice she said, 'Sorry, miss.' But what she thought was: You're a shame and a disgrace, Claudia Marshall, and it's *you* who should be apologising to *me*.

Claudia was not altogether satisfied, for she detected a rebellious note in Jenny's voice. However, she had done what she set out to do, and that was to cause turmoil. It was plain from the pained and defiant look in those blue eyes that Jenny was upset by this little episode. 'Help me dress, then you can go,' snapped Claudia impatiently. 'After that you had better keep out of my way for the rest of the day.'

Keeping her thoughts to herself, Jenny gathered the discarded silk slip from the carpet and placed it on the chair ready for the wash. She was burning with anger at Claudia's wanton behaviour; downstairs the wash-tub was already bursting at the seams, and it went against the grain to fill it with clothes that were hardly used.

Half an hour later, at precisely ten o'clock, Jenny laid the silver-backed hairbrush on the dressing-table and stepped away. Claudia remained seated on the stool, admiring her long sweep of brown hair that shone from Jenny's vigorous brushing. 'I always look lovely in this dress, don't you think?' she remarked, cocking her head to one side and examining the emerald green dress with its loose cowl neck and scalloped sleeves. She stood up and ran her two hands over the smooth material, her fingers sensuously following the lines from the straight skirt to the hem, which fell just below her knees. 'You think I wear my clothes too short, don't you?' she demanded when Jenny looked away in disgust.

'It isn't for me to say, miss.'

'Too damned right it isn't!' Flicking her hair back from her face, Claudia glared at Jenny with hatred. 'Get out!' she spat.

Without another word, Jenny thankfully departed. 'Little cow!' she muttered as she went down the stairs. 'Mark my words, Miss High and Mighty, one of these days you'll get your comeuppance.' Only that fervent hope, and thoughts of kindly Mrs Marshall, persuaded Jenny to remain in this house.

As she came to the bottom of the stairs, the bell above the front door clanged loudly. It was the postman. Hurrying across the wood-panelled hallway, Jenny swung the great door open. Bill Saxon was a local man with a splendid physique and an attractive smile, but few brains. 'Miss Claudia not up yet?' he asked, withholding the letter as though he might snatch the opportunity to hand it to the young mistress herself. She had often given him the glad eye but as yet he hadn't found full favour with her, though he knew one or two who had. And from their graphic descriptions, he couldn't wait to get his share.

Snatching the letter from his hand, Jenny told him sharply, 'You'd do well to mind your own wife instead of making eyes at other women. Shame on you, Bill Saxon.' With that, she closed the door in his face. 'Better to be insulted by me than ruined by *her*,' she told his departing footsteps.

Outside, Bill paused and turned around to look at the house. At one time the dwelling had belonged to the local squire, but he was long gone. It was nearly five years now since the Marshalls had moved here from London; 1914, the same year war started. It was said that Mr Marshall was a high-ranking officer in the forces. There had been certain rumours since the war had ended, unkindly whispers that spoke of his having deserted his wife and daughter. It was true that folk expected to see him round these parts once the war was at an end, but there had as yet been no sighting of him.

It was also said that he had fallen on hard times and lost the fortune his father left him. And that was why there were now only two servants at the big house, Jenny and a scullery girl. But rumours were rumours, and often they came to nothing.

However, it *was* true that he had returned from the fighting some two years ago, a hero but badly wounded. Mrs Marshall herself had told that to the vicar's wife, and it was borne out by the letters which various postmen had delivered, because on the backs of the earlier ones was written the address of a certain military hospital. The impressive handwriting on the front was very striking and bespoke a man of authority. Nowadays the letters were fewer and there was no hospital return address. The only clue to Mr Marshall's whereabouts was a London postmark.

'It's a funny kettle o' fish and that's a fact,' the postman muttered. He wondered whether Mr Marshall was quietly planning on taking the family back to London. He hoped not. At least, not yet. He chuckled, glancing again at the proud house. Certainly Mr Marshall couldn't have done better than to fetch his family here. This was beautiful, peaceful countryside, and Tall Gables was unquestionably the best house in the village of Woburn Sands, perhaps the finest in the whole of Bedfordshire.

It was a grand place, with high black and white wooden gables and a look of splendour about it. The Marshalls owned land all around this beautiful Tudor place, with more than fifteen acres of open fields extending beyond. Sometimes, in the early hours, the magnificent Claudia could be seen astride that big bay stallion of hers, driving it mercilessly over the rough ground. Every time he'd seen her whipping that horse and squeezing it with her legs, he'd longed for it to be him beneath her. But it never was.

As he prepared to move away, his attention was attracted by someone at an upstairs window. It was her! She smiled at him. Astonished, he waved back. Happen she was coming to fancy

7

him after all. By! If he got a chance to bed her, he wouldn't turn it down, no matter *what* Jenny Dickens said. Besides he knew Jenny was a good sort and would never tell tales. And, what his wife didn't know couldn't hurt her.

As he went away, merrily whistling, it was a pity he didn't hear Claudia's cruel laughter. But it was *he* who would have the last laugh, for at some time in the future, and because of unfortunate circumstances, Bill Saxon would get his just rewards.

'I've got a feeling this won't be an easy day,' Jenny told herself as she hurried towards the drawing room with the letter. Thanks to Claudia, the morning was nearly gone and she was behind with her work. Mrs Marshall would be wanting her tea and biscuits, young Meg still hadn't turned up, the washing was soaking in the tub, the potatoes weren't peeled, and there was a whole multitude of errands to be run. Thank God for Frank, who had offered to fetch her main supplies on his way back from the blacksmith.

The thought of seeing him across the kitchen table, when the two of them could sit and have a quiet chat, brought a smile to her pretty face. He'd be back from Bedford by midday, rightfully expecting a bite to eat. 'And my own tongue's hanging out for a cup of tea!' she muttered, tapping on the drawing-room door with unusual vigour.

'Yes?' Elizabeth Marshall's voice enquired.

Gingerly, Jenny pushed open the door. 'There's a letter for you, Mrs Marshall,' she said, coming into the room.

Elizabeth was seated in the tall-backed chair to the left of the firegrate. 'Thank you, dear,' she said, looking up with a warm but weary smile. When the letter was put on the low table beside her, she glanced at it and the smile faded from her face. A troubled frown creased her pale forehead as she recognised the handwriting.

Charles was due to come home tomorrow, and so she was not expecting a letter from him. She couldn't hide her despair as she imagined the contents. Her hands rose to cover her eyes before, with trembling fingers, she took the letter and pressed it close to her breast. 'Oh, Charles,' she murmured forlornly.

'Are you all right, ma'am?' Jenny had seen the colour drain from Elizabeth's face, and was genuinely concerned.

At once Elizabeth regretted showing even the smallest sign of emotion before the perceptive maid. In her usual forthright manner she asked, 'Is my daughter out of bed?' Slipping the letter into her skirt pocket, she waited for Jenny's response. At forty-two years of age, Elizabeth Marshall was some three years older than her husband. She was a handsome woman, small and slim, with masses of rich auburn hair and vivid green eyes. She was known hereabouts as a warm and gentle person, a 'deep thinker' who bore her troubles with quiet dignity.

'I've just this minute left Miss Claudia,' Jenny replied. 'She had her breakfast in bed and now she's washed and dressed. I'm sure she'll be down any minute.'

Elizabeth sprang out of the chair. 'Oh, Jenny!' She clenched her fists. 'I gave instructions that she was *not* to have her breakfast in bed. If she can't come down in the morning and sit at the table with me, then she must go without.'

'Yes, ma'am.' Jenny was reluctant to reveal how Claudia had threatened to 'turn this house inside out' if her breakfast wasn't taken to her room. But the truth must have betrayed itself in Jenny's pretty face, because now Elizabeth's green eyes were studying her hard.

'I understand,' she said presently. Her voice was soft and forgiving. 'And I'm sorry she's so difficult.' She looked away and her spirits fell as she remembered the letter in her pocket. So many letters. So much disappointment. Suddenly she felt Jenny's sympathy and it shamed her. When she looked up again she was smiling, beaming at Jenny as though she hadn't a care in the world. 'I know you have a great deal to do, so I won't keep you,' she said brightly. 'If you see Claudia before I do, would you ask her to come and see me?'

'Of course, ma'am.'

'And you are not to serve her breakfast in bed again. Not under *any* circumstances.' She smiled knowingly. 'Not even if she threatens to burn the house down.'

Jenny's smile was equally knowing. 'Very well.'

'Has Meg arrived?'

'Not yet.'

'Then *Claudia* must help with the housework.'

Jenny was speechless for a moment, unsure whether she'd heard right. Quickly recovering herself, she said in a firm voice, 'I'm sure that really won't be necessary, ma'am.' She was horrified at the thought of Claudia being made to work alongside her. What! It would be unbearable. 'Meg will turn up soon, I'm certain. I can manage 'til then,' she frantically assured her mistress.

'Nonsense. You're shockingly overworked as it is.' Elizabeth regretted having to dismiss the cook and house-keeper recently, but financial uncertainty had given her little option. More than once she had given thanks for Jenny but it hurt Elizabeth to think that this fine young woman should be saddled with so much responsibility, though she did seem to thrive on it and never complained. If only her own daughter had been blessed with the smallest part of Jenny's admirable qualities, there might be hope for her. As it was, she had shown herself to be bone idle and too full of her own importance. Some of the blame for that must lie with her father. He had treated that young madam as though she was royalty itself, and now he had created a monster. 'If Meg isn't here within the hour, you must inform me.' She seated herself in the chair, a sign for Jenny to leave her alone.

Stunned at the idea of Claudia's reaction to her mother's unthinkable suggestion, Jenny quickly departed, heartily praying that Meg would soon show her face. 'I'd best get a move on and see all the work done,' she told herself, 'or there'll be murder in this house!' The thought made her shiver. *It was almost as though she had felt a premonition.*

No sooner had Jenny cleared the dining-room table and set about the washing-up, than she heard the familiar clip-clop of hooves outside in the yard. Frank! Standing on tiptoes, she could see out of the kitchen window, and there he was. Her heart leapt with joy as she followed his every move. In that moment he saw her there and gave a cheeky, charming wink.

Frank made a fine figure of a man as he manoeuvred the horse and wagon into the cobbled yard. Though the month was December, the sun was shining down. His thick mop of fair hair and warm brown eyes glinted, and his strong features broke into a wide smile as he jumped down on the cobbles, his loving gaze fixed on Jenny's face and his arms open to her. Frank Winfield was twenty-four years old, mature and reliable. A man among men, he worked close to the earth and was part of nature itself. He was rugged and straight, proud yet humble. And Jenny adored him.

Wiping the suds from her arms, she sped across the kitchen, up the stairs and out through the back door. He was about to unload the wagon when she ran full pelt into his arms. 'I thought you'd never get back,' she cried. When he swung her round in his embrace, she laughed with sheer pleasure. And when he pressed his lips to hers, she clung to him as though she would never let him go. She hadn't forgotten what Claudia had said: '*I could take him away from you any time I wanted.*' Suddenly her happiness was cruelly curtailed.

'Well now! If that's the kind of welcome I get when I fetch

your supplies, I'd best do it more often.' Frank laughed. He had not seen the dark shadow pass over her bright blue eyes.

'Did you get everything?' she wanted to know. Going to the front of the wagon, she stroked the horse's long soft face. Not too long since there had been four work-horses. Now there was only one.

'Are you saying I haven't done the job right?' he asked with a twinkle in his eye. When she laughed, he suggested, 'What say you get away in and put the kettle on for a thirsty man while I load this little lot into the pantry?' No sooner had the words left him than she was on her way. He watched her pretty trim figure until it disappeared into the house. 'Aw, Jenny lass, yer a real beauty and it won't be long before I make an honest woman of you,' he promised lovingly.

Soon his voice was raised in a merry Irish ditty as he finished the unloading. His father had been Irish, but his mother was born within the sound of London's Bow bells. Folks said he had his daddy's beautiful singing voice and winning ways, and was blessed with his mammy's deep love of life. His parents were long gone now and, like Jenny, who had fled a brutal father, he was alone in the world.

He sang as he put the horse into its stable. He sang all the while he loaded the goods into the pantry, and was still softly singing when he came into the kitchen. Pausing at the door, he sniffed the air. 'By! Something smells good,' he declared, going to Jenny and wrapping his strong arms round her waist. Lifting her clear off her feet, he kissed her full on the mouth. 'What else could any man want?' he asked. 'But a grand-looking lass who can fill a kitchen with delicious smells to turn a man's stomach . . . then greet him with a kiss exciting enough to turn his happy heart?'

As always when he flattered her with such blarney, Jenny's face went all shades of pink. 'Away with you, Frank Winfield!'

she told him with a girlish giggle. 'You're only after the scones I'm baking for tea.'

Hugging her harder, he whispered in her ear, 'I can promise that ain't *all* I'm after.'

Laughing, she pushed him away. 'Well, one small scone is all you're going to get,' she said. 'And you can think yourself lucky. Happen when the shortage is over and the shops are stacked with good food, I might let you have *two*.'

'Jaysus, but yer a cruel, heartless woman,' he groaned. With a face that told of tragedy, he dropped into a chair and, leaning his arms on the table, looked up at her with soulful brown eyes. 'Have you no pity at all?' he asked in a sorry voice. 'And here's me in terrible agony after lifting them heavy groceries.' He rubbed at his shoulder and winced with pain. Then, when she seemed unsure as to whether he was play-acting, he burst out laughing and she threw the wet dish-cloth at him.

In no time at all, the two of them were seated at the table with a fresh baked scone and a steaming mug of tea before them. 'Five minutes,' Jenny told him in a stern voice, 'then I've to get back to my work. Mrs Marshall's threatened to send Claudia down to help me, so I've to get it all done before that lazy article decides she's had enough of admiring herself in the mirror.' Her blue eyes rolled heavenwards. 'Dear God! Can you imagine *that one* up to her armpits in potato peelings?'

The idea brought a smile to his face. 'Heaven forbid,' he remarked. Then he grew serious. 'Did Mrs Marshall really say that she would get Claudia to help with the housework?'

'She did.'

He shook his head and thoughtfully sipped his tea before saying in a hushed voice, 'By! Things must be going from bad to worse.'

'She had a letter this morning.'

'Oh?'

Jenny took her time buttering a scone. She didn't like to discuss the family's affairs, although Frank would never repeat anything she told him. The butter melted away and she took a bite. Presently she revealed, 'Judging by the writing, I reckon it was from Mr Marshall.'

Having finished his tea and scone, Frank collected his plate and mug and carried them to the sink where he put them into the sudsy water. 'I suppose that means he won't be coming home tomorrow? That's a shame.' He turned to face Jenny. Taking out both pipe and baccy from his coat pocket, he bit the pipe between his teeth and proceeded to pack it. 'She'll be disappointed and no mistake.'

Jenny brought her own cup and plate and sank them in the bowl. 'What's going to become of us?' she asked. Lately, there were things going on here she daren't think about.

Absent-mindedly taking the tea cloth and proceeding to wipe the dishes which Jenny put on the drainer, Frank thought for a moment, then puffed hard at his pipe and was lost in a billow of sweet-smelling smoke. After a while he answered in a sombre voice, 'There'll be trouble, I reckon.'

Jenny swung round, her bright blue eyes big with surprise. 'What do you mean?'

'Well, lass, think of it,' he prompted her. 'The war's over . . . armistice was signed on the eleventh of November, more than six weeks back. Them as fought and were left able like myself, thank God, are coming home and trying to pick up their ordinary lives. Even them as were wounded are beginning to return from France, determined to forget what they've been through.' He bowed his head. 'But I dare say not all of 'em will make it. It's especially hard for some.'

'You're getting at Mr Marshall, aren't you?'

'No, sweetheart. I'm not "getting at" him. He's a good man. When I could find no work, he was quick to set me on here. I'll always be thankful for that.' His smile was wonderful. 'After all, if I hadn't come to work here, I would never have met you.'

She came to him then and they embraced in poignant silence; Jenny thinking how empty her life would be without him, and Frank wondering whether the officer who had seen his men through bad times would ever be well again. 'Do you think he'll come home soon?' asked Jenny, as though reading his thoughts.

He shrugged his shoulders. 'Who knows? No man can easily shake off the horrors of war.'

Even now, Frank would wake in the night, sweating and terrified, thinking himself trapped in a darkened trench with the awful sounds of killing echoing from all sides, and the bodies of his friends rotting beside him. 'Captain Marshall was badly wounded. It takes time.' Suddenly the carnage was too alive in his mind. Gently he pushed her away. 'We'd best get on, lass. There's a deal to do.' When she looked up at him, he kissed her tenderly on the mouth. 'If you're not careful you'll have Claudia finishing that washing-up for you.' His smile widened, then it became a soft laugh. 'Go on,' he told her, making for the door. 'I'll see you later, eh?'

Before he went, she had to voice what was on her mind. 'You don't think he'll *ever* come home, do you?'

He shook his head. 'I don't know, and that's the truth.'

'If he doesn't come home, do you think the family will move back to London?' Suddenly she was afraid for the future. 'If they do, we'll be out of work.'

He came to her in a stride and, placing his two hands on her shoulders, said in a firm voice, 'I've told you before, you're not to worry your pretty head about such things. We'll cross that bridge if we ever get to it. All right?'

She gave no answer and he knew she was not altogether appeased. Feeling the need to lighten her mood, he asked, 'Do you want me to call at Meg's house and find out what's keeping her?'

'No. She'll be along, I'm sure. Being late is becoming a habit with her.'

'Then you'll have to speak sharply to her.' His mischievous smile belied his true feelings. 'Unless you want Mrs Marshall to give the job to Claudia?'

'If that's all the comfort you can give me, then you'd best take your leave,' she told him, but she was sorry when he did.

A short time later, the kitchen door opened to admit a plump young girl with flyaway dark hair and small frightened eyes. 'I'm sorry I'm late,' she moaned in a breathless voice, 'only me mam and dad were fighting all night and I didn't get a wink of sleep.' She slung her coat off and hung it in the pantry. 'I'm ever so sorry,' she kept saying over and over.

Coming out of the pantry, she presented herself to Jenny who had finished the washing-up and was on her knees at the sink cupboard. Without immediately answering the girl, she took out the box which contained the polishing materials, then she closed the doors and scrambled to her feet, with the box in her hand. 'Oh, Meg!' she said, shaking her head. 'That's the best excuse yet.' Everyone knew how devoted Meg's parents were to each other.

'It's true. Honest to God!' she cried. And for a minute Jenny thought the girl was going to burst into tears.

'We'll talk about it later,' she said. 'Right now, the dining room needs polishing out.' She thrust the box of polishing rags and such into Meg's hands. 'You'd best be quick,' she warned, 'or we'll not get through it all before this time tomorrow.'

'But I can't polish 'til I've emptied the grate and laid the fire.'

'I've done that.'

'The breakfast things?'

'I've already cleared them away.'

'Oh. And what about the bedrooms?'

Jenny was rapidly losing patience. 'No, I'm sorry, but all I've managed to do since getting out of bed at five o'clock this morning is clean my own room, cook and serve breakfast, taking her ladyship's up to her room, clean out the drawing-room grate and light the fire there. And I've cleaned and prepared the grate in the dining room, and delivered a letter to Mrs Marshall. I've washed the breakfast things and scrubbed the kitchen floor too. Now! Do you think you could do what you should have done hours ago? After that, we might just get the bedrooms done before it's time to serve lunch.'

One look at Jenny's flustered face told the girl she had better make herself scarce. While she herself had been lazing in bed, dreaming of her new boyfriend, it was plain that Jenny had been working her fingers to the bone. 'I'll be quick as I can,' she promised. Without further ado, she clutched the box to her and went smartly out of the room, leaving Jenny flushed with shame for having been so sharp.

Hunched in her chair with the letter crushed in her hand, Elizabeth looked a dejected figure. 'What's happening to us, Charles?' she murmured. Everything was changing so quickly, and for the first time in her life Elizabeth Marshall was afraid. 'I don't want to lose you,' she whispered, her quiet voice betraying her fears. 'I want things to go on the way they were . . . before.' She thought of the splendid man who had gone to war, and pictured the sorry creature who had lain in a hospital bed all those agonising months. Then there was the other man, one who appeared to have lost all sense of direction, a stranger who had found every excuse under the sun not to come home to his family. Three men. Not the same. Never again the same. It was torture to her.

When she first opened the envelope and tore out the letter, she

17

had prayed her suspicions were wrong. Now, with the opening words written on her heart, she couldn't bear to read past those first two lines. They told her all she needed to know.

For a while she just sat there, staring, her face set like stone. Then, at the sound of someone's footsteps approaching, she stiffened and sat upright. 'Claudia!' However unpleasant, the girl would have to be told.

The footsteps came closer, striking the tiled hallway with sharp angry clicks. Elizabeth's hand flew to her throat in dismay. Hurriedly, she wiped her eyes and nervously straightened her dress. 'Don't let her see your weakness,' she muttered. She knew instinctively that Claudia would tear her to shreds if she ever thought herself the stronger of the two. Lately, she had seen a side to her daughter that was deeply disturbing.

Forcing the ghost of a smile to her face, Elizabeth rose from her chair and thrust the letter deep in her pocket. Afterwards she went to the fireplace where she picked up the poker and feverishly prodded the coals. She felt unusually cold, surprised to find herself shivering.

She had only just replaced the poker, when the door burst open and in rushed her daughter. She remained at the door for a moment; Elizabeth couldn't help but think what a strikingly lovely creature Claudia was, with her gleaming brown hair tumbling over her shoulders, and wicked elfin face. Her long slim fingers curled and uncurled around the door-knob as she boldly regarded her mother through suspicious grey eyes. 'You're hiding something, aren't you?' she asked in an aggressive voice. 'I know there was a letter,' she continued, scowling as she entered the room and closed the door behind her. 'I saw it being delivered.' Her hard eyes went from her mother to the table, then to the fire. 'What have you done with it?'

Elizabeth was not intimidated. With equal boldness she faced her daughter. 'Explain yourself,' she demanded. As always, she felt the confrontation with her daughter was a test of her strength, and she must not be seen to be afraid.

'You know what I mean,' Claudia retorted angrily. 'I know you've had a letter from Father, and I think you've burned it.'

'Oh? And why would I burn it?'

'To keep me from seeing it.'

Elizabeth kept her waiting. There were times when she could have taken that brazen young woman and shaken her by the throat. 'You're right about one thing. There *was* a letter from your father.'

'I knew it!' Claudia's smile was triumphant.

'When you know what it says, you may not be so pleased.'

Something in her mother's tone made Claudia think. For many long months now she had waited patiently for her beloved father to return, until at last he had sent news some weeks ago that he was arriving home on 29 December, in time for New Year. Today was 28 December. So why should he be writing, when he could tell them everything tomorrow? 'What are you trying to say?' Her hard grey eyes froze with anger.

Just for a brief moment Elizabeth's heart went out to her daughter. Charles was her father and she idolised him, but he had hurt her too. 'Your father isn't coming home for the New Year.'

'I don't believe you! You're a liar. Why should I believe anything you say? You tell me that we have less money to live on, and that we have to cut down on everything. You've dismissed all the servants except that stupid scullery girl and that awful Jenny Dickens. I want my own personal maid back! If things aren't rectified, I shall make it my business to let Father know what you're up to. I don't suppose he knows anything of what you're doing. You're making my life a misery with your penny-pinching. I want a new saddle for the hunter but I'm denied even that. And I haven't had a new dress in months.'

'We can't afford to indulge your whims and fancies any longer. There isn't the money.'

'We've *always* had money.'

'There's been a war. Things change.'

'I still think you're doing it all behind Father's back. When I tell him, he'll be furious. And you can be sure I will tell him how you schemed to keep us apart all this time.'

Elizabeth forced herself to make allowances. With calm deliberation she plucked the letter from her pocket and held it out. 'Parts of it were not meant for your eyes, but it might be as well if you read it for yourself. Everything I've told you is the truth. This letter will bear me out.' It was also bound to reveal things which Claudia would be shocked to hear.

In a sudden movement that took Elizabeth completely by surprise, Claudia sprang forward and snatched the letter from her. With a choked cry she flung it into the open fireplace. 'You're a liar!' she shouted, swinging away to run from the room. 'And I won't listen to you!'

In an instant, Elizabeth retrieved the letter before the flames could devour it. Quickly she straightened the crumpled paper in her hands and proceeded to read aloud. Her soft determined voice caused Claudia to pause at the door where she remained with face turned away and eyes tightly shut until the last word was spoken:

'My dearest Elizabeth,
'Writing this letter was not an easy thing to do.
Forgive me, but I can't return home. Not yet. I intend to
remain here at my London club for a while longer.
'After all that has happened, rest assured that my
affection for you has not changed. You are my wife, and
I know how my continued absence must be heartbreak to
you. But I know you will understand. I so much *want* to
come home, and I will, but there is much for me to think

about. Before I can resume a normal life, I must resolve the personal problems that haunt me.

'Added to which, our financial security is of great concern to me. In spite of all my efforts, things have gone from bad to worse. The aftermath of war has struck deep at the heart of our economy. There is a growing sense of uneasiness in the City and a loss of old markets. The disruption is far reaching and, for all our sakes, I must keep a close eye on the holdings left to me by my father.

'I know I have let you down in many ways and ask your forgiveness. Before all of this, we had a good marriage. I pray you will remember that. Meanwhile, please explain to Claudia. It would be wiser if I did not see her yet. She does have a tendency to ask awkward questions. If she is finding it hard to go without her little luxuries, I'm afraid the fault is mine. It seems I may have spoiled the goodness out of her. I hope you can find it in your heart to forgive me,

'Yours, Charles . . .'

When the last word was spoken, a bitter silence descended. For what seemed an age neither of the women moved. Elizabeth was the first to speak. 'I know how much you were looking forward to his homecoming, and I'm truly sorry.' She did not regret that Claudia had learned a few home truths, although she doubted her daughter would be a better person for knowing them.

'You're not sorry!' Claudia slewed round to accuse her mother. 'It's *your* fault that I haven't seen him in almost a year. When he was wounded, I could have gone to France with you but you refused. Then, when he was brought back to London, you refused to take me again. You deliberately kept us apart, and I know why. YOU'RE JEALOUS! You've always hated it because

21

he loves me more than he's ever loved you. That's why you don't want me seeing him!'

'Talk sense, Claudia. The reason I wouldn't take you to France was because your father expressly forbade it. He didn't want you to visit him in that hospital.' Her own memories of that sad place had haunted her ever since. Good brave men had been horribly mutilated, and young fresh-faced boys were dying all around. Charles was gaunt and desperately ill. It was a shocking experience that she must carry to the end of her days. 'It was right that you were kept away.' It was also true that Charles idolised his daughter, but it was Claudia's love for him that bordered on obsession. That was why his prolonged absence was particularly hard for her to bear.

'And why was I not allowed to see him when he was brought back to London?'

'For the same reason. Your father was not recovered enough. It was his wish that you be kept away.'

'I only have your word for that.'

'It's the truth.'

'And why am I *still* kept from him? He's been out of the hospital for nearly six months, and you keep fobbing me off with lies . . . telling me he's coming home, when you know he isn't. Lies! Always lies!'

'How can you say that? You read his last letter. I too believed him when he said he would be home for the New Year.'

Claudia was crying now, bitter angry tears that burned her face and fuelled the hatred inside her. 'I don't believe anything you say. And I don't believe what you've just read. My father would *never* say those unkind things about me.'

'He didn't mean to be unkind.'

'How do I know that my father wrote that letter? Or any of them? Perhaps you wrote them? I wouldn't put it past you. You've always been jealous of the way he dotes on me.'

22

'You don't know what you're saying.'

'Oh yes, I do! And you won't keep us apart any longer because I'm going to London. I'll find out once and for all why he doesn't want to come home.' A wicked thought occurred to her. 'Have you got a lover? Is that why you don't want him home? Oh, of course, I see it all now. It's that gentleman farmer who owns the land adjoining ours. I've seen you talking and laughing with him in the fields.'

Elizabeth was visibly shocked. 'You're a wicked, evil-minded girl. You know very well that Jacob Laing is a lonely old man who likes to pass the time of day.' In fact he had become a dear friend, but that was all.

At last Claudia had found a way to pierce her mother's armour, and she wasn't about to let go. 'Not such an old man, Mother. On the contrary, he's quite tall and handsome, even if he does have grey hair. Oh, I see it all now. Father's found out, hasn't he?' Claudia was well aware that Jacob was nothing more than a friendly neighbour, but she was delighting in goading this gentle woman. 'What was it Father said in that letter . . . "After all that has happened, rest assured that my affection for you has not changed"?'

'Your father was referring to the war, and his own difficulties in coming to terms with it.'

Claudia laughed and shook her head. 'No. There's more to it than that, and I mean to find out. I can see now that you're not the puritan you would have people believe. You once said I had the heart of a whore. Well, now I know who I take after!'

'GET OUT!' Elizabeth had seen the depravity of her own daughter many times before, but she had never known such evil as she saw in her face at that moment.

'Oh, I'll go. But you haven't heard the last of this, Mother dear.' With those words, Claudia stormed out of the room.

With a heavy heart, Elizabeth read the letter through once

more. It still told her the same thing. Charles was not coming home. Perhaps he would *never* come home. And now there was something else for her to worry about. It seemed their money troubles had become an even greater cause for concern. Charles would never have mentioned it unless he felt the need to prepare her for the worst. Oh, he hadn't said as much in so many words, but the implication was there right enough, and the tenor of his letter was that of a man deeply disturbed.

She would have gone to him, but he would not welcome her, she knew. Charles was a man who preferred to fight his battles alone, and she was used to being shut out. If he wanted her by his side, he would send for her. Until then, she must be patient as always . . .

'Give us the strength to help each other, Lord,' she whispered. Only the crackle of the coals answered her. With calm deliberation she leaned forward and dropped the letter into the fire. She watched it curl and blacken.

When it had smouldered to bright grey ash, she leaned back in her chair and stared up at the high ceiling and the framed landscapes hanging from the picture rail. She turned her head this way then that, gazing thoughtfully at the heavy tapestry curtains and the strong dark furniture that was characteristic of this house; the tall dresser with its many cupboards and shelves had been her own mother's. The crystal and silver it displayed were valuable heirlooms handed down through generations of Charles's family. Maybe soon they would have to be sold. Suddenly, it meant nothing to her. She was lonely and afraid. In the early years her marriage had been her life and Charles her mainstay. Now all that was over. Battle had taken the soul from him. 'I'll always love you,' she murmured, and the tears welled in her eyes. She dropped her head to one side and let the weariness flood over her. For some reason beyond her understanding, she sensed a catastrophe brewing.

A short time later, when Jenny peeped into the room, Elizabeth was gently sleeping. 'That's it, ma'am,' she whispered, quietly banking the fire. 'After that unholy row with *her*, you need to recover your strength.' The argument had carried through to the kitchen where Jenny was preparing lunch, and now she wondered how she might tell Mrs Marshall, when she woke, that her peevish daughter had already left for London – and with a look on her face that would make the devil cringe.

# Chapter Two

Claudia stepped down from the cab. The street lights threw strange shadows and the buildings seemed to hem her in. For the briefest moment she was unsure of herself.

The driver climbed out of his cab and came to stand beside her. Taking off his flat cap, he scratched his balding head and studied her face in the half-light. Certain that she had given him the wrong directions, he told her in a shocked voice, 'This is an officers' club, miss.' Reluctantly he reached into the cab's interior and brought out the bulky tapestry portmanteau. 'Are yer sure this is the right place?'

He slammed the cab door shut and stared across the pavement at the softly lit façade. The building was old, fronted by tall fluted columns and long windows fortified by stone mullions. He'd been astonished when this young toff asked him to take her to the officers' club on Argyle Street. This was a grand establishment where women were not welcome, and rightly so in his opinion. Women were best kept in their place. He wouldn't be surprised if they didn't show her the door.

'Don't be impertinent!' she snapped. 'Kindly take my bag inside.' Claudia was not in the best of moods. The train journey from Bedford had been long and arduous. She ached through every bone in her body, and this common little man was irritating her with his gabbling.

'As yer say, miss,' he mumbled. 'As yer say.' He thought of his own four daughters and vowed that if they ever spoke in such tones to an elder, he would smack their arses good and proper. In angry silence he followed her up the short flight of steps and into the lobby. The man at the desk jumped out of his seat and gawped at them open-mouthed. 'Can I help you?' He directed his question to the driver but he got his answer from the woman.

'A moment,' she told him with a sweet smile. Turning to the man who had delivered her here, she said sourly, 'How much is the fare?'

'A shilling, miss, if yer please.'

'Daylight robbery!' Digging into her purse she brought out the necessary coin. When he deliberately lingered, she said curtly, 'I hope you don't expect a tip?' She stared at him until he was out of sight and then informed the other man, 'My father is Charles Marshall. Inform him at once that I'm here.'

The man's eyes popped open and he stiffened to attention. 'Sorry, miss, but I'm afraid your father has retired for the night.' He carefully omitted to reveal that Charles Marshall had been drinking since early morning. When they carried him to bed at midday, he could hardly put one foot before the other. That was six hours ago, and there hadn't been a peep out of him since.

'But it's only six o'clock. You must be mistaken.' Claudia was out of patience. 'Do as I ask and tell him that I'm here. *Now*, if you please.' She glanced around. 'Is there a lounge where I might wait . . . perhaps you could serve me with tea and sandwiches?'

'Sorry again, miss.' He was red in the face and visibly flustered. 'I can't allow you to go through. You see . . . women aren't allowed in this establishment.'

'What nonsense!' She leaned close to the desk and drew out

27

the long needle-thin pin from her wide-brimmed hat. For one awful minute he was convinced she was about to stab him with it. When she merely swept the hat from her head and laid it on top of the tapestry bag, he breathed a sigh of relief. But it was short-lived when she declared, 'On second thoughts, I won't wait. You may collect my bag and show me to his room.'

He coughed and spluttered and spread his white-gloved hands on the desk. 'I can't do that, miss.'

'Then bring someone who can, you bloody fool!'

Her shrill voice carried into the library behind her. There were two men in there, each with his head buried in a newspaper. They stared at each other but didn't speak. The round bespectacled fellow sat up in his chair and peered towards the door with horror, while the tall white-haired gentleman rose from his seat and went across the room. At the door he turned and smiled at the other man, causing him to grunt and retreat into his newspaper. The round man had never married and so knew nothing of women and children. The tall gentleman came of a large and noisy family. A woman shrieking was nothing new to him, although he had never heard the like inside these hallowed walls.

When he emerged from the sanctity of the inner chamber, he was astonished to see Claudia angrily pacing the area in front of the desk. The frustrated clerk addressed him in a rush. 'It's a visitor for Mr Marshall, sir. I've already told her she can't come into these premises.'

The tall white-haired gentleman smiled benevolently. 'It would appear she is *already* in.' When Claudia glared at him, he assured her, 'He's right, you know. I don't believe I've ever known a woman get beyond those doors.' He inclined his head towards the front of the building.

'Well, I'm not leaving.' She turned her wrath on the clerk. 'That fool won't tell my father I'm here, and I have no intention of going until I've seen him.'

28

The gentleman opened his mouth to speak. The clerk antici-
pated his question. 'She's Mr Marshall's *daughter*, sir.' Behind
Claudia's back he winked and wiped his brow. The message was
clear.

'Oh, I see.' The gentleman collected Claudia's bag and took
it to the settee on the far side of the foyer. He placed it on the
floor there and invited her, 'Wait here. I'll see if I can rouse your
father.'

'Take me to him.' She rammed the long thin pin in and out of
her hat.

He shook his head. There was something calming about his
countenance. 'No, my dear. It's best if you wait here.' Claudia
didn't argue. Instead she sat on the settee, her steel grey eyes
following that tall distinguished figure as it went away. He
reminded her of her father. The same dignity. The same proud
authoritative bearing. She could wait. And meanwhile she would
get it all straight in her mind. There were so many things she had
to say to him: the way she had missed him; the dreadful time she
had been put through at the hands of her mother, and the lies she
had been told just to keep Claudia and her father apart; the way
her mother had cut back on her daughter's every little pleasure.
Oh, and of course, he would have to know about his wife's affair
with the neighbouring farmer. And if *that* didn't make him come
home, she didn't know what would.

It seemed an age before the tall gentleman returned. 'Your
father will be down shortly,' he promised her. He seemed worried,
but gave nothing away. Addressing the clerk, he ordered, 'Tea for
the young lady, I think, and a bite to eat.' With a smart little bow
from the waist and a certain look that told her not to wander, he
returned to his newspaper. He hoped she might not have to wait
too long. He hoped also that the poor haunted fellow he had just
woken could gather himself together long enough to welcome her
with open arms. Charles Marshall was a hero, but he was also a

wreck, a drunkard, a man who had allowed life to grind him down. God only knew he needed someone to take him in hand.

At first he'd been shocked to the core on being told that the daughter he idolised was actually here, waiting downstairs in this very club. In fact, he had buried his head in his hands and seemed like a man about to face a firing squad. But then, when the truth dawned, he laughed out loud, behaving like a young man getting ready for his first date. It was good to see his spirits lift because over these many months he had been through a bad time. It didn't help that his fortune was diminishing with every day. Times were bad, there was no denying that.

Charles Marshall bent his head to the sink and splashed water over his face a dozen times. With a comb he slicked back his greying hair and tidied his thin drooping moustache. Then, fastening the buttons on his shirt, he put on his coat, straightened the collar, and regarded himself in the wardrobe mirror. 'What kind of man are you?' he asked his reflection. It was a shocking image, that of a man dejected. The eyes were dull and stricken with pain. His clothes were shabby, his shoulders drooped, all trace of pride was gone. 'She can't see you like this, man. Get a hold of yourself!' he groaned. He felt ashamed. He should have been stronger. But she was here. Claudia was here! It was the spur he so desperately needed.

For one awful minute doubts assailed him. Would she understand? Could he really explain what was in his heart? For so very long now he had shirked his family and his duty. Everything had crumbled around him; the very fabric of his existence had rotted away and he had wallowed in self-pity. No! It was more than that. Yet it was over. He *must* start again. He owed it to them. 'She came to find me!' Somehow he had never thought she would.

Suddenly his mind was made up. 'She's got to know how bad

things are. I can't protect her any more.' He pulled himself up and straightened his clothes, all the while muttering to himself, 'They've forgiven me. I owe it to them to try again.'

Claudia's gaze remained fast on the door through which the gentleman had returned. Her father would come through that door. Any minute now, he would come to collect her. Hurriedly, she ran through all the things she had prepared to tell him. Wicked things every one. But she *must* make him come home. She had grown to hate her mother, and hoped to oust her from their home. Then there would be only the two of them, her father and her. The thought brought a smile to Claudia's face.

It was still trembling on her lips when Charles Marshall came into the foyer. It froze when she saw him there, and became a gasp of disbelief when he called out her name.

For a moment she didn't recognise him. Here was a creature who looked no better than a tramp. It was obvious he had been drinking; he clung to the door-jamb as though without its support he might fall over. She recoiled in horror. Even when he rushed forward and took her in his arms, she couldn't accept that this was her father. 'Oh, Claudia, you look lovely as ever.' His breath sickened her.

Charles could hardly contain his joy. He had been afraid and ashamed to meet her. The taste of booze was still on him, and his brain was befuddled. He didn't even know if he was making any sense. But now, holding her softness in his arms and wallowing in the gentle waft of her perfume, he realised what he had missed. With a small cry he buried his head in her hair. 'You shouldn't have come here,' he moaned. 'But, oh, I'm glad you did. I'm so glad.' Suddenly he saw a light at the end of the tunnel.

Whatever happened he would always have his family. Together they could cope with anything. He knew that now. Proudly he held her from him. Her face betrayed such bewilderment that his heart went out to her. 'I didn't want you to see me like this,' he murmured, easing her on to the settee and sitting beside her. It didn't occur to him that she was shocked and stunned into silence. He wasn't even thinking straight. He held her hands in his. They were warm and soft, melting his heart. 'Things have been bad, my darling, but I was wrong to stay away. I was afraid, you see? There have been things on my mind for a long time now, and I couldn't shake them off. I should have realised that a man can recover more quickly in the bosom of his family.'

He had kept his thoughts buried deep, and they had buried him too. Suddenly the sight of Claudia, and the knowledge that she had come here to find him and take him home, stirred him to tears. Unaware that she had stiffened and inched away from him, he let the bad things spill out. 'We may not have the sort of money we've been used to, and things will get worse before they get better, but I promise you this, my sweet – I'll make our fortune again. I'll work my fingers to the bone.' His blood was still fired by the whisky he had downed during his long lonely vigil. 'Help me,' he pleaded. He was crying like a baby, long overdue tears flowing down his face as he begged her forgiveness. He had been all kinds of a fool. Now, with God's help and the strength of his family, he must pull through. Why hadn't he seen that before? Why had he isolated himself? Oh, what a fool he'd been. What a blind, selfish fool.

'GET AWAY FROM ME!' Wrenching herself from him, Claudia was on her feet, her face twisted and ugly. 'I hate you!' Her voice fell to a hiss.

He grabbed at her. 'No. Please don't say that!' He was a sorry sight as he reached out for her.

'Don't put your filthy hands on me! You're drunk. I wish I'd never come here. I wanted you to come home, but not now. You're worse than *she* is.' Claudia backed away. 'I DON'T CARE IF I NEVER SEE YOU AGAIN!'

'You don't mean that, sweetheart?' Charles shook his head in disbelief, his hands falling to his sides as she recoiled from him. 'Can't you find it in your heart to forgive me?'

'I'll never forgive you . . . either of you!'

He stared as though seeing her for the first time. 'That's so unfair. I know it must have been a shock to you, finding me like this, and I can't blame you for feeling repulsed, but, please . . . I think I can find the courage to go on if you help me. Won't you give me a chance to put things right? Haven't I always been a good father in the past? Haven't your mother and I always given you the very best?' Realising that he was beginning to whine, he closed his mouth and lowered his gaze. 'I'm sorry,' he muttered finally. His heart was like a stone in his chest and he felt more desolate than ever. Yet he must hope. In spite of her hard face and stiff countenance, he must hope. But when she spoke again, raising things from the past that had haunted him too, he knew all hope was lost forever.

'So you think I'm being "unfair", do you?' she sneered in a low voice, bending her head so that he could see her face more clearly. 'And what about you? What about all those times when you were unfair to me? Cast your mind back, Daddy dear, to when I was small, to when I begged you to stay . . . to when I needed you more than anything in the world. But you didn't care, did you? All those times I sobbed myself to sleep, needing you so much . . . on my birthdays . . . at Christmas . . . when *she* had been especially irritating. You were never there to love and comfort me.' She paused to let her words sink in. She wanted him to remember too.

'Don't be cruel,' he pleaded softly. 'It wasn't my fault. When you're a soldier, you go where you're sent. In the middle of the night, at a moment's notice.'

'That was always your excuse.' In a voice trembling with loathing, she wounded him as he had wounded her. 'Surely you

33

remember my first real birthday party? I was five years old, and had just started school. I told all the children my daddy would be there, because you had promised and like a little fool I believed you . . . just as I believed you all those times before. At first I was proud of you, boasting that you were a soldier, and that you adored me above all else.' She laughed, a dark sinister sound that caused him to raise his head. 'I was lying, you see. I knew it wasn't true. How could it be when all the time you loved only your precious uniform. 'Oh, and *her*!' Jealousy invaded her very being and she visibly trembled. 'You always loved her more than you loved me, didn't you?'

'Please, Claudia, don't do this. And don't blame your mother, who has always been there for you, loving you, watching out for you, making up for my enforced absence.'

'Suffocating me, you mean!' Her eyes blazed into his. 'Oh, you're right, she *was* always there – first thing in the morning and last thing at night. She was there when I went to sleep and there when I woke, forever watching . . . afraid I might make a wrong choice, afraid to let me have even the smallest measure of freedom, criticising my friends until I wanted none at all, saying they were a bad influence. Well, maybe they were and maybe they weren't, but the choice should have been mine, not hers! She tried to be mother and father, fussing and touching until I couldn't bear her near me. The more I tried to distance myself from her, the more she resented it. In a different way, she hurt me as much as you did. But then I found a way to hurt her: by being especially unruly and refusing to be moulded into what she wanted me to be.' Claudia remembered how it had been, and was delighted all over again. Chuckling, she told him, 'You were not there to be punished so I punished her instead, and always enjoyed it. Because, you see, I knew you loved her more than you loved me.'

His face was wrung with despair. 'Oh, Claudia, you were so

wrong. Of course I loved your mother, but I loved you too – though not in the same way, of course.' Suddenly he could see it all, and his guilt was overwhelming.

'I *know* how you loved her.'

Something in the change of her tone made him study her more closely. 'What are you trying to say?'

'I saw you!' Her eyes narrowed as she returned his curious stare. 'You and her together . . . in the bedroom . . . I saw you.' She made a grimace. 'Naked, wrapped round each other, and so engrossed in what you were doing you didn't even notice me.'

His face was suffused with shame. He made no sound but slowly shook his head from side to side, his gaze appalled as he continued to look at her.

She laughed, a soft satisfied sound that struck him to the heart. 'Like I said, I *know* how you loved her. And now I believe you know how much I loathe you!'

A strange thing happened then. Suddenly his shoulders became square and straight and his face reflected a kind of pride. 'Go home,' he said. 'You are wrong about your mother. She's a good woman and has always loved you. It wasn't she who bred this shocking hatred in you, it was me.' Against his better judgement he asked once more, 'Will you ever find it in your heart to forgive me?'

'Never!' Veering away, she ran from him. He could hear her sobbing as she sped into the road.

'CLAUDIA!' He rushed forward, stumbling, crying out to her. But she was gone. His shocked eyes looked up the street and there she was, scrambling into a horse-drawn carriage. He called her name but the carriage sped by, taking her away. Taking his sad heart with her.

'Come on, old fellow.' Strong comforting arms gathered him in. 'Let's get you to your room, eh?' Dejected, he collapsed against the bulky form of the clerk. Together with the tall white-haired gentleman, he led Charles back to his room. There they laid him on the bed and softly crept away. 'My God, the things she said.' The clerk shook his head in pity as they went down the stairs.

'What can you say?' the other man asked. 'It must have been a shock to her. After all, he's not the man he was.'

'Well, I for one think she should have had more compassion. He's not the only one to come home from the war in a bad way. But not all of them lose their fortune as well.'

'Unfortunately, Charles was never a businessman. He'd tell you that himself. He was badly advised. It's a sad thing, but there's little he can do now. The market's shaky and we all have to tread carefully.' At the foot of the steps the gentleman paused and looked up. 'Poor blighter. It seems even his own have turned their back on him now.'

Upstairs in his room Charles relived the awful incident with Claudia. Over and over he saw how she had looked at him, with horror and repugnance on her face. Her last words echoed in his brain like giant hammers: 'I DON'T CARE IF I NEVER SEE YOU AGAIN!'

Incredibly calm now, he sat on the edge of the bed, his eyes staring round the room. '*This* is what you've come to, Marshall,' he told himself. 'A room no better than a prison.'

He walked to the window and looked out across the night sky. From here he could see the chimney-tops. *She* was out there, his beloved daughter, and she had gone away loathing him. After all he had been through, it was more than he could bear. Like a man in a trance, he slid open the window. It stuck halfway. He laughed. *He couldn't even do that right!*

He was still laughing when his feet left the ledge and he launched himself into the darkness. As he fell through the air he made no sound. There was no fear, no regret. Instead, he felt an odd sense of elation, as though a great crippling weight was lifted from his broken heart. The last words that left his lips were these: 'Forgive me, Elizabeth. I love you.'

As the cab crossed the busy road and drew into the kerb outside King's Cross Station, the ambulance almost collided with it. 'God Almighty!' the driver said in a shaking voice when he held the door open for Claudia. 'He's in a desperate hurry, ain't he? Must be some poor begger in a bad way.' When she showed little interest, he held out his hand. 'Ninepence, if yer please,' he muttered, thinking what a surly bugger she was.

Claudia had only just realised that she had left her tapestry portmanteau behind, but the small envelope bag in which she kept her personal things was still clutched in her hand. She opened it now, took out the ninepence and thrust it into his fist before rushing away to catch the first train to Bedford.

Once on the train she sat back in the chair, her eyes glittering with tears. They might have been tears for her father and for the callous way she had treated him. They might have been tears for her mother and the worry she had endured. But they were not. Claudia's tears were for herself. And all she could think of was that Charles had confirmed what her mother had been saying all along. *They were in financial trouble*. Everything she cherished was under threat. No more expensive outfits. No splendid parties of the kind she used to enjoy, and which had already been sacrificed by her miserly mother. No chance of getting back her personal maid or filling the house with servants like before. No new leather saddle for the hunter. In fact, she was mortified by the possibility that she might not even be able to keep the magnificent beast. She didn't doubt for one moment that her mother would use any excuse to get rid of him. Already she was whining about the cost of his keep and the huge veterinary bills.

She was convinced that her mother was at fault too, or why

had she not seen it all coming? Ah! Maybe she had, though. A cunning thought came into her mind at that moment.

Deep down Claudia still couldn't bring herself to accept that the Marshalls were without money, and it occurred to her that her mother was deliberately exaggerating the situation. In fact, it wouldn't surprise her if that devious bitch had kept a sizeable sum of money to one side. That was it, of course! Elizabeth Marshall was trying to keep it all for herself. 'Well, I won't let you spoil my life,' Claudia promised under her breath. 'I'll see you in hell with *him* first.' In her rage and selfishness she was totally beyond reason.

# *Chapter Three*

On Friday 10 January 1919, Charles Marshall was laid to rest in the grounds of St Mary's church. The bells rang out and the villagers hurried through the high street of Woburn Sands, up the hill and into the pretty church.

He had been a soldier of the highest rank. The Mayor told everyone so, and the Brigadier read a passage from the Bible that made them cry.

After the service, everyone filed behind the coffin and watched them lower it into the ground. There were those who thought he had taken his own life and so should not be laid into sacred ground, but they remained silent, because the coroner's court had decided that there was not enough evidence to suggest suicide. It was known that Charles Marshall was heavily intoxicated, and so a verdict of 'accidental death' was recorded.

If Claudia suspected she had played a part in the tragic demise of her father, she told no one, and at no time did she feel any semblance of guilt.

Now, three days later, at four o'clock on Monday afternoon, the solicitor and his colleague were fed and rested after their journey from London. Not used to being away from his beloved city, Mr Oberson was anxious to get on with the task in hand.

Several times he took out his pocket watch and scanned it with a frown. He had the departure time of the train imprinted on his mind . . . at precisely five-thirty the London train would leave the station. And, come hell or high water, he meant to be on it. Woburn Sands was a pretty little village, but after being raised in the smog of a great city he had developed a peculiar allergy to open fields and blue skies. He wanted to be gone from here, and the sooner the better.

Clearing his throat and shuffling the papers before him, he prepared to read out the will. 'If I may begin?' He perched tiny rimless spectacles on the edge of his nose and, squinting over the top of them, regarded the three persons whom he had called together. Already he had taken stock of their nature, and his sympathies lay entirely with the woman of the household. As for the daughter, he saw her as a sharp and painful thorn in the woman's side.

Seated directly opposite at the other end of the table, Elizabeth grew aware of his discreet attention. She gave a nervous half-smile, and he responded with a slight nod of his rather large head. His figure was a study in comparisons, because while his head was over-large, his appearance was diminutive. Mr Oberson was a comical fellow with grey bushy mutton-chop whiskers and the small quick presence of a child. Ancient and unpredictable, he was well-known and greatly respected for his legal expertise.

A glance around the table told him that all were now ready. His sharp eyes went from Elizabeth, who was feverishly wringing a small lace handkerchief between her long strong fingers, to Claudia's bold and beautiful face, and finally to his own clerk who was every bit as anxious as his master to be seated on that train and speeding on his way home. 'I think we're all ready,' he answered, bestowing a sparse dutiful smile on one and all.

'For goodness' sake, get on with it!' Claudia rudely interrupted. 'No doubt you'll present a handsome bill for your troubles, and no doubt it will grow longer the more time you waste.' She sat upright and stiff, her hands spread palm upwards on the table, almost as though she was preparing to catch a fortune.

'Claudia, please mind your manners,' Elizabeth curtly reminded her. 'For whatever reason, these men are guests in our house.' Turning to Mr Oberson, she murmured, 'Please excuse my daughter. She's been through a particularly bad time since losing her father.' She could have said that she too had been through all kinds of heartbreak. She could have said also that Claudia's 'bad time' had little to do with losing her father, and more to do with the awful prospect of losing the material things that gave her so much pleasure. Instead she remained silent and waited for the reading to begin. Her hopes were not as high as Claudia's. She was sensible enough to know that from now on life could never be the same again.

Mr Oberson began. In a soft, firm voice he relayed the wishes of Charles Marshall, occasionally glancing up at the women's faces when he reached a particular point which he believed might prompt a question. When there were no questions, he went on. When at last he was finished, the final word seemed to hang in the air, suspended in the heavy silence which hung over the dining room like a thick dark cloud.

'I'm sorry,' he said honestly. He was always genuinely uncomfortable when a will took more than it gave. This particular will was short and simple. Any holdings that Charles Marshall had inherited were virtually gone, as much a casualty of war as he himself had been. In the early days when that unfortunate man had remained in London, trying to recapture both his own soul and the Marshall fortune, he had kept his wits long enough to secure the house on a prepaid lease of twenty-five years. He had also made a modest financial allowance for his wife and daughter. Compared to the Marshall family's past affluence, though, the allowance was shockingly meagre: a mere twenty guineas each month.

There was also a capital sum of five hundred pounds. This money was to be wisely invested by Mr Oberson and placed in trust for Claudia. It was to remain in trust until she reached the age of thirty, when it would be turned over to her; unless she married before that age. In this event, it would revert to her mother, Elizabeth. And only on her mother's demise would Claudia then have access to the capital.

Slowly removing his spectacles, Mr Oberson regarded first one woman then the other. Elizabeth was leaning back in her chair, her face white as chalk and her pale hands limp on her lap. Claudia had remained stiff and attentive throughout the reading. She was the same now, but her face was tight with rage and the upturned palms were clenched into small hard fists. With round accusing eyes she stared at the man who had delivered the crippling news. In just ten minutes he had confirmed everything that Elizabeth had feared and which Claudia refused to accept, even though she should have been prepared. '*I'm glad he's dead,*' she said in a harsh whisper that shocked everyone.

'You had better go to your room,' Elizabeth ordered. Her green eyes were moist with tears. Inside she was still trembling at the knowledge that they were almost destitute. Yet when she spoke her voice was unwavering.

In an instant Claudia was on her feet, hammering the table with both fists and facing her mother with unveiled hostility. 'Don't tell me what to do!' she cried. 'You're no better than him or you wouldn't have let him lose all our money!' The tears were flowing down her face, leaving thin rivulets of mascara that gave her a clownish appearance. 'We're paupers, aren't we?' she cried bitterly. 'No better than the servants.'

Elizabeth stood up then. She made a fine and dignified figure as she calmly faced her daughter. 'I said, go to your room. When you're calmer, we can talk.' Her quiet authoritative voice belied the churning of her stomach. When it seemed as though Claudia would defy her, she leaned forward. 'GO TO YOUR ROOM. AT ONCE, CLAUDIA!'

Something in her mother's demeanour struck deep. It might have been a legacy from the time when she was smaller, when her father was away and her mother's word was law. Or it might have been the unaccustomed force of her mother's voice, usually so calm and deliberate. For just the briefest moment, Claudia was taken aback. Then, with a broken cry and a vicious glance at Elizabeth, she ran from the room.

'Forgive her,' Elizabeth asked, turning to Mr Oberson. 'I can't think what came over her,' she lied. She knew *exactly* what had come over her daughter, and it made her ashamed.

Mr Oberson beamed at her with genuine affection. 'There is nothing to forgive. You've both been through a trying time and I do understand, believe me.' He thanked his lucky stars that he had never married, because if he had then he might well have fathered such a hostile and precocious creature as this gentle woman's daughter. The thought was repugnant to him.

Overcome with gratitude and sympathy, he hurried to Elizabeth's side and, taking her hand in his, bent his head and brushed a small quick kiss against her knuckles. It was an uncharacteristic and chivalrous gesture that shocked him almost more than it shocked the other two present.

When it was done, he blushed to the roots of his bushy mutton-chop whiskers and hurriedly backed away. 'Goodness me!' he declared, snatching out his pocket watch and peering at it with surprise. 'Have you seen the time?' Swamped with embarrassment, he swung round to stare at his companion, who was still open-mouthed at the actions of his employer.

Much to the delight of Mr Oberson, the other fellow answered cunningly, 'If we're to catch that train we had better leave without delay.' He couldn't think what had caused his usually restrained and proper colleague to behave in such a way. But then, he reminded himself, Mr Oberson could afford to be magnanimous, because not only was his task here accomplished, he could look forward to a healthy commission on Claudia's invested capital.

The very same sentiments were running through Mr Oberson's mind. He adored his profession, and received a very comfortable lifestyle from it. Still and all, he believed wholeheartedly that he deserved it. In this instance he had invested the five hundred pounds wisely, and was convinced that the returns would make the small inheritance grow to Claudia's advantage. Although the little bitch doesn't deserve it, he thought sourly.

'Can I offer you some tea before you leave?' Elizabeth felt she had to make amends for Claudia's shameful behaviour.

He shook his head. 'Thank you, no, Mrs Marshall. My colleague and I will take our leave, I think.' He hastened to put on his hat and ushered the other man across the room. 'Duty calling and all that,' he apologised.

Elizabeth stood on the front doorstep and waved the two men away. Long after they had turned out of the drive and gone down the high street, she remained there, a slim solitary figure, her thoughts steeped in memories of the way things had been. It seemed only yesterday she had had everything a woman could want. She had a strong marriage and a good husband, she was the proud mother of a small and beautiful daughter, with the security of wealth to cushion her and her family from the harsh realities of life.

But all that was long ago. Now her husband was gone and that small child had grown into a selfish young woman who had destroyed any warm feelings that had once existed between them. The money was gone too, and already the harsh realities of life were creeping up on her. 'All the same, I have much to be thankful for,' she assured herself. They still had an income, though it might be drastically reduced. And they had the security of this lovely house for the next twenty-five years. Beyond that, she wouldn't let herself think. She turned her face up to the sky. It was growing chilly. The afternoon was still fairly bright, but soon the dusk would come gently over the valleys and hide everything in shadow. She shivered, wrapped her arms across her breast, and went back inside. Already she was mentally preparing for the confrontation with Claudia.

As always, Elizabeth tapped politely on her daughter's door, and as always was told: 'Go away.'

'Not this time, my girl!' she replied. 'We need to talk, you and I.'

'I've got nothing else to say to you,' came the churlish reply.

Elizabeth tried the door. It was unlocked. Softly she stepped inside the room. Claudia lay face down on the bed. 'I know it's come as a shock to you,' Elizabeth started gently. 'But there is nothing we can do now except to live according to our means. Certain plans need to be made . . . a tighter budget. It will be difficult, I know. But it has to be done.'

Claudia spun round. 'I won't let you sell the hunter,' she growled threateningly.

Over these past weeks, Elizabeth had turned her mind inside out trying to find a way to keep that magnificent beast, but there was no way that she could see. 'I'm sorry, Claudia. We can't afford to keep him. The cost of his food alone would cripple us.' Now she dared to voice what had come to mind as a kind of solution. 'Of course, there *is* one way you could keep him.' It would be a solution to many things and would give Claudia a sense of purpose in her lazy life. 'You could apply for the position of clerk to the village solicitor. It's advertised again this week and I know you could do the job well. You have a quick brain, when you choose to use it, and the wages would be your own, to do as you like with.'

Claudia was horrified. Swinging herself off the bed, she

remarked in a bemused voice, 'You're asking me to *work*?' The thought shocked her. Suddenly she was laughing out loud. It was an awful, frightening sound. But the silence that followed was even more unnerving. With narrowed eyes, she studied her mother, then in a chilling voice she whispered, 'Get out.'

At first it seemed as though Elizabeth would stand her ground. She knew all too well what the consequences might be if she let Claudia think she was compromised. However, she was wise enough to realise that this was not the time to discuss certain delicate matters that affected both their futures. In a strong voice she told her, 'I have other things to attend to. But you need to give careful consideration to what I've said. We can discuss it further when I have the time.' With that she went sedately from the room. Once outside she sagged against the wall and put her hand to her heart. One of these days that poor heart would give out. She was in no doubt that her daughter would find that a cause for celebration.

Jenny was crossing the hall below when Elizabeth started on her way down the stairs. Their eyes met, and in that same moment Claudia's door was flung open. 'To hell with you!' she snapped, running down the stairs towards her mother. Dressed in riding boots and jodhpurs, her slim figure was shown to perfection.

Taken by surprise, Elizabeth turned round, losing her balance as Claudia deliberately pushed by. Only her iron grip on the banister stopped her from falling headlong down the stairs. Out of the corner of her eye she saw Claudia career into Jenny, who gave a startled cry when the tray she was carrying went spinning across the carpet to the sound of shattering crockery.

Without a backward glance, Claudia fled out of the house and down to the stables. She was livid with rage. Things were happening all around her. Unsettling things over which she had no control. Uppermost in her mind was the ludicrous idea her mother had put to her just now. How dare she suggest that her daughter should take up a clerical position in the village! Did she want to make a laughing stock of her? Of course, that was it. Well, she would be disappointed, because Claudia had no intention of becoming one of the working class. She was never meant for that. As for the hunter, if *she* couldn't keep him, then she would make sure he would never belong to anyone else.

In the stable she took a moment to look into his brown soulful eyes. There were no kind words. No regrets. No compassion in her soul as she quickly saddled him. At least she could do that with some degree of competence, because she had sat on the railing and watched Frank do it time and again. She rode out of the yard like someone demented, wildly jumping the fence that bordered the field, and yelling at the poor frightened creature as she cracked the whip hard against his withers and forced him on over the rough terrain.

In the growing dusk, Frank bent over the engine of his tractor; he could hardly see. Astonished by the thunder of hooves close by, he looked up and was even more astonished to see Claudia gallop past him, head down into the wind and grim determination on her face. Alarmed, he called after her, 'God Almighty! Take it easy, you little fool.' When she ignored him, he shouted again, 'You'll answer to me if you bring him to any harm!' He had a mind to saddle the cob and chase after her. 'Spiteful bugger. You don't deserve a fine animal like that,' he called. In a mumble not meant for her ears, he added, 'It wouldn't hurt *you* to feel the cut of the whip across your bare arse, damn and bugger you!' Angrily throwing his spanner to the ground, he prepared to return to the stables. Almost at once he reminded himself that he was only an employee here. The likes of her had never listened to the likes of him before, and what made him think that would suddenly change? 'If he throws you, that might teach you a lesson you'll not forget in a hurry,' he chuckled. The hunter was a strong beast. Far stronger than its rider. 'Aye. He'll only put up with so much, that he will,' he promised himself. All the same, the thought of that magnificent animal being treated in such a way made his blood boil.

He peered into the distance, but horse and rider were only a speck on the horizon now. The skies were grey and the shadows closing in. Shaking his head in frustration he picked up the spanner and applied his attention to the spluttering engine. It was no good. He'd have to see to it in the morning.

Climbing into the seat he eased the ailing machine along the rough earth, but it went only a short way before it gave a mighty sigh and came to a stop. Reluctantly he set back to the stables on foot. His thoughts were on Claudia and the hunter. He couldn't understand folk like that. But then, they weren't like *ordinary* folk. They'd had it too easy all their lives. For one fleeting shameful moment, he sensed a deep envy inside. But it was only fleeting, and the anger Claudia had raised in him was a far stronger emotion.

'Are you all right, my dear?' Elizabeth was full of concern for Jenny, who was on her knees in the hallway, carefully collecting the broken fragments from the carpet.

'I'm just a bit winded, that's all,' Jenny told her with a reassuring smile. 'But there's no harm done, apart from to the tea-cups.' She gave a regretful glance at the broken cups. The sugar bowl and milk jug were fortunately still on the tray, but the rose china teapot had rolled on to the floor and was on its side with a long dark stain running from its spout. It was surprisingly intact. 'I was just taking the tray to the drawing room,' she explained. Elizabeth always had a pot of tea brought to the drawing room at this hour of the day. 'I'm sorry, but I couldn't hold on to it.'

'I know you couldn't.' Elizabeth touched her hand against Jenny's shoulder. Her smile was warm. 'You're not to worry about it,' she said. Stooping from the knees, she collected a number of jagged china pieces and placed them carefully on the tray. 'Ask Meg to attend to that,' she said, pointing to the tea stain. It was still hot to the touch. 'And we need the lights on. It's growing dark outside.'

'Right away,' Jenny promised. 'And I'll make you a fresh brew.'

'That would be nice,' Elizabeth remarked wearily. She looked down on Jenny's pretty face; such a bright eager face, she thought kindly. It hurt her to think she must cause this lovely young woman a degree of disappointment. But her course of action was painfully clear. She had a duty to perform, however unpleasant. She couldn't do it today though. Not today, when she was bone tired and reeling from the catalogue of events that had overwhelmed her. In her foolish heart she had hoped that Claudia might at last be a source of friendship and comfort to her, but it was not to be. Claudia thought of no one but herself. Elizabeth realised she was on her own. There was no one for her to turn to. No one whose shoulder she could cry on. Jacob Laing was a kindly soul, but he owed her nothing.

'I'll be in the drawing room,' she said quietly. 'Mind you don't cut yourself now.' With all the worry on her mind, two broken tea-cups was a trivial thing. Tomorrow she would have to talk to Jenny and Meg on that more serious matter, and she was not looking forward to it.

Pausing in her task, Jenny watched Elizabeth walk away. 'Poor thing,' she murmured. Then, recalling how much work she still had to do, she frantically cleared the mess and hurried to the kitchen, switching on the lights as she went.

When Frank returned after his day's work, Elizabeth had enjoyed her fresh pot of tea and was upstairs in her room. She was reading a copy of her husband's will. Even now she found it hard to believe that he was lying in the churchyard. He had been such a strong, fine man.

49

Meg was setting the table for dinner and Jenny was downstairs in the kitchen. She was peeling the potatoes and dreaming of her sweetheart when he pushed open the door. The cold blast of evening rushed in with him.

'You're early,' Jenny commented, her heart leaping at the sight of him. Even in his grimy overalls, he was a fine figure of a man. 'I didn't expect you for a while yet,' she remarked.

Jenny always looked forward to the day's end when he would come into the kitchen, hungry and weary from his labours. It was almost as though they were already wed. 'Sit yourself down,' she said. 'You look frozen to the marrow.' The heat from the oven made the kitchen cosy. The delicious aroma of baking rose into the air and permeated every corner.

Straight away Jenny knew that Frank was in a bad mood because normally he would sniff the air and say something like, 'By! There's a smell to warm a man's heart.' But not tonight. Tonight he was scowling and deep in thought. 'The tractor's on the blink,' he answered in a quiet voice.

'Well now, that's a nice face to bring into my kitchen, ain't it?' she chastised. Her smile though was warm and welcoming.

'I could wring her bloody neck!' he moaned, flinging off his coat and hanging it on the back door. Going to the sink, he reached over Jenny to turn on the tap. Rinsing his hands beneath the running water, he bent his head and kissed her softly on the top of her head. 'It's a good job I've got you, my lovely,' he said in a brighter voice, 'or I might strangle her anyway and to hell with the consequences!'

'Oh?' Jenny rinsed the potato dirt from her nails. 'And what's "her ladyship" done now?' she wanted to know. She didn't need to ask who had upset him, because it was the same person who upset *everyone* round here.

'She's a wicked bugger is that one,' he answered, slowly

shaking his head from side to side. 'How mother and daughter could be so different, I'll never know.'

Turning the tap off, Jenny plucked a small towel from the window-sill. She wiped her own hands and gave the towel to Frank. 'You'd best sit down and I'll make you a brew. You know dinner won't be ready for an hour yet.' The main meal of the day was served to Elizabeth and her daughter in the dining room at seven o'clock. Meg left for home straight after, and Jenny sat down at the kitchen table with Frank, as soon as the dining-room table was cleared. The big wooden clock on the wall above the pine dresser told him it was five minutes to six.

'I'll be starved to death before then!' he moaned. 'It's a known fact that fresh air makes a man wild and hungry.'

Jenny laughed out loud. 'Well, I can't have you going wild in *my* kitchen,' she said. 'And I'll not let you starve neither.' Pointing to the pantry, she told him, 'You'll find some beef sandwiches I made for Mrs Marshall. She didn't want 'em though . . . on account of Claudia upsetting *her* too. Oh, and there's a chunk of apple pie left over from last night.'

When he disappeared into the pantry, she called out, 'So you see, you're not the only one madam's crossed today because she's upset me an' all . . . cost me a lot of precious time she did. Thankfully though, Meg turned up early and she's working like a thing possessed, so if you give us a smile, happen I'll spare a few minutes to sit with you.'

She laughed softly as he emerged, carrying a plate of food and wearing a smile that made her heart bounce. 'You're a little beauty, Jenny Dickens, what are you?' His brown eyes sparkled with the love of a man for his woman, and not for the first time, Jenny asked herself how such a good and handsome man had come to be hers.

'A fool to myself, that's what I am,' she answered cheerfully, glancing at the great chunk of pork pie on his plate. 'I should make you put that back right now,' she said, 'I was keeping it for your lunch tomorrow.'

'Aw, now you said yourself you wouldn't refuse a starving man,' he coaxed with a charming wink. 'It's your own fault anyway. You should never have left it where I could see it. You know I could never resist your delicious pork pie.'

Jenny's heart melted beneath that wonderful smile. Oh, how she adored him! 'Go on then, you devil,' she laughed. 'You'll have to make do with cheese sandwiches tomorrow.'

With the kettle already simmering on the gas ring, it was only a minute before she and Frank were seated at the big old table with a piping hot cup of tea each. 'Right then,' Jenny started, looking at him across the table. 'Now that you've wolfed all them sandwiches and finished off my pork pie, you can tell me what she did to send you back here in such a bad temper?' She raised her cup and slowly sipped at it, her soft blue eyes focussed on his face. 'Anyway, you shouldn't let her rile you like that.'

Suddenly she found herself thinking of what Claudia had threatened: 'I can take him from you any time I want.' She shivered. Life without Frank would be unbearable. He wasn't her husband yet, although it was only a matter of time. A church wedding cost money, and they wanted a little place of their own. It was no good the way they were, with him living in that draughty old outhouse and her with that cramped room at the top of the house. They still had a deal of saving to do before her dreams came true. Jenny told herself that she could wait because he loved her. She knew that beyond a doubt. But he was only a man, whereas Claudia was a very determined and beautiful woman. Frightened by her own fears, she thrust Claudia's shocking threat out of her mind.

'Sometimes I wonder if she's a demon.' Frank grasped the cup until his knuckles drained white. It was almost as though he had his fingers round that slim white neck. When he looked up,

Jenny was astonished at the hostility in his brown eyes. 'She passed me a while back . . . riding like a thing possessed.' Thumping his fist on the table, he said through gritted teeth, 'If there's anything that makes my blood boil, it's seeing a horse flogged like that. Don't these hard-hearted buggers know the animals are just flesh and blood like themselves?' He winced as though he could feel the whip across his own shoulders.

Jenny shivered at the idea of such cruelty, 'You've seen how she treats her own mother,' she pointed out. 'Why should she be any different with animals? The truth is, she's cold hearted. In a way I pity her, because she doesn't know *how* to be kind.'

'Then somebody should teach her!' He stared at her, his brows furrowing. 'What made her go off crazy like that, Jenny? What in God's name happened here?'

She shrugged her shoulders. 'I'm not certain. All I know is that she and her mother had a row . . . I could hear raised voices coming from Claudia's room. I was taking Mrs Marshall's tea-tray to the drawing room when she came out of Claudia's room and began her way down the stairs. The next thing I knew, Claudia was bouncing out of her room. Oh, she was a sight to see, I can tell you. Mad as a hatter she was, her eyes sticking out of her head like hatpins.' Jenny paused, the scene vivid in her mind. 'She nearly sent her mam headlong to the foot of the stairs, and she knocked the tray right out of my hands. It was a dreadful mess . . . two best china cups broken and tea spilled all over the carpet. It took poor Meg twenty minutes to soak that stain out.'

Frank took a gulp of his tea and wiped his mouth with the back of his hand. 'Do you reckon the row was anything to do with Mr Marshall's will?'

'Bound to be.'

'Hmh. I've a feeling we could *all* be affected by Mr Marshall's will. Happen it won't be for the best neither.'

'Why do you say that?'

'Well, look at what's happened already. All the work-horses bar one have been sold; the tractor's been on its last legs these past weeks and I'm not allowed to buy spare parts for it; the field's in dire need of a load of fertiliser, and tradesmen are complaining to me that their bills haven't been paid. Did you know that Thomas Orkot won't supply oats unless he's paid first?' He sighed and swilled down the last of his tea. 'The old cob's all right because he'll do well on anything. But that hunter's a streamlined fellow, and he needs the very best.'

'You don't have to tell *me* that things are bad, Frank,' Jenny reminded him. 'Since there's been only me and Meg, it's been real hard.' She gave a small harsh laugh. 'But all our hardships are nothing compared to *hers*,' she added with unusual sarcasm. 'What! The poor thing hasn't had a new outfit for at least four weeks. And she's had to learn how to dress herself all over again since her personal maid was dismissed.' It wasn't in Jenny's nature to be bitchy, but Claudia had a way of bringing out the worst in everyone. 'I thought I'd have a fit when Mrs Marshall threatened to make Claudia help in the kitchen.' She rolled her eyes to the ceiling. 'Heaven forbid!'

'It's her mother I feel sorry for. She's a good woman.' Frank pushed his chair back and rounded the table. Sliding his arms round her waist, he eased her gently from the chair. 'I love you, Jenny Dickens,' he whispered, nuzzling his face into her thick fair hair.

She leaned into him. The hardness of his body felt good against hers. But the pleasure was spoiled by what he had said. Suddenly she was fearful for the future. 'Do you really think things will get worse?' she asked in a quiet voice.

'Aw, stop your worrying, woman!' he chided, squeezing her tight and kissing her neck. 'Haven't you a strong handsome man to take care of you?' He put his fingers beneath her chin and tipped her head back, until her pretty blue eyes had nowhere else to look but into his face. 'Worrying gives a woman wrinkles, isn't that so?' he teased.

Her whimsical smile touched his heart. 'There y'are then,' he told her. 'It'll be fine, you'll see. Happen I'm wrong after all, and the fellow's left a fat fortune to be shared between the lot of us.'

At that, Jenny burst out laughing. He could always make her feel good. That was one of the reasons why she loved him so. 'Away with you, you rascal,' she chided. 'I can't be doing with you under my feet. Haven't you got work to do?'

'That I have,' he confessed. 'There are the stables to muck out before I've earned my dinner, and if that crazy woman's got back with the horse in one piece, he'll be in a right sweat, I'll be bound. He'll need a thorough grooming before he's bedded for the night.'

'I'll see you later then.'

He kissed her long and passionately. This past week they had both been kept so hard at work, that they'd found little time to be alone. He had almost forgotten how soft and warm her naked body was. 'Are you sure we haven't got time to make love in the pantry?' he chuckled. But he ached so much for her that he wasn't altogether joking.

Jenny pushed him away. Just now when he pressed her tight to him, she had blushed pink at the touch of his hard member against her thigh. 'Shame on you, Frank Winfield!' she gasped in a shocked voice. But her blue eyes were twinkling. She too had felt the stirrings of passion deep inside. This was her man, and it was only right that they should want to be together.

'I'll see you later, won't I?' he asked meaningfully. 'After you've finished for the night.'

She nodded coyly, adding in a firm voice, 'Dinner will be within the hour. Don't let it waste now, will you?'

Holding her tight, he swung her round, then brought her to a standstill in his arms and kissed her again. 'I'd best be off,' he said, and before she could get her breath, the kitchen door was flung open, there was the low whistle of cold air rushing in, and he was gone.

For a long moment Jenny stood where she was, her thoughtful blue eyes roving the kitchen; the air was still filled with that delicious aroma, the table where they had sat was still the same, except for the empty tea-cups and the chairs haphazardly pulled out. The floral curtains were extremely pretty with their flouncy tie-backs, and the dresser boasted the same number of willow-pattern plates and dainty little china cups. Everything was the same. Yet something was missing. And Jenny felt lonely without him.

Elizabeth was seated at the long dining table. In spite of the fact that she was only forty-two, she felt incredibly old. Claudia had been gone for over an hour now, and it was pitch black outside. The skies were heavy with snow, and it was no weather for a dog to be out in, let alone a horse and rider; although of course Claudia was very experienced and capable. All the same, Elizabeth was quietly concerned. In spite of the dreadful things that young woman had said to hurt her, she couldn't help but feel partly to blame. When all was said and done, she was Claudia's mother. Nothing could ever change that. Being a mother brought its own kind of responsibility, and more often than not it was an unbearable and crucifying weight.

From the far side of the room, where she was preparing to serve the first course, Jenny peeped at her mistress. In the light from the lamp, she saw how the narrow straight shoulders had stooped, and how those pale fingers constantly fidgeted, and she realised that Elizabeth had been badly shaken by recent events; first the loss of her husband and then the perpetual friction between herself and her daughter. Sadly though, there was no one that poor woman could confide in. Oh, there was Jacob Laing, but then he was a man known to prefer his own company, and though he might chat over the hedge and be persuaded to help those less fortunate than himself, he was not a man who visited others, and he did not encourage them to visit him.

As she busied herself with the tureens and plates, Jenny could sense Elizabeth's awful loneliness, and thanked her own lucky stars for bringing Frank to her. She wondered whether Elizabeth would ever marry again. Oh, but how could she, when she hardly ever left the house, except to wander the fields and tend to sick animals? It was this particular passion for bringing home wounded creatures that had brought her to the attention of Jacob Laing. He had always believed that animals deserved more help than humans. 'Will Miss Claudia be joining you, ma'am?' Jenny was surprised when only Elizabeth came to the dining room.

'She isn't back yet. I dare say she'll show her face soon enough,' came the curt reply.

Jenny let her thoughts wander. Wouldn't it be wonderful if this lonely soul could find someone to love her? After all, she was a very attractive woman, with that restrained mass of titian-coloured hair and those strong green eyes. She had her health and strength, and she was a warm-hearted soul.

'Just a *little* soup.' Elizabeth's voice startled Jenny as she scooped out a ladleful of celery and stilton soup. 'I have small appetite this evening, I'm afraid.'

'Very well, ma'am,' Jenny answered, serving the tiniest portion and thinking a mouse would eat more. Even then, the delicious broth was hardly touched. Neither was the baked salmon, nor the light as gossamer apple strudel. When the cheese and biscuits were brought, Elizabeth sighed wearily. Pushing her chair away, she stood up. Without looking at Jenny she said, 'If you could just serve a pot of tea in the drawing room?' She delicately dabbed the soft white napkin to her mouth, then dropped it to the table and hurried from the room, leaving Jenny vaguely disappointed. Most foodstuffs were still on ration. She had worked hard to produce a meal fit for a queen and it had been all but ignored.

'Still, I expect you've got a great deal on your mind,' she murmured after the departing figure. 'No doubt Claudia will have it in for you now, she'll be a pig to live with. So it ain't *me* that should feel put on, is it?' As for any salmon that was left over, Jenny supposed she could find it a good home in these hard times. Besides, salmon wasn't a dish that kept easy, and it was against Jenny's nature to throw it away.

'Thank you, Meg.' Jenny came in from the dining room with the last of the dishes. She put them down on the drainer where Meg was already preparing to wash up. 'No, that's all right,' Jenny told her. 'You get yourself off home. Your mam will be waiting for you.' Meg's father had suddenly left the area to search for work, and the girl hadn't smiled since. There were three other children at home, all growing fast and all hungry as birds in the nest.

Meg was reluctant to leave. Since her dad had gone, her mam was miserable company. 'I can make a start on these if you like,' she offered, beginning to roll up her sleeves. Even dirty dishes were better company than her mam.

'You'll do no such thing, my girl!' Jenny scolded. 'I'm not having you wearing yourself to a frazzle doing over-time. Especially when you won't get paid for it.'

'I don't mind. Honest.'

'Well, *I* do.' Jenny put a comforting arm round the girl's plump shoulders. 'I know things aren't easy at the minute, luv,' she said kindly, having already been made aware of the situation at Meg's house. 'But your dad'll be back, you'll see. He'll get a job in the London Docks and everything will work out fine.'

Meg smiled weakly. 'Oh, I know. I keep telling me mam the

very same, but she sulks an' yells an' snaps me head off. Honest to God, I can't do nothing right for her.'

'I expect she's missing him, that's why. It can't be easy for her . . . nor for *him* neither. Can it, eh?'

Meg thought hard on Jenny's wise words. She hadn't really seen it that way. 'Well, it's true they ain't never been parted in all the years they've been wed,' she admitted.

'There you are then. You'll have to make allowances for her. Give her a bit of extra loving on your side, eh?' A thought suddenly occurred to her. 'I'll tell you what. You can take home a little treat to cheer her up. I dare say money's a bit short too, what with your dad away looking for work.' She went to the pantry and brought out the dish of baked salmon. 'I'll keep back just enough to serve Claudia when she gets home.' Slicing a generous chunk, she placed it into a smaller dish and wrapped it in a piece of clean muslin. 'Get your coat on now, and be off with you,' she told the delighted girl.

'Aw, you're a good kind soul,' Meg told her, grabbing her long tweed coat from the dresser cupboard and slinging it over her shoulders. The coat had been her mam's and her late gran's before her. It was thick and warm on a winter's night. 'If that fat salmon don't cheer her up, I don't know what will!' she laughed, snuggling into the coat and doing up the big bone buttons.

When Meg had gone, with the dish tucked securely under her arm, Jenny thought how good it was to see her smile again. She told Frank when he came in a short while later, and he agreed. 'You did right. After all, it were *me* who caught the salmon, and if there's no one here that wants it, then it makes sense to give it to someone who does. I dare say Meg's mother's finding it hard to make ends meet since her fella's been away.'

Jenny's guilt melted with his generous words. 'I could have saved it for you,' she teased, watching him enjoy his own meal.

'No. You did right,' he assured her. Happy in each other's

company, they talked a little, laughed a lot, finished their meal, and then the two of them cleared away the dinner things. Afterwards he lit his pipe and stood by the sink while Jenny began the washing-up. 'Mrs Marshall was worried, you say?' He regarded Jenny with serious eyes. 'Didn't she eat *anything*?'

'Oh, I didn't say that,' Jenny protested. 'She ate a little, I suppose. But mostly she just played with her food.' She glanced up at him. 'The other one's not back yet, is she?'

He sucked on his pipe and blew the smoke above his head. 'No.' His voice was sombre. After a while he brought his gaze to bear on Jenny. For a moment he said nothing, then, 'I reckon I'll have to go and find her.'

It was Elizabeth who answered. She had come into the kitchen so quietly that neither of them had heard her. They were both astonished to see her there. 'I was about to ask you if you would go and look for her,' she said softly. 'I know my daughter is a superb horsewoman, but she went away in such a rage I'm afraid she might be hurt.' In her heart she believed that Claudia was deliberately staying out to worry her. If that was the case, then she had certainly succeeded. Mingled with her concern was a rush of anger. Why was it that parents must take the blame for everything on to themselves? But they did. They *always* did!

'I'll saddle the cob and get after her then,' Frank assured her. 'Don't you worry, ma'am. She won't have come to any harm, I'm certain.' In two strides he was at the fireplace where he tapped the bowl of his pipe against the grate. When the lighted baccy fell into the glowing coals, he straightened up and laid the pipe on the mantelpiece. Quickly then, he took his jacket from the back of the chair, putting it on as he crossed towards the back door. 'She'll be fine,' he said again, nodding his head and politely smiling at Elizabeth as he closed the door. She didn't see the cheeky wink he gave Jenny.

Still blushing pink, she asked Elizabeth if she would like a hot drink in the drawing room. 'It'll only take a minute, ma'am,' she assured her. It hurt her to see how pale and distressed her mistress was.

'Later perhaps,' Elizabeth answered, going from the room. 'When Claudia is home safe and sound.'

With Elizabeth gone to wait for her daughter, and Frank out searching, Jenny was left alone again. 'That blessed woman wants her arse leathering,' she muttered angrily, plunging her arms into the soapy suds, and slapping the dishcloth against the plates. 'Never satisfied unless she's the centre of attention,' she grumbled. Up on her tiptoes she stared through the window at the night.

Only the shaft of light from the kitchen penetrated the immediate darkness. There was a soft yellow glow from the lamp in the outhouse which Frank had made his home, and high above the trees the sky lay heavy and brooding. Jenny shivered. 'Brr! Shouldn't be at all surprised if there weren't a foot of snow before morning.' In the distance she could hear the soft thud of horse's hooves. Frank had lost no time in saddling the cob and making off across the fields. Jenny said a little prayer that he would soon be back. There was no such prayer for Claudia.

Frank was used to the cold outdoors. He was weathered by it, and deep in his soul felt part of it. Tonight, though, he bitterly resented being called out. In his mind he could still see Claudia's wicked face. He could see her flogging that helpless creature without a care for the damage she might be inflicting, and the anger he had felt then bubbled to the surface now.

Still he pressed on because it was his duty, and because he was a man of great sensitivity. For all her selfish ways, Claudia was only eighteen years old. She had never mastered the art of making firm friends and so she led a lonely life. Recently she had suffered the loss of many privileges that were as much part of her existence as Nature was his. Then there had been that awful business when it was unclear whether her father had committed suicide or died by accident. It was bad enough losing a father without all of that.

As he rode, searching the ditches and scanning the horizon, he found every reason to forgive her. But he could not easily forget how she had thrashed the horse. Whatever she had been through, it was no one's fault, least of all that poor animal's. He couldn't understand what had happened to make her behave towards the hunter like that, because of all creatures she loved that beast the most; even above her own mother. But then, he mustn't forget that she was grieving, and grief took folk different ways.

Time passed and he grew weary. The night was deepening and the skies pressed down on him, laden with snow, and hanging low like the belly of a cow when she was flush with milk. They had covered the land as far as Ridgmont and then to the outer fields of Salford. At every turn Frank had called out Claudia's name, but there was no sign of her. He was desperately worried now and considering whether to go back and recruit more help.

They were deep in the Woburn Woods when he brought the cob to a halt and climbed down. His legs were stiff and his lips cracked with cold. At first the snow had been just a trickle, covering the earth with a sprinkling of crystal dust. Suddenly the flakes were big and fluffy, billowing down in a gathering breeze, settling thick on the earth and making it dangerous underfoot; potholes and gulleys pitted this land, and though the cob knew his way, the snowfall was like a camouflage to his old eyes. He stared up at his master as though to say, 'Take me home. I'm cold and I'm tired.'

Frank affectionately rubbed his hands across the cob's broad neck. 'Sorry, my beauty,' he said through numb lips. 'But the way that reckless young fool was riding, she might be in trouble. We'll give it a while longer, then we'll head back. We need a few more men. Happen they could fan out and cover a larger area than the two of us can in one night.'

His next stop was Jacob Laing's farmhouse. He hadn't made his way there earlier because he felt Claudia was safe and deliberately staying out to cause others inconvenience. Besides, Frank was well aware of how Claudia felt about Jacob Laing. She had made it known more than once, and at the top of her voice, how she believed her mother was having an affair with the old farmer. 'Vicious little bugger!' Frank muttered beneath his breath. 'More's the pity they're *not* sweet on each other, because he's a good man who might give Elizabeth Marshall the contented life she deserves.'

The lights from Jacob Laing's farmhouse were a comforting sight, spilling into the darkness and mingling with the snow to create a beckoning halo. 'If she's taken shelter there, old fellow,' Frank told the cob, 'our work will be done, and we can make our way home to a warm bed.' He stroked his hand against the hairy snow-covered withers. 'What do you say to that, eh?' The cob's answer was to put his head down and thrust forward with greater determination, his large hooves making a sucking sound as they were drawn deep into the snow.

Claudia saw him coming. In her devious mind she had known that her mother would send Frank looking for her. At first she had waited on the upper ridge above Aspley Hills, but when the snow threatened she had made her way here. *Watching. Waiting.* Her instincts had been right. She smiled to herself as he came nearer.

Quickly now, she prepared herself for him. Taking the sturdy stick she had collected earlier, she used it to stab wildly at her clothes. When her riding breeches were shredded with long jagged tears, she cut into the sleeve of her blouse until the blood spurted up in small red fountains. Afterwards she spattered her face with muck and dust, scraping her sharp nails along her cheekbone until she was made to cry with pain.

As they drew close to the big barn, a sound from inside urged Frank to draw the old cob in. 'Shhh,' he whispered, remaining still for a moment. In the breeze he thought he heard a kind of whimper. But he wasn't certain. All the same, he swiftly dismounted to lead the cob across the uneven ground. The barn door was open. Gripping its edge with frozen fingers, he peered inside. There was someone there he felt sure. 'Is that you, Miss Claudia?' Bringing the cob into the shelter, he let loose the reins and hurried forward.

The whisper startled him. '*Frank*!' At first he didn't recognise the voice, but when it came again, this time more urgent, 'Frank . . . I'm hurt,' he realised it was Claudia's.

Fear for her safety overriding all else, he rushed forward. 'It's all right,' he cried, falling to his knees before her. 'You're safe now.'

Her sobs were as real as the pain in her body, where she had wildly cut into her own flesh. 'I knew you'd find me,' she said softly, clinging to him. Her blood smeared his face. The fresh damp smell of his hair heightened her senses. 'Don't leave me,' she begged.

'Can you walk?' He was angry and amazed that she could believe he would leave her there.

'No.'

He braced himself to lift her in his arms, but laid her back down when she cried out. 'Where are you hurt?' In the shaft of moonlight that filtered through the window to bathe them, she looked a sorry sight. Her face was grazed and she was shockingly dishevelled. *And yet he was moved by her stunning beauty*. The exquisite pale eyes stared out at him like those of a wounded creature. Her brows were dark, like perfect crescents, stark against her forehead. The long brown hair cascaded over her shoulders, almost as though it had been carefully arranged, its warm chestnut hues accentuating the pallor of her skin. 'I'm so cold,' she said, shivering against him. Through his coat she could feel the muscular hardness of his body. It roused her deep down inside.

Ripping off his coat he wrapped it round her. 'Where are you hurt?' he asked, his eyes scouring her body.

She didn't answer. Instead, she pulled back the coat and lowered her eyes to the torn breeches. Taking hold of his hand, she placed it tenderly on her bruised skin. He shivered inwardly. He was so cold and she was so warm. So soft and smooth, like the touch of silk. 'Feel me,' she whispered. 'Make love to me.' When his eyes widened with surprise, she undid the buttons of her breeches and slid his fingers inside. Her legs were open wide. His fingertips slid into the moistness there. She groaned, pushing up to him. 'You don't hate me, do you?' she murmured. '*They* do, I know. But please . . . not *you*.' She was crying now, tearing him apart. At the back of his mind he told himself that she was the devil. But her skin was like velvet. So inviting. And he was only a man after all. A sense of loathing rose in him. Loathing her. Loathing his own weakness.

'No!' His voice grated in the hush of that great barn. Confused, he began to move but she held him there. He didn't resist. It was already too late for that.

In only a heartbeat she was naked under his coat. Now, in the moonlight, she plucked the coat away and lay open beneath him. 'Love me,' she pleaded, her quick fingers fumbling at his trousers. Her legs were wrapped around him. Her small pert breast was touching his mouth. He could feel himself growing bolder, his thighs tightening and tingling as he grew bigger with the passion she aroused in him.

He knew he should tear himself away but his whole body was aching for her. Suddenly all reason was gone, and he was on her. He heard her gently laugh as he gripped the inner softness and parted her thighs wide. Then, with a groan that came from deep

65

inside, he pushed his erect member into her. Skin and wetness lapped over him. He was beyond redemption now. Greedily she rose to him, taking him deeper, engulfing him in a wave of overwhelming sensation. She was all over him, desperate, hurting him like he had never been hurt before. But it was a pleasurable, bitter-sweet pain. His tongue found her nipple, hard and pointed. Her buttocks in his hands were round and firm, thrusting up, tight strong muscles holding him inside, hungry for him.

It was a fever. A fever that must run its course. All too soon it was over. In that moment he despised her more than he thought possible. He despised himself too. 'You're not sorry, are you?' she purred. Her pale eyes were smiling as she stretched out like a satisfied kitten. In that moment he knew she had deceived him. '*I'm* not sorry,' she murmured, straightening her tattered clothes.

Shame and regret would not let him answer. Silently he put on his trousers and turned away. It was then that he saw the long dark shape lying a short distance away. 'It's *him*,' she said, her arrogant eyes following his gaze. 'He stumbled back there. It's a wonder he didn't kill me.' Her words were lost in the gloom as Frank bent to the animal. His shame was tenfold. In the throes of passion he had forgotten the hunter.

'What in God's name have you done to him?' he asked. His voice was low and disbelieving. The animal was on its side, hardly breathing and covered in a film of fetid sweat. Running tender skilful fingers over the hot flesh, he feared the worst. 'He's in a bad way,' he said, half turning his head. 'Why the hell didn't you tell me?' His fingers came to the rear legs. There was something awful here. Shifting himself so that the moonlight fell full on the animal, he saw why the proud hunter shivered with pain. The bone was jutting through his flesh. 'God Almighty, you bloody vixen, you!' He wanted to kill her.

Suddenly she was beside him. 'Stop fussing. He'll be fine,' she said callously, laying a hand on his shoulder.

'Get out of my way!' Thrusting her aside, he ran to the farmhouse. In a matter of minutes he returned still running, but with Jacob Laing alongside. Frank was carrying a lighted lamp. The older man was carrying a shotgun.

A quick examination, then Jacob shook his white head. There was no need for words. Frank had seen the extent of the damage for himself. 'I'll be the one to do it,' he said, choking back the tears in his eyes.

Outside a lone hare was startled by the loud shattering explosion. Inside the barn, the old cob stayed in the corner, safe in the dark. Frank let the shotgun fall to the ground. 'Will you take *her* back?' he asked brokenly. He didn't look up. He didn't want to see her face, and didn't want the other man to see the truth in his. What had happened here was his punishment for lying with the devil.

'Aye.' Jacob Laing looked from one to the other, and he knew. 'Don't worry. I'll get her home safely,' he promised.

In the dark early hours, Frank came home. Anxious and afraid, Jenny longed to run out to meet him but something about his downcast eyes, something about the way Claudia smiled at her when she took the hot drinks in . . . something about the way she told her mother, 'Frank found me. He'll be along later,' made Jenny stay in the shadows. In her frantic mind she heard Claudia's boast: '*I can take him from you anytime I want.*' Unsure, she crept into her bed. Frank didn't cross the paved yard to come to her. Not that night. And never again.

He stood the letter against the mantelpiece clock, and then he left, pausing only to raise his sad brown eyes to Jenny's bedroom window. Come the dawn he was many miles away. He might have stayed had he known that it wasn't only Jenny he had left behind, because now another being was conceived. *His child and Claudia's.* An innocent. Born to serve. And destined to change all of their lives.

# *Chapter Four*

'Packed his things and gone, you say?' Elizabeth was shocked. She had asked Jenny to bring Frank to her so that she could thank him for seeing Claudia safely home, although to tell the truth she believed it was more than that irresponsible girl deserved.

'I knew straight away,' Jenny replied. 'The door was left open and the bed hadn't even been slept in.' When Elizabeth looked at her curiously, she cast her gaze down. Her eyes were still red raw from crying. In spite of her determination not to let her feelings show, a small sob escaped her.

Elizabeth was mortified. 'What an insensitive fool I am,' she murmured. 'This must be a dreadful blow for you.' She came to Jenny and softly touched her shoulder. 'If a man chooses to leave without telling anyone, he must have a strong reason. No doubt time will reveal the truth.' She knew something of losing her man, and knew how painful it was. 'Leave me now,' she told Jenny. Suddenly she had her suspicions as to why Frank had departed in such a hurry. There were things she had to say to Claudia. Intimate things that would not do for Jenny's ears. 'Is Meg in yet?'

'No, ma'am.' As always, Jenny covered up for that feckless girl. 'I expect her mam's not too well again.'

Elizabeth was not fooled. Meg was as lazy as Jenny was hard-

68

working. 'I need to talk to you both . . . before lunch, I think.'
The sooner she got it over with the better. 'Twelve o'clock. Bring
her to the drawing room.' She pondered a moment. Then: 'How
unlike that responsible young man to sneak away in the dead of
night. Obviously he came home after finding my daughter or the
cob wouldn't be in the stable.' She peered at Jenny. 'You did say
the horse was back in his stable, didn't you?'

'Yes, ma'am. I've already given him a feed of sugar beet,'
Jenny assured her. 'I haven't put him out to the field yet because
the snow's still deep on the ground. Later though I'll let him have
a little run while I muck out the stables.'

Elizabeth thought of her daughter lying warm and lazy in her
bed, and was ashamed. 'What would I do without you?' she said
quietly. When Jenny looked embarrassed, she added in a firmer
voice, 'But you have enough to do without taking on stable
duties. I won't allow it. Something will have to be done, and
quickly.' She frowned. 'I haven't quite decided what to do about
the cob. With the hunter gone, well . . .' She suppressed the anger
within her. She also had her suspicions about the hunter's awful
injuries. Claudia could be an out and out bitch. All the same,
knowing how Jenny's fellow felt about that fine animal, both
Elizabeth and Jenny knew it must have broken his heart to shoot
it. 'What I'm saying is, perhaps we don't need the field any
more.' She shook her head and lapsed into deep thought. 'Heaven
only knows what we'll do without Mr Winfield,' she murmured.
Realising that Jenny was still waiting, she said in a brighter voice,
'But we mustn't worry too much, must we? Everything will turn
out for the best, I'm sure.'

'Yes, ma'am.'

'I'll think of something before the day's out.'

It wasn't a question, and it didn't need an answer, so Jenny
gave none. Instead she declared, 'Breakfast won't be long,
ma'am.'

'I have no appetite for breakfast,' Elizabeth replied. 'My daughter is still in her bed, so there is no need for you to cook.' She smiled fondly. Jenny's list of duties were a mile too long, and no doubt she had a great deal on her mind where Frank Winfield was concerned. 'A pot of tea will suffice.'

With a polite nod of the head, Jenny departed the room. Downstairs in her beloved kitchen, she doggedly went about the motions of boiling the kettle, laying the tray, and finally taking it to the drawing room. Elizabeth was not there, but Jenny thought nothing of that. No doubt she would be back any minute.

She was grateful that breakfast wasn't wanted. If they didn't feel like eating it, she certainly didn't feel like cooking it. In fact, she was in half a mind to pack her own things and chase after Frank. With this thought uppermost, she even went to her room and stacked a few articles on the bed: four pairs of clean panties and her two cotton slips with the rosebuds on the hem. Frank had bought them for her last Christmas. She sat on the bed and lovingly stroked her hands over the delicate pretty things. Tears ran down her face. 'Where are you, Frank?' she sobbed, going to the window and looking across at the outhouse. It was empty, she knew. Just like her heart. 'What made you run off like that?' she asked. Wiping away the tears with the back of her hand, she spun round, her sad gaze hardening as she stared at the small pile of clothes on the bed. 'Was it *her*?' she asked in a harder voice. 'Is that why you couldn't face me in the light of day?'

Suddenly she laughed. It was a bitter sound. 'What happened out there in the night? Something *bad* happened, didn't it, Frank? Or you'd be here telling me about it, just like always. You'd be telling me what a disgrace she was, and how you felt she should have been left out there to freeze. After all, it was her own fault. That's what you'd be saying. And you'd be swearing about the shocking way she treated that magnificent beast . . . an animal

70

she never deserved. Isn't that what you'd be saying, Frank? But you're not, are you? You've sneaked away because something *shameful* happened between you and her.'

Sitting on the bed, she gave herself up to deeper thoughts; bitter-sweet thoughts, memories of her and Frank together. 'How could you go away like that?' she murmured. It was all beyond her. And yet she knew why. Deep in her soul, Jenny knew why he had gone.

Raised voices carried up the stairs and into her room. It was Claudia. Curious, Jenny came out on to the landing. There was a fearful row going on in Claudia's room although Elizabeth's voice was lower, dignified as always. 'Sometimes I despair of you,' she was saying.

Claudia resented her mother's intrusion into her room. When Elizabeth strode over to the windows and flung the curtains back, she sat up in bed and bawled at her, 'Get out of my room. I don't want you in here.' She had already guessed the reason for her mother's visit, and though she wasn't in any mood to be questioned, it gave her a measure of satisfaction to know that she was the centre of attention.

'I'll go when I'm good and ready, and not before.'

It was a rare thing for Claudia to see her mother so angry, and it had a strange sobering effect on her. 'What do you want from me?' she said sullenly, falling back against the pillow. 'I'm very tired.' She folded her arms behind her head, looking at her mother with an injured expression. 'You don't realise what a dreadful experience it all was.'

Elizabeth softly laughed. 'I don't think so, my dear. You forget, I know you very well.'

Undaunted, Claudia turned over and smiled sweetly. 'So you do, Mother dear,' she said slyly. 'And what else do you think you *know*?' She stretched her long slim body, deliberately exposing

71

her bruised breast, hoping it would offend this gracious woman whose morals she could never live up to.

Knowing Claudia's intention, Elizabeth kept her eyes on that brassy face as she went on in a cool cutting voice. 'Is that what you did to *him*?' she asked. 'When he found you, did you bare yourself to him?' When Claudia merely laughed, she silenced her by coming closer to the bed. 'You did, didn't you? *Like any woman off the streets, you offered yourself to him.*' Her green eyes glittered angrily as she thought of how she herself had sent Frank out searching. 'I was a fool to send him after you. I should have known that you were never in any danger. Wild cats and foxes have a way of looking after themselves.'

'I don't know what you're getting at!' Feeling unusually threatened by her mother's closeness, Claudia sprang out of bed. Though she was naked and it was cold in the room, she made no attempt to cover herself.

Elizabeth stood her ground. She had only suspected, but now her awful suspicions were confirmed. It was there in her daughter's bold eyes. 'You know very well what I'm getting at,' she snapped. 'I've seen the way you look at him. How you shamelessly flaunt yourself at him. You weren't lost last night, were you? I couldn't be certain then, but I am now. You knew full well that if you didn't return on such a foul night, I would send him out after you. The whole thing was a plan, wasn't it? Like the good man he is, Frank Winfield spurned your previous amorous advances, so you used *me* to trap him.'

Claudia stared at her for a while. Her mother was hurt and bitterly ashamed. That pleased her. 'All right,' she proudly admitted, 'maybe I did. What of it? I've wanted him for a long time, but he was too wrapped up in *her* to look at me. Trapping him was the only way.' She smiled and licked her lips. 'It was worth it too.'

Even though she had known all along, Elizabeth was so

distraught that she couldn't look on that brazen face. With downcast eyes she murmured, 'How could I have given birth to such a wanton as you?'

'Have you ever thought there must be wantonness in *you*?' Claudia cruelly replied. 'Perhaps it's *your* badness that's shown up in me.' Snatching her robe from the bed and throwing it over her nakedness, she looked into her mother's face. 'Do you know that I've always hated you?' she taunted callously.

Elizabeth met her wicked gaze with suspiciously bright eyes. 'I'm used to your destructive ways,' she told her, raising her head proudly. 'But what about that poor girl downstairs? The man you seduced was promised to Jenny. She's never done you any harm. In fact, there have been times when I've wished that you were more like her. She's a good, loyal soul with little in life. But she had her man, and a future to look forward to. You've ruined all that. Doesn't it even bother you?'

Claudia laughed out loud. 'Oh, Mother, what a fool you are. Why on earth should it bother me? I got what I wanted. No, it doesn't bother me one little bit! In fact, I don't see why it should end there. It isn't many men who would put themselves out to search for me. Strange, isn't it, Mother, to discover that a servant can be a real man after all? I found that out last night,' she said meaningfully.

'Mr Winfield may be an employee in this household, but he's far too good for you.' Elizabeth had never been so incensed.

'Servant . . . employee, it's all the same.' Claudia tossed her head in triumph. 'Do you want to know what happened when he found me?' Before Elizabeth could stop her, she went on, 'It was wonderful! Better than I had imagined it would be. We lay on the ground in Jacob Laing's big barn. We were both stark naked, Mother. He took me then and there . . . oh, but he was magnificent. I can see you're shocked – a servant of this household and your own daughter. What you think doesn't concern me. I'll do what

I like, and have whichever man takes my fancy. I'm sorry if that wasn't what you wanted to hear. Does that shock you even more, Mother?'

'Nothing you could say would ever shock me,' Elizabeth replied in a hard voice that betrayed something of her fury. 'You will ruin your own life, I have no doubt about that. But to come between a young couple who loved each other and planned to marry . . .' She shook her head in disgust. 'Don't you feel any shame at all?'

'None whatsoever. On the contrary, Mother dear. I expect Frank Winfield and I will get to know each other even better. After all, he enjoyed it as much as I did. And I'm so easily bored, a passionate affair will help me to while away the time. The fact that he belonged to someone else will only make it that much more exciting, don't you think?'

'You wouldn't want to know what I think,' Elizabeth said sharply. 'But I'll tell you this . . . if I see that you're making her life unbearable in this house, I'll make certain you leave before she does.' Lately she felt old and spent, and if she had to choose a companion, she would rather it was a good and kind servant like Jenny than her own daughter. 'Do you understand what I'm saying?'

For the first time, disbelief and astonishment registered on Claudia's face. 'Are you saying you would turn your own daughter out in favour of a skivvy?'

'Something like that, yes.' While Claudia's mouth was still wide open and her eyes big with surprise, Elizabeth added, 'That girl is worth ten of you, and if I find you deliberately hurting her, I myself will pack your portmanteau and see you through the front door.'

'You wouldn't dare!' Claudia jerked her head back as though she had been physically slapped. 'You *couldn't*.'

'Nonsense. There is nothing in your father's will to say that we must live together in this house.'

Claudia was speechless. It had never occurred to her that she could be turned out. Now that she came to think of it, her mother was right. It was like a bolt from the blue. This was a bad situation, and it set her scheming. She didn't care for the idea that her mother had the upper hand here. Something would have to be done. Quite what she didn't yet know. But it would have to be something drastic. A plan of sorts, to ensure that never again could her mother threaten her with eviction.

'Tell me, Claudia,' Elizabeth needed to know, 'Jacob Laing explained the hunter had to be shot. According to what you have just told me, you were not lost or hurt . . . so how did he come to be so badly injured?' In the back of her mind she wondered whether Claudia had deliberately driven the horse to his death. It was such a terrible thought that she wanted a measure of reassurance.

Claudia was in the mood to make her mother suffer. 'You still don't understand, do you?' she goaded. 'I wasn't going to let you sell him to anyone else. He was mine. If I couldn't have him, then *no one* would.'

Elizabeth went cold inside. Was there no end to her daughter's badness? 'What did you do to him?' she demanded in a low voice. When Claudia hesitated, she cried out, 'WHAT DID YOU DO TO HIM?'

Startled by her mother's outburst, Claudia snapped back, 'I sent him on and on until he was exhausted . . . through the spinney and over the hedges. I heard his leg tear on the gate post, and knew it was splitting open the further we went. He stumbled, almost throwing me off. I was angry, don't you understand? He could have killed me. He wanted to stop, to lie down, but I wouldn't let him.' She was sobbing bitterly. Only now did she realise how much she'd loved him. 'It's *your* fault,' she yelled, hitting out with her fists. '*You* said he would have to be sold. He was *mine*! You had no right. I hate you! Do you hear me, I hate you!'

When one of Claudia's fists caught her on the temple, Elizabeth brought her hand up and slapped it hard across Claudia's mouth. She reeled back, clutching her face and staring at her mother with eyes that were black with loathing. Yet she remained silent when Elizabeth told her in a harsh whisper, 'What an evil person you are, Claudia. How can you bear to admit that you deliberately caused that proud animal's death? God help me, but you could be right. It may well be *my* fault, because I've raised a monster when I should have drowned you at birth!'

Filled with despair, she dropped her gaze and went slowly to the door. Before she left there was one more thing she had to say. She hoped it might cause Claudia at least some regret. 'I'm sorry but you won't be able to continue what you've started with Frank Winfield because he's gone. I like to think he was so ashamed of what you and he did that he's done the honourable thing. I won't deny it takes courage. I don't altogether blame him for he's only a man like any other. All the same, you've caused Jenny a great deal of unhappiness, between the two of you.'

'If he were *my* man, I'd know how to hold on to him.'

'You still don't feel any remorse, do you?' Elizabeth didn't wait for an answer. Instead she declared forcibly, 'I meant what I said. If I find that you're deliberately setting out to cause her any more pain, you will leave this house and never come back.' With those words still ringing in the air, she went on to the landing, leaving the bedroom door wide open. Somehow her daughter's privacy didn't seem to matter any more.

As she made her way downstairs, the sound of Claudia's door slamming behind her echoed round the house. Elizabeth paused and gripped the banister, half turning back. It was then that she saw the small figure in the shadows of the upper landing. 'Jenny!' She was momentarily taken aback.

She came slowly down the stairs. Seeing the stricken look on her face, Elizabeth knew straight away. *Jenny had heard*

76

*everything!* It was then that she realised the maid meant to confront Claudia. 'No!' Elizabeth swung round and rushed up the stairs. Outside Claudia's room, the two of them faced each other – Elizabeth silently pleading with her not to enter that room, and Jenny filled with such bitterness that all reason had fled. 'It won't solve anything,' Elizabeth assured her kindly. 'Come downstairs with me. We'll talk. Please.' She could see that Jenny meant to burst into that room and confront Claudia and if it had been Elizabeth herself she would probably have done exactly the same. But to what purpose? 'Please?' she urged again. 'Won't you come down to the drawing room where we can talk?'

At first it seemed as though Jenny would refuse. She glared at the bedroom door and imagined Claudia behind it. Jealousy and hatred raged through her. The woman had deliberately set out to seduce Frank. Thoughts of what had taken place burned in her mind. Yet somehow Elizabeth's calm and gentle presence tempered her fury. She began to realise Frank's part in it all. After all, he could have walked away but he hadn't. He'd stayed with her. Made love to her. All the awful rage seemed to melt into a corner of her heart, settling there like a dead weight. If she were to go bursting into that room, Claudia would have won again. But how could she stay in this house? It would be impossible to live under the same roof as the woman who had ended her happiness. Yet Frank was as much to blame. She must be careful not to forget that.

Now, when she looked at Elizabeth's worn and anxious face, the tears broke from her eyes and blinded her. In her misery she felt the other woman's hand on her shoulder, tender and comforting. 'Come with me, child,' her mistress said softly. Reluctantly, Jenny turned away from the bedroom.

Together they went down the stairs, Elizabeth slightly ahead. She could hear Jenny treading the steps behind her, and her heart went out to that sad creature. She imagined Claudia laughing at them both. Her own daughter, yet she was a stranger. Moreover, she was a stranger Elizabeth did not care for. 'God help us, what have we come to?' she murmured softly. In times such as these, mother and daughter should be a great strength to each other. Yet here they were, bitter enemies.

Claudia's hatred followed them like a dark shadow. It was almost more than she could bear. As they descended the stairs, each woman was moved by the same emotions. Jenny's thoughts echoed those of Elizabeth. In all her life she had never felt so lonely.

By the time they reached the drawing room, Jenny felt more able to take control. 'Please, ma'am . . . I don't really want to talk about it. Not now,' she pleaded. She wanted to think a while longer. To understand how this had happened. Maybe it wasn't just Claudia and Frank to blame. Perhaps it was *her* fault too. Somehow she wondered now whether she was responsible for Frank's going. Was she so unforgiving that he couldn't come to her and explain? Oh, but how could she have forgiven him such a dreadful thing? She felt inadequate, broken inside. She didn't want to talk with anyone about it. A strange sense of shame came over her. 'Thank you all the same, ma'am,' she said. 'I'm grateful that you stopped me from going into your daughter's room.' Apart from anything else, such a confrontation would only have caused this poor woman a great deal more anguish.

In the face of what had happened, Elizabeth seemed lost for words. She merely smiled and nodded, and Jenny gratefully took her leave. Both women had momentarily forgotten that Jenny and Meg had been summoned to the drawing room at twelve o'clock. That was another matter that was bound to cause hardship.

Meg was frantic. 'What does she want to see me about?' she asked. 'It weren't my fault I were late, honest to God it weren't.'

Her bottom lip was trembling and she was close to tears. 'If I'm dismissed for being late, our mam'll kill me . . . Oh, Jenny, what am I to do, eh?' She fell into the stand chair and dropped the dustpan on her lap. 'I won't dare go home, I won't. She'll kill me, I'm telling you!'

Jenny was used to Meg's dramatic outbursts. 'Take hold of yourself,' she told her, replacing the sprouts in the colander and wiping her hands on her pinny. 'I've no idea what Mrs Marshall wants to see us about but we'll soon find out. She doesn't only want to see you but me as well, and I'm not carrying on, am I?' She had done her carrying on, and now there were no tears left. Later she had to decide where she would go, for it was hardly likely that she could stay in this house after what had happened.

Meg knew nothing yet of the saga which had played itself out while she was slumbering in her bed. 'It's all right for you, 'cause you ain't got a mam to go home to.' Even before the last word was spoken, Meg's face fell with horror. 'Oh! I'm sorry. I'm really sorry. What a thing to say,' she moaned, crying all over again.

Going to her, Jenny put a comforting arm round her shoulders. 'It's all right,' she murmured. 'It's been so long since I had a mother, I've forgotten what it's like.' In fact, Jenny still had vivid memories of her mother. She remembered her as being a very beautiful woman with long dark hair and a wide wonderful smile. As she grew older, though, the image became dimmer. Jenny supposed there would come a day when she could no longer picture her. The thought was saddening.

Suddenly, Meg was curious. 'How old were you when your mam died?' Though Meg was vaguely aware of Jenny's background, it was a subject that was hardly ever mentioned.

'Oh, I don't know.' She cast her mind back. 'Three . . . four maybe. All I know is that they took her away in a long box. After that, I never saw her again.' Suddenly she was overwhelmed by the recollection. The past was a nightmare she would never forget. When she eventually found a position here in this house, she was incredibly happy. Then, when Frank told her he loved her, she was constantly afraid that one day it would all vanish into thin air. Now it had, and she didn't know which way to turn. What with Frank's leaving her like that, and then the shocking conversation she had heard between Claudia and her mother, her whole world had collapsed yet again. All the old feelings of loneliness and confusion washed over her, and she was that same helpless little girl who had been dragged, screaming, from the body of her mammy. 'Look, Meg, there's no use worrying. It's time we made our way to the drawing room.' She took off her pinny and patted her short fair hair. 'And for goodness' sake, stop thinking the worst.'

'I can't help it,' Meg whimpered, visibly trembling as Jenny looked her over and straightened her white mob-cap. 'I just *know* she means to dismiss me.'

'You don't know any such thing.'

'What does she want me for then?'

'She wants us *both*!' Jenny reminded her. It was only a few minutes ago that she'd remembered they were summoned to the drawing room at twelve o'clock. There was no denying she herself had been curious as to Mrs Marshall's reasons. Now it didn't matter any more because in a few days, when she had decided which direction to take, Jenny meant to be gone. 'If she was going to dismiss you, why would she want to see me as well?'

Jenny's comment appeared to soothe Meg. She even managed a little nervous smile. But a short time later, when Jenny knocked on the drawing-room door and Elizabeth's voice called for them to enter, Meg began trembling all over again.

'I'm sorry. I had completely forgotten I'd asked you to see me.' Elizabeth had been taken by surprise when the two of them walked in. Jenny couldn't help but notice how deeply troubled she was. It occurred to her that while she herself had nobody in the world, neither had Elizabeth Marshall. In a strange way they were companions.

'Would you like us to come back later?' Jenny put the question and Meg silently thanked her.

Elizabeth dismissed the idea. 'That won't be necessary. You have quite enough to do without running backwards and forwards. No, now that you're here, I might as well tell you the worst.' When Meg made a nervous little noise, she hated herself for what she had to do. 'Please . . .' She gestured to the settee. 'I'd like you both to sit down a moment.' It was such an outrageous suggestion that both Meg and Jenny looked aghast at her. 'Please,' she insisted. And they did as they were asked.

Seated opposite them, Elizabeth explained, 'Without going into personal details, I'm afraid I have to tell you that this family is not as well off as it once was. But then, no doubt you already suspected that?' She looked from one to the other and the strain of this interview was evident on her face, though Jenny knew it had much more to do with the whole sequence of events rather than what she was saying now especially. 'There is only the cob left and he will have to go. Mr Laing has often stated an interest in him, and I have no doubt he will also be happy to take over the lease on the field.' Here she paused and glanced anxiously at Jenny. 'Sadly Mr Winfield is no longer with us, and there will be no need to take on another man of his skills, though of course it will be necessary to employ a handyman of sorts, for the heavier tasks about the grounds . . . keeping the hedges cut, cleaning the windows and chopping wood, that sort of thing.'

She noticed how Meg stared with astonishment at Jenny, and was filled with remorse at being the one to break the news about Jenny's young man. Quickly now she went on, 'As you may have guessed, there is another reason why I asked you to see me.' She looked from one to the other. Swallowing hard, she continued in a softer voice, 'I'm sorry but it isn't good news. I have had to make a very difficult decision.' She brought her sad gaze to Meg. 'I'm afraid I must let you go at the end of the week.'

Meg had been expecting it, and now was too upset to speak. Instead she stared at the ground and fidgeted with her skirt. 'I'm so sorry, but I'll see to it that you're paid a full month's wages,' Elizabeth promised. She didn't like what she had to do but with her depleted finances there was no other course left open to her.

Her gaze went to Jenny. She had asked her to bring Meg here before that awful business with Claudia. Now she felt awkward, and yet there were other matters that must be dealt with if she and her daughter were to survive. 'I asked you here because I wanted you to know the situation. Though I can't afford to keep Meg on, I need someone to help me run this house. Someone I know. Someone meticulous in their work, someone wholly trustworthy and reliable.' She paused to let the words sink in. 'That someone is you. I won't pretend it will be easy. Indeed, the work will be much harder with Meg gone. But I know I would never get anyone more capable or dedicated.' Her spirits fell as she realised that Jenny might not want to remain in this house now. 'I can't even offer to raise your wages,' she apologised. Without giving too much away to the listening Meg, she suggested kindly, 'Perhaps, after all that's happened, you might need some time to think about it?' Apprehensive, she waited for Jenny's answer.

Jenny had been thinking all the while Elizabeth was talking. Two things occurred to her. First she wondered if there was any way that Meg could keep her position here, and secondly she was unsure of what she herself must do. The thought of leaving without anywhere else to go was terrifying to her. The world was a cold cruel place when you were on your own. She had already been through that and the memories were still too fresh. And yet she was afraid of what might happen if she was to stay here. Claudia would always be a thorn in her side, and with her vindictive nature would find every way to remind Jenny of what had taken place that night.

On the other hand, Jenny asked herself whether she could really leave this woman who, in her own gentle way, was begging her to stay? She had a real affection for Elizabeth Marshall. While Claudia's animosity towards her mother had grown, Jenny's affection had deepened. This wasn't a decision she could reach in a matter of minutes. 'Thank you, ma'am,' she replied, rising from the settee. 'I *would* like to give it a deal of thought.'

'Then you and I will talk again, the same time tomorrow.'

There was a wonderful moment when each woman knew what the other was thinking. Their eyes met and Jenny gave a half-smile. 'Thank you, ma'am,' she murmured. With that she turned away and left the room. Subdued and tearful, Meg followed her.

In spite of Jenny's reassurances, Meg remained upset for the rest of the day. She cried all the while she was laying the dining table for dinner, and she cried when Elizabeth sat fifteen minutes waiting for her daughter to join her there. She sulked when Elizabeth left her own meal untouched, and brooded when strict instructions were given that: 'Nothing is to be served to my daughter while she remains in her room.' She sobbed while she helped to clear the table and afterwards, when Jenny was brewing a pot of tea for the two of them, constantly wiped her red eyes while she reluctantly black-leaded the kitchen range. 'I didn't tell you our dad came back from London, did I?' she said. 'There ain't no work there neither, so my wages are *still* the only money that's coming into our house. Oh, Jenny gal, I daren't go home,' she groaned. 'Our mam'll skin me alive.'

'Don't tell her.'

'What d'yer mean?' Meg's eyes grew round like two full moons. 'I've *got* to tell her.'

'Don't tell her until tomorrow.'

'Why not?'

'I have an idea, that's all.' While Meg had spent the day feeling sorry for herself, Jenny had given a great deal of thought to what had been said in the drawing room.

For the first time that day, Meg managed a smile, though it was a weak and wan expression. 'D'yer reckon yer can get the Missus to keep me on?' she asked hopefully.

Jenny shook her head. 'I'm not saying that. In fact, I'm not saying *anything*. It's no good getting your hopes up. All I'm asking is that you don't tell your mam until tomorrow.' She helped Meg into her coat and fastened the buttons up. 'Do you think you can manage that?' She sighed at the sight of Meg's red-rimmed eyes. 'If you keep crying, she'll guess anyway.'

Suddenly, Meg's smile was brighter. 'She won't know, cross my heart. Oh, Jenny, if only you can get the Missus to keep me on, I'll never be late again.'

Jenny laughed. 'Don't make promises you can't keep,' she chuckled, pushing her out of the door. 'Away with you, and remember what I said. Don't go worrying your mam tonight. Happen you'll have to tell her the worst tomorrow anyway, but like I say, I've an idea. It might not come to anything but it's worth a try.' Before Meg could reply, she gently closed the door with the warning, 'Don't get your hopes up now.' Meg mumbled something but it was lost in the night.

'I hope I've done the right thing,' Jenny told herself as she went across the kitchen. There was still a deal of work to be done, cupboards to be cleaned out and silver to be polished.

It was half-past nine when Jenny went to her humble quarters. Earlier she had served Elizabeth's hot drink, and was not surprised to find that dear woman slumbering in her chair. She didn't wake her. Instead, she placed the tray closer to the hearth and quickly took her leave. As she passed Claudia's bedroom, she felt the strongest urge to rush in and tell that young lady exactly what she thought of her. She even lingered outside, turning the events over and over in her tortured mind until her blood was fired and she wanted to maim the person who had taken Frank from her.

'It wouldn't do any good, you know.' When Elizabeth's soft voice spoke from directly behind, she was visibly startled. 'Don't bring yourself down to her level,' Elizabeth told her as she spun round. And Jenny was shocked by such a telling statement.

In her heart, she knew that Elizabeth was right. What good would it do? It wouldn't change what had happened. Nor would it bring Frank back. Claudia was beyond redemption. She *enjoyed* being bad, and for her mother that was the worst thing of all. 'Good night, ma'am,' Jenny murmured, preparing to turn away.

'Good night,' Elizabeth replied. 'We'll talk tomorrow. In spite of everything, I hope you will decide not to leave me.' It was a pitiful remark, and one that told Jenny how deeply Elizabeth Marshall had come to rely on her.

She couldn't sleep. Many times Jenny was persuaded to the window from where she gazed at the outhouse which had been Frank's home. She pictured him there as she had seen him so often on a winter's night such as this, sitting in the deep armchair, with his long legs stretched in front of the stove, and his pipe clutched between those strong white teeth. More often than not she would be curled up on the floor beside him. His arm would be round her shoulders, his long capable fingers playing with her hair. There was such harmony between them. Such love. How could it all be so quickly gone? Disillusioned, she turned away, only to return moments later, allowing the bitter-sweet memories to torture her again.

Soon the night was spent. The dawn came up with a warm sun

and the world was covered in brilliance. Even as she watched, the snow began to melt and the song of the birds moved the quiet air. She stayed by the window a while longer, steeping herself in Nature's beauty and wondering how, in all this splendour, she could have imagined her own affairs to be important.

Raising her eyes to the skies, she gave up the smallest prayer. 'Which way shall I turn?' she whispered, and for one strange, inexplicable moment felt stronger in spirit. Even without her realising it, her mind was already made up. *She would stay!* If she chose to leave because of Claudia, she would be doing an injustice to Elizabeth. Somehow, after all that woman had been through, it didn't seem right.

Her soft blue eyes reached beyond the shifting clouds. Maybe she wasn't alone after all. For in these virgin magical moments of a new day, who could deny the presence of a mightier force at work?

Elizabeth was thrilled. 'I know it's a lot to ask of you, but I'm so glad you've decided to stay.' Jenny couldn't wait until midday to tell her. Instead, the moment she heard Elizabeth come down the stairs and into the drawing room, she went to her.

'You mustn't worry about Claudia,' Elizabeth declared. 'I've already spoken to that young lady and there will be no mention of what happened the other night. I'm sorry to say that Claudia can be evil and vindictive, but she knows the consequences of waging a vendetta against you.'

'It's all right, ma'am,' Jenny assured her. 'I've had time to think and I know this much – Frank is gone. He went of his own accord. I don't imagine Claudia forced him to leave so I won't hold her to blame for that. I thought I knew him, but happen I didn't know him at all.' In fact, Jenny wondered whether she wanted a man who could first deceive her with another woman, and then up and go without so much as a by your leave. 'As far as what happened between them, ma'am – well, it's done now, so whatever your daughter does or says, it can't hurt me more than I've already been hurt.' She sensed Elizabeth's helplessness and was made to voice the only reservation she had about staying in this house. 'The last thing I want to do is cause bad relations between you and your daughter.'

Elizabeth lapsed into a thoughtful silence at Jenny's words. Presently she looked up to say in a determined voice, 'I'm afraid it's too late for that, my dear.' Beyond that she wasn't prepared to speak because, although Jenny was more than a servant in this house, Elizabeth could not altogether forget the restraints of her upbringing. It was not done to talk about the failings of one's own family. Not even to friends. But then, she had no friends. There was only Jacob Laing and Jenny.

She understood. 'I'm sorry, ma'am,' she murmured.

'Thank you for deciding to stay. But you do realise that the workload will be heavier with Meg gone?'

Jenny bit her lip. 'I wanted to talk to you about that, ma'am,' she began. 'If there is a way of keeping her on, would you do it? Y'see, her dad's back from London and he's not found any work so Meg's wages are all that comes into that house. I know how frustrating she can be, and I know she hardly ever arrives on time, but she's a good girl, and works hard.'

'I'm aware of all that,' Elizabeth reminded her. 'Of course I would keep her on if I could.' She thought for a moment, and then slowly shook her head from side to side. 'No it isn't possible.'

'If you'll pardon me, ma'am,' Jenny ventured anxiously, 'there *is* a way.'

'Oh?'

Quickly now, before she lost her nerve, Jenny explained, 'Well, what with one thing and another, I've been up most of the night and I've done a lot of thinking.' She winced inwardly. 'Now that Frank's gone, I won't need to scrimp and save for a wedding, will I, ma'am?' Without waiting for an answer, she went on, 'I'm willing to take a cut in my wages . . . so that Meg can be kept on. Only I wouldn't want you to tell her, ma'am, because it wouldn't sit right.' If Jenny had learned anything from Meg about her mam, it was her fear of charity.

Elizabeth stared at her in disbelief. 'Are you saying you want me to *share* your wages between you and Meg?'

'If that's all right with you.'

Elizabeth was adamant. 'No. It is *not* all right with me. As it is you aren't paid anywhere near your worth.' She couldn't believe that anyone could be so unselfish, and so she mistakenly put it down to the fact that Jenny wasn't yet thinking straight, and who could blame her? 'I won't hear of such a thing,' she declared. Her tone betrayed a trace of anger. 'Meg will have to go and that's an end to it.' It was obvious that she was dismissing Jenny.

However, Jenny had allowed for every contingency. In the event that Mrs Marshall might not agree to that particular idea, she had come up with a second plan. 'Excuse me, ma'am, but there's something else.'

Elizabeth didn't speak. She merely nodded. Hopefully, Jenny went on, 'After Frank went, you said you would need a handyman. I wondered if you might kindly offer the job to Meg's dad. He's known to be a good and reliable worker, and – well, that way there would still be a wage going into the house.'

'I see.' Elizabeth's face had been grim but now it broke into a warm smile. Stepping away from the fireplace she stood before Jenny, her inquisitive eyes searching the girl's face; such a proud and lovely face, with those sky-blue eyes and small square chin. In that young face she saw a strength that warmed her heart. Somehow this house would not be the same if Jenny were ever to leave it. 'You're a fine young woman,' she said softly. 'You have been in this house almost as long as I have. When you came for the post of housemaid, you were so young, so very pale and undernourished, I was tempted to turn you away.' She inclined her head and raised her eyes upwards as though seeing it all in her mind's eye. Returning her gaze, she said softly, 'If I had turned you away, it would have been the worst thing I ever did in my life.' In her heart she couldn't help but compare Jenny to her own daughter. 'Things haven't gone well for you, have they? But I believe it will all come right one day. Frank Winfield is sure to realise what a treasure he's left behind and he'll be back, I know he will.'

Jenny did not have the same conviction. 'I don't think so, ma'am,' she said. Besides, she'd already made up her mind. However empty and painful it might be, she had no intention of living out her life in the hope that one day he might return for her. *She* had done nothing to be ashamed of, so why should she punish herself? 'So will you do that, ma'am?' she asked politely. 'Can Meg's dad have the job of handyman?'

Elizabeth nodded. 'Yes, I don't see why not.' When Jenny's eyes sparkled, she added, 'Of course, I'll have to see him first, to make certain he's suitable.' She sighed wearily. 'No doubt he's a good worker as you've already said, but like you he'll have a great deal of responsibility on his shoulders. I need to know he's man enough.' She returned to the fireplace. Being in Jenny's company was always a tonic. 'Do you know,' she said brightly, 'I think I'm ready to eat a hearty breakfast this morning.' It was only after Jenny had departed to prepare the meal that she realised what she had said. 'A hearty breakfast.' Wasn't that what a man sentenced to the gallows was allowed? 'Hmh!' she chuckled wryly. 'In fact, there is very little difference between us.'

Jenny was cooking the kippers when Meg came in from outside where she'd been emptying the scraps in the midden. Her eyes flooded with tears as Jenny explained, 'I'm sorry, Meg, but Mrs Marshall can't find no way to keep you on.'

89

'God help me then!' she cried, rubbing her eyes on the corners of her pinafore. 'We'll all starve, and it'll be *my* fault. If me mam skins me alive, it ain't no more than I deserve.' When Jenny laughed, she was shocked. But when she was told, 'You *won't* starve, because your dad is to come and see Mrs Marshall about the handyman's job,' her face crumpled into a grin. Squealing with delight, she lunged forward and flung her arms round Jenny's neck. Unfortunately, Jenny was caught by surprise, and as her arm went up, the pan went with it. The kipper did a somersault before flying through the air and landing face up on the floor, from where it stared at them through accusing eyes.

Mortified, Meg backed to the wall, her hands spread over her mouth and her eyes big as dinner plates as they followed the thick greasy trail of cooking fat, from the top of the stove and all the way down to the tiled floor. A shocked silence settled over the kitchen as she looked up at Jenny's face. Jenny stared back. She was smiling, then she was laughing, and everything was all right.

Meg was all for putting the kipper back in the frying pan but Jenny told her, 'We're not that hard up yet.' A short time later the mess was cleared and breakfast was ready. 'Oh, Jenny, you don't know how happy I am.' Meg grinned. 'If me dad gets the job here, me mam'll be so pleased she'll forget to have a go at me. Anyway, I expect he'll get a bigger wage than me, won't he?' She went on and on, merrily chattering, and Jenny couldn't get a word in.

Breakfast was served and Claudia showed her face. It was a glum and sullen face, and throughout the meal she never said a word. Once or twice she glared at Jenny. Then Elizabeth glared at Claudia, and the message was understood.

Jenny was grateful for she had never wanted to leave this place. Claudia, on the other hand, was inwardly seething. She knew her mother had meant it when she warned: 'I'll see *you* leave this house before her.' She knew without a doubt that, while her mother was alive, she must guard her tongue or face the consequences. She consoled herself with the knowledge that nobody could live for ever. *Least of all Elizabeth Marshall.*

With this delightful prospect in mind, she tucked into her food and made her wicked plans.

# Chapter Five

'I'm just off to the village, ma'am. Is there anything special you want me to fetch?' Jenny stayed by the drawing-room door while she waited for Elizabeth's answer.

'No, I don't think so.' Elizabeth turned from the window and studied the pretty face that looked at her with such loyalty. She knew what a burden she had put on those slender shoulders, and, though she had no alternative, it was a source of regret to her. 'Have you much to carry?' she asked with concern. 'Because if so you really ought to let Mr Taylor collect it. I'm sure he wouldn't mind, once his own work is finished.'

Jenny shook her head. 'Oh, no, ma'am,' she answered with a bright smile. 'It ain't much at all. As for Meg's dad, he's got his own work cut out. Besides, I've been through the house from top to bottom, and there's half an hour to spare before I need to start the dinner.' She glanced beyond Elizabeth to the window. 'It's such a beautiful day, I fancied a little walk.'

Lowering her gaze, Elizabeth said in a solemn voice, 'You're right, Jenny. It *is* a lovely day. One of those special April days that make you feel life is worthwhile.' She smiled to herself. Her life was not worthwhile. Not now. She fell quiet then, her thoughts turning inward as she recalled her own youth, and the way Claudia's father had walked arm in arm with her on such a day.

'If that's all, ma'am?' There was no reply. Realising she was no longer needed, Jenny softly departed.

In the kitchen, she made a small list of what she needed: a pound of white flour, some brown sugar, a measure of yeast, two bars of carbolic soap and some soda. That done, she put on her best cream shawl and collected her large wicker basket from the pantry. After satisfying herself that she had the necessary coins in her purse, she set off.

The path meandered through the flower beds and down to the kitchen garden. As she came closer, her quick eyes caught sight of the man in the vegetable garden. Mr Taylor was bent to his labours; a sturdily-built man with thin fair hair, he kept himself to himself and got on with his many duties. When she called out a cheery, 'Good morning', he straightened up, holding his hand to the bottom of his back. 'Morning, m'dear,' he returned, groaning as he stretched. 'This ground is hard as granite.' He regarded her curiously. 'Are you sure it were dug last year?'

Jenny nodded. 'Like I've already said, the man who worked here before you . . .' Painful memories of Frank made her pause. 'What I mean is, we always got a good crop of fat vegetables.'

'In that case, I'll just have to keep at it.' He chuckled and came to stand before her. 'Truth is, I'm not really used to digging. You step out of our front door and you're on the pavement. The backyard is flagged over, and to tell you the truth, I don't really know a carrot from a turnip. I've allus been a factory man.'

Jenny turned her attention to the flower beds. The sun had brought out the many colourful blossoms while here and there clusters of new buds were shooting through the crumbled earth. 'Look how you've tended the flower gardens,' she said kindly. 'They're so beautiful.'

'Aye. They've come up grand,' he admitted proudly. 'By the time I got round to 'em, they were overrun with weeds and the like. Oh, but the fella that were here afore did a good job with

93

them or my own work would have been that much harder.' He saw how the sunlight heightened her loveliness, and he knew the goodness inside her. 'He were *your* young man, weren't he?'

His direct question made Jenny swallow hard. She thought she had come to terms with Frank's being gone, but sometimes a word or a thought was too much for her. 'He's been gone some three months now. It doesn't matter any more,' she lied. It would always matter. She could never stop missing him.

Aware that he had touched a tender spot, he apologised lamely. 'I allus open me mouth afore I think. Meg's told us how you and the fella were planning to wed until he upped sticks and left here. All I can say is this . . . he couldn't have been in his right mind to leave a woman like you behind.'

Jenny knew he meant well but he was innocently opening up old wounds. 'I'd best be off,' she said, 'or the dinner'll be late on the table.'

He hadn't finished. 'I want you to know that me and the missus are very grateful. We've a lot to thank you for,' he murmured shyly. 'Our Meg reckons it were you as got me this work.'

'That's not altogether true,' Jenny protested. 'Mrs Marshall was looking for someone, and I just mentioned your name, that's all.'

'Aye, if you say so,' he replied with a knowing smile. 'Well, I won't let you down, I can promise you that. I may be an old dog, but I ain't so old I can't learn a new trick or two. What!' He glanced at the stiff ground. 'I'll have it soft as butter in no time,' he promised.

'I'm sure you will.' With a word of encouragement, Jenny went on her way, leaving him chipping at the earth and cursing under his breath. Meg's father was a good man, and she had taken a real liking to him. Sometimes, when she caught sight of him at work, images of Frank would flit into her mind and her spirits would dip. But she was learning to cope. With every day that went by Jenny taught herself to believe that he could never really have loved her at all.

As she came down the hill towards Woburn Sands, Jenny passed the thick shrubbery that led to the woods. A strange cry attracted her attention, and, thinking an animal might be caught in the many snares hereabouts, she parted the tangled foliage and peered in.

It was no ordinary animal she saw, but a half-naked couple in the frenzied throes of mating. The man's bare buttocks rose and fell repeatedly. A pair of eyes glanced up, momentarily astonished to see her there.

Ashamed and horrified, Jenny quickly retreated and hurried on her way. Her face was burning with shame as she recalled the mocking eyes that had stared up at her from beneath the man's body. *Claudia's eyes.* Claudia with her limbs wrapped round her mate while the two of them coupled on the ground like wild beasts.

The shop was full. Jenny didn't mind. She had a great deal to keep her thoughts occupied while she waited. All manner of questions flowed through her head. What depths would Claudia sink to next? What in God's name would happen if Elizabeth were to find out? Or did she already know? Certainly their relationship had worsened, until now they hardly ever sat at the table together, and when they spoke it was only to row. While Claudia became more and more rebellious, Elizabeth drew into herself, like a snail into its shell. And Jenny's heart went out to her.

'Wake up then!' Nan Demmy's voice cut across Jenny's thoughts. 'Thought you'd fell asleep on your feet,' she laughed. The shopkeeper was a big lady in every way, big-boned, big-hearted, and big of voice. Everyone knew and liked her.

'Sorry,' Jenny laughed, 'I was miles away.' She put her wicker basket on the counter and took out her purse. After reciting her shopping list to Nan, she watched the big woman go from shelf to shelf collecting her wares. She didn't follow her chatter though, because she was still haunted by what she had seen. Oh, she was well aware that Claudia wantonly took up with one man after another, but she had never dreamed it had come to this. As far as Claudia was concerned, Jenny didn't care a fig. But she loved Elizabeth more than she could ever reveal and it was to her that all of her sympathies went. 'Where will it all end?' she asked herself.

Jenny was caught unawares when Nan remarked, 'What was that you said, dear?' Flustered, she looked around at the shelves. 'A pound of carrots,' she answered calmly. It would never do for Nan to know what she had been thinking. She was a kindly soul, but she was a terrible gossip. 'I'm hoping we'll have a good crop of vegetables this year,' she offered.

There then followed a conversation about Mr Taylor and his progress with the vegetable garden. The conversation took another turn when an elderly man came into the shop and launched into a long tirade about: 'This new housing act, which promises local councils the money to build decent housing for ordinary working folk.' Another customer reminded everyone not to forget the shame of Lloyd George's rash promise on the very same issue. 'And nothing came of that either!' The two men were quickly served and went on their way still debating the possibility of new low cost council housing.

'MEN!' Nan shook her head. 'All they ever do is *talk*. And half the time they're spouting rubbish.' She then went on to enquire after the mistress of the house. 'Mrs Marshall is well respected round these parts,' she commented. 'Though I can't say the same for that daughter of hers.' When Jenny feigned ignorance and wanted to know what the other woman meant by that, Nan told her straight. 'What! I'm surprised you don't already know . . .

living at the big house and all. She's the talk of the villages. Claudia Marshall don't care *whose* husband she pairs up with. I'll tell you this, and make no mistake . . . if that little hussy don't put a stop to her gallivanting, there'll be blood spilled and that's a fact.' Having said her piece, and seeing that Jenny had no intention of giving her any juicy snippets of gossip, Nan gave her her change and bade her good day. 'Look after yourself,' she said as Jenny left the shop. It was well known that the lovely Jenny Dickens had been deserted by her intended, and the fact that she had no other family made it especially cruel.

On her return home, Jenny took the long way round, up Aspley Hill and across the top of the long bank. At the highest point, she halted and sat herself on the trunk of a fallen tree. The sun was warm on her face as she stared out over the hills and valleys. In the distance she could see the many herds of cattle, haphazardly spread across the fields like tiny toy creatures. A farm-worker on his tractor covered the ground with zig-zag markings, while in one farmyard the children played and fought. She envied them all.

The shopkeeper's words ran through her mind. 'Little hussy . . .' 'Make no mistake, there'll be blood spilled.' With only the trees and the skies to hear her, Jenny muttered, 'Where will it all end?'

Taking off her shawl, she draped it over her filled basket. The sun was bright in her eyes and so she lay back in the soft lush grass, absent-mindedly staring at the fluffy white clouds through half-closed lids. The blueness of the sky reflected in the soft azure of her eyes, making them tired and lazy. Now, with her eyes closed, she could still see it all: the landscape that dipped away as far as the eye could see, the small figures going about their business, moving on the face of the earth like ants on a mound. God's children all.

Before she realised it, Jenny had taken up her shawl and basket and walked along the path that led to St Mary's church. The inside struck cold after the warm sunshine. She stayed at the back, her eyes fixed on the crucifix above the altar. She wasn't praying, nor was she thinking anything in particular. It was just good to be here. She felt safe. *Wanted*. Here, in God's house, her soul always found a lasting peace. And so she stayed awhile, and thought, and dreamed.

Inevitably, her thoughts turned to Frank. Frank whom she had loved and still loved; a man she had trusted above all others. She could see him now, almost as though he was here with her, tall and strong, with his mop of fair hair dipping over his eyes, and his smile so real that it touched her heart. 'Oh, Frank.' Her voice caressed his name. 'Where are you, I wonder?' She felt his essence all around her, yet she was wise enough to know that such memories would only bring heartache.

Dismissing him from her mind, she dwelt on other things: Elizabeth and Claudia, and the awful atmosphere in that house. Was Nan Demmy right? Would there really be bloodshed? Oh, she hoped not. For Elizabeth's sake, she hoped not. And yet she sensed something awful, some shocking thing that was already in the making.

She contemplated where her own life might be leading, and suddenly wondered whether it was all worthwhile. Her quiet gaze fell on the cross and she was ashamed. 'Be thankful for what you have, my girl!' she chided herself. In a moment she had emerged into the sunlight again. Her spirits were restored, and she was ready to face it all. Quickly, she followed the path back to the big house.

Claudia was beside herself with rage. 'What are you saying?' She stood before her mother, hands on hips and a look of defiance on her face. Her pale eyes were round and staring as she waited for an answer.

'You know very well what I'm saying.' Elizabeth's voice was steady and firm. Inside she was made to tremble by Claudia's vicious manner, but outside she gave no quarter. 'As you refuse to take up any form of study, and your time is wasted between wandering the woods and losing yourself for hours on end, doing God only knows what . . . I've decided that you can help to maintain this house. From tomorrow morning, you will take on the task of keeping the dining room cleaned and polished.'

Claudia laughed out loud. 'You *are* mad! I always knew it.' Her laughter gave way to a chilling threat. 'Don't dare to treat me like a common servant, Mother. I have no intention of doing what you ask.' She raised her head high, staring at Elizabeth through hostile eyes. 'There's nothing you can do about it either. You must know you can't *make* me do what I don't want to.'

'You'll do as I ask or leave this house.' Elizabeth was never more serious. 'It needn't necessarily be housework but I insist that you find something useful to occupy your time.' Her next words carried a clear meaning. '*Something you and I have no need to be ashamed of.*'

For what seemed an age those telling words hung in the air. The two women challenged each other in silence; Elizabeth standing by the fireplace, and Claudia with her back to the dresser. She was smiling to herself, softly chuckling as though someone had whispered obscene things in her ear. Lately this cunning expression had become a habit – a disgusting habit which deeply offended Elizabeth. 'Leave me now,' she ordered impatiently. 'There's nothing more to be said.'

Claudia was defiant. 'So you really mean to throw me out?' She was still smiling.

Elizabeth faced her with a stern expression. 'If I have to.'

'Because I shame you?'

Elizabeth momentarily lowered her gaze. 'I think you know

the answer to that.' She raised her eyes and pleaded with her daughter. 'I don't want to sound cruel, Claudia, but you force my hand. There's been . . . gossip.'

'Oh?' Claudia came closer. She chuckled a little. 'Gossip, you say?'

'You've brought disgrace on your father's house.'

'Ah! Well now, I mustn't bring shame on Father's house, must I? Even though he was a coward and a drunk and lost all our fortune . . . I must not bring shame on him!' Her pale eyes were like chiselled ice and her voice was trembling. 'He brought us to this, and I hate him!' She fell backwards when the force of Elizabeth's hand caught her full on the mouth.

Her mother was enraged. 'Your father was a fine man who made me proud.' This time Claudia had gone too far.

'You're a fool!' For some time now, a cruel plan had been flowering in Claudia's black heart. 'I won't leave this house, and you won't throw me out.'

'*You're* the fool if you believe that!'

'Whatever would the neighbours say? I can just hear them now . . . "What a heartless woman that Elizabeth Marshall is. Did you know she's thrown her own daughter on to the streets? *And her with child too!*"'

Ashen-faced, Elizabeth opened her mouth to speak but the words stuck in her throat. Disbelieving, she stared at her daughter with wide stricken eyes.

Delighted to see how her words had shocked the older woman, Claudia confirmed, 'That's right, Mother dear, I'm going to have a child.' Before Elizabeth could recover, she went on with glee, 'What would you say if I told you that the spawn inside me is *Father's* spawn?' Elizabeth's obvious distress spurred her on. 'He was not the fine man you think he was. Charles Marshall was a failure . . . a drunkard. I went to see him on the night he died. I wanted him to side with me against you. You see, I was sure you were lying to me when you said we weren't rich any more. I wanted him to reassure me.'

Her mouth twisted in disgust. 'He was dishevelled, unshaven, and smelling of booze. No better than a tramp. When I saw him, I hated him more than I hate you.' Lunging forward, she took her mother by the wrists. 'Oh, but he was pleased to see *me*. He wouldn't leave me alone. Do you know what I'm saying? Do you? Your husband bedded me . . . his own daughter. *I'm carrying my father's child!*'

She was shaking Elizabeth now, pushing her violently backwards and forwards. 'Throw me out and I'll tell the world,' she threatened, and her laughter was terrible to hear.

With tears flowing down her face, Elizabeth shook Claudia from her. 'God forgive you for such lies,' she said in a broken voice. 'For I never will.' She stood proud and straight, but her whole body was trembling and she was badly shaken. 'I want you out of this house today.' Her fists clenched and unclenched by her sides. For the first time in her life, there was murder in her gentle heart.

Astonished, Claudia looked at that calm dignified woman whose heart she had broken so many times. 'Every word is true,' she insisted. 'See.' Tearing at her clothes, she exposed the rise of her belly. 'See that?' she demanded. 'That's *his* child growing there. And I'll tell you something else. Afterwards he was so frightened of the consequences that he jumped to his own death. They said it was an accident, but you and I know better, don't we? He killed himself, like the coward he was!'

'NO!' With a cry like that of a wild animal, Elizabeth sprang at her. Grabbing the astonished Claudia by the hair, she thrust her forwards over the fireside chair, and, taking up the poker, began to lay it across her shoulders. Time and again she brought the poker down. Again and again, until the screaming and struggling had stopped and Claudia lay face down, broken and almost lifeless, her arms hanging limp and her brown hair stained with blood.

When Jenny came to the dining room, she was horrified by the scene. The small round table was overturned where Claudia had kicked out, and the floor was littered with shattered ornaments. White-faced and sobbing, Elizabeth was seated amongst the broken fragments, rocking herself back and forth and staring across the room with unseeing eyes. The bloodied poker was still clutched in her hands. Claudia was stirring, moaning with agony as she righted herself in the chair. In that moment, she caught sight of Jenny coming into the room. She looked at her stricken face, and then she looked at her mother – a woman who had been pushed beyond sanity. It was a pitiful sight. But when Claudia turned to Jenny again, she was smiling. And Jenny's heart turned cold.

Later, when the doctor had attended Claudia's injuries and Elizabeth was sedated, Jenny sat by her bedside until she woke. 'Don't leave me!' Elizabeth's first words were a desperate plea.

'You're not to worry,' Jenny told her softly. 'You know I won't leave you.'

'And *her*? Promise you won't leave her. She can't help the way she is. It's not her fault. And whatever she says or does, I have to love her. Don't you see, Jenny, she's my only child? *I have to love her!*'

When Elizabeth began crying and working herself up to a fever, Jenny reluctantly gave the promise. If she had her way, Claudia would be made to suffer a great deal more than a poker across her back. But Elizabeth had pleaded on her daughter's behalf, and Jenny would not do anything that might cause that dear woman any further torment. 'It's all right,' she murmured, 'I won't leave her.' Such a promise went against all of her instincts. But it was given now, and Jenny knew she would abide by it.

Satisfied, Elizabeth fell into a troubled sleep. In her deep fear and confusion, she cried and muttered, and little by little the story of what had taken place in the drawing room was revealed.

Jenny heard every word and was stunned. She didn't believe for one minute that Charles Marshall had made his own daughter with child. What she truly believed was this: if Claudia *was* carrying a child, it could belong to one of many men. And one of those men was Frank.

In her heart of hearts, Jenny knew the unborn innocent belonged to the man she loved. And she realised that, regardless of any promise she had made, she was now obliged to remain in Elizabeth Marshall's house.

# *Chapter Six*

Elizabeth had lost her will to live. For months now she had lain in her bed and nothing Jenny could say would persuade her from it. 'It's a beautiful day, ma'am,' she said cheerfully one day, opening the curtains to let the morning sunshine flood in. 'Why don't you let me dress you and we can take a stroll through the gardens?' Though her work was piling up, she would willingly spare a while to walk arm in arm with Elizabeth.

'No.' Her mistress's voice came across the room in a whisper. 'I don't want to.'

Sighing, Jenny returned to the dresser and collected the tray. 'Well, won't you at least eat a little breakfast?' she asked, putting on a bright smile as she laid the tray on the bedcovers. 'See what I've made for you. I've boiled your eggs just the way you like them. Then there's a heap of toasted soldiers and a piping hot brew of tea.'

'Bless you, but I don't want anything.' Elizabeth had been looking away but now she turned her face to look at Jenny. 'I know you mean well,' she murmured. 'But I've no appetite.' Her once vivid green eyes were dull and filled with pain just as they had been since the day she took to her bed. 'Leave me,' she asked now. 'I'll sleep awhile.'

It was a deliberate lie. Elizabeth wouldn't sleep. She couldn't.

For endless weeks now she had only drifted fitfully in and out of slumber, her mind tormented by what Claudia had told her on that April day four months ago. Deep down Elizabeth knew it was only her daughter's wickedness talking, but the germ was planted and its invasive roots had eaten their way into the darkest recesses of her soul, sending her back through the years to when Claudia was small and Charles doted on her. He had been utterly obsessed with his beautiful daughter, dwelling on her every word, her every smile; each insignificant action was a cause of joy and pride to him.

Elizabeth told herself over and over that any father would love his daughter in the same way, but God forgive her she still couldn't convince herself of his innocence. In the light of Claudia's shocking accusation, and even though she felt the truth in her every bone, Elizabeth now saw his innocent actions as menacing and unnatural. Her emotions were torn every which way, and now she wanted only to be left alone with her crucifying thoughts.

All the while their daughter was blossoming into womanhood, and right up to when he was sent home from the war, a broken man, Charles and Claudia had been two of a kind, strong and independent. Elizabeth had always felt herself an outsider, never sharing what they shared. But how could she believe that they shared an indecent love? NO! She must not let herself believe such an odious thing. Claudia was capable of untold evil, she knew that. But not Charles. Not that gentle dignified man. Yet she must not forget that he had changed drastically from the man she had known and loved. Before his downfall Charles had been a hero, a man of pride and great principles. He was not capable of anything bad. But what of the sorry creature he'd become? Could *he* force himself on his own daughter? Could *he* take his own life? Oh, if only she could be sure. But she couldn't. And she never would be. Dear God, what was she to believe?

'Won't you try to eat a little?' Jenny persevered. 'A piece of toast?' Elizabeth shook her head. 'A cup of tea then?' Jenny had brought the doctor out before, and she would not hesitate to do so again, but it never made any difference. If anything it made matters worse, because Elizabeth had only grown more stubborn.

'Later. I'll try something later.'

'You always say that,' Jenny reminded her. Now it was *her* turn to be stubborn. 'No, it won't do. I'm not leaving this room until you've had something to eat, even if it's only a spoonful of egg.'

'That's for *me* to decide,' Elizabeth protested.

'That may be, but it's for *me* to decide whether you're ill enough to warrant the doctor calling.' She saw at once that Elizabeth took her meaning. Though she mostly ignored his advice, Elizabeth hated the doctor calling. 'It's either me or him,' Jenny warned. Sometimes she was surprised and ashamed by her own boldness, yet she had grown more assertive in her new role. Big with child and loathing herself for it, Claudia cared nothing for the house, and even less for her mother. Consequently responsibility for the running of this house and the welfare of those in it fell on Jenny's small capable shoulders. 'Will you have a bite to eat then or do you want me to fetch the doctor?' she insisted.

Elizabeth laughed softly. It was a sound to warm Jenny's fearful heart. 'You're a bully,' Elizabeth told her, but there was affection in that quiet voice.

Jenny gave no answer. Instead she placed the tray on the dresser then set about making Elizabeth comfortable. With one arm supporting her mistress's head, she plumped up the pillow with her free hand. 'Up you come,' she chided kindly, sliding her two arms around Elizabeth's thin body and easing it to a sitting position. 'There!' She surveyed the pathetic bundle lying back against the pillow. It hurt her to see how that fine woman had come to this; a pathetic sight with green sunken eyes and a white frightened face that was wistfully childlike. Even now though she was stunningly beautiful with her finely chiselled features and that rich mass of fiery hair, like a burning sun against a pale cloudless sky.

While Jenny put the tray on the eiderdown, Elizabeth took the time to study her. She thought Jenny such a pretty little thing. Her short fair hair sprang about her face and ears with a life of its own, unruly as always. The pretty blue eyes were tired, yet she always managed to smile as though the morning sun was rising in her face. Jenny deserved better, she thought sadly, and her heart was flooded with guilt. Since the first day she had seen Jenny she had known straight away the value of this homely soul. There was something about Jenny that was very special. Some people buckled beneath their burden. Others carried it well. Jenny was such a person and Elizabeth thanked the Good Lord for her. She had come to love and cherish this young woman, and dreaded the thought of her not being here. Suddenly the words that Elizabeth was thinking came to her lips and made themselves heard. 'You're young with your life ahead of you, child. Why do you stay?' she whispered.

Jenny was taken aback. For a moment she was lost for an answer. But then she said simply, 'Because there is no one else. Nowhere for me to go. And because I promised.'

Elizabeth remembered, and was saddened. 'Because Claudia came between you and him, and he left you,' she corrected. 'And because I made you promise.'

'I'm here because I want to be with you,' Jenny explained. What Elizabeth said was true, but nothing on this earth would have dragged her from her mistress's side now.

'I don't deserve you.'

Jenny smiled. 'No, you don't,' she teased, 'especially when I take the trouble to cook you a special breakfast, and you refuse to eat it.'

'I'm sorry. Just a spoonful then.'

Jenny sighed. 'That's all I ask,' she said. 'If you eat, you'll soon be well.' Afraid of embarking on a deeper conversation, she sliced off the top of the egg, then dipped the spoon in and scooped out a measure of the congealed yellow yolk. With her free hand she placed the bib beneath Elizabeth's chin, and pressed the tip of the spoon to her partly opened mouth, 'Meg's Dad got this egg fresh from under the hen this very morning,' she explained. Elizabeth took three mouthfuls before she pushed the spoon away. 'No more,' she said. 'Please. No more.' It had been an effort. Now she was weary.

Reluctantly Jenny replaced the spoon on the tray. 'At least you've had something,' she remarked gratefully. Almost half the egg was eaten. That in itself was an achievement. 'How about the smallest drop of tea to wash it down?'

Elizabeth nodded. The salted egg had made her thirsty.

Jenny lifted the cup and touched Elizabeth's lips with the fine rim. Slowly, she sipped and swallowed until it was all gone. Afterwards, she looked up with imploring eyes, and even before she spoke, Jenny sensed what she was about to ask. 'Where is she?' The question was the very same that had been asked every morning for the past four months.

In her mind, Jenny pictured Claudia as she had seen her time and again. She saw her frantically pacing the garden, backwards and forwards, backwards and forwards, constantly glancing over her shoulder and quickening her steps, as though she was pursued by some unseen demon. She hadn't changed. Claudia was even more aggressive, more violent, and more abusive than she had ever been. As the child inside her grew, so did her hatred of it. Jenny could see her now, standing in the drawing room and staring out of the window. Sometimes she was beside herself with rage. At such times she became deeply agitated, morose and dangerous, one minute hurling ornaments across the room and the next clutching at her stomach as though she might tear the child out with her bare fists.

'She's in her room.' Jenny leaned over to make Elizabeth more comfortable. 'How's that?' she asked, drawing the patch-work eiderdown up to the other woman's chin. It was a glorious day and the room was warmed by the sun, but lately Elizabeth seemed to feel the cold.

'That's fine.'

'Good.' Collecting the tray, Jenny told her, 'I'll be back shortly to wash you. Afterwards you can sit by the window in your dressing-robe.' Elizabeth nodded and Jenny ventured hopefully, 'Better still, I'll dress you and we'll go for a walk round the garden, eh?'

'No. I won't go out. But I'll sit by the window for a while, if you insist.'

'I do.'

'Jenny?'

'Yes?'

'Is she well?'

'Well enough.'

'The child?'

'What about the child?'

Elizabeth shook her head. 'It doesn't matter.'

Jenny sat on the bed. Placing the tray on her lap, she said kindly, 'If it's playing on your mind, then it *does* matter.'

'I'm afraid.'

'You mustn't be.'

'She hates the child, doesn't she?' When Jenny was loath to confirm such a terrible thing, Elizabeth insisted, 'I know she hates that poor innocent child. Even more than she hates me.'

'You shouldn't say such things.' Jenny prepared to depart from the room, but Elizabeth hadn't finished. 'You will stay, won't you? You wouldn't leave me now?' When Jenny assured her that she would stay, Elizabeth went on, 'We both need you. But . . . the child will need you more.'

Cold fingers gripped Jenny's heart. 'What are you saying?'

'I'm afraid she'll harm it, even *kill* it.' She struggled up against the pillow, her eyes big with fear. 'Claudia is capable of anything.' Her voice fell to a whisper. 'Don't let her do that, will you? *Don't let her kill it.*'

'Shh now.' Jenny leaned over to cover the narrow white shoulders with the eiderdown. She knew she must calm the poor woman's fears. 'She wouldn't harm her own flesh and blood.' Suddenly she felt Elizabeth's fear as though it was her own. There was no doubt that Claudia was bad all the way through. 'It's all right, ma'am,' she said softly. 'You can rest easy. No harm will come to the newborn.'

Elizabeth visibly relaxed. 'God bless you for that,' she said. Then she closed her eyes and was lost in deeper thought.

When Jenny glanced back from the door, she saw how the older woman lay against the pillow with her eyes closed and long pale fingers interlocked across her breast. Jenny was shocked to the core for in that brief moment Elizabeth Marshall looked like a corpse ready for its shroud. 'I'll be back in a while,' she called. There was no answer so she went quietly from the room.

Downstairs in the kitchen, she piled the breakfast crockery into the sink. As always her day would be frantic. There was Elizabeth to be washed and settled, then there was the ritual with Claudia, when she would criticise everything on her breakfast plate before picking at it like a bird and angrily pushing it from her; occasionally she would fling the remains across the carpet and storm out to lock herself in her bedroom. Other times she would flee from the house and not be seen again until the day turned to twilight.

By contrast, Jenny's routine seldom varied. After the worst of Claudia's tantrums, the carpet was scraped, then the breakfast table had to be cleared. The crockery was washed, dried and stacked away. The kitchen was made spick and span, and then came the cleaning routine which took Jenny from one room to the other until the whole house was presentable. There were nine large rooms in this great house, four downstairs and five upstairs; each room had a thorough going-over once a week, with the daily dusting being done by rota. Yesterday Jenny had dusted upstairs, and today she would dust downstairs. After that, she would collapse at the kitchen table, refreshing her aching body with a scone and a piping hot mug of tea. Sometimes Mr Taylor joined her there, and sometimes he didn't. It all depended on how their considerable duties coincided.

There was shopping to be done, vegetables to be prepared, lunch and dinner to be cooked and served. Then the same ritual of washing, drying and stacking more crockery away. And somewhere in between the laundry was washed, hung out, brought in again and pressed. Jenny's life was hard and thankless, and when the day was over she would crawl into bed and sleep soundly until dawn. But she was a contented soul, glad of her work, for it gave her little time to think. In those all too rare and quiet moments when Frank came into her mind, her heart began longing and she knew it was futile. Little by little, she pushed him to the back of her memories; and though he was always there, she learned not to let him hurt her.

The morning flew by. Before she could turn round it was midday. Upstairs, Elizabeth was content by the window, while downstairs, with the main bulk of her work behind her, Jenny went to the window-ledge where the apple pie was cooling. As she cut herself a small slice and placed it on the rose-patterned plate, she looked across the yard, searching for Mr Taylor's familiar figure. Her pretty blue eyes reached beyond the washing that was blowing dry in the warm summer breeze. The sight of it gave her a feeling of accomplishment. She took a great pride in her duties for she had little else to love.

There was no sign of Mr Taylor. Jenny wondered whether he was still turning the ground over in the kitchen garden. He had produced a fine crop after all, and now the earth was to be got ready for planting the winter greens.

As she was about to turn away, Jenny caught sight of him, hurrying towards the kitchen and carrying what appeared to be a letter. When he saw her there, he waved the paper in the air and quickened his steps towards her. In a minute the kitchen door was open and he was inside. 'Here you are,' he said, putting the small white envelope down on the table. 'The postman gave it me.'

Jenny thought nothing of it. 'Another bill, I expect,' she muttered. When Elizabeth first took to her bed, the running of this household was a nightmare to Jenny. Claudia had no sense of money, no time for anything other than her own sorry predicament, and no wish to deal with what she arrogantly called 'tiresome little tradesmen'. Consequently, the bills poured in and Jenny was forced to raise the matter with Elizabeth.

Being loath to trust Claudia with the money put aside for living expenses, Elizabeth placed an even greater responsibility on Jenny's shoulders by making an arrangement with the bank manager. Together with her own wages which she collected weekly from the bank, Jenny was paid a domestic allowance. Out of this she was to buy groceries and keep the wolf from the door. To an outsider it might have seemed an odd arrangement, but to Jenny it was only another step in the natural order of things. Besides, if she didn't do it, who would?

Every bill and receipt was carefully recorded in the house-keeping ledger, and this was kept upstairs by Elizabeth's bed. But, like Claudia, though for very different reasons, she showed little interest. Jenny did the best she could, and though there was hardly enough money to go round, she soon learned the art of 'robbing Peter to pay Paul': economising wherever possible, bartering when she could, and buying her dairy produce at favourable prices from Jacob Laing. One way or another she managed well enough. The bills were paid, if not a day early then a day late. The traders knew Jenny from old, and they trusted her.

'That were all the mail he had,' Mr Taylor said. 'I got it from him at the top of the path. Thought I'd save him a few steps, but I might as well not have bothered.' He sat down, took his cap off and placed it on the nearby chair. 'He came to the house all the same,' he added scornfully. '*She* let him in, and he hasn't come out yet.' He jerked a thumb towards the door which led from the kitchen to the inner hallway. 'If you ask me, Claudia Marshall's a bad lot.'

Putting a plate of pie before him, Jenny sat down opposite. 'It doesn't do to talk about our employers like that,' she warned kindly. Wrapping her two hands round the warm cup, she glanced at the letter and her heart almost stopped. The letter was addressed to her! What was more, she recognised the handwriting. *It was Frank's* . . .

'Aye, you're right,' Mr Taylor went on. 'It's none of our business, I suppose, but it's disgraceful all the same.' He tasted the succulent pie and a broad smile creased his face. 'By! It melts in your mouth,' he told her. But Jenny wasn't listening, so he quietly paid attention to his pie and made a mental plan of what he might plant in the vegetable garden.

All the while he had been talking, Jenny's eyes never left that envelope. She wanted to tear it open, then she wanted to throw it, unopened, into the midden. Her mind was alive with all manner of pictures. Frank sitting in the very same chair that Mr Taylor was in now; Frank smiling at her through the window as he unharnessed the old cob; Frank teasing and kissing her, and swinging her round this very kitchen. Like it was only yesterday she could see the two of them, running through the heather and

Josephine Cox

playing hide and seek like two excited children. The letter was from Frank. After all these months he had remembered her. She felt numb inside. Long after Mr Taylor had gone, she still couldn't bring herself to pick up the letter from the table.

She washed the crockery, brought in the clothes from the washing line and folded them ready for pressing. She peeled the potatoes for dinner, filleted the fresh cod bought from Nilgett's fishmonger's, and split a whole pan of garden peas from their pods. Leaving the letter where it lay, she returned to Elizabeth's room. 'Are you feeling strong enough now to take a little walk?' she asked hopefully. 'The sun's warm as toast, and there's no breeze to chill you.'

Elizabeth smiled wanly. 'Help me back to my bed,' she said. 'I'm bone tired.' It wasn't her bones that were tired, it was her heart, and all the sun in the world wouldn't cure what ailed her. But didn't they say that time heals? Maybe they were right. 'Perhaps another day,' she told Jenny. Even now, she hoped there *would* be another day. But it was too early, and she still hadn't found the courage to face her own daughter or her own weakness.

'Please, ma'am.' Jenny felt so lonely then. Elizabeth was afraid to face one truth. Jenny was afraid to face another. She saw this anguished woman as her only friend, and she truly believed that the two of them could help each other. 'A walk will do you the world of good.'

Elizabeth wouldn't be persuaded, and so Jenny made her comfortable in her bed. When she was about to leave, Elizabeth grabbed her wrist and kept her there. 'She has a man in her room, you know.' Her wide green eyes brimmed with tears. 'What am I to do about her, Jenny? How can I make her see that what she's doing is shameful?'

She realised Elizabeth must have seen the postman come into the house. 'I wasn't aware that we had a man in the house,' she lied light-heartedly. 'Apart from Mr Taylor, who's just wolfed down the greater part of my apple pie.'

Elizabeth was used to Jenny's little ploys. 'I'm sorry,' she said, falling back against the pillow. At once she regretted appealing to Jenny in such a way. Only Claudia herself could supply the answers. Jenny had done more than anyone had a right to ask of her. 'Please leave me now.' Elizabeth buried her face in the pillow, her sad eyes watching as Jenny went from the room.

Outside, Jenny lingered awhile on the landing, her face turned towards Claudia's room. The soft lewd laughter rose and fell, filling the air with a sense of shame. Quickly Jenny continued downstairs. In the kitchen she stood for what seemed an age, just staring at the envelope on the table. When she picked it up, it was cold in her fingers. She turned it over and over, feeling his presence. Her pretty blue eyes swam with tears as she remembered how he had gone. So cruelly. How could she ever forgive him?

Curiosity gripped her. Love was always stronger than regret. Happen the child wasn't Frank's after all? Happen he had something to explain that she should hear? Encouraged, she slid her thumb beneath the fold in the envelope and slit it open. The address at the top of the letter told her that Frank was now in the North.

The familiar handwriting was strong and firm with each word imprinting itself on her heart as she read:

Dearest Jenny,

I've spent days thinking about what I would say to you. You've been in my thoughts every minute of every hour since I left. Nothing I can say will alter the fact that I deserted you, and that in a moment of weakness I became the worst coward.

I lived like a vagabond for many weeks before finding work in the North. I'm presently lodging with a widow, a kind, understanding soul who has been through her own

115

bad times and has been a godsend to me.

I've told her how you and I had planned to be wed. She knows what I did to spoil all that, but she makes no judgements.

If you're wondering how I've the nerve to put pen to paper after all this time, it's because I've never stopped loving you.

Doreen has made no secret of her affection for me, but I'm torn two ways, Jenny, and this is why I'm writing. I'll always love you, in spite of the shocking way I treated you. Claudia meant nothing to me. What happened was a spur of the moment thing which I have deeply regretted ever since.

What I'm saying is this: can you forgive me?

I would understand if you could not find it in your heart to forgive me, Jenny. Although I pray you can.

If I don't hear from you within a month, I'll know that it really is over between us, and I'll make a new life with Doreen. She's a good woman, and loves me in spite of the fact that I may never be able to return that love.

The next month will be the longest of my life. But I won't blame you if you cannot bring yourself to forgive me.

Yours ever,
Frank

Jenny sank into the chair, her hands trembling as she held the letter. 'Oh, Frank, what do you expect of me?' she whispered. Didn't he know how hard it had been for her to come to terms with what he had done? Couldn't he realise how her world had been turned upside down? How she had cried herself to sleep night after night, wondering whether she would ever see him again, or whether she even *wanted* to? Even now she couldn't rid herself of that picture in her mind, the picture of Frank and Claudia making love in Jacob Laing's barn. It was a picture that she might *never* be able to rid herself of.

Her face as white as chalk, Jenny read the letter again and again, and each time it became harder. 'He wants me back,' she whispered, 'Frank wants me back.' She should have been exhilarated but she wasn't. Oh, she loved him as much as ever, it was true. But something had been spoiled. The magic was gone, and in its place there was a deep down anger.

Suddenly it all came back to haunt her. The long dark hours of that awful night when she had waited for him to return. How she had been frantic with worry for his safety, when all the time he was with *her*. The memory was like a giant hand squeezing her heart. She wasn't ready to forget. It was too soon. Too alive in her mind. Slowly, the agony left her eyes and her face became a grim mask to hide the hurt beneath. 'I do love you, Frank,' she whispered. 'But you chose her over me, and I can't forget that. Not yet. Maybe never.'

Quickly now, before she could change her mind, she crumpled the letter and dropped it into the waste bucket beneath the sink. 'There's nothing you can say to change things now, Frank,' she murmured tearfully. 'You said it all when you walked out on me.' All the same, throwing that letter away was the hardest thing she had ever done.

Thinking it might have been better if she had never read those painful words, Jenny put on her shawl and took to the path which led out towards Jacob Laing's farmhouse. For the moment she had more pressing things on her mind than a letter out of the blue, although she couldn't deny that its arrival had thrown her emotions into turmoil. Her love for Frank was still as strong as ever. With every step she had to fight the instinct that told her to turn back, retrieve the letter and write to him.

As she hurried along the narrow path through the woods and

out to the open field, Jenny forced herself to concentrate on Elizabeth's predicament. Her mistress was getting worse, not better. Her illness was not a physical thing, it was the aftermath of a terrible shock, an inner malaise, a weariness with life that had taken a dangerous hold on her. Jenny had tried everything she knew to shake her out of it. 'Happen Jacob Laing could talk with her,' she muttered. 'After all, he was a friend in the past; the only real friend she had.'

Jacob Laing was not one for visiting, but it was well known that he had taken a liking to Charles Marshall's widow. When she was first struck down, he had sent flowers and sympathy, but the one and only time he had chosen to visit, Claudia sent him on his way with harsh words. He had never returned. Jenny hoped he could be persuaded to try again, for Elizabeth's sake.

The noises grew louder. Cries of passion that came through the walls to invade Elizabeth's restless sleep. She stirred, her face pressed sideways into the pillow, and her green eyes turned towards the far wall. She knew what was going on in her daughter's room, and her heart broke because of it.

Claudia laughed out loud. She loved a man's hands on her skin. It made her feel good, wanton. She liked that. 'You're insatiable,' he told her, dropping to his knees and pushing his tongue between her legs. When she fell back on to the bed, he shuffled forward, his large red hands spread across the mound of her belly. 'When my own wife was pregnant, I wasn't allowed to touch her,' he said sourly, poking the tip of his tongue into her swollen naval. 'Months before and months after, she starved me of my rights.'

Snatching away from him, Claudia snapped, 'I don't want to hear about your wife!' She stood before the mirror, naked and unashamed, examining herself from every angle. Her young body was never more beautiful, yet all she could see was ugliness. Her

118

legs were long and slim, the ankles still pretty in spite of the weight they carried. Her shoulders were straight and small, mantled in the magnificent tumble of long brown hair. The eyes that stared into the mirror were unnervingly pale, but strangely mesmerising to the man who watched. 'You're so beautiful,' he gasped, coming up behind her and rubbing his erect member against the small of her back. 'I still don't know what you see in me.' His rough red hands slid round her swollen body and up to the small taut breasts, where they softly pinched the stiff brown nipples. 'Won't it hurt the child if we make love?' he asked naively.

Swinging round, she pushed him from her. Her eyes glittered angrily as she snarled, 'If it killed the little bastard, it wouldn't matter. And if you think it does, you'd best get out. Go on. GET OUT!'

Leering, yet afraid he had spoken out of turn and spoiled his chances, he pressed himself on her, forcing her back towards the bed. She laughed again, making him angry, playing with him. 'I could tell your wife what you've done here today,' she threatened softly. 'It might be fun if I were to ruin your miserable life.' She sniggered at the fleeting look of horror on his face.

'You're too clever to do that,' he bluffed. 'It could work both ways. After all, I don't suppose your mother knows what *you're* up to either, eh?'

She smiled then, twining her fingers round the hairs on his chest. 'I wonder if I should tell you whose bastard this is?' she mused aloud, glancing at her own belly, her long fingers reaching down to toy with him. When he gasped with pleasure, she quickened her actions. But not so that she couldn't share his final throes of rapture. When she abruptly stopped, he dropped his head, his body still shivering with delight.

'For pity's sake,' he groaned. Every time he surged forward, she inched away, until he was almost out of his mind. She

119

wrapped herself round him, her every limb enfolding him like the tentacles of an octopus, and he was amazed that a woman so heavy with child could be so strong. Suddenly he was underneath and she was on top, sitting astride him with her belly jutting across the flat of his hard stomach. 'How much do you want me?' she teased. When he closed his eyes, she put her two outstretched hands on his broad shoulders and pushed her weight down, down and forward, causing him to slide into her with exquisite pain.

As he penetrated deeper, she studied his face with amusement, her avaricious eyes greedily following the changes in his expression. His small dark eyes grew round to match his mouth as he cried out with pleasure. Tiny droplets of sweat erupted all over the surface of his skin and he began whimpering like a baby. Desperate now, he pushed up, driving himself into her, groaning with frustration when she drew away. Tormented beyond endurance, he jerked forward and locked her into his arms. It was what she wanted. And now her frenzy matched his own. Thrusting herself down on to him, she jerked backwards and forwards, her small white teeth nipping at his lips, making them bleed, and her legs bent at the knee as they drew him deeper. The louder he cried, the more excited she became. In their ecstacy, neither of them realised that Elizabeth had entered the room.

In her worst nightmares, she could not have imagined the extent of her daughter's debauchery. To see her own flesh and blood, big with child and stripped naked while she coupled with a man who was little more than a stranger, was more than she could endure. In that initial moment she leaned on the door-jamb, her weight supported by the stout stick which Jenny had brought to her room some weeks back. Summoning every ounce of her remaining strength and urged on by her sense of outrage, she crossed the room. When she was close enough, she brought the full force of her stick across her daughter's bare shoulders. 'GET OUT OF MY HOUSE!' she cried. 'BOTH OF YOU!'

The first to recover from the shock was the man. 'Christ Almighty!' he yelled, springing from the opposite side of the bed and crouching in the corner. White-faced and drained, Elizabeth would have brought the stick down again across her daughter's bare shoulders, but Claudia was too quick for her. 'Not this time, you witch!' she cried, grabbing the stick in mid-air and wrenching it from her mother's hands. 'You beat me once before, but that was the last time. You'll never again see the day when you beat me like that!' She smiled with glee at her mother's feeble attempts to hurt her, and she laughed in her face when Elizabeth almost stumbled. 'You can't do anything to me,' she boasted, prodding at Elizabeth's breast with the tip of the stick.

Gripping the bed-end to steady herself, Elizabeth told her in a firm voice, 'You're no daughter of mine. I want you out of this house. Now.'

'If you want me to leave, you'll have to *make* me!' Scrambling to the edge of the bed, Claudia opened her legs, deliberately exposing herself and taking a wicked delight in the way Elizabeth averted her eyes. 'But you can't make me leave, can you? No more than you can tell me who to sleep with. I'll do what I want, and I'll stay in this house for as long as it suits me. And you won't be able to do a thing about it, because you haven't the strength you once had.'

'You bring nothing but shame and disgrace to our name, and I won't stand for it any longer.'

'Oh, and what is it you plan to do then?'

'All you need to know is that I'll be writing to the solicitor before the day is out.' Shocked and exhausted, Elizabeth could feel her senses fading but did not intend to give Claudia the satisfaction of watching her crumble. With as much dignity as she could muster, she began to walk away.

At once Claudia pounced. Standing brazenly before her mother, she goaded, 'It serves you right, you know. A lady should always knock when she enters another lady's room. If you didn't like what you saw, you've only got yourself to blame.' She put out her hand and pressed it against Elizabeth's shoulder, holding her back.

'Get out of my way.'

'Oh, I will. I will, Mother,' Claudia chuckled. 'When I'm good and ready.' Suddenly the smile was gone from her face and she was scowling, her pale eyes glittering with rage as she demanded in a low voice, 'Did it shock your gentle nature to see your daughter having such a good time?' When Elizabeth appeared to sag before her eyes, she went on eagerly, 'It was the same with him . . . with the bastard's father. But then, you know who *he* was, don't you?'

Seeing how Elizabeth was devastated by the meaning in those cruel words, Claudia glanced at the man who was still crouched in the corner, his nervous eyes uplifted as he slid his legs into his trousers. He had hoped to sneak quietly away. He didn't like the way of things here, because there was something between these two that frightened him. Claudia was angry that he meant to leave. 'Oh, surely you're not going, are you?' she mocked. 'I thought you wanted to know who made me pregnant?'

He shook his head, inching forward, desperate to get away, but he was still when she quickly warned, 'You're not leaving here until the truth is out.' Grabbing Elizabeth by the neck of her nightgown, she stared into those stricken green eyes, her every word uttered with slow deliberation. 'It was my own father! *He* made me pregnant.' She turned her head to see what effect her words were having on the man. He was open-mouthed and visibly shocked. 'Tell them all!' she laughed. 'Tell them how the eminent Charles Marshall seduced his own daughter.'

Elizabeth was beside herself with grief. 'You're a liar!' she cried, lashing out and losing her balance. Leaning against the fireplace, she cried like a child, 'How could you defile your father's memory?'

Like a predator, Claudia delighted in her mother's growing weakness. 'He always wanted me, you must know that,' she lied mercilessly. 'What you saw here was nothing compared to how it was with my father. It was so much more exciting with him. He was a *real man*, you see . . . rotten to the core, like me. He knew how to give a woman pleasure.'

Distraught and confused, Elizabeth put her hands over her face, but Claudia tugged them away and thrust herself closer. 'Oh, but I forgot. I don't have to tell *you* that. You *know*, don't you? Because you and he made love often enough, I dare say. I mean, you made love when you created *me*, didn't you? How many times, Mother? How many times did you and he strip naked? Did you like it, I wonder? No, somehow I don't think you did. In fact, it wouldn't surprise me if you lay there stiffer than he was.' She laughed then. 'No wonder he wanted me. Any man would prefer a soft pliable body to love, don't you think, Mother?'

'Leave her be, you wicked little sod!' Though he was guilty of many things, the man who had entered this house for one purpose only was shaken to his roots by what he was witnessing. 'She's your mother, for God's sake.'

Claudia turned on him with a fury that silenced him. 'Don't forget I know where you live, and would enjoy paying a visit to your wife. There are things I could tell her that would cause you more grief than you could ever imagine.' It was enough. He bowed his head and gazed at the floor. In the end, he was no better than any of them.

Elizabeth grasped her chance to take a frail step sideways. She had to get away. But there was no escape, for when Claudia realised what was happening, she pounced, pinning her fast. 'I haven't finished yet,' she snarled, pushing her so hard that she reeled back against the wall and slithered to the ground. 'Get up, you bitch!' she ordered. But Elizabeth didn't move and Claudia was incensed. Putting out a bare foot, she poked her mother in the shoulder. 'I SAID, GET UP!' Still, Elizabeth didn't move. It was then that Claudia turned to look at the man, and his words sent a shiver of fear down her spine. 'You've killed her,' he said in a hoarse whisper. *'You've killed your own mother.'* Bare-chested, with his trousers half open, he padded across the room. Narrow-eyed, Claudia followed his progress until he was standing beside her.

Together they stared down at Elizabeth; she was oddly twisted, with one leg bent beneath the other, and her thin arms stretched out. Her eyes were open, green emerald pools that were never more beautiful. They flickered for the briefest moment, staring first at Claudia and then at the man. In the fading light, Elizabeth mistook him for the only man she had ever loved. 'Charles,' she murmured. She saw his face clearly. She felt the strength of his love, and in that moment knew he could not have done the things he was accused of. There were no more doubts. Her heart was at peace. At long last she could go to him. With a long shuddering sigh, she closed her eyes and her suffering was ended.

The man knelt down, and he knew straight away. 'She's dead,' he told Claudia. 'God forgive you.'

She was momentarily horrified. But it was only for a moment, because her quick brain was already searching for a way out. 'You'd best keep your mouth shut,' she answered, grabbing her robe and wrapping it tightly round herself. 'She was ill ... everybody knew that. She could have died at any time.'

The man stared at her, a look of disbelief on his face. 'What are you saying?'

'I'm saying, no one need ever know what took place here.'

'You're mad!'

'Pick her up.'

'What?'

'Pick her up and take her to her room. She'll be found in bed . . . dead of a heart attack in her sleep. Nobody could ever prove otherwise.'

He straightened himself up and fastened his trousers. 'Oh, no. I'm having nothing to do with it.' Striding across the room, he collected his clothes from the floor and quickly dressed. 'It was *you* who killed her, not me. You'll not involve me in no murder, I can tell you that.'

'It's your word against mine,' she reminded him. 'You're here, aren't you? In my room? I could scream right now and bring someone running . . . claim that you forced your way in.' She knew well enough that no one would come running. They had no immediate neighbours, and Jenny must be out or she would have heard the row and come to Elizabeth's aid. 'You'll be hanged.'

'You bloody witch!' He rued the day he had ever clapped eyes on her. Deep down he had always known she was trouble, but sometimes a man preferred it that way. A man with his brains in his arse anyway!

She had won and she knew it. 'Like I say, keep your mouth shut and no one will ever know. Do as I tell you and I promise you'll hear no more of it.'

She watched him collect her dead mother into his arms, and as she followed them into the other bedroom, felt a sense of triumph. When he laid Elizabeth in the bed and reverently laid the eiderdown over her breast, Claudia knew not the slightest compassion. And as he said a small prayer over the woman who had earned a good name in the village, Claudia could think of only one thing and it was this: the house and everything in it was now hers. She would have control of her inheritance, and never again need she rely on her mother's handouts.

Knowing how they would swing from the gibbet if this dreadful deed was ever discovered, Claudia and her unwilling accomplice checked every little detail. The stick which Elizabeth had carried was set against the bed where it was kept. Her robe was taken from her body and laid across the back of the chair, and her long auburn hair was fanned out as though she had been serenely sleeping when her heart had given out.

Certain that all seemed tragically natural, the guilty pair slunk away: the man, with a thankful if frightened heart, back to his wife; and Claudia to dress quickly and wander the gardens before Jenny arrived.

Mr Taylor had been at the far end of the grounds, tending to some broken tools inside his shed, when Claudia came to tell him how she'd been sitting in the orchard for some time, feeling strangely unwell. 'I knocked on my mother's door,' she lied, 'but she's obviously sound asleep and I wouldn't want to wake her, not when she's been so ill.'

'Quite right, miss,' he agreed, loudly hammering at the neck of his spade. 'All the same, happen you should have a word with the doctor if you feel unwell yourself . . . if you don't mind my saying?' He felt uncomfortable in her company, and wanted her to go. He wondered at her pleasant manner because it wasn't natural to her. At the back of his mind, he also hoped it was because she had seen the folly of her behaviour and sent the postman on his way after all.

From the way he looked at her, Claudia wondered whether he'd seen her visitor come into the house. With this in mind, and knowing how it might confuse matters if the snippet of information got out, she said softly, 'I find it so hard to make friends, you know. It's difficult being on your own for most of the time. What with Mother being ill, and Jenny tied down by her many duties, and the fact that I'm now too heavy to walk into the village – well, I'm starved for someone to talk to. Only this morning I invited the postman in for a chat. But he's a boring fellow with little to say.'

'Aye, he's that right enough,' Mr Taylor readily agreed. He

felt foolish for having jumped to the wrong conclusions that morning. He might have said more, but at that minute Jenny and Jacob Laing passed by on the path. 'Why, good morning, Mr Laing,' Claudia said, stepping out from the shadows.

At first he appeared startled, and it was no wonder when the last time he'd showed his face here he was swiftly despatched beneath a volley of abuse. 'Good morning, Miss Marshall,' he replied warily, taking off his cap and tucking it beneath his arm. 'I've come to see your mother, I hope you don't mind?'

Claudia smiled her most charming smile. 'Of course not. It will be nice for her to have a visitor.'

He returned her smile and nodded to the other man, then he continued along the path. 'Well now, that was a warm enough welcome,' he told Jenny.

'Must be the sunshine,' she laughed. But she was puzzled. Claudia's sudden change of heart where Jacob Laing was concerned was astonishing. But then again, she reminded herself, Claudia was only a matter of weeks away from birthing and some women had violent swings of mood when they were with child. It was a known fact.

Jenny led the way up the stairs. 'Oh, it'll be a real tonic to her when she sees you, Mr Laing,' she chatted. 'She gets no visitors at all these days, and you were always a good friend to her.'

At the top of the stairs, he paused to get his breath. 'Hold on a minute, young lady. I'm not as young as I used to be,' he chuckled. Then he brushed his grey hair, straightened his blue tie and rubbed the toes of his shoes against the back of his trousers to buff the shine. 'Lead on,' he said, walking behind with straight shoulders and a lighter heart because he was about to see Elizabeth whom he'd always believed was a most gentle and beautiful woman.

Jenny tapped on the bedroom door and waited for an answer. When none came, she tapped again. Still no answer. Jacob Laing

127

stepped forward. 'Perhaps I should come back later, don't you think?'

'No. I'd never hear the last of it if I let you go without seeing her.' She pushed the door open and glanced across the room. The silence was almost deafening, and Elizabeth was so still. 'She's sleeping,' Jenny told him. 'But I'll wake her because I know she would want to see you.'

The two of them went into the room together, Jenny in front and he behind. 'It's Mr Laing to see you, ma'am,' Jenny said softly, touching the auburn hair and winding it round her finger. She stroked the pale forehead. 'Shall I fetch you both some tea?' On the last word she bent forward, stroking the back of her fingers against that lovely quiet face. 'ma'am?' She was afraid then. 'MA'AM!' Something about Elizabeth's pallor and the awful stillness in that room turned her heart over.

Jenny felt a strong hand on her shoulder. 'Come away, child,' Jacob murmured. Easing himself between Jenny and the bed, he leaned forward. When he turned round again, there was a look on his face that told her all. She could hear her own voice, yet it was strange to her ears. 'No. Oh, dear God . . . no!' She looked at Elizabeth, but she could hardly see for the tears that brimmed in her eyes. She brushed them away and gazed on that kindly face, willing her to move, to open her eyes and smile that familiar gentle smile.

'I'm so very sorry, my dear,' said Jacob. He was more than sorry, he was saddened by such a waste. 'Stay with her while I fetch the doctor,' he said tenderly. In a moment he was gone, leaving Jenny holding Elizabeth's hands and crying until she thought her heart would break. 'I've never told you this,' she whispered through her tears, 'but I love you as though you were my own mother. You've been kind to me, and I won't forget that.' She stroked Elizabeth's face. It was still and cold, like alabaster. 'I'll miss you,' Jenny said brokenly. For the moment all she could think of was that Elizabeth Marshall was gone forever. It was a loss that Jenny felt to the bottom of her soul. Later she would be made to think about the deeper consequences for herself.

Jenny couldn't yet know it but the tragic events of this day would shape her own life, in more ways than she could ever have imagined.

On 15 August, beneath an overcast sky and the threat of a storm brewing, Elizabeth Marshall was put to her rest beside her beloved Charles. It was a moving service, attended by many villagers. The church was overflowing with flowers, and the grave itself was piled high with colourful blooms and little white cards written with kind affectionate words. 'They didn't know her too well,' said Mr Taylor. 'But she was known to be a kindly soul, and never had a bad word to say about anyone.'

Others said they had been proud of her husband, and were honoured to see her laid beside him. While some, like the newsagent and the man who had mended her shoes, told those who listened, 'There was a lovely lady.' That was all. A lovely lady. And one who, unlike her daughter, had never put on airs or graces, or talked down to them as though they were lesser beings.

Claudia sobbed throughout. To those who didn't know better, she was stricken with grief, the devoted daughter Elizabeth had always wanted. Inwardly, though, she was counting the minutes to when it would all be over and she could return to the house as mistress. With her mother gone and her inheritance under her own control, there was nothing to stop her from leading the life she wanted.

Jenny watched while people filtered past and gave their condolences to Elizabeth's only child. In turn, Claudia thanked them softly, pale tearful eyes hiding so much cunning. But Jenny saw through those false tears. And she despised her more than words could say.

# *Chapter Seven*

Claudia dabbed at her mouth with a napkin before pushing her chair back from the breakfast table and addressing Jenny in a clipped voice. 'See me in the drawing room in five minutes,' she said, going out of the room at an ungainly pace and muttering to herself as she went.

Jenny shook her head as she watched that hated figure make its way to the drawing room. 'What now?' she wondered aloud. 'What have I done now?' Hurriedly she collected the breakfast crockery and went into the kitchen where she piled it up on the drainer. 'Hmh! She won't be the only one who'll be glad to see that baby born,' she grumbled, taking off her apron and patting her bobbed fair hair. 'Happen she'll be in a better mood once she's able to wear her best frocks again, and make eyes at herself in the mirror.'

It was two weeks now since Claudia had become mistress of the house, and in that time she had filled out to enormous proportions until she found it difficult to do even the most mundane of things. She was eaten up with bitterness. Bitterness because the solicitor had been slow in transferring the inheritance to her personal account; bitterness at the way she saw herself in the mirror . . . a large and clumsy object made to dress in clothes which, to her mind, took away the last ounce of her femininity.

She was bitter at being without a man, alone in this great house apart from Jenny, who was the butt of her sour temper from morning to night. And she was irritated by every little thing that unfortunate soul did. Most of all, she resented the fact that lately she could not wash her hair, bathe herself properly or put on her clothes, without Jenny's assistance.

Unlike Jenny, Mr Taylor managed to keep out of her way most of the time, but even he was made to tremble at Claudia's approach. 'I pity the fella who finds himself in her clutches,' he told Jenny. 'She might be a beauty on the outside, but inside she's a bad bugger.'

Jenny knew exactly what he meant. 'And I'd best be on my way or she'll give me what for and no mistake,' she told herself as she left the kitchen to tread the familiar path to the drawing room. So many times she had walked along this passage; first to Elizabeth, and now to her daughter. So many times she could have walked it blind-fold. So many times that the red roses on the carpet were worn almost threadbare beneath her feet.

There was a growing air of neglect about the old house now. When Elizabeth was mistress, the house was cloaked in love. Now there was none, apart from Jenny's, and somehow the house seemed to know it.

Claudia waited until Jenny was inside the room and the door closed behind her. 'I told you five minutes,' she snapped, fidgeting awkwardly on the edge of the chair as though suffering a form of torture. She indicated the clock on the mantelpiece. 'That was *eight* minutes ago.'

'I'm sorry, miss,' Jenny apologised. Both she and Claudia knew the clock in the drawing room always ran a few minutes ahead of the one in the dining room. Wisely, Jenny made no mention of that. She had learned long ago not to antagonise this petulant woman. 'It won't happen again,' she promised.

Claudia studied her for a moment, then, struggling to stand up and with her eyes held fast on Jenny's, she said through a wicked grin, 'You still don't like me very much, do you?'

Jenny was tempted to speak her mind, but she had fallen for Claudia's little games before and lived to regret it. This time she decided to answer only, 'I'm sorry if you feel that.' She had neither denied nor confirmed her dislike of Claudia, but both women knew the truth. It was there like a physical block between them, simmering in the air and tainting the very room in which they stood.

Claudia smiled, a tight unpleasant expression that put Jenny on her guard. 'You're a cunning little bitch, aren't you?' she hissed. 'Know when to hold your tongue, don't you?' When still there was no reply, she taunted angrily, 'You remind me of my dear departed mother. I'm sure she would turn over in her grave if she knew how I bring money into this house.' The idea made her chuckle. 'I don't mind taking money from men. I earn it, wouldn't you say? What's more, I *enjoy* it immensely.' She clicked her fingers at the stiff little figure. 'Shock you, don't I? Well, to hell with you, and to hell with her. If I want to entertain men in my own bed, and charge them for the pleasure, what right have you to scowl, damn you?' Jenny infuriated her by standing firm, her expression giving nothing away.

'The feeling is mutual, you know,' Claudia kept on. 'I find it loathsome to be in the same room as you.'

'Yes, ma'am.' Time and again Jenny had to remind herself of the promise she had made to Elizabeth. If it wasn't for that, she might have left long ago.

Claudia rudely regarded her. 'Whether you're happy here or whether you're not, doesn't really matter to me. I don't particularly like you living in this house. I never have. In fact, I had thought of getting rid of you, but I'm forced to admit you're a good worker and you do run this place remarkably well.' She laughed. 'I wonder though, perhaps it wouldn't be hard to find someone else to do the work you do, for the same money?'

This time Jenny was made to defend herself. 'I don't think so, ma'am,' she said firmly.

'Oh?' Claudia walked to the fireplace where she put one hand on the mantelpiece and leaned her weight against it. The other hand was stretched across her stomach, stroking up and down as though trying to still the turbulence inside. She was obviously very uncomfortable. 'I'm tempted to put it to the test,' she warned. 'I could get Mr Taylor to place an advert in the local shop windows. There must be plenty of women who can run a house of this size.' She would have given anything to send Jenny on her way, but Claudia was no fool. She knew it would be impossible to get a more efficient housekeeper. Besides, better the devil you know, she reasoned.

'As you say, ma'am.' As always, Jenny let Claudia play her little game.

'You may *want* to leave when I tell you why I've sent for you.' Claudia came back to seat herself in the chair. As she sat down, she gave a small cry, grasping her stomach with both hands. Since early that morning, and all the while Jenny was dressing her, she had been plagued with tiresome pain that came and went. Her attention wandered for a moment while she closed her eyes and let the pain pass. Presently she raised her head and looked at Jenny. 'It's bad news, you see,' she began. 'As you know, the solicitor came to see me yesterday.'

Jenny nodded, wondering what kind of trouble was brewing now. For the moment though she was concerned about Claudia herself. 'Are you all right, ma'am?' she asked. It was obvious that Claudia was in a deal of pain.

'Yes,' she retorted, straightening herself and focussing her pale eyes on Jenny. It was irritating to think that Jenny might feel pity for her. 'What I'm saying is this. I simply cannot afford to pay you the same wages you're getting now.'

Jenny was taken aback. 'Begging your pardon, miss, but they're pitifully small as it is.' When Frank first walked out on her, Jenny hadn't bothered about saving anything, because there seemed no point. Since then, however, she had come to realise that there might be a time when she would have to live on what meagre funds she could manage to put by. With this in mind she had begun to put a few shillings away, but with her wages being so small it was hard and there was never anything left over for new clothes and small treats. She didn't mind that so much because she made most of her own clothes anyway and she had neither the time nor the energy for going out. But if Claudia was to cut her wages further she would be little more than a slave in this house.

'Nonsense!' Claudia replied. 'You have free bed and board, and I can offer you wages of four shillings a week.' She was on her feet again. 'Take it or leave it,' she said. There was nothing in her manner to suggest that Claudia was frantic in case Jenny should refuse her offer.

She thought long and hard. Claudia was using her again. Four shillings a week was disgraceful. It was on the tip of her tongue to refuse. But then she thought of Elizabeth, and the child that was soon due. Could she break that promise she had made? Could she leave the child to whatever fate Claudia chose for it? And anyway, Jenny asked herself, what did it matter how small her wages were? As Claudia pointed out, she had bed and board, and little purpose in life other than to look after this grand old house and wait for the child which she believed to be Frank's. All of these things raced through her mind and she knew she would stay. But she wouldn't let Claudia win too easily. 'How long will it be before I'm paid a proper wage again?' she asked boldly.

Claudia only smiled. She opened her mouth to say something. But, ever so slowly, the devious smile changed to a grimace as she fell into the chair and crouched forward, both hands clutching her stomach and a low growl issuing from her as she began rocking herself back and forth. Suddenly she jerked upwards, her eyes raised in agony. 'I think it's started. FOR PITY'S SAKE, HELP ME!' she cried, her body writhing and tears rolling down her twisted face.

At once Jenny was at her side. 'It's all right,' she said calmly. 'You'll be all right.' She hoped the baby hadn't started because it wasn't yet time. With strong hands she took Claudia by the shoulders and walked her across the room towards the door, 'Can you make it to your bed?' she pleaded. Claudia's answer was a deep groan and a shake of her head. Her weight was crippling as she collapsed into Jenny's arms.

Without another word, Jenny helped her to the settee where she laid her down with great gentleness. Then, while Claudia lay there, stretched out and groaning, Jenny ran to the window and flung it open. 'Mr Taylor!' Her voice carried over the grounds and into the shed where he was sorting his seeds.

He came running up the path towards the house where he saw Jenny hanging out of the window. 'Fetch the doctor!' she told him, her firm voice belying the fear inside her. 'Miss Claudia needs him right away.'

'I'll have him here afore you know,' he promised, and with that he took to his heels. Relieved, Jenny returned to Claudia's side. 'He won't be long now,' she said soothingly. She slid her hands round Claudia's back and began massaging. 'It'll be all right,' she told her. 'You'll be fine.' She knew instinctively that the child was weary of waiting to be born and was already on its way. Claudia was beginning to panic, so Jenny forced herself to be calm for both their sakes. 'It would be better if you could make it to your room,' she explained. 'Please, will you try?'

Encouraged by Jenny's soothing manner, and unable to settle, Claudia nodded her head. For the first time since Jenny had come

135

to this house, she was grateful to have her there. 'Good,' Jenny said, taking Claudia's weight again. 'By the time we get you into your bed, the doctor will be here, I promise.' The pace was frustratingly slow as they went into the hallway and up the stairs, taking each step as though it was the side of a mountain, and with Claudia shaking and sobbing all the way. After what seemed a lifetime, Jenny had her undressed and lying in her bed.

Just as Jenny had promised, the doctor burst into the room almost as soon as Claudia was laid in the bed. He gave her a swift examination. It was enough. 'The child's early,' he said grimly. Turning to Jenny, he instructed as he rolled up his sleeves, 'Fetch the midwife.' As Jenny fled from the room, he shouted, 'We'll need clean towels . . . You know what to do?'

'I know,' she confirmed. She had made herself ready for weeks now. There was no point waiting until the last minute. But it was too early, she thought with a shock. Claudia had gone into labour almost six weeks too early.

At the bottom of the stairs, she almost bumped into Mr Taylor. He was white-faced and nervous. Before he could say anything, Jenny repeated the doctor's instructions. 'The child's being born,' she told him. 'Quick now. You're to fetch the midwife.' On her words, he slewed round, running from the house as though the devil was on his heels. He didn't like these things. God only knew he'd seen enough of his own young 'uns come into the world, the latest a little lad only two months back, and still it all frightened the hell out of him. Babies and such were not men's business. He didn't care for being around at such a time, and he was thankful to be sent on an errand that took him out of it.

The minutes ticked by, and turned into hours, and still there was no news. Mr Taylor kept well out of the way, yet close enough at hand for Jenny to call him if he was needed. As for herself, she followed the midwife's instructions to the letter, going up and down the stairs until she was worn out, ferrying clean towels up, fetching soiled ones down and keeping her supplied with hot water and soap. She made sure the baby's cradle and blankets were aired, and laid the shawl within easy reach of the bed. Now there was nothing left to do but wait. It was as if the waiting went on forever.

All day, Jenny kept herself busy. She washed and dried every item of crockery and took her time in putting it away. After finishing her normal duties, she polished the silver until she could see her face in it, she rubbed wax into the drawing-room furniture until her arms were ready to drop off, and she rinsed every item of porcelain in the display cabinet. After that she tackled the long tapestry curtains with a feather duster, then taking all the mats outside to the washing line, she beat them until the air swelled with dust. Twice she washed the kitchen floor, and umpteen times she went to the bottom of the stairs where she listened for the sound of a newborn. All she could hear was Claudia, screaming and yelling enough to frighten the dead. Now and then a terrible hush would fall over the house, and that was even worse than the noise.

Twice the doctor came, washed his hands at the kitchen sink, and went away. 'I have a patient to see,' he explained, seeing Jenny's surprised expression. 'The child won't be born for a while yet, I think. But your mistress is in very capable hands. Don't worry, I'll be back shortly.' And he was. The first time he was gone for only an hour, and the second time he was back in a remarkably short time, bringing with him a long brown box. It was probably as well that Jenny couldn't see the instrument inside.

The day lengthened, evening came and the night crept in. Claudia slept from exhaustion, and then she woke. And when she woke, she began screaming again. It was unnerving. Mr Taylor stayed as long as Jenny wanted him, and then he took himself off home, grateful that *his* day at least was at an end.

In the gaslight, Jenny crouched over the kitchen table, with her hands to her ears. 'Dear God, let it soon be over,' she asked. For though she disliked Claudia, it was pitiful to hear her in such agony.

With her eyes closed and her thoughts so deeply occupied, Jenny didn't hear the midwife come into the kitchen. 'We can't wait any longer,' she said, startling Jenny out of her reverie. She was a small woman, but strong and stiff, like a little terrier. Her hair was steel grey and her eyes were like brown currants in a mound of pale dough. 'We'll have to bring the child out quickly now,' she told Jenny. '*Or lose it.*'

Droplets of sweat trickled down each side of her face as she made for the pan of water simmering on the stove. 'Fill the kettle again, and then come upstairs,' she ordered Jenny. 'We might have need of you.' Before Jenny could recover from the shock of being summoned into that room where Claudia was undergoing such terror, the midwife quickly poured the steaming water into the prepared bowl, gripped it with strong fingers and, taking it with her, went from the room without another word, leaving Jenny rushing around to refill the kettle and put it on a slow light. That done, she went after the little woman at a hurried pace, not wanting to go into that room where Claudia lay, and not wanting to stay out.

Jenny was shocked when she came into the bedroom. Claudia was stretched out on the bed, with her nightgown rolled up to her breasts and both doctor and midwife stooped over her lower half. Her legs were wide open and bent at the knees, with her ankles tied to a chair either side of the bed. Her screams were ear-splitting.

While the doctor and his assistant worked with desperation, Claudia struggled and fought, tearing at the bolster and writhing every which way, until the ropes round her ankles were stained with blood. Flustered and impatient, the midwife was made to slap her hard on the face. 'If you want this child born, you'll have to help us,' she told her. 'You're only making matters worse!' All she got for her troubles was Claudia's long fingernails down her face.

Jenny was a welcome sight. 'Quickly!' The midwife impatiently beckoned her into the room. 'Stay with her. Hold her tight,' she pleaded. Jenny saw how she tenderly touched her face where Claudia's sharp nails had scored four red weals from cheekbone to chin. The skin was raised, with small crimson bubbles peppering the gash. The look she gave Claudia was withering.

Without hesitation, Jenny did as she was told. With no chair for her to sit on, and her instincts telling her to keep off the bed, Jenny dropped to her knees beside Claudia. 'It won't be long now,' she whispered, taking hold of her hand and keeping it tightly clasped in her own. Never having been in such a situation before, she was nervous and unsure as to what she could do.

'Bitch! Claudia lashed out with her free hand. Suddenly her whole body was pouring sweat and violently jerking, as though she was in some kind of convulsion. Jenny was adamant. 'You can do it. You can bring this baby safely into the world,' she told her in as calm a voice as she could, when all the while she was terrified inside. Thanking her lucky stars that it wasn't *her* who was going through this awful nightmare. Grabbing Claudia's other hand, which was flaying the air, Jenny held them tight in one fist while she gently stroked Claudia's forehead. 'It won't be long, I promise,' she murmured, sending up a silent prayer that it would soon be over.

As though in answer to her plea, the midwife cried jubilantly, 'That's it! That's a good girl!' and immediately there was a flurry

139

of excitement, before the room echoed to the rhythmic sound of flesh slapping flesh. Glancing up, Jenny could see the doctor holding the bloodied infant upside down in the air. With swift firm movements he brought his flat palm down time and again on the small reddening buttocks.

The midwife looked on, wiping the back of her hand across her face to mop the beads of sweat. 'You've got a daughter,' she called out, turning to Claudia with a smile. But Claudia didn't even look. All she knew was that the pain was over. The child had caused her pain, and she wanted nothing to do with it.

Suddenly the unmistakable cry of a newborn filled the air, a small angry protest at its harsh treatment on entering the world. In that moment it was as though the long desperate hours had never been. 'Oh, Miss Claudia!' Jenny couldn't take her eyes off that tiny pink bundle. 'It's a little girl, and she's so beautiful.' Scrambling up from the floor, she stretched her stiff aching knees. 'It's a little girl,' she kept saying, her eyes misting over as she gazed on that tiny new creation.

With his work done, and all danger passed, the doctor made ready to leave. 'I'll leave them in your capable hands,' he told the midwife, who in turn told Jenny, 'Here, wash the child while I attend to its mother.' She pinched the child's nose with her finger and thumb until the black mucus that had accumulated there was emitted, then she bundled the crying infant into a white cloth and handed it to Jenny. 'Gently now,' she warned. 'Wash the little darling gently, then the mother can hold her.'

When Jenny thought about it later, she knew that if she lived to be a hundred years old, she would never experience anything so wonderful as the feel of that child being placed into her arms. As soon as the baby was in Jenny's embrace, it ceased crying. Instead it looked up at her with wide-awake eyes, seeming to study her face with great curiosity.

Filled with wonder, she held the child close to her breast. She couldn't believe how tiny it was. So uniquely perfect: its every limb, the exquisite fingers that tapered to a fine point, the way it jiggled its little body and kicked its legs as though it felt glorious to be free. 'Oh, but you're beautiful,' Jenny breathed. Reverently, she laid the child on the dresser and began washing the blood and mucus from it. She stroked the brand new skin with the tips of her fingers, and it felt like silk beneath her touch. She held its tiny toes between finger and thumb, and wondered how anything so small could be so complete.

But the most astonishing thing of all was the little face because the child was the mirror image of her grandmother. For a newborn she had a generous growth of hair. It was the same warm shade of auburn, glowing like fire in the lamplight. And the eyes that twinkled up at Jenny were Elizabeth's eyes. They shone like the brightest emeralds, touching her heart in a way she had never before experienced. 'Dear God above,' she murmured, 'you're Elizabeth Marshall born all over again.' And she was overwhelmed with such love, it was like a physical pain inside her.

When the child was ready, the midwife placed it beside Claudia. 'Isn't she lovely?' she asked warmly.

She gave no answer. Instead she remained sullen, with her face turned away from the child and her body making no contact.

The midwife was not unduly concerned. She had seen it before when the birth had been particularly difficult. 'All right, dear. I'll put the child in its cradle,' she told Claudia. 'When it cries for a feed, you must put it to your breast straight away.' She tucked the infant into its bed and made certain that everything was tidy before she left. 'Make your mistress a cup of strong tea,' she informed Jenny. 'Then let them sleep. They're both exhausted.'

Jenny saw the woman from the house. Then she put the kettle on and prepared a tray for Claudia. 'Oh, it'll be grand, having a baby in the house,' she said aloud. In fact, with the baby looking so much like Elizabeth, it would be like having a part of that dear soul back again. Into Jenny's mind crept another thought, more disturbing. There was nothing in the child's features to say that it was Frank's, but in her deepest heart she knew he was the father. The realisation was strangely sobering.

Just as she was about to pour the boiling water over the tea-leaves in the big brown pot, Jenny felt her senses tingle, as though someone was watching her. Alarmed, she swung round, and what she saw made her drop the kettle with a clatter on the stove. 'MISS CLAUDIA!' She couldn't believe her eyes.

Her long brown hair was matted and caked with sweat, and her pale eyes seemed lost in the grey pallor of her face. Dishevelled and stooping from the shoulders, as though the weight of the world was on them, Claudia glared from the doorway. 'Get it out of my room,' she murmured. Her voice was low, but more frightening than if she had raised it from the rooftops.

Jenny was horrified. 'What . . . the baby?' Somewhere inside she laughed out loud. What was she thinking of? Claudia couldn't possibly mean she wanted the *baby* taken out of her room.

Claudia stared at her, and then stumbled away. Mesmerised, Jenny followed. At the top of the stairs, Claudia fell against the wall. Jenny went to help her, but she pushed her away. 'Do it now.' The words were spat out. 'Or I won't be responsible for my actions.'

If Jenny had doubted Claudia's intentions, she couldn't doubt them now. Hurriedly, she went into the room and scooped the child into her arms. 'You're coming with me, little one,' she murmured. 'Later your mammy will want you back.'

As she went past Claudia, their eyes met. There was murder in Claudia's face as she glanced briefly at the baby. When she saw how like her own mother it was, she gasped aloud and cringed away. 'Don't bring it near me,' she told Jenny. 'Don't *ever* bring it near me again.'

142

Trembling in every corner of her being, Jenny went to her own room, where she pressed the sleeping child into the corner of her own small bed. Quickly now, she returned to Claudia's room. Shivering and exhausted, Claudia had climbed back between the bedcovers. From there she watched Jenny collect the child's belongings. When they were placed in the cradle, Jenny lifted the whole ensemble into her arms and placed it outside the room. Going back, she dared to tell Claudia, 'Tomorrow, you'll feel different.'

'I meant every word I said. I want no part of it.'

Still convinced that it was only a temporary madness, Jenny forced a small smile. 'You need to rest, miss. I was starting a tray for you. I'll fetch it now, shall I?'

'I don't want it. I don't want *anything*.' She rolled over so that she was facing Jenny full on. 'Most of all, I don't want that bastard.' She smiled then, and it was a terrible sight to see. '*You* can have it if you want. After all, it's yours by rights because it belongs to the man who promised to marry you.' She chuckled when the colour ebbed from Jenny's face. 'Surely you must have guessed?' she taunted.

'I thought it might be,' Jenny said flatly. She didn't want to give Claudia the satisfaction of showing too much distress.

'Do what you like with it, but it's never to know that I'm its . . .' She couldn't bring herself to say 'mother', and so she snapped, 'I don't even want to talk about it, and I won't feel any differently tomorrow. Do you understand?'

'Yes, miss.'

Suddenly a look of fear flitted across Claudia's face. 'You'll stay?'

'Yes, miss.'

'At the lower wages?'

'If that's all you can afford. For now.' She wanted Claudia to know that she wasn't satisfied with the terms of her employ, and would bring the matter up again when the time was right.

Claudia seemed surprised that Jenny had decided to stay. 'I don't understand you,' she said, regarding her closely, and her devious mind examining every angle. Then, as if a light was lit in her thoughts, she knew. 'My mother asked you to watch over me, didn't she?' Excited, she leaned up on one elbow. 'And you promised to stay, didn't you?'

Jenny's instincts told her that it would not be wise or dignified to disclose what had taken place between her and a sick woman. Besides, she owed no explanation to Claudia Marshall. 'You've asked me to stay on, and I will. That decision is my own,' she said truthfully. 'And if you want me to care for the child, I can do that too.'

Claudia was impressed by Jenny's proud manner, but she would not have said so for the world. She also suspected that Jenny *had* given a promise to stay and watch over her . . . and possibly the child. The thought infuriated her and then it amused her. And it gave her a strange sense of power. 'So you will stay, and the little bastard is your concern from this minute on,' she remarked. 'You're to say nothing of this arrangement to anyone. Whatever happens in this house is to remain within these four walls. Is that clear?' Claudia was no fool. She knew the enormity of her shocking plan.

'As you say, miss.' Jenny could have argued with her. She could have pointed out that rejecting your own flesh and blood was monstrous, but she knew that it would all be to no avail, so she simply inclined her head in acknowledgement and departed with a heavy heart.

The dawn was creeping over the rooftops when Jenny hurried through the deserted streets, down the main road and past the school, then on towards Russell Street where the Taylor family lived.

'Isn't it beautiful?' she said to the bundle wrapped securely in her arms as she looked up at the rising sun. The early morning sky was shot through with slivers of gold that glittered and danced in the burning light. 'Like your hair,' she whispered. 'And your grandmother's before you.'

When the child began whimpering again, she held it tighter, saying soothingly, 'All right, sweetheart. It's not far now.' She was so afraid for that little mite, and she was so helpless. She'd tried everything she could think of to make it feed, but everything had failed. Jenny had made a jug of warm fresh milk, with a drop of honey, and had tried for an hour to coax the child to suck it from her finger. At one stage she had gone to Claudia's room and asked her to take the child, but she had reacted like the mad woman she was, and Jenny was forced to think of other ways to satisfy the bairn. She even bared her own breast, in the hope that she might pacify the child, and for a while it sucked on the barren nipple until it realised it was being fooled.

Finally, a possible solution occurred to her. She wrapped the child in layers of blankets that would protect it against the morning air, and set off for the village.

'All right! All right!' Mr Taylor's voice went before him, down the narrow passage and out to the doorstep where Jenny stood. 'Is there a fire or summat?' he demanded, inching open the door. His eyes popped open and he flung the door wide to let her in. 'Good God, whatever's happened?' he asked, quickly fastening his trouser buttons and ushering her down the passage.

Mrs Taylor came rushing breathlessly down the stairs, a large round woman with wild hair and big eyes. 'Jenny Dickens, ain't it?' she commented, screwing up her eyes and peering at Jenny in the gaslight. Her surprised gaze fell to the child, and at once she pounced forward, ushering the two of them into the parlour. 'Whatever possessed you to fetch a newborn out at this hour of a morning?' she demanded.

Before Jenny could answer, Meg appeared. When her mam glanced at her, she reassured her, 'It's all right, Mam. The young 'uns are sound and fast asleep.' She was amazed to see that it was Jenny who had got them from their beds.

'I'm sorry, but I couldn't think where else to go for help. This is Claudia Marshall's newborn, and she won't feed her. The poor little mite's been crying for most of the night, and now she's worn herself out. Oh, Mrs Taylor, I've been at my wits' end.'

Mrs Taylor fell backwards into a chair as though she'd been pushed. '*What* did you say?'

Quickly, Jenny went on to explain, but left out all the sordid truth. 'It isn't really her fault, because she had a real bad birthing and the midwife says that sometimes it makes a woman reject her baby.' She thought enough of an explanation had been given without defiling Claudia's character too much. Besides, at the bottom of her heart, Jenny hoped that Claudia would come to regret having rejected the baby.

'Oh, well, we'll soon see to this one.' Mrs Taylor sprang forward to collect the child from Jenny's arms. In a minute she had undone the front of her nightgown and unleashed a mound of soft pink flesh. Murmuring endearments, she rammed the plump brown nipple into the child's mouth and settled back in the chair. 'There. My own little lad's fast asleep with a full stomach, and there's more than enough left over to satisfy this little 'un,' she declared proudly.

Fascinated, Jenny watched. It gave her a good feeling to know that the bairn was content at last.

An hour later, they all stood at the front door. 'Mind, she won't be satisfied for long,' warned Mrs Taylor. 'You'll need to see the midwife. In fact, Mr Taylor can call on her as he comes to work.' She smiled a wrinkly smile. 'She was right, you know, and you mustn't worry. I've known women who turn against their newborn and can't show their affection for days, even weeks.'

'It's the same with pigs,' Mr Taylor said absent-mindedly, looking embarrassed when everyone stared at him.

'Thank you,' Jenny told them both. 'I don't know what I would have done without you.' Turning to Meg, she remarked, 'I'm so glad you've got a good cleaning job at the Swan Inn, but you really must find time to come and visit up at the house. It gets lonely, you know.' She had been astonished to discover that Meg was earning almost twice as much as her, for half the work.

'I'll try, but I don't get all that much time,' Meg apologised. She had a fancy fellow, but it was still a well-kept secret from her parents.

Addressing Mrs Taylor, Jenny pleaded, 'I would be grateful if you could say very little about what's happened?'

'We'll say nothing at all,' she promised. 'We're not given to gossip in this house.'

With that assurance, Jenny made her way home. Once the child was laid in its cradle, she peeped into Claudia's room, and seeing her still asleep, wondered how it was that someone so callous could sleep so soundly.

At six-thirty, when Jenny was beginning her work, Mr Taylor arrived at the kitchen door. He had the midwife with him, and a younger woman – thin, with rolled black hair and a sour-looking face. 'This is the wet-nurse,' the midwife explained. 'I understand your mistress is having trouble feeding the child.' Without waiting for an answer she marched upstairs, and within minutes marched down again. 'Nasty young woman,' she muttered angrily, adding in a brighter voice, 'Still, perhaps it's to be expected. There's no sign of any milk, and perhaps she may not have any at all. We'll see. We'll see.'

She then departed, leaving behind the wet-nurse and a list of instructions: when to bathe the child; when to blanket-bath the mother; what to feed her and when; how to make a broth which would induce a flow of milk; and what to do in an emergency. 'We must all do our best,' she said, then promptly departed and never set foot in Claudia Marshall's house again.

Jenny watched while the thin woman fed the child. It amazed her how two women could be so different. With Mrs Taylor it had been a labour of love, while this woman was stiff and unloving. When Mrs Taylor fed the child, it snuggled into a warm yielding titty, but this woman held the child on the edge of her bony knee, only allowing it to suck at her sharp pointed nipple from an uncomfortable distance.

Before she left, the woman gave the child to Jenny. 'Hold it upright and let out the air,' she said.

Jenny walked the child up and down, murmuring words of comfort. 'Let the air out?' she repeated. 'Anyone would think you were a balloon. By! It's a wonder she didn't turn her own milk sour,' she chuckled.

Afterwards, she held the child on her knee and gazed at its beauty. 'What shall we call you, eh?' she mused. 'As you're so like your grandmother, happen we should name you after her?' She laughed aloud. 'No. Better not. That would really put the cat among the pigeons, eh?' She thought awhile, and the name fell from her lips. 'Katie,' she murmured. 'We'll call you Katie.' It was a lovely name, and somehow it was made for this darling little girl-child.

The tiny features grimaced, and Jenny swore it was a smile. 'So you think it's a good choice, eh?' she laughed, nuzzling her face into the baby's neck. Holding the child at arm's length, she gazed on it with tenderness. 'I'll tell you this much, Katie sweetheart,' she said, 'you've come into a harsh world, and your mammy doesn't want you. But I can promise you this.' She looked into those emerald green eyes and recalled another promise. She didn't regret that one, and she would never regret the one she was about to make now. 'While I'm alive, you'll never go short of love.' Then she held the child close, letting the warmth flow between them. It was a warmth that would last a lifetime.

# Part Two

## *1921*

## MEMORIES

# *Chapter Eight*

Frank had been busy all day. With the snow thick on the ground, the tradesmen's horses were more prone to lose their footing. Often they would catch their large hooves under a tram rail, and that meant a visit to Frank Winfield's yard on Peter Street. No sooner had he fitted a set of shoes to one horse, than there was another waiting. His back had been bent to his labours from five o'clock on this Saturday morning, and it felt like he would never be able to straighten it again.

'If I don't stretch up for a minute, you'll be carrying me out crooked,' he told the latest irate customer. 'Look, join me in a brew, eh? It won't take long to boil the kettle.'

Without waiting for an answer, he scuttled into the recess at the back of the shed, and it was only a minute before he came out again, his two hands on the small of his back and his eyes closed as he raised his head and groaned. 'God Almighty! What a day,' he declared. 'Here it is . . . four o'clock of a Saturday, and I should have closed the doors long since.' Normally, he shut shop at noon on a Saturday, and didn't open again until first light on Monday.

'Bloody weather!' The driver jumped down from his perch atop the brewery wagon, stamping his feet and clapping his gloved hands together in an effort to warm his frozen fingers. He was a huge mountain of a man, with a long drooping moustache and thick hairy eyebrows that poked out from above scowling dark eyes. He was smothered against the cold, wearing a tattered blue scarf round his throat, an old grey overcoat that scraped the ground as he moved, and a brown hat with a limp brim that made a wavy umbrella over his glowing face. 'Can't remember such a long cold winter,' he grumbled, beginning to unshackle the big grey cob. 'I shan't get the rest o' these barrels delivered on time, I can tell you that. Roads clogged up. Every wagon going at a snail's pace, and kids making slides so you can't stand up straight when you're offloading. And as if that ain't enough to test a man's good nature, I very nearly had a run-in with one o' them fancy motor vehicles . . . damn' near frightened the horse half to death!'

Frank knew the man well. He was a good sort but easily put out. 'That must be Squire Pitt's vehicle,' he commented. 'As far as I know, he's the only one to have such a monstrosity.'

'Aye, but I dare say he'll not be the last. Some folk have got more money than sense. I read somewhere that London's roads are seeing more o' them bloody contraptions every day. Though I don't reckon the day will ever come when they take over from the tram and horse-drawn wagon.'

'I wouldn't put money on it,' Frank warned. 'It seems to be gaining interest in the South, and I imagine it won't be long before the novelty's spread throughout the country.' He lapsed into serious thought, adding in a quiet voice, 'Happen I'd best change my trade, because they'll not be wanting blacksmiths *then*, God knows.'

The older man was flabbergasted. 'Damn and bugger it! I hadn't thought of that. And what about folks such as myself, eh?' he wanted to know. 'I've driven nowt but horses and wagons since I were no taller than one o' them there beer barrels.' He pointed a cold stiff finger at the neat rows of wooden barrels lined up on his cart. 'By! It don't stand thinking about.'

While the fellow had been grumbling on, Frank had disappeared. Now he emerged with two mugs of steaming hot tea, one of which he placed on the rim of the wagon, within the fellow's reach. 'Maybe not,' he replied, leaning on the wagon and sipping gratefully at the warming liquid. 'But it'll come. Mark my words, the day will come when the roads are filled with these newfangled vehicles.'

The other fellow stared at Frank in disbelief. Then he shook his head and the snow that had accumulated on his hat fell round his ears in a fine white shower. 'Well, you can keep the blessed things as far as I'm concerned, because I wouldn't be seen dead in one o' them smelly noisy articles, not even if me life depended on it.'

While Frank reflected on the wisdom of his own words, the disgruntled fellow continued muttering under his breath, taking occasional gulps from his mug, then returning it to the wagon and clapping his hands together while he blew into them from raspberry red cheeks. 'By! I'll be glad when spring comes and that's a fact,' he commented as Frank set about preparing a pair of new shoes for the old cob.

With practised skill, the big fellow loosed the cob from his harness and walked him forward on a halter. 'Come on, me beauty,' he coaxed. 'We'll have you right in no time.' He and the cob had been together a long time now, and like tried and true friends trusted each other implicitly. Beginning to whistle a merry tune, he fastened the halter to the iron ring in the wall. When the cob jerked his head high and impatiently stamped his hoof on the hard ground, he chided, 'Now, now! We've done this often enough to know what's expected. I know you're itching to be on your way, and so am I, but we're not leaving here till you've got yourself a set o' pretty new shoes. So be patient, yer old bugger.'

'I expect he's tired, like me,' Frank chipped in. 'Had a long day, has he?'

'You could say that, Frank,' replied the big fellow. 'We've already made four deliveries today.' He glanced at the smith and made a grimace. 'Drunken buggers,' he laughed. 'What with Christmas only a few days away, every inn in Blackburn must have a cellar stacked to the ceiling with booze.' He looked fondly at the cob. 'It's been a busy day, and that's a fact. Poor bugger's getting old, that's the trouble. We both are. Oh, I know there'll come a day when we'll have to part, but I try not to think too hard on it. What! I'd rather part with the missus than with old Jack here.'

'He's a good 'un,' Frank agreed. Looking over his shoulder, he told the cob, 'Don't worry, old fella, I'll have you finished in no time at all.' He sighed wearily. 'God only knows, I'm as anxious to get home as you are.'

At this, the other fellow collected his mug of tea before ambling over to where Frank was poking the bellows into the coals and intermittently squeezing air through them. The coals grew gradually redder until the heat emitted was almost unbearable. The fellow drained the remainder of his tea into a wide-open throat and put his mug down on the floor against the wall. 'By, that's grand!' he remarked with an appreciative grin, at the same time spreading his enormous palms before the heap of coals. 'It might be bloody freezing outside, but it's warm as toast in here.'

'*Too* warm,' Frank explained. 'It's not so bad on a day like this, but in the summer, even with the doors wide open, it's worse than hell itself.' Plying his attention to the task in hand, he pinched the piece of misshapen iron between the prongs and placed it on the stone edging the furnace. Tapping at the iron with his hammer, he began to tease it into a recognisable shape; every now and then thrusting it deep into the burning coals, until the iron glowed white hot. With incredible speed, the iron became more curved until it was a perfect horse shoe. That done, he took up another piece and enacted the same procedure.

The big fellow was fascinated. 'You're a bloody good blacksmith,' he said. 'The best.' Frank went on working without comment so the fellow continued, 'Yer never have said what made you leave the South to come and live here in Blackburn. Were it because you saw how them motor vehicles might take your trade away?'

Frank shook his head. 'If that ever does happen, it'll be *years* from now.' The memories were never far away. Memories of his lovely Jenny, and of how he'd let her down badly. 'Besides, I wasn't a blacksmith at the time. I were a blacksmith before, and I've been a blacksmith since, but . . .' He didn't want to give too much away, because so far he'd managed to keep his past life to himself. 'Well, every man yearns for a change at some time or another,' he said, hoping that would be an end to the other fellow's penetrating questions.

'You never wed then?'

Frank appeared not to hear, hammering harder on the shoe and keeping his eyes averted from the fellow's prying eyes.

'Well, that does surprise me . . . a man like yourself.'

'How's that?' Frank wondered then how many times he'd been the subject of gossip over a pint of ale.

The big fellow stroked his chin and stared Frank up and down, taking account of the big muscular shoulders and the straight broad back. It was not long ago that Frank Winfield was a stranger in Blackburn town. There were some strangers you instantly took a dislike to, and then there were those who put you at your ease straight away. Frank Winfield was such a man. With his honest brown eyes and thick mop of fair hair, he was now a familiar and welcome sight throughout the town. Through sheer hard work and determination, he had carved a niche for himself here. He

157

asked for no favours and he gave none, but he was known to be a good and decent man.

He kept himself to himself though, quiet spoken and self-sufficient, yet there wasn't one man who'd made his acquaintance who didn't have a good word to say about him. 'Well, you've come up from nowhere and earned yerself a respectable place in these 'ere parts,' the big fellow went on. 'Yer business is thriving and yer seem like a man who'd put money aside for a rainy day. On top o' that, yer young and a strong handsome fellow. It's no secret that's how yer landlady sees yer,' he intimated knowingly.

At this Frank stopped work. Glancing sharply at the older man, he reminded him, 'Doreen Craig is a fine woman and I'll not have her name bandied about.' His eyes darkened with anger. When he was a stranger in this town, Doreen Craig had given him lodgings. Ever since then, she had been a good and stalwart friend to him.

'Oh, now, don't get me wrong. I didn't mean nothing by what I said.' He smiled a secret smile while Frank turned away and resumed his labours. 'She *is* a fine woman, and nobody knows that more than I do. As a younger man I delivered coal along Jubilee Street, an' Doreen Craig were one o' my best customers. When she were widowed, I saw for myself how the loss turned her life upside down. She had no other family except her young son. There was no man to look after 'em, and precious little money to keep the wolf from the door. But she never complained. Instead, she just got on with life the best she could, taking in lodgers, such as yourself, and raising her lad without asking for nothing from nobody.' He pursed his lips and sent his mind back over the years. Presently he explained, 'She were widowed six year ago, an' if my reckoning's right, young Rodney's about eighteen now. It's because of Doreen's upbringing that he's turned out a fine young man.'

'Aye.' Frank hung the four horse shoes from his belt, then put the long file in his overall pocket, collected his small hammer and came towards the cob. 'You've known them both a lot longer than I have,' he apologised. 'So I don't have to tell you what a kind soul Doreen is.'

'Kind, yes . . . but she's nobody's fool, isn't Doreen. It were real hard for her in the early years, what with no proper income and a lad to raise. There were plenty who offered to help, but she'd have none of it. She was determined to do it on her own.' He clicked his tongue and tipped his head to one side, a look of admiration on his face. 'And, by God, she did an' all.' He remembered how Doreen's husband, Lou, had always been a delicate soul, even when they were lads at school together. If he ran he coughed, and when he coughed he took ill for weeks on end. Later, when he was a husband and father, he seemed to do better, holding down a job at Markham's warehouse, and appearing to thrive on family life. But he was never what you'd call strong, so when the tuberculosis took him, nobody was surprised.

Not wanting to discuss Doreen's private affairs in such a way, Frank remained silent, stooping until his head was close to the cob's withers, and raising the fetlock so that the enormous hoof was tucked securely between his own knees. After a brief examination, he told the other man, 'There's no damage to the hoof, but the shoe's been ripped away and bent.' He cocked his head sideways, looking up with an expression of concern. 'You're lucky it didn't split the hoof from one end to the other.'

The big fellow came to take a peep. 'By! No wonder the poor bugger were hobbling.' He straightened up and put his great hands on the cob's back, rubbing them backwards and forwards in a fond gesture. 'Bloody tram rails. Happen it might be better if them noisy motor vehicles did take over, eh? At least there wouldn't be no tram rails to contend with, eh?'

'Happen there wouldn't be any horses either,' Frank reminded him wryly as he prised the old shoe off and began filing the cob's underfoot.

At Frank's words, the other man lapsed into a deep silence. His thoughts went from one thing to another, and it wasn't long before they returned to Frank himself. 'What made yer leave then?' he asked.

'Leave where?'

'The *South*. What made you leave the South to come here? You ain't got no relatives in Blackburn, have yer?'

'No.'

'So what made you leave the South to come here?' he persisted.

'Oh, this and that.' Impatient to be rid of this well-meaning but nosy fellow, Frank pressed on with his task. He had replaced the worst shoe so the rest shouldn't take too long, he thought thankfully.

'Don't want to talk about it, eh? Well, I can't say I blame yer. All the same, when a man decides to up sticks an' mek for strange parts, there's allus a good reason for it.' He rubbed a thick coarse finger along his chin. 'Aye, there's allus a good reason, and more often than not it's a woman who's at the bottom of it all.' He chuckled, not knowing how his words were disturbing Frank. 'That's it, ain't it, eh? It were a *woman* as made yer take off.'

Frank appeared not to have heard him, and his silence only convinced the other man that he'd hit the nail right on the head. 'I'm a nosy old sod,' he declared. 'So you'd be in yer rights to tell me to mind me own business.' But what he really hoped was that Frank would confide in him.

'Wouldn't dream of telling you to do any such thing,' he returned, at the same time quickly tapping on the third shoe.

The big fellow waited for an admission of sorts. All he got was the sound of Frank merrily whistling. 'Aye,' he moaned, 'the wife's right. I've a bad habit of poking me nose in where it don't belong.'

Realising he was getting nowhere as far as Frank's affairs were concerned, and being sorry that he'd caused an awkward atmosphere between them, the big fellow moved on to other topics; mainly Germany's determination to seek a moratorium on war reparations, and how the League of Nations had refused Russia's entry.

Frank made suitable responses, but he wasn't altogether interested. His attention was elsewhere. Certain things the big fellow had said were playing on his mind ... 'It were a *woman* as made yer tek off.' Well, he was almost right. In fact, it had been *two* women. One who deserved the best, and one who was a devil in disguise.

'There you are,' he said, straightening from his labour. 'Good as new.' He patted the cob on its withers. 'Keep your eyes peeled, old son,' he light-heartedly warned the beast, 'because if you get caught under the tram rails between now and Monday morning, you'll have to find another blacksmith. Once I've locked these doors today, nothing short of murder will make me open them until first thing Monday morning.'

'Don't you worry, I'll keep a sharp eye on him,' interrupted the big fellow. 'Come on, my beauty,' he coaxed. Walking the cob back to his wagon, he reversed it in between the shafts and quickly coupled the harness up. 'Shan't be sorry to get to my bed tonight and that's a fact,' he grumbled, leading the whole equipage out across the cobbles. Once clear of the big doors, he returned to pay Frank the one shilling and sixpence for a good job done. Then he clambered high into his seat where, taking up the reins, he clicked the cob away. 'If I don't see yer afore, have a grand Christmas,' he said with a chuckle, and Frank knew he was hinting about himself and Doreen. For a brief second he was angry, but then he laughed and shook his head in mock frustration. 'You old sod,' he muttered beneath his breath. 'Still, I don't reckon you mean any harm.'

\* \* \*

The snow was falling thick and fast as Frank locked the big gates and set out for home. It was a brisk ten-minute walk to Jubilee Street, and he was glad of that because it would give him time to think before seeing Doreen. Four months ago he had sent Jenny a letter, hoping to put things right between them. In the weeks that followed he waited anxiously for her reply. It never came, and he wasn't all that surprised. Since then, he had managed to push thoughts of Jenny and his old life to the back of his mind. The big fellow's remarks had stirred him up again, and all the old longings were back. Dark and painful feelings which he had foolishly believed were under control.

In those first lonely weeks of settling in Blackburn, there was hardly a night when he didn't pace his bedroom until the dawn broke. He felt lost, adrift in a strange land, and there was a restlessness in him that threatened to send him down the road again. Jenny was as real to him as a physical presence, yet he couldn't speak to her, couldn't hold her – and, oh, he so much wanted to.

In his despair, he had even toyed with the idea of going back and asking her forgiveness, pleading with her to leave Woburn Sands so the two of them could make a new start somewhere else. But he was afraid. Afraid that she would slam the door in his face, and God knew he would have deserved it after what he had done. Her lovely face haunted him until he thought he'd go completely mad. Then, when he secured work at the Preston blacksmith's, he poured all his energies into his labours, working from dawn to dusk and wearing himself out so that he had neither the time nor the energy to think too deeply. He replaced thoughts of a reconciliation with Jenny with another ambition, a determination that eventually brought him his own blacksmith's yard. Slowly, he learned to live without the hope that somehow he and Jenny could get together again.

Now though the pain of losing her was as strong as ever. It was like a great leaden hammer striking right in the middle of his heart. 'You've been fooling yourself, Frank,' he muttered against the growing breeze. 'You haven't forgotten her, and you never will.' Somehow the knowledge was strangely comforting, almost as though by loving her, he kept her close. The pain melted into memories – warm, delightful memories of his time with Jenny – but though they gave him immeasurable pleasure, all the memories in the world were a poor substitute for the real thing which, because of his own shameful actions, he believed was denied to him forever.

Not for the first time he was made to wonder how, if it was Jenny who had cheated and then deserted him in such a way, he would have reacted. One thing was for sure, it would have broken his heart. But *he* was the bastard who had done those unspeakable things, and his heart was broken anyway. But then, wasn't it written that you sow only what you reap?

The breeze became fierce and the snow poured relentlessly from a darkening sky. Drawing the brim of his cap further over his brow, he bent his shoulders into the cutting wind, then quickened his footsteps and hurried on his way. The faster he went, the harder he tried to shut Jenny from his mind. But it was impossible. She clung to him, drowning his senses, until he could think of nothing else.

When he approached Jubilee Street and saw the small dark-haired figure standing in the doorway, he realised that he was only causing himself a deal of anguish and that it would never bring Jenny back to him. More than that, the sight of the familiar slight figure on the steps made him feel instantly ashamed. 'Take hold of yourself, Frank Winfield,' he snapped angrily. 'You've let *one* woman down, and you must be careful never to let it happen again.' Doreen Craig and he had a kind of understanding. She had come to rely on him, to make him feel like a man again.

She had been there for him when he was desperate, so while Doreen needed him he would be there for her. He owed her that much.

Doreen Craig's house was situated right at the top of the street and straddling the corner. Most of the properties in this part of Blackburn were rented out either by the Corporation or by private landlords. Doreen's house was different because it was her own. The house had been built by a millowner some fifty years ago, a quiet little man who later became a recluse. He lived in the house until he died, when his solicitors put it on the market. Doreen's father bought it with fifty pounds which he borrowed from his employer, the local candle-maker. The house eventually came to Doreen, and she always said she would end her days there.

Number one Jubilee Street was a fine strong house, the kind of house that would stand forever. It had a long frontage, a wide oak door with a stained glass panel on either side, four double bedrooms, two living rooms, a dining room with a large bay window, and a spacious kitchen which was the heart of the house. Every room was furnished exactly as it had been since Doreen's mother first moved there, with strong wooden furniture that was as stalwart as the house itself and long tapestry curtains that were as good as the day they were hung. The big beds were all brass-ended, with pretty ceramic knobs atop each post and firm iron springs beneath the mattress. The floors were covered in plain linoleum, with rugs scattered here and there, and the walls were painted in varying shades of green, a favourite colour of Doreen's. The house was friendly, and welcoming, much like Doreen herself.

'Wherever have you been?' she cried as Frank mounted the three steps that led to the front door. 'I've been worried sick,' she said anxiously. She was a slightly built woman in her mid-thirties with a round plain face and shoulder-length dark hair tied at the back of her neck in a thin brown ribbon. She had on a floral wrap-round pinafore with only the hem and sleeves of her green frock showing.

'Never mind me,' Frank told her, at the same time gently ushering her inside, 'you shouldn't be out here, Doreen . . . and with no coat on.' When they were both inside, he took off his overcoat and shook it from the outer step before closing the door on a hostile night. 'What in God's name were you thinking of?' he asked, hanging his coat on the peg above the hallstand. 'It's a wonder you haven't caught your death o' cold.'

Taking off his cap, he hung it over his coat before placing his hands on her shoulders. 'I'm sorry I'm late,' he apologised. 'You must have known I'd be home soon as ever I could.' Awful regrets stabbed inside him as he looked into her speckled dark eyes. They were nothing like Jenny's, which were blue and soft as a summer sky, but they reflected her concern for him. 'I don't want you worrying about me.'

'But I *do* worry, Frank,' she objected. 'Rodney was late as well . . . a train derailed or summat. I worried until he came home, and then *you* were late as well.' She threw her hands wide in a gesture of despair. 'I can't help but worry, you should know that by now.'

He smiled and placed an arm round her shoulder, leading her down the passage towards the sitting room. 'I know,' he said fondly. 'All the same, I *can* find my way home, even in the dark and through a snow-storm.'

'I know,' she answered. 'And I'm a silly woman.'

He pecked her on the cheek. 'You're no such thing, Doreen Craig,' he chided.

She looked from him to the young man seated at the fireplace, a long-legged young man, with carrot red hair and big soft freckles. Tired from his long day as a porter at the railway station, he had fallen asleep. In the dancing heat from the fire his freckles had taken on a deeper hue, as though someone had splashed nutmeg all over his face. 'Rodney said he'd wait, and we could all sit down to supper together,' she explained.

'Oh, he shouldn't have done that,' Frank protested. 'The pair of you should have enjoyed your meal without me.' It was on occasions like these that he felt himself being sucked deeper into emotional ties, and still he wasn't sure how to handle it all.

Returning her attention to Frank, Doreen protested, 'I've done us a hot-pot so nothing's spoiled. You get off and wash yourself, and it'll be on the table when you're ready.' He nodded and went towards the door which led into the outer scullery. 'You'll find your clean clothes on the airer in front of the fire.'

With Frank gone, she went to her son and gently shook him. 'Rodney, wake up. Frank's home.'

The young man woke with a start. 'Good. I'm starving,' he said, stretching long bony arms above his head and yawning aloud. 'I'm tired an' all. I had thought of going to a show at the Palace, but I think I'll go to my bed early instead.'

'If you ask me, bed's the best place for you,' she answered. 'There's nothing on at the Palace Theatre that won't wait, and anyway it's no place for a dog outside. The snow's an inch thick on the ground and the skies are full of it. There's no sign it'll let up before morning, that's for sure.'

On Sundays, Doreen and the two men had their main meal in the dining room, but on weekdays they ate at the round oak table in the sitting room. Before Frank arrived there were three other lodgers; a young woman who worked as a clerk at the Town Hall, a middle-aged man by the name of Mr Wright, and a peculiar, elderly gent who was called Arthur Bedford and played the banjo at all hours of the day and night. But they had all moved out. According to Rodney, the young woman was 'more trouble than she was worth', so she was long gone and Frank was given her room. The latest lodger went only two weeks ago, and now there was only Frank, Doreen, and her son. Frank had come down last Sunday morning to find that he had been promoted to the head of the table. He didn't like the idea, but Rodney insisted. 'Mam and I like you a lot,' he declared proudly. So that was that.

Frank washed and shaved, and came back into the kitchen. 'Sit yourself down,' Doreen told him. She let her eyes rove over his upright muscular figure. He had changed his overalls for brown cord trousers and a white shirt with a turned back collar and sleeves rolled to his elbow. His thick fair hair was still damp, falling down to his ears and tumbling over his forehead as always. She thought him the most handsome man she had ever seen.

'Something smells good,' he observed, returning her smile with honest brown eyes. Addressing Rodney, who was already seated at the table, he said, 'Sorry, young fella, you must be starving. But to tell you the truth, I began to wonder if I'd ever get away.' He inched the chair out from the table and fell into it. 'By! Every bone in my body aches.'

'I know how you feel,' Rodney replied. 'The station's never been so busy, what with folks arriving and leaving to be with family at Christmas. There are two porters off sick, so that meant the rest of us had to work twice as hard.' He glanced appreciatively at his mother when she came to the table with a big earthenware dish which she brought straight from the oven. Placing the dish on the mat in the centre, she quickly removed the cloth which had protected her hands. '*I* were late home as well, weren't I, Mam?' Rodney continued, as he sat up straight in readiness for his meal.

'It's to be expected now and then, I suppose,' Doreen replied, taking the lid off the dish and placing it upside down on the cloth. At once the rich brown gravy could be seen bubbling to the rim of the dish, and the air was filled with the mouthwatering aroma of chunky meat and vegetables simmering in their own juice.

With practised skill, she took up one plate at a time and filled it with a generous scoop of hot-pot. The two men watched as the gravy spilled to the plate edges while the chunks of meat and vegetables made a steaming mound in the centre. When each man had his plate before him, she handed round the wicker basket which was filled with plump barm-cakes; the men took two each, which they placed on small sideplates. Doreen took one and broke it in half, leaving one piece on her plate and dipping the other into her gravy. For a while there was a contented silence as they each enjoyed the meal.

There then followed a brief exchange on Rodney's day compared to Frank's. Doreen had little to tell except: 'There was a woman here today, asking after lodgings . . . a big bossy type she was, with a little man in tow. She all but forced her way in. "I were told we'd find a room here," that's what she said, and a right nasty sort she was too.'

'Did she give you any trouble?' Frank wanted to know.

'Oh, no. I soon put her right. "I don't take lodgers in any more," that's what I told her, and she went away cursing and moaning at the little fellow.' She chuckled at the comical image in her mind.

Rodney beamed from ear to ear. 'Quite right!' he declared. 'You've no need of lodgers now, not with Frank and me looking after you. We both pay our way, and to tell you the truth, Mam, I never did like strangers living in our house.' He cast his eyes downwards and seemed to be deep in thought before proudly telling Frank, 'Anyway, we're more of a family now, aren't we, Frank?'

Frank nodded slightly and stuffed a piece of barm-cake into his mouth. He hated it when Rodney put him on the spot like that. But the lad meant well, and it was good to see him contented. It couldn't have been easy for him, growing up with different strangers in the house.

Rodney wasn't so easily put off. 'Our mam's a changed woman since you came to live here,' he went on, smiling knowingly at Doreen.

She blushed a fierce shade of pink. 'Behave yourself, young man,' she chided light-heartedly, at the same time grinning foolishly. 'Let Frank enjoy his tea in peace.'

Rodney winked at Frank, and wolfed down a forkful of leeks. 'You've changed our lives, and you'll never know what that means to me,' he muttered in a serious voice. Suddenly his mood brightened and he smiled at his mother who was quietly studying him. 'You've even put the roses back in our mam's cheeks,' he said with a cheeky wink.

Frank leaned back in his chair. 'I'm glad of that,' he remarked. Turning to Doreen, he murmured, 'You're a good woman, Doreen, and I was fortunate that the cab driver directed me to this house. I honestly don't know what I would have done without you all these months.'

'Give over, Frank!' she protested. 'It wouldn't have mattered *which* door you knocked on that night, because what you've achieved has been through your own hard work and determination. You don't owe that to me, nor anybody else.'

'Maybe, but it's good for a man to have someone beside him when he's struggling to make good. It's been a long hard road, and it would have been a lonelier one without you and Rodney to come home to.' Even while he spoke those truthful words, he couldn't help but think how wonderful it was when he came home to find Jenny waiting in the kitchen. How he'd swing her round and they'd kiss and hug, like they hadn't seen each other for many weeks when it might have been only a matter of hours. He could feel her slender waist even now, and later, when she came to his bed, he would hold her in his arms and think himself the luckiest man in the whole world. There had been something magical about the love between himself and Jenny. A love that could have lasted a lifetime, if only he hadn't been such a bloody fool!

Thinking of it now, he was consumed with a burning anger. How in God's name could he ever have fallen for Claudia's evil little scheme? But however devious she was, he couldn't blame her. *He* was the one who made love to her in that barn, and *he* was the one who could have walked away as soon as he guessed what she was after. It was he who had walked out, instead of facing Jenny with the truth. How could he have been such a gutless coward? Oh, if he could turn the clock back, God only knows he would, but he couldn't. It was done, and Jenny had chosen not to answer his letter. All he could do now was to wish her well and put it all behind him forever. Or else go quietly crazy. Jenny deserved better than him. He would have gone to her on bended knees if she would only have had him, but he had thrown it all away and now he was paying the price.

'Are you all right, Frank?' Doreen had seen how his fists clenched on the table, and wondered at the strength of his thoughts that they could torment him like that.

'I'm fine,' he answered, returning his attention to the wonderful meal she had prepared. 'It's been a long hard day, that's all.'

The conversation took an unexpected turn when Rodney asked: 'Why don't you and Mam get wed?'

'RODNEY!' Doreen was shocked and angry. 'That's enough. Eat your dinner and get about your business.' She dropped her knife and fork on to her plate and stood up. Her face was scarlet as she addressed Frank. 'I'm sorry. I can't think what made him blurt that out,' she apologised. 'Certainly *I've* never given him cause to think such a thing.' In a fluster, she began to gather the crockery together, deliberately averting her eyes from both men.

As he looked on her, it occurred to Frank that he could do worse than look after this good woman who had been such a friend. He didn't love her in that way, it was true. He could never love anyone except Jenny like that, but she was already lost to him and it would be some small reparation for his sins if he could make Doreen happy. Lately, the idea of him and Doreen getting wed had crept up on him. She wasn't Jenny, yet she loved him, he was sure. More than that, she and Rodney needed him, and he felt responsible for them somehow. It was impulse that made him answer now, '*Will* you marry me, Doreen?' The minute the words left his lips he regretted them, yet he knew also that he was committed to do the right thing by her.

Doreen stared at him as though she'd eaten a hot potato, with her mouth wide open and a look of disbelief on her face. It was Rodney who broke the silence. 'GREAT!' he yelled, dancing out of his chair. 'That's bloody marvellous.' He was laughing and crying all at the same time as he threw himself into his mother's arms. 'Oh, Mam, I knew it. I just knew it,' he said, swinging her round and putting Frank in mind of himself and Jenny.

Doreen composed herself enough to tell her son, 'Watch your mouth, my lad. I'll not have you using bad language in this house.' She pushed him away and for the briefest moment their eyes met; his were smiling while hers betrayed a deeper emotion. 'You had no right to embarrass Frank like that,' she said stiffly.

He was so excited he couldn't be silenced. 'Say yes, Mam,' he urged, his gaze intense as he stared at her, willing her to accept Frank's offer. 'Please?' he begged, and she was astonished to see his eyes grow moist with the threat of tears.

Looking at her son now, Doreen realised just how much he had been through since his father's death, and she blamed herself for his deep-seated grief. 'All right, son,' she whispered, putting a hand on his shoulder and smiling warmly. Turning to Frank she said, 'I'm very fond of you, Frank, and if you're sure it's what you want, then yes . . . I'd be very happy to be your wife.'

In an instant, he was by her side and she was in his arms. 'It's what I want,' he answered, but his voice said one thing while his heart said another.

Rodney laughed out loud. 'Oh, Mam, you can't know what this means to me,' he told her. Then, after shaking hands with a bemused Frank, he rushed to put on his coat. 'I'm off to the Robin Hood,' he said excitedly. 'I'd not be half a man if I didn't celebrate because it's the best news I've heard in a long time.' As he added the next words, his voice faltered and he was momentarily morose. 'It's been difficult since Dad . . . well.' He shrugged his shoulders and looked from one to the other. 'You won't be sorry, Frank,' he promised. 'I've always known you'd be good for each other.' With that, he was gone, racing down the passage and out of the front door, leaving Frank and Doreen staring at each other with a deal of embarrassment.

'He thinks the world of you,' she explained. 'Ever since his father died, he's been desperate to fix me up with the right man.'

'It's only natural that he wants to see you taken proper care of.'

'You don't have to, you know.' Quickly, before he could interrupt, she went on, 'I mean, he did push you into it, didn't he? So if you want to change your mind, you've only to say.'

Sitting her down in the chair, Frank told her sincerely, 'Like any normal man I've made mistakes . . . done things that I'm not proud of. But I've asked you to wed me, and I'll not go back on that.' He glanced at the door and chuckled. 'Besides, I wouldn't dare. What would Rodney say?' he teased.

She merely smiled, a secret little smile that made him fleetingly curious. 'Oh, he'd get over it,' she answered. 'I've got a sneaking feeling that you might have proposed to me on the spur of the moment, and I wouldn't be offended if you changed your mind.'

'Anyone would think you didn't want to wed me.'

'I just want you to be sure.'

He knew that his life might begin or end right here, and he

was aware that she was waiting for his reassurance. He would be less than a man if he changed his mind now. 'I am,' he answered softly. Gripping her by the shoulders, he eased her from the chair until she was looking up into his eyes. With careful deliberation, he bent his head and pressed his mouth to hers. She shivered beneath him, but sadly he felt only fondness for her. In that moment he vowed not to let that stop him from being a good husband. 'How soon?' he asked. Now that it was decided, he wanted it over and done with.

She drew away, her hands closed in his. 'Let's make it an Easter wedding,' she suggested, and so it was agreed. In three months' time Frank would take her to be his lawful wedded wife. 'We'll mark the moment,' he told her. 'Get your hat and coat on, and we'll join Rodney in the Robin Hood.'

'No. Let's stay here,' she whispered, pulling at the top button of his shirt. She had her own reasons for not wanting to go out.

With her fingers touching his throat, and her body pushed close to his, he found himself thinking of Jenny. Suddenly he was filled with an angry passion. Without a word he swept Doreen into his arms and carried her from the room. He took her up the stairs and laid her on his bed. There, with great tenderness, he stripped her naked. Afterwards, when he began taking off his own clothes, she watched him, her eyes following his every move, quietly admiring his handsome frame and manly physique.

When he lay between her thighs, his warm moist mouth on hers, with his strong hands roving her nakedness, she was greatly excited. It had been a long time since she felt like a real woman. Yet amid the excitement and the passion, there were other, more disturbing emotions. While she moved with his body, pushing into him, then holding on when he drew away; when he was kissing her, raising a longing in her like no other man had ever done, she prayed that everything would work out all right – for both their sakes, and for the sake of her son who had known too much unhappiness in his young life.

They fell asleep there. When she awoke, it was dark. Not wanting to wake him, she got quietly out of the bed and dressed. He didn't stir. On tiptoe, she went out of the room and down to the kitchen where she sat at the table until Rodney came in. He was merry from the drink. 'When will you wed?' he asked, falling into the chair opposite and staring at her with bleary eyes.

'You were wrong to say what you did,' she told him quietly.

'He would have asked you anyway, Mam,' Rodney argued. 'It were only a matter of time.'

'You don't know that.'

'Please, Mam.'

'You had no right.'

He hung his head. 'I didn't mean no harm, you know that.'

'Don't try to live my life for me, Rodney.'

'You *are* getting wed though, aren't you?' He was out of his chair and suddenly sober. 'Frank asked you and you said yes, so you *are* getting wed, aren't you?' he asked again.

She nodded and clasped her hands together on the table. 'Easter,' she replied. 'The date's been set for Easter.'

At this, he visibly relaxed. 'Oh, Mam!' he murmured, shaking his head and staring at her. 'Oh, Mam, I'm so glad. Frank's a fine man, you can't deny that?'

'No, I can't deny that,' she agreed. 'But you should not have interfered. I've told you before, don't try to run my life.'

Angered by her words, he scraped the chair back and stood up. 'What am I supposed to do, after what happened?' he demanded. 'What would any *other* son do?'

Her mouth was set in a thin line and her eyes glittered as she stared back at him. 'Maybe Frank intended asking me to wed and maybe he didn't,' she said presently. 'It would have been better if the idea had come from him. Don't you understand what I'm saying?'

'Oh, I understand all right!' he snapped. Leaning forward, he loomed over her. 'You're my mam and I love you more than anyone else on God's earth,' he admitted. 'If I spoke out of turn, I'm sorry, but as far as I'm concerned, the end justifies the means. You've agreed to wed him, and that's the best thing that could happen to this family. If I put the idea of marriage into his head, then I'm not sorry I said what I did. Happen I should have said it sooner.'

'That's enough, Rodney.' She stood up to face him. 'He could wake at any minute, and I don't want him to hear us falling out.' She glanced nervously at the door.

'Well, of course you don't,' he jeered. 'Happen I'll open my mouth and let slip one or two things that might send him back up the stairs to pack his bag.'

'Let it be, eh?'

Ignoring the plea, he went on, 'Happen he should know anyway, Mam.'

'It wouldn't serve any purpose.' Her eyes silently pleaded with him.

He dropped his head in shame. For a moment he remained that way, with the two of them inwardly regretting the heated exchange, until at length he sat heavily in the chair, muttering beneath his breath, 'You're right, and I'm sorry, Mam.'

She came to him then, lovingly sliding her arm round his shoulders. 'It's all right,' she murmured, laying her face against his and holding him close. 'I don't want to hurt you, you know that, don't you? I never wanted to hurt you.'

'I love you, Mam.'

'And I love you, son,' she answered. 'That's why I'm happy to be Frank's wife. Like you said, we'll be a family again, and that's good.'

He turned in his chair and looked up into her face. It was a while before he spoke. In the ensuing silence each seemed to know what the other was thinking. 'I won't tell him,' he promised. 'I would never tell *anyone*.'

She hugged him gratefully. 'That's right, son. *We'll keep it our little secret, eh*?'

He nodded and she moved away, softly laughing as she spun round, asking light-heartedly, 'What colour dress do you think I should wear for my wedding?'

'Blue,' he said. 'You look lovely in blue, Mam.'

She came to a halt and gripped the table top with both hands. 'Blue it will be then,' she said breathlessly. 'When me and Frank get wed, I shall wear the prettiest blue outfit in the whole of Lancashire.'

He jumped out of the chair and skipped round the room with her, until he became too dizzy to stand. 'Oh, Mam, it'll be grand, won't it?' he laughed, throwing himself into the horsehair armchair. 'You, me and Frank . . . a proper family at long last.'

Upstairs, Frank heard the laughter. With his hands clasped behind his head and an ache in his heart, he lay there deep in thought, his empty eyes staring at the window. The curtains were open and the flickering light from the street lamp was creating weird shadows on the wall. He let his gaze move with the gently meandering shapes until gradually his turbulent soul became calm.

He knew he should go down and share in the joy, but how could he when his only joy was Jenny, and she was hundreds of miles away?

# *Chapter Nine*

The sun was just peeping over the horizon when Jenny opened her eyes and looked towards the window. For so many years she had woken with the dawn, and now it was as natural to her as the air she breathed. Propping herself up on one elbow, she turned the bedside clock towards the window and focussed sleepy eyes on the thick ornate hands. 'Time to get up.' It seemed only a minute since she'd come to bed worn out by the day's labours. But now it was five o'clock, her normal rising time.

Falling back against the pillow, she closed her eyes for a moment, to gather her thoughts. There was so much to be done in this great house, she reminded herself. 'So much to be done,' she muttered, sighing noisily.

Turning her head sideways Jenny gazed at the little face pressed into the pillow beside her; a small heart-shaped face, with a full soft mouth and a tumble of rich auburn hair that prompted Jenny to whisper, 'Oh, Katie, you'll never know her, but you're the image of your grandmother.' Entwining her fingers in and out of the auburn curls, she continued to gaze on that exquisite sleeping face. 'God only knows what Elizabeth Marshall would have said about your own mother turning you away,' she murmured with disgust. 'I'm just thankful she didn't send you away altogether, because you've been such a joy to me.' A great

177

well of love flooded her heart as she gathered the child to her. 'I could never imagine life without you now,' she said simply, as the child nestled against her.

Somehow, having Katie had come to mean almost the same as having Frank. The child smiled in the same slow easy manner, and had a way about her that was reminiscent of Frank: the way she slept with her arms above her head; the way she woke with a smile as bright as a summer's morning; the way she inclined her head to one side when studying the sky or touching a wild flower, and the joy she expressed whenever they walked through God's green fields. Katie had auburn hair and green eyes like her grandmother before her, but there was no doubt that she had the same nature and mannerisms as her daddy, and even if Claudia had not admitted that Katie was Frank's child, Jenny would have known. Katie was a darling, and so much a part of her life now that Jenny trembled at the thought that one day, for whatever reason, Claudia might find delight in parting them.

Easing out of bed, she was careful not to wake the child. 'Sleep while you can,' she whispered, looking down on the small sleeping form. 'She'll run us off our feet soon enough.' The thought of Claudia had brought a shadow into the room, and as though to dispel it with a rush of fresh air, Jenny pulled back the curtains and inched the window open a little. The sunlight was struggling to break through. Night and day mingled to create even more shadows, and though the sun was climbing higher and the air was already warm, the world was suspended between darkness and lightness. It was the time of day Jenny loved best.

Now and then the sweet song of a bird sailed over the morning. Leaning out on the sill, Jenny took a deep invigorating breath. Already she felt wide awake. Soon the sky would open and the air would be busy with the sound of a new day; dogs barking in the distance, the unmistakable rattle of the milk churns as the wagon came up to the house, a growing chorus of bird-song, and the occasional curious creature who might saunter across the yard at the back of the house.

'A new day,' she murmured softly, looking at the child. 'A *special* day, Katie luv, because it's your fourth birthday.' She smiled at the thought. It seemed only yesterday she had held that newborn in her arms. 'I promise you the best birthday party you've ever had!' she whispered. Jenny had been planning the event for weeks now, and it had been the devil's own job keeping it a surprise for the girl. Now, quietly closing the window, she came back to the bed. Reaching into the cupboard beside it, she took out a small parcel and a large envelope which she placed on the pillow where she herself had been sleeping. When the child woke, she was bound to see them.

Going to the wash-stand, she poured a jug of cold water into the basin and proceeded to wash her whole body, from her forehead to her toes. After drying herself, she put on her underclothes, then came the long dark stockings, blue skirt and freshly starched white blouse. She then slipped her feet into their black ankle strap shoes and smartly fastened the button across her ankle. Next she brushed her fair hair into a bouncy bob, and clipped it back at one side with a pretty tortoiseshell slide. 'There!' she exclaimed, studying herself in the long mirror. She was ready now to face the world. 'Let her complain about you today, if she can.' Claudia had grown increasingly bitter, and delighted in picking fault with every little thing, particularly with Jenny herself though she did her best to stay one step ahead.

It was nearly five years since Frank had gone away, and Jenny was twenty-eight now. She worked a long hard day, and had had very little time to call her own, but in those years she had seemed to grow even prettier. Her fair hair held a glint of sunshine, her skin shone with a girlish hue, and her figure was just as trim as it had been when she was a young girl. 'It's all the work Claudia sets you,' she told herself. 'Hard work will leave you no time to grow old.'

Coming out of the bedroom, Jenny softly closed the door behind her. Satisfied that Katie slept on, she went to the big old dresser and, after replacing the candle-stub with a new candle from the drawer, she took a match out of the box and held the flame against the wick until it spat into life. Taking up the candle-stick, she hurried down the stairs and into the kitchen.

As the day wore on, the kitchen was the warmest place in the house, but first thing in the morning, before the stove was lit and the oven grew warm with rising bread, this place with its high ceiling and cold tiled floor was enough to freeze the bones in your body.

As Jenny pushed open the kitchen door, the icy air enveloped her, making her shiver through every inch. However warm it was outside, this wing of the old house always struck chilly of a morning. 'Best get that fire going,' she told herself, putting the candle-stick down in the centre of the pine table; experience told her that she would need the candle alight for at least another hour.

Making first for the windows, she flung back the curtains to let the morning in. 'It's going to be a glorious day,' she muttered, momentarily fascinated by a hare as it sprang across the back field. Suddenly the sky was marbled with silver trails and the night was quickly falling away.

Collecting a small shovel and bucket from under the sink, she carefully scooped out the cold spent cinders from the grate. That done, she took a box of matches from the shelf above the oven and set about kindling the stove. A sheet or two of yesterday's newspaper and a handful of sticks from the basket in the grate would soon get it going. Jenny laid them into a small pyramid and struck a match to it all. The paper curled and blackened, lighting the thin splinters of wood. Soon the flames were licking nicely, so Jenny dipped her hands into the coal-scuttle to pick out the smallest pieces. She then began building the flickering pyramid into a wigwam, leaving a hole in the top to let the grey swirling smoke escape. The coals began to glow red and the heat emitted was sheer pleasure. 'Grand!' she said, feeling pleased with herself. 'We'll have a blazing fire in no time at all.' She rubbed her hands and warmed her face in the heat, before clambering from her knees and enacting the very same procedure in the grate beneath the oven.

Soon the kitchen was homely and comfortable, and the daylight was strong enough for her to snuff out the candle. From the pantry she brought all her mixing bowls, the rolling pin, two deep pie plates, three bread tins and a cluster of trays. A second trip produced all the ingredients for her morning's baking, some of which she had been hiding from the curious Katie. 'You're in for the surprise of your life, Katie darling,' she said, rolling her eyes to the ceiling and thinking of that innocent little soul lying up there, asleep to the world. 'Sleep for an hour or so,' she pleaded, tying her pinafore over her clothes, 'when it'll all be done and hidden from you until four o'clock this afternoon.'

By quarter past six, the back of the pantry was filled with little delights: tiny cup cakes with cherries on top; deep apple tarts with pretty swirling ridges of pastry round the edges; gingerbread men with big currant eyes and white icing for teeth; and a big brown jug filled to the brim with home-made sarsaparilla. Jenny stood back to admire her handiwork. 'There's two months' savings in that little lot,' she reminded herself, 'but it'll be worth every penny to see Katie's eyes light up.' Covering it over with a white cloth, she returned to her baking. There was bread to be put in the oven, the vegetables to be done, and the meat pie to be prepared for dinner that evening. Then there was breakfast to be got ready for eight-thirty when Claudia came down.

It was quarter past seven when the kitchen door opened to

admit Katie. As always she had washed and dressed herself, and as always she had her frock on back to front, her shoes on the wrong feet, and her hair falling over her face. On seeing Jenny she came at a run into the kitchen, holding the parcel in both hands. 'Look, Jenny! Oh, look!' she cried, as Jenny scooped her up. 'It's my birthday and I'm four.' She held the parcel out. Jenny took it from her and placed it on the table. 'Did you get me it, Jenny?' she wanted to know. 'Did you?'

Jenny laughed aloud. 'Well, let me see now,' she teased. 'Who *else* could have brought you that, I wonder?' She put her finger to her mouth and pretended to think hard, her face filled with confusion as the child giggled helplessly. 'Perhaps the fairies sneaked in when we were asleep?' she suggested to Katie's obvious delight. 'Or maybe Father Christmas got his dates wrong and came down the chimney with it?' She shook the child gently. 'What do you think to that, eh?'

Katie's answer was to throw her arms round Jenny's neck. 'NO!' she protested. '*You* gave it me, didn't you?'

The two of them laughed together as Jenny admitted, 'You've found me out, and I wanted you to think it was the fairies who brought it.' Keeping the child on her knee, she sat down in a chair and pointed to the present. 'I can take it back if you don't want it,' she said with mock innocence.

At this the girl grabbed hold of it. 'It's *Katie's*!' she cried in horror. '*Katie's* birthday.' Her tiny fingers tore at the wrapping paper, but they were still tired. 'Will *you* open it for me?' she asked, yawning widely, her shining green eyes pleading.

Seating the little girl on the chair beside the table, Jenny sat opposite and opened the present. When the last layer of paper remained and the box was partly revealed, Katie could contain herself no longer. 'I can do it, Jenny,' she cried. Scrambling down from the chair, she ran round the table. 'Lift me up! Let *me* do it, please!' she begged.

With a laugh, Jenny seated her on the table beside the present and slid the box closer. 'Bet you can't guess what it is?' she said with a smile.

Katie pulled the last piece of paper away and there it was, a huge blue and white box with no indication of the treasure inside. Suddenly wide awake and beside herself with excitement, Katie dug her fingers beneath the rim of the lid, preparing to prise it back. Pausing to look at Jenny, she asked breathlessly, 'Is it a hairbrush?'

'No.'

'Is it a new frock?' Her fingers were itching to rip the lid away, but she was enjoying the game too much to end it yet.

'No, it isn't a frock,' Jenny told her. 'Why don't you open it and see?'

Katie could wait no longer. Taking the lid off, she peered into the box. When she saw what was there, she gasped aloud, pressing her hands to her mouth. Her eyes grew big and round as she stared into the box. The doll was beautiful, with long dark hair and black eyes that were fringed with thick lashes; she had on a red dress with a frilly lace collar, and she was smiling at Katie as though she had known her all her life. 'Oh!' She reached into the box, touching the doll as though she was afraid it would melt away. 'Oh, Jenny!' she kept saying. 'Oh, Jenny!' Then she had the doll in her arms, hugging it to her and rocking from side to side, laughing and crying at the same time.

'You like her then?' Jenny teased. That present had cost her the price of a new shawl, but the look on Katie's face was more than reward. It did her heart good to see the child laughing with sheer joy.

Katie flung her arms round Jenny's neck. 'I love you,' she said, and Jenny was moved to tears.

Normally, Katie would help Jenny about the kitchen, getting under her feet and doing little things that often created more work for her. Katie so loved to feel useful that Jenny hadn't the heart to refuse her. Besides, it was better for Jenny to know where the child was rather than going about her work feeling frantic if Katie disappeared for any length of time.

Today was different. It was Katie's birthday and Jenny had no intention of setting little tasks to keep the child busy. 'Soon as ever it gets warmer outside, you can take your new friend for a walk,' she promised. 'So long as you don't wander too far away. 'Til then you can stay here in the kitchen with me, where it's warm. First, though, let's get you properly dressed, eh?'

'*I* can do it,' Katie protested, beginning to pull off her dress with one arm, while with the other she held on tight to the doll. 'I know how.' Her muffled voice emerged from beneath a ruche of material which was now twisted round her throat. The hem of the dress was over her shoulders, and the whole thing was suffocating her.

Without a word, Jenny took hold of the dress and loosened the whole thing, then swivelled it back to front and slipped it over Katie's squirming form. She smiled sheepishly. 'I can put my own shoes on,' she declared, promptly sitting on the ground with the doll leaning against her as she took off both her shoes. 'Watch me, Jenny,' she said, moving the shoes round several times and appearing totally confused.

Jenny watched until the shoes were in front of the matching stockinged feet. 'Good girl,' she said, pouncing on the shoes before Katie could switch them again. The child beamed up at her before sliding her feet into the shoes. 'I can't fasten them though,' she confessed, grabbing the doll to her and absent-mindedly sucking its hair.

'That always takes a little longer,' Jenny said encouragingly, at the same time dropping to her knees before the child and quickly fastening the laces of her shoes. 'This afternoon we'll have a little practice, shall we?' Katie shook her head, pulling a sour face that made Jenny laugh. 'All right then,' she conceded. 'Another day, eh?' Katie grinned and it was agreed. After all, today was her birthday and she had just made a new friend. She and the doll had a great deal to talk about.

At eight-thirty Claudia walked into the dining room. She had on her favourite blue dress with its scalloped hem and neckline of dark blue beads. Jenny had been summoned earlier to roll Claudia's long brown hair into a soft mound at the nape of her neck. Her pale eyes were swollen from lack of sleep, and she was obviously in a sour temper.

'I don't want any of that!' she snapped, glaring at Jenny who was placing a dish of freshly scrambled eggs on the sideboard. 'Tea, that's all I want.' She looked impatiently at the silver teapot on the table as she sullenly waited for Jenny to serve her. When she dutifully poured a measure of the tea into Claudia's china cup, all she got was a volley of abuse. 'It's cold, damn you! Fetch a fresh pot, and don't be all day about it.' She actually smiled. 'I've got someone coming to see me this morning,' she said coyly, then in a sharper tone ordered, 'so you had better see to my room, then keep out of my way.'

Muttering to herself, Jenny carried the teapot back to the kitchen and quickly brewed a fresh pot of tea. Katie was seated at the kitchen table, talking to her doll. 'You're nearly as pretty as Jenny,' she was saying. 'If you're a good girl, me and Jenny might take you for a little walk.' When she saw Jenny come into the room, she said hopefully, 'We might even be able to go to the shops and I can show you to Mrs Arnold.'

'Why not?' she answered as she bustled about making a fresh brew of tea. 'I need to get some groceries, and the fresh air will do us both good.'

'And it will do Dolly good too, won't it?' Katie insisted.

'So that's her name, is it? Dolly, eh?' She nodded her approval.

185

'Yes, you're right, sweetheart, a walk to the shops will do us *all* good. First though I'd best get this tea into Madam.' She deliberately emphasised the word as though it was of immense importance. 'Before she has a blue fit,' she finished, rolling her eyes to the ceiling and giving a small smile as she hurried away.

When the door swung to behind her, Katie stared at it for a minute, wondering about Jenny's words and afraid that if Madam was to have a 'blue fit', it might mean that Jenny would have to look after her and so she wouldn't be able to take her and Dolly for a walk. 'Don't you worry, Dolly,' she told the toy. Then she scrambled down from the table and followed Jenny into the dining room.

Claudia grunted appreciatively while Jenny poured the tea. 'When my visitor calls, you're to show him straight up to my room,' she instructed.

Before Jenny could answer, a small voice piped up, 'It's my birthday and I'm four.'

Both women swung round, and both were horrified to see Katie standing there. 'Dolly's my new friend, and we want to go to the shops with Jenny.' In that vast open doorway, the child herself looked like a little doll with her cascade of auburn hair and those magnificent green eyes that always looked a little sad. Clutching the doll to her breast, she started forward.

In that moment, Claudia could see Elizabeth in the child. Awful images of her dying mother came into her mind to haunt her; images that spoke of murder, and a deep guilt that would scar her forever. 'GET HER OUT OF HERE!' Her scream echoed round the room, frightening the child who ran to Jenny and clung to her while staring at Claudia with frightened eyes.

In that instant, when Claudia and Katie looked at each other, something snapped in Claudia. Knocking her chair over as she clambered up, she rushed across the room. Taking both Jenny and the child by surprise, she raised her hand high in the air and brought the flat of her palm down on the child's face. The sound of that slap was like the crack of a whip. 'Don't *ever* come into a room where I am!' she screamed. When Katie began sobbing, she glared at Jenny. 'You know my orders. See it doesn't happen again.'

Pressing Katie behind her, Jenny stretched herself to her full height. In a low trembling voice, she said, 'If I had my way, Katie wouldn't even be in this house, let alone be forbidden to come near you.' She could feel her emotions raging inside her; emotions which she knew she must keep under control. There was such hatred, such disgust of this woman who was Katie's mother. Yet Jenny knew that if she was to overstep the mark, Claudia might send her away, and then Katie would have no one to watch out for her.

As though reading Jenny's thoughts, Claudia began to laugh. 'Be very careful,' she warned in a harsh meaningful whisper. 'I think you're in danger of forgetting your place here.' She glanced at the sobbing child. 'Just because *I* don't want her, doesn't mean to say she's yours.' She saw how Jenny trembled with rage, and for one shocking moment she was afraid. Jenny knew too much. She was too strong-minded and intelligent. Yet it was more prudent to keep her here than to send her away. The two women silently challenged each other; Jenny bold and accusing, with the child secured behind her, and Claudia looking forward to the day when she could rid herself of this woman without too much fuss.

'Stand the girl out,' she ordered, stepping back a pace. 'Let me look at her.'

Jenny felt the child tremble at Claudia's words. Her love for the little girl made her bold. 'I think she should be allowed to leave now,' she said hopefully. More than that she dared not say because Claudia was the child's mother after all and could do far worse than slap her if she put her mind to it.

187

'I'm not interested in what *you* think,' Claudia snapped. 'I said . . . stand the child out.'

Reluctantly, Jenny edged her forward, but Katie would not be pushed away. She clung to Jenny's skirt, quiet now but staring at Claudia with intense dislike. 'It's all right, sweetheart,' Jenny told her softly. 'It's all right.'

Claudia smiled at that, but her smile fell away as she studied the child, inwardly flinching when she saw at close quarters how Katie was her own mother reborn. She forced herself to look a moment longer. Somehow, amid the fear and the guilt, there lurked a feeling of immense satisfaction. 'I don't understand a woman like you,' she told Jenny slyly. 'How can you bear to look at her when you know how she was conceived . . . when he turned his back on you?'

'I love her, that's why,' Jenny returned simply. If Claudia was waiting for her to say more she was disappointed. Jenny had suffered long enough because of what Frank did, and she had come through it all with a quieter heart. Now that she had found a measure of peace, she wasn't going to let Claudia open up old wounds.

Claudia looked at Jenny's grim face and was amused. 'You're all kinds of a fool,' she said. When Jenny appeared unmoved, she went on, 'If I thought you had put her up to coming in here this morning . . .' She took a deep breath. 'You must know how the very sight of her upsets me . . . it's uncanny how like my own mother she is.' She gasped as though cold water had been poured down her back. Shifting her attention to the child, she stared her up and down. Presently she said in a stiff hostile voice, 'She seems sturdy enough. Put her to work.'

Jenny was horrified. 'Work?' She looked from Claudia to Katie and back to Claudia. 'What do you mean?'

'I mean exactly what I said. You've intimated often enough that you would welcome some help in this house.' She gestured to Katie and the child visibly cringed. 'Train her to fetch and carry. Surely she can do simple tasks, like emptying the fire-grates and cleaning the silver? She might even be trusted to fetch the shopping, leaving you to get on with more important work.'

Jenny couldn't believe her ears. Opening her mouth she prepared to argue Katie's case, but Claudia interrupted. 'Do as I say. If you recall, my mother once treated me in the very same manner.' Memories rushed back, fanning her rage. 'She would have had me working like the lowest servant . . . doing menial tasks below my station.' She laughed softly. 'Perhaps she didn't die a moment too soon.'

Jenny was frantic. 'The child is very intelligent. I was hoping to put her to school within the year.'

'Really! But then it isn't up to you, is it? No, I want you to train her. Make a good servant of her. After all, what other use is she? She eats my food and sleeps in my house. It's time she was made to earn her keep. Look at her.' She studied Katie's straight shoulders and that strong upright little frame. 'Why, she's *made* for manual work, anyone can see that.' Stooping to the child, she said, 'You and Jenny are two of a kind. *Born to serve.*' Straight-ening herself up, she swept to the door. 'Train her to be a loyal servant,' she said crisply. 'And you can start today, birthday or no birthday.'

Jenny took it upon herself to ignore Claudia's orders, at least for today. 'It's your birthday,' she reminded Katie, 'and I so much want you to enjoy it.' She turned from the cupboard, where she was stacking away the clean crockery. 'You can play outside while I finish the housework,' she suggested.

Katie was seated on the rug beside the range. 'We don't wan to play,' she murmured, undressing the doll for the umpteen' time. For hours after the incident with Claudia, Katie had follow Jenny everywhere. She was on her heels as Jenny went backwa and forwards to the dining room, and she even insisted on carr the smaller items from the table. 'The lady said I have to,' she told Jenny, and Jenny could have strangled Claudia with her bare hands.

All the while Jenny was washing up, Katie was there making sure she was part of it, standing on a chair and handing Jenny the plates. She cried a little, and every now and then a small sob would catch in her throat. 'I don't like her,' she murmured once, and Jenny was in no doubt as to whom she meant.

Now, as Jenny took up the kitchen mats and carried them out to the washing line where she proceeded to beat the dust from them, Katie found a long thick stick and pretended to do the same. Jenny was greatly tempted to send her back inside, but resisted for two very good reasons; firstly, she knew that if she herself was in Katie's shoes, she would want to be with someone who loved her. There was no doubt that Katie was intelligent enough to realise that Claudia was capable of doing something terrible if her wishes were not carried out. Secondly, Jenny instinctively knew how desperately Katie needed to be near her right now, and could not bring herself to deprive the child of that reassurance. However, she had to clean Claudia's room before the visitor arrived, and Katie must not be seen to enter that room. 'Will you and Dolly do something for me?' she asked, taking Katie by the shoulders and smiling down on her. 'Something very important?'

'Yes, please,' came the enthusiastic answer, and for the first ince Claudia slapped her, Katie's face broke into a smile.

want to go into the village, don't we?'

ou do know I can't go until I've finished all the work?'

. That's why me and Dolly want to help.'

ou *can* help, Katie, because you see I always wear my when going to the village. It's a fair walk, and the rd beneath my feet.'

'Can I wear my boots?'

'Well, of course you can, sweetheart, and I want to wear my strong brown shoes, but I can't find the laces, you see.' She frowned and glanced at the bottom drawer in the old dresser. 'I've looked everywhere except in that drawer.' She gazed into those uplifted, serious green eyes and her love was tenfold. 'I wonder if you and Dolly could find them for me?'

Katie beamed from ear to ear. ' 'Course we can,' she said.

In a minute, Jenny had seated the child at the table with the doll beside her. Then she pulled the drawer all the way out and carried it to the table where she placed it before Katie. 'There's all sorts in this drawer,' she explained. 'It's a bit of a jumble because with one thing and another, I've not had time to clean it out.' The drawer was packed with all manner of things . . . a pile of old socks and stockings, bits of cotton wound round pieces of cardboard, a tiny bunch of dried lavender, ribbons, buttons, and a batch of old shoe-laces tied together.

'Don't forget the ones I want are *brown*,' she told Katie. 'Like my shawl, do you see?' She pointed to the garment hanging on the nail behind the door. 'That's the colour. Remember?' She had spent a deal of time teaching Katie different things, how to write her own name and the colours all around her. She was amazed at how quickly the child learned.

'I know,' Katie confirmed proudly. Turning to her doll, she said, 'Brown is like the leaves when the wind blows them down.' She hadn't forgotten what Jenny had taught her.

'Good girl. Now take your time, sweetheart, because I've a lot to do. And don't put anything in your mouth, especially the buttons.'

Katie looked at her then. 'Jenny?'

'Yes, sweetheart?'

'Are you a servant?' Claudia's cruel words had cut deep Jenny had hoped that memories of the awful incident

191

passing, but it was obvious that there were questions still to be answered. 'Yes,' she answered truthfully. 'That's what I am, a servant.'

'That lady isn't a servant, is she?'

'Oh, Katie, I always knew there would come a day when you needed to know more,' Jenny groaned under her breath. Yet when she spoke now, neither her voice nor her manner betrayed her deeper feelings. 'No, Miss Claudia Marshall is not a servant. She owns this house.'

Katie thought on this awhile before asking in a serious voice, 'Does she own us?'

Jenny was taken aback at the child's innocent remark. 'People don't own other people,' she explained, thinking of Frank and how she had imagined they would spend the rest of their lives together. 'Miss Marshall pays me to keep her house clean and look after her.'

'But why do we have to live here?'

'Because it's easier, and because this is our home, Katie.'

'I don't like it here,' came the studied answer. 'I don't like that lady.'

'Then we'll keep her away from you, shall we?' Jenny went to the child and held her tight. How could she explain that Claudia was her mother, and that the only reason she herself remained in house was because she wanted to be near Katie, to protect ve her? If she left, God only knew what would happen to But it would not be easy, Jenny knew that. Katie was 'ng awkward questions, so how would she cope when to wonder about her parents?

d given strict instructions that the child was never ruth. Yet it was something that would be very hard ause the villagers were aware that Katie was timate child. Up to now, Katie had got by without but that couldn't go on for very much longer.

Within the next year or so, she would be starting school, and children could be cruel when they sensed a misfit. So what was Jenny to tell her when the time came? It haunted her day and night.

Suddenly, in that unpredictable way children have, Katie glanced at the mantelpiece where Jenny had stood her birthday card. '*She* never gave me a present,' she remarked.

Before Jenny could stop herself, she replied angrily, 'And she never will!' When Katie looked at her with curious eyes, she quickly added, 'But you never know, she might.'

'Well, if she does, me and Dolly will give it right back,' declared Katie, digging into the drawer and taking out the posy of lavender which she stuck in the doll's hair.

Jenny took the opportunity to leave, thankful for the moment anyway that the conversation didn't go any deeper. After collecting clean sheets and a towel from the landing cupboard, she made straight for Claudia's room. From the window she could see Claudia seated on the bench in the orchard. 'Pity you couldn't take root and stay there forever,' she muttered. In that instant Claudia glanced up to the window and Jenny looked away.

She threw open the window to let the warm sunshine flood in, then stripped the bed, pummelled the mattress and put on clean sheets. She shook the mats out of the window and replaced them beside the bed, then dusted all the surfaces and the window-ledge, giving each and every ornament a quick flick with the duster. That done, she wiped the soiled towel over the jug and bowl, soaking up the remaining drops of water until the jug was bone dry, then replaced the soiled towel with a clean one, closed the window a fraction and, bundling sheets and towel together, tucked them under her arm and went out on to the landing. 'Spick and span for you and your man!' she chuckled. Her voice rose to a light-hearted melody. She wouldn't let Claudia spoil Katie's birthday. The sun was shining, and soon she and Katie were off to the shops. This afternoon there was to be a party and Jenny was looking forward to it immensely. It was more than enough to sing about.

Deep down, though, she was disgusted at Claudia's antics. Since Elizabeth's demise, Claudia's appetite for members of the opposite sex had grown insatiable. Jenny wondered whether there wasn't some medical term for it. Certainly her shocking behaviour went far beyond that of any normal woman.

Jenny swept through the house in record time. 'Did you find my laces?' she asked, coming into the kitchen. Her fair hair was stuck to her forehead. She was red in the face, hot and exhausted. 'By! I could do with a dunk in the horse's trough,' she said, smiling at Katie.

She was still seated at the table, surrounded by paraphernalia. At Jenny's remark, she began to giggle. 'Me and Dolly don't want to go in the horse's trough,' she said, pushing her face into the doll's and laughing until Jenny touched her on the shoulder. 'What about my laces, young lady?' Jenny didn't want the laces, but she couldn't let the child know how she had been duped.

'Dolly found them.' Katie held up a ragged pair of laces, one black and one brown.

'Thank you very much.' Jenny stuffed the laces in her pocket. 'I'll go and put these in my shoes,' she said. 'Then I'll have a wash while you and Dolly put everything back in the drawer. What do you say?'

'We say we want to go to the shops.'

'Are you hungry?'

'No.'

'All right then. The sooner we get ready the better, eh?' She laughed aloud when Katie began a frantic scramble to put everything away.

Going up to the small room which she and Katie shared,

Jenny took her brown walking shoes out of the wardrobe. They were well-polished and stout, with a strong square heel, and fitted with a brand new pair of leather laces. 'Sorry, sweetheart,' she whispered as she plucked the odd ragged laces from her pinnie pocket and squashed them into a drawer.

Washed and refreshed, Jenny entered the kitchen. She looked very pretty in a clean white blouse and blue skirt, with her light grey shawl draped over her shoulders. 'Ready, are you?' she asked, her gaze going before her to the table.

There sat Katie, breathless but very pleased with herself. She had put every item back into the drawer, and Jenny wondered whether she hadn't taken everything out of the other drawers and packed them into this one too. It was piled high, with everything standing on end and bits hanging out all the way round. 'Can we go to the shops now?' she wanted to know.

'I don't see why not,' Jenny told her, taking the drawer over to the dresser. 'You climb down and fetch the shopping basket from the pantry, then we'll be on our way.' She was satisfied that Katie couldn't see the goodies she'd baked earlier that morning, because not only were they on a high shelf but she had covered them with a cloth. 'This drawer doesn't want to go back,' she grunted, making a determined effort to push the thing into place. Later, when Katie was asleep, she would have to clean out the drawer and repack it.

Ten minutes later they went out of the front gate and down the path that led into the village. They were so busy chattering that neither of them saw the ruddy-faced young man go in through the gate behind them. Claudia was waiting for him, and it wasn't long before the two of them were upstairs in her room, laughingly roughing up the bed which Jenny had so carefully made.

'What a glorious day,' Jenny breathed deeply, looking up through the tree-tops as they passed beneath and thinking how fortunate she was. 'It's true, Katie . . . if the good Lord deprives you in some ways, he makes up for it in others.'

She glanced up at Jenny's words. She didn't understand them, but she was content just to be holding Jenny's hand in hers. 'Can we go and watch the trains?' she asked, squinting her eyes against the sunlight.

Jenny shook her head. 'Not today, sweetheart.'

'Why not?'

'Because I have a great deal to do.'

'What?'

'You'll see.'

'Tomorrow then?'

'Happen.'

Katie appeared satisfied, at once indulging in a long conversation with her doll which was securely tucked under her arm. 'You'll like the trains,' she whispered, going into a lengthy description of the noise and steam when the train pulled out of the station.

After visiting the ironmonger's, where Jenny chose a new teapot, they went to the butcher's and purchased a pound of best tripe. Next Katie was taken to the draper's to decide what colour ribbon she wanted; the green took her fancy so Jenny bought two short strips. Finally they came into Mrs Harold's general stores. 'My, you do look well,' she told Jenny. 'And aren't we a pretty girl today?' She leaned over the counter and beamed at the child, her ill-fitting false teeth hanging loosely in her large mouth.

Katie stared at Mrs Harold with some surprise because the balding woman was thin as a match-stick, with a long bony nose and small close-set eyes. She was astonished to learn that Mrs Harold thought herself to be pretty. She told Jenny as much after the basket was filled with various weights of cheese, butter and sugar, and the two of them were outside.

Jenny laughed until she cried when Katie said, 'I don't *ever* want to be "pretty" like Mrs Harold.' It took only a moment for Jenny to explain it was Katie herself whom Mrs Harold had thought to be 'pretty'.

'Oh!' Katie looked at Jenny, then she looked at her doll, then she felt foolish and giggled.

'One more call before we head back,' Jenny declared, heading into the post office where she beckoned Miss Mackeson to one side. 'Did you do it?' she asked anxiously, making sure that Katie couldn't hear.

Miss Mackeson was the postmistress, a kindly soul with a heart of gold. 'Don't worry, my dear,' she told Jenny. 'I kept the notice in the window all last week, and various young mothers commented on it so I'm certain the little one will have a few friends arriving for her birthday tea.' She beamed at Katie who promptly sat herself on the floor and began to plait the doll's long hair. 'Little darling,' the woman went on. Leaning towards Jenny, she said, 'Forgive me if I'm poking my nose where it doesn't belong, but why is it that her mother never comes into the village with the child?'

This wasn't the first time one or other of the shopkeepers had made the same remark, and Jenny knew it wouldn't be the last. 'No reason,' she said cautiously. 'It's just that Miss Marshall doesn't care much for going out anywhere . . . hardly ever leaves the grounds of the house.'

'Really? How sad.' She tutted and gazed down on Katie with a grim expression. 'Of course, that's why the child has no friends. It's such a pity.' She covered Jenny's hand with her own, her homely face wreathed in a smile as she said softly, 'You're a real godsend to that woman, my dear. I've often thought how bleak young Katie's life would be without you.' She looked at Jenny in a strange manner, almost as though she suspected the truth. 'They do say you're more of a mother to Katie than Claudia Marshall will ever be.' Like everyone else in the village, Miss Mackeson had heard the rumours with regard to that shameless young woman.

Jenny took Katie back by way of the woods, but they didn't stop as they had done on many previous occasions because there wasn't enough time. It was quarter to two when they left the post office, and the children would be arriving in less than two hours for Katie's birthday party. Before then there was the washing to be brought in and pressed, vegetables to be got ready for the evening meal, and all manner of finicky little jobs like kneading the dough for tomorrow's baking and setting the table afterwards for the party. As she hurried Katie along, Jenny took a deep breath then blew it out in an exclamation. 'Hmh! It's a good job Madam never bothers about lunch, or I'd catch myself coming back and no mistake.'

The sun was high in the heavens and the heat was stifling when Jenny flung open the kitchen door. 'At least it's cooler in here,' she told Katie.

'Can me and Dolly play out?'

' 'Course you can, sweetheart,' Jenny said, dropping the heavy basket on to the kitchen table. 'Don't wander off though. I want to see you from the kitchen window.'

'Can I go to the greenhouse? Mr Taylor said I could help him to pick some tomatoes today.'

'All right, but you're not to get under his feet, and you're to come straight back afterwards.' Jenny had seen Mr Taylor in the greenhouse as they came through the garden. Whenever Katie 'helped' him about the place, he always saw her safely back to the house afterwards.

Jenny watched the small figure toddle off down the garden path. How she loved that child, nobody would ever know. Her mind flew back over the years and she found herself thinking of

Katie's daddy. 'Oh, Frank, why did it all go so wrong?' she murmured, a great sadness overwhelming her. She choked back the tears and stared after Katie until she went out of sight behind the shed. 'It's your loss, Frank Winfield,' she said in a sterner voice. 'You have a lovely little daughter, and you'll probably never know her.'

While she was fetching the washing from the line, Jenny's attention was caught by a peal of laughter emanating from Claudia's bedroom. She glanced up in time to see a ruddy-faced young man swing the window shut. 'God almighty!' she breathed, wiping the sweat from her brow; the heat was unbearable, and there wasn't a breath of wind. 'The pair of you deserve to suffocate,' she muttered. Then she shook her head and cast a derisory glance at the closed window. 'Shame on you, Claudia Marshall!' she said beneath her breath. 'Your mam would turn over in her grave, and that's a fact.'

Gathering the remainder of the washing, Jenny folded it into the basket. Securing the basket under her arm, she hurried back into the kitchen. Once there, she was tempted to put the basket in the cupboard until later, when all the children had gone home and Katie was asleep in her bed. 'No!' she told herself. 'If I don't press it now, I'll not keep up with it all.'

It was quarter past three. Jenny was ironing the last garment when Mr Taylor brought Katie to the kitchen door. 'I'll not come in,' he said. 'I've been digging the soft ground down by the hedge, and my boots are thick with mud. It's thirsty work, though, so I'll drop by later for a brew o' tea if that's all right?' He lifted Katie inside. 'Beats me how that part of the garden is always wet, even when we've had days o' sunshine.' With that, he bade Jenny good afternoon, and went on his way. His many duties, like Jenny's, left him little time to indulge in small talk.

Katie was asleep on her feet. 'Come on, my girl. Off you go to bed for a little while,' Jenny ordered, taking the child in her arms and whisking her up the stairs. Katie didn't object. Instead, when Jenny laid her on the bed, she looked up with weary eyes, then yawned widely and fell into a deep sleep. 'That's it, sweetheart,' Jenny said, as she laid a blanket over her. 'I had thought of asking Mr Taylor to keep you busy until I'd laid the table, but you might as well sleep now. It'll give me time to get your surprise ready before the children arrive.'

At ten minutes to four, Mr Taylor peered in through the open kitchen door. 'By! You've worked hard, gal,' he remarked, his eyes roving the table. The whole thing was a sight to behold. The table was laid with a clean white cloth and spread from end to end with plates and dishes of the delicious little niceties which Jenny had spent so much time over. Right in the centre was Katie's birthday cake, written in icing with her name and decorated with four pink candles.

Jenny blushed pink, 'Thank you. It *does* look lovely, though,' she agreed. 'I hope Katie likes it because it's her very first real birthday party and I do so want it to be a day to remember.' While she was talking she poured him a mug of freshly brewed tea and brought it to him. 'Miss Mackeson said there was a lot of interest in the note I put in her window . . . asking the village children to Katie's party. As we don't know the villagers very well, Miss Mackeson thought that would be the best way of doing it.'

'She's right, I reckon.' He took his mug of tea and sat down on the stone step. Taking a great gulp of the hot liquid, he sighed aloud. 'I shan't be sorry to get home today, I can tell you,' he moaned, stretching his legs out. 'I'm not one for heat. It wears me out.' He turned to look up at Jenny who was standing by the door, staring at the table and wondering if she'd forgotten anything. 'Honest to God, I don't know how you do it,' he told her, shaking his head in disbelief. 'You work your fingers off morning 'til night, seven days a week, and never a thank you for it. Don't you mind that you've got no life of your own?'

Jenny turned her head to look down on him. For a moment she didn't say anything, but then she raised her eyes to the ceiling and smiled. 'Katie's my life,' she said simply, and he knew she had spoken from the heart.

He sat quiet for a while, supping his tea and reflecting on Jenny's words. Somehow he was humbled by her love for the child. Presently he asked, 'When do you intend to wake her?'

'I wondered whether she should be here when the children arrive, but when I went up just now, she was still hard and fast asleep, so I think I'll leave her until they're all here. It'll only take a minute to put on her best frock and fetch her down.' She smiled at the idea. 'I can't wait to see her eyes pop open when she sees them all seated round the table.'

He laughed. 'I'd rather you than me. In my experience, when a clatter o' childer get together, it's like all hell let loose.'

'I've set the table for eight,' Jenny explained, 'but I can always fetch more chairs from the dining room if needs be.'

He brought her attention to the time. 'It'll not be long now,' he said, gesturing to the big round clock on the wall above the dresser. 'It's nearly five to. I'd best take myself off or I'll be trampled underfoot.' As he stood up and handed her the mug, he asked, 'Where are they?' His expression left Jenny in no doubt who he meant.

'Still in her room. One minute they're giggling like two year olds, and the next they're as quiet as church mice.' She felt the hot blush of shame riding up from her neck. 'It's none of my business when all's said and done.' She rolled her angry eyes up to the ceiling. 'Just as long as Katie isn't affected by it all.'

'Aye, well, like you say, it's none of us business.' He gestured towards the table. 'You've done a grand job,' he declared proudly. 'Them childer don't know what a treat they're in for, and that's a fact.' With that he went away, heading for his shed and whistling all the better for the mug of tea Jenny had made him. Not for one moment did he imagine that the rumours he'd heard could be true. Not even Claudia could be that callous . . .

As the minutes ticked away, Jenny grew more and more excited. 'Anybody'd think it were *my* birthday party,' she laughed, looking at herself in the mirror and straightening her pinnie. She couldn't stand the waiting. She must have gone to the door umpteen times; she rearranged the plates and dishes; she took Katie's best frock from the cupboard and hung it on the kitchen dresser. It was a pretty little thing that Jenny had made herself, red in colour, with a cream lace collar and big flouncy bows decorating each pocket.

When the clock chimed four, her excitement dimmed and she became nervous. 'Where are you?' she muttered, going to the door and staring anxiously down the empty drive. She walked down to the road but there wasn't a soul in sight. Dejected but still hopeful, she walked slowly back to the kitchen where she remained at the door, her eyes ever turned towards the curve in the drive where any visitor would be seen approaching. 'Please don't let her down,' she murmured. 'You can't blame a child for what its mammy does.'

Four o'clock had come and gone. Then it was ten past and Jenny's heart was in her boots. But still she stayed by the door, hoping and praying that she was wrong. When the clock chimed the half hour, she went inside and closed the door. 'How could they be so cruel?' she cried, her clenched fists hard on the table as she sat down in front of Katie's birthday cake.

Jenny was visibly startled when the door opened. 'It's only me,' said Mr Taylor. His face said it all as he stepped inside the kitchen. For the last half hour he had watched Jenny go up and down that long drive, and his heart went out to her. He was angry. So the rumours were right. Claudia really had let it be known that any villagers who came on to her property uninvited by her, children or otherwise, would be treated as trespassers and severely dealt with. Disgusted that anyone could behave in such a fashion, he toyed with the idea of telling Jenny but thought better of it. After all, it would serve no real purpose because, like himself, there was nothing Jenny could do about it.

She had kept back the tears but now they ran down her face as she told him sadly, 'They're not coming.' She smiled painfully. 'I should have known.'

'It's their loss, not yours,' he assured her. 'I'm only sorry my lot had to go and get poorly or they'd have made up for them as didn't come.'

'I know,' she said, pushing back the chair and wiping her face with the back of her hand. 'They must be disappointed to miss a party.' She went into the pantry and came out again with a large dish and a muslin cloth. 'I want you to take some of these goodies to them.'

He watched her gathering the sandwiches and cakes, which she carefully placed into the dish. 'I don't know what to say,' he muttered. 'People can be so cruel.'

'It's all right,' she assured him. 'I'm leaving just enough on the table so Katie can still have a little party. There's no need for her to know what's happened here today.'

'Well, she won't know from me, that's for sure.'

'Will you stay?'

He nodded. 'Why not? I like a party as well as the next,' he lied.

'Then it'll be just the three of us, eh?' Smiling now, Jenny replaced the dish in the pantry then she took away all but the usual four chairs, setting the other four against the wall in the dining room. 'Get ready to light the candles,' she told him brightly as she collected Katie's frock, 'and I'll fetch her down.'

As she went up the stairs, Jenny felt lighter of heart. 'A little party's better than none at all,' she told herself, 'and Katie won't know any different.'

She knew something was wrong as soon as she turned the corner on the landing because her bedroom door was half open. Running forward, she rushed into the room. The bed was empty and Katie was gone. 'Katie,' she called out, but there was no answer. Puzzled, she came back out on to the landing. It was then that she caught sight of the familiar little figure, standing in the open doorway of Claudia's room.

Frantic, Jenny ran along the landing, her eyes fixed on Katie, her only intention being to get the child away before Claudia woke. But she was already awake. When Jenny came to the child's side, she saw what Katie saw: Claudia and the ruddy-faced young man were lying stark naked on the rug; he was on top of her spreadeagled body, and they were deep in the throes of love making. Claudia's head was turned towards her daughter and she was actually beckoning her to enter the room, her face wreathed in a cunning smile. When she saw Jenny, she laughed out loud, pushing herself against the young man and making deliberately animal-like noises.

Snatching Katie away, Jenny slammed the door on them. Claudia's laughter rang in her ears and for the first time in her life, Jenny had murder in her heart.

By the time she got Katie back to the kitchen, Jenny had dressed her in her best frock and chatted enough to erase the memory from the child's mind. 'What surprise?' Katie kept asking, her curiosity fired by Jenny's teasing.

Her questions were answered when Jenny flung open the kitchen door. The cake was lit, and the table was set for something special; though not for the special event that was originally planned. Mr Taylor and Jenny called out together, 'HAPPY BIRTHDAY!' and Katie ran forward, whooping and shrieking.

It was a lovely tea, and Katie enjoyed every minute. An hour later Mr Taylor went home with the big dish of goodies for his own family, and soon Katie was washed and put to bed. Jenny sat by her for a while. 'I won't be long before I come up,' she promised. 'But if you wake, I want you to stay in your bed. All right?' First, she had to get the evening meal, before which no doubt Claudia's 'visitor' would be gone. They were usually gone by early evening. When Katie nodded her answer, Jenny kissed her good night.

As she went across the room, Katie called out, 'Jenny?'

'Yes?'

'I love you best in all the world.' Yawning, she turned over and fell asleep.

Downstairs, Jenny reflected on what had happened earlier. 'I love you too, sweetheart,' she murmured, 'and things can't go on the way they are. Somehow I have to get you away from here, but God help me, I can't see how. She doesn't want you, but she would never let me take you from her.' Claudia got immense pleasure out of using Katie to torment Jenny. More than that, she hated the child as much as she had hated her own mother; in her wicked eyes, Katie and Elizabeth were one and the same, and it suited her to belittle the child in the same way she believed her mother had belittled *her*.

'There has to be a way,' Jenny vowed. 'I won't let her ruin your life.'

She couldn't know it, but very soon one of Claudia's 'visitors' would turn all their lives upside down.

# Chapter Ten

'No, you fool, I asked for my *boots*!' Claudia kicked the shoes across the floor and slammed her fist down on the dresser. 'Do I have to explain everything twice over?' she snapped. 'How do you expect me to walk through the woods in shoes?'

Muttering under her breath, Jenny collected the shoes and took them back to the cupboard. She wasn't in the best of moods herself. For some reason, she had suffered a bad night, tossing and turning until the early hours, and then sleeping so lightly that every little sound woke her again. It could have something to do with the fact that she had made up the room next to her own and moved Katie into it. After all, she was reaching the age when she needed a room of her own.

Replacing the shoes, Jenny reached to the top shelf and took down the long pair of lace-up boots. While she crossed the room before falling to her knees at Claudia's feet, Jenny was ashamed at her own malicious thoughts because she had visions of wrapping the laces round Claudia's neck and choking the life out of her.

'That's better,' Claudia declared as Jenny drew the laces into a pretty bow. 'Why couldn't you have done that the first time?' She swung round on the stool and studied herself in the mirror.

'I must look my best,' she crowed. 'I never know who I might meet on my little walks.'

'Will that be all?' Jenny asked, getting to her feet and itching to get back to her kitchen.

Claudia turned her gaze on Jenny's tired face. It was a moment before she spoke, and then it was to say something very cruel. 'You look old and weary. What's the matter with you?'

This time Jenny couldn't hide her intense dislike of this woman who held her in the palm of her hand. 'As long as I do my work, you shouldn't mind whether I look old and weary,' she said sharply. Standing straight now, she returned Claudia's curious stare. 'Will that be all for now, miss?'

Claudia laughed and swung herself round on the stool. 'My, my! You really do despise me, don't you?' She watched Jenny through the mirror.

'Yes,' she admitted. 'It's true I have no regard for you.'

'You're too honest,' Claudia said sourly. 'One of these days it will get you into a deal of trouble.'

'I'm sure you're right, miss.' Jenny's face was grim as she looked directly into Claudia's pale smiling eyes. 'But you did ask, and I'm not about to lie.'

'Brush my hair.'

Taking up the silver-backed brush, Jenny did as she was bid. As she swept the brush down the long brown tresses with strong deliberate strokes, she wondered how much longer she would be able to bear living in this house, being at this shameless woman's beck and call. But then she remembered Katie, and she knew she would always want to be wherever Katie was.

Claudia's next words not only gave Jenny her own answer, but made her stiffen with fear. 'You wouldn't like it if you couldn't see your precious Katie any more, would you?' Looking in the mirror she saw how those words had taken the colour from Jenny's face, and was immensely proud of herself.

'What are you saying?' The brush lay still in Jenny's hand.

'Brush my hair, you fool. I haven't got all day.'

'What did you mean . . . if I couldn't see Katie any more?'

'I said, brush my hair!'

Jenny resumed the brushing, but she had to know. 'What did you mean?'

'MISS!' Claudia swung out with the flat of her hand, catching Jenny a light blow on her shoulder. 'It's MISS when you address me. I'm your employer, and I won't have you forgetting your place. Do you understand?'

'What did you mean . . . miss?'

'Exactly what I said. I could send you away tomorrow if I wanted to. Any number of women would gladly take on the work of housekeeper, and make the brat a good servant into the bargain.'

'But you wouldn't do that, would you . . . miss?'

'Oh? And why not?'

Desperation made Jenny bolder. 'Because I know too much, and besides, I doubt if you could find anyone to take on the considerable duties in this house, at the wages you give me.'

Claudia was frantic. She could never be certain but she had always been afraid: did Jenny know Elizabeth had been murdered by her own daughter? '*What* do you know?' she demanded, flicking Jenny's hand away and slewing round to face her. This time it was *she* who turned pale.

'You know what I mean . . . miss,' Jenny replied. Much more than that she was not prepared to say. After all, it was not for her to remind Claudia of all the men who had thrashed about in her bed; of the wives who would string her up if they knew how she had deliberately enticed their men, taking a good part of their wages in payment for her favours. 'There are many things I could spread about if I had a spiteful tongue,' Jenny threatened. 'Not least the fact that you gave away your own child, and ordered that she be made a servant in your own household. If that were to become known, you might very well find yourself having to answer to the law . . . *miss*,' she added with a wry little smile.

'You're a sly thing and no mistake.' Claudia still couldn't be certain that Jenny didn't know the truth about Elizabeth Marshall's death.

'I don't mean to be, but if you try and part me from Katie, there's no telling *what* I might do.'

'Who do you think would believe you? You're only a maid in this house. I could have you thrown in prison for spreading wicked slander.'

'By then the damage would be done, wouldn't it, miss?'

Claudia was mortally afraid and there was little she could do about it. She couldn't very well ask Jenny whether she was suspicious about Elizabeth's death. Nor could she be certain that Jenny was deliberately using that information against her now. All she could do was play her at her own game. Her mood changed and her tone was deliberately kinder. 'You can't expect me to feel anything for her. I never wanted children, and she put me through so much pain. Besides, she's really more yours than mine, especially as her father was your intended.' She studied Jenny's impassive features and felt a pang of jealousy. In spite of the dark shadows beneath her pretty blue eyes, Jenny possessed a special loveliness, a kind of inner beauty that shone through. 'How can you love her?' Claudia asked. 'When you know how Frank deceived you?'

'I can love her for herself.'

'Then you're a fool.'

'Yes, miss.'

'I loathe her.'

'I know.'

'We need each other, you and I.' Claudia was already regretting having threatened Jenny. It was a dangerous thing to do, especially when she wasn't certain just how much Jenny knew.

'I don't need *you*.'

Claudia bristled at that. 'But you need the child?' Her tone was sharper and her pale eyes glittered angrily.

'I need the child.'

'Then you need *me*!'

'Yes.'

'We'll say no more of this.' Claudia sprang from the stool and strode across the room. 'Get about your work.' She flung open the door and Jenny went through it at a steady walk. 'Remember what I said . . . I don't want her, but she isn't yours. My orders concerning the child still stand.' When it seemed as though Jenny would go without acknowledging her, she called out, 'Is that clear?' There was no answer and so she slammed the door. Banging her fist on it, she muttered, 'If I thought you knew nothing of how I murdered her, you would be out of this house before you could turn round. *Then* we would see about the brat.' She smiled slyly. 'All the same, while I have what you want, I have *you* too.' It felt good, having power over another human being. That was one of the reasons why she so enjoyed the company of men.

Jenny was in the middle of hanging pretty floral curtains at Katie's bedroom window when the young man arrived. It was a lovely October day, crisp with the onset of winter, yet still warm enough to leave the kitchen door open. Jenny often did her sewing while sitting on a chair by the back door; from there she could see Katie and Mr Taylor in the garden, and there was something wonderful about sewing in God's own light instead of straining your eyes under a lamp. This very afternoon she had finished the rose-patterned curtains, and now she stood back to admire them. 'By! They look real pretty,' she told herself, with a little pride.

Peering out of the open window, she saw Katie in the distance; she was seated on the step of the shed, helping Mr Taylor to string some onions. Jenny's face lit up at the sight. 'I do miss your being in my room, Katie luv,' she muttered. 'But next year you'll be going to school, and you shouldn't have to share with me.' She tutted loudly. 'If *she* had her way, the pair of us would be squashed in that one room forever and a day, but you've got your very own room now and I've made it pretty as a picture, just like I promised.'

The room was next to Jenny's, at the back of the house, and overlooking the garden. It had been a junk room, damp and cold. But now the junk had been taken away to be burned by Mr Taylor and Jenny had transformed the room until it was unrecognisable from the miserable little place it had been. Today it was bright and fresh, with the window open and the frilled curtains tied back with a matching sash. On the floor beside the bed lay the peg-rug which Jenny had taken from her own room. 'I can always make myself another,' she told Katie, but she wondered when she would ever find time.

She found the time, though, to make an eiderdown cover which matched the curtains, and after searching long and hard she discovered a set of lace doilies at the bottom of a drawer in the drawing room; these she lovingly positioned on the little sideboard which held Katie's few possessions. There was a cupboard in the wall where Jenny hung Katie's best frock, and a chair by the bed which she had 'borrowed' from the kitchen. 'We don't own much, sweetheart,' she said now, glancing round the room. 'But while we've got each other, we won't want for nothing.'

She fussed and polished and sang as she worked, until at last she was satisfied. 'Wait 'til you see it,' she murmured, going once more to the window to make sure Katie was still safe. She hadn't moved from the shed step. Quickly gathering her polishing rags, Jenny placed them in her work basket and began on her way downstairs. 'Miss High and Mighty will soon be back,' she muttered. 'Demanding this and that, and expecting me to have her dinner on the table.' The grandfather clock in the hall told her it was almost five-thirty. 'Don't know where the day goes!' she remarked, rushing towards the kitchen.

When the sound of the front door-bell echoed down the hallway, Jenny was visibly startled. Swinging round, she dropped her work basket to the ground and pushed it with her foot until it was almost out of sight beneath the hallstand. 'Who the devil's that at this time of day?' she asked herself, quickening her footsteps as she hurried along. Before opening the door she brushed her hands down the front of her apron and patted her short fair hair, then she wiped her warm face to smear away any smuts of dirt or dust. After glancing at her boots, she took a quick look in the mirror. 'You'll do, gal,' she told herself.

Satisfied that she was presentable, Jenny painted on her best smile and opened the door. 'Yes?' She was surprised to see a young man there. He wasn't the usual type of man Jenny had grown used to seeing in this house. Of medium height, stocky and pleasant-looking, he was smartly dressed in a dark suit and trilby. His eyes were light hazel and he was clean shaven. Jenny guessed him to be in his late twenties.

'Good afternoon,' he said with a quick smile. 'I hope I'm at the right place?' He peered into the hallway and asked anxiously, 'Is this the Marshalls' residence?'

'It is, sir.' Jenny liked him straight off, and her smile deepened. His next question, though, wiped the smile from her face.

'Thank goodness! It isn't an easy address to find, is it? And I've come a long way to see the lady of the house . . . Mrs Elizabeth Marshall.'

'Oh!' All the old memories came flooding back, and Jenny saw Elizabeth clearly in her mind. The memory brought its own pain. This gent had come a long way, he'd said, and he wanted to see Elizabeth. She wasn't quite sure how to break it to him. 'I'm sorry, sir, but you see – well, Mrs Marshall passed away some time ago.'

He was shocked speechless, and though she was curious as to his identity, Jenny's heart went out to him. He had a kind and honest face. 'You'd best come inside, sir,' she invited, opening the door for him to pass. 'Mrs Marshall's daughter will be back shortly, and you should talk with her.' Poor bugger, she thought, wondering whether Claudia would seduce *this* young man and take his money. Judging by the motor vehicle parked outside, he wasn't short of a shilling or two.

'You'll be comfortable in the drawing room,' she said, leading him across the hall. 'You say you've come a long way, sir?' She glanced back over her shoulder. The preoccupied look on his face told Jenny that he still hadn't recovered from the tragic news about Elizabeth.

'London,' he replied. 'I've travelled up from London.'

'In that case, you must be tired? You won't have long to wait, though. Miss Marshall's usually back before six.' Showing him into the drawing room, she urged him to sit in the most comfortable armchair by the fireplace.

He graciously declined. 'I've been sitting in the motorcar and my legs are a little cramped,' he explained.

She laughed a little. 'I shouldn't want to travel far in one of them things. Come to think of it, I don't reckon I'd want to travel *anywhere* in one.'

He smiled and she wondered again what he could have wanted with Elizabeth. 'Would you like a bite to eat and a cup of tea?'

'That would be lovely. Thank you.'

After Jenny departed from the room, he strolled to the casement windows and stared along the drive, his eyes resting on the motor vehicle. It was a big black Ford and very expensive. He smiled at Jenny's caustic remarks. Then he remembered that the lady he had so wanted to see had died before he could make her acquaintance. 'I'm sorry, Father,' he muttered. 'I would have got to her sooner if only I'd known.' He wondered about the daughter, and his imagination ran away with him.

Like Jenny, Mr Taylor was curious. 'Who is he?' He drew out two chairs from the table, sitting himself in one and Katie in the other. Two pairs of eyes watched her as she bustled about making the tea.

'I've no idea,' Jenny replied, placing a plate of jam tarts in front of them. 'There weren't no sense asking for his name because there's nobody here to tell it to.'

'What does he want?'

'I don't know that neither.'

'Is the man pretty?' Katie wanted to know. She loved taking part in a conversation.

Jenny smiled and tapped her on the head. 'Men aren't pretty,' she laughed.

'What are they then?' Katie asked, stuffing the greater part of a jam tart in her mouth.

'They're *handsome*.'

Katie had to think about that. 'Well, is he handsome then?'

Jenny was deep in thought as she put the china cup and saucer on the tray, but Katie didn't seem to mind when she didn't get an answer. Instead, she helped herself to another jam tart.

Mr Taylor chuckled as he watched Katie. Taking one of the tarts and nibbling at it, he thanked Jenny for the pot of tea she put before him, then told her through a mouthful of crumbs, 'I heard the motorcar coming up the drive, so I took a peep. It's a real beauty. That type cost a fortune, you know.'

'I dare say.' Jenny sliced the sandwiches and arranged them prettily on the plate. She put the plate on to the tray. 'He's well off, anyone can see that.'

'He asked for *Mrs* Marshall, you say?'

'That's right.' Jenny shook her head and looked sad. 'It was a shock to him when I told him.' She polished the dainty knife and placed it beside the plate. 'Happen he knew her a long time ago. After all, he said he comes from London and that's where *they* lived, before they came to Woburn Sands.'

'But you reckon he's not yet thirty? That's a great deal younger than either the late master or his wife.'

Jenny took the tray into her hands and went to the door. 'That don't mean to say he couldn't have been a friend.'

Mr Taylor leapt from his seat and opened the door for her. 'Aye, happen,' he agreed thoughtfully.

The young man thanked Jenny kindly and watched her with interest as she poured the tea. 'Were you here when Mrs Marshall died?' he asked in a kindly voice.

'Yes, sir. She'd been ill for some time, and the end came peaceable like.' She made no mention of the fact that Claudia had fought and argued with her until the poor tormented soul took to her bed. Nor did she say how Claudia had cruelly led her mother to believe that the late master had seduced his own daughter and made her with child. As far as Jenny knew, Claudia had sent her mother to the grave, still believing that awful lie. But she made no mention of any of it, for to Jenny's mind such shocking things did not even deserve to see the light of day.

'I understand that Mrs Marshall's daughter is an only child?'

Jenny was surprised. 'Why, yes, that's right, sir.' Thank God, she thought, because Claudia Marshall had been more heartache to her mother than a dozen children.

He sipped his tea and thought of the woman he had so longed .

to meet, but now it was too late for that. 'What was she like . . . Mrs Marshall?'

His question shattered Jenny's idea that he was an old friend. It was obvious that he didn't even know her. 'She was a lady, sir,' she replied, indulging in thoughts of Elizabeth.

'You were fond of her then?'

Jenny's eyes filled with tears. 'I loved her like a mother, sir,' she answered truthfully.

He smiled to himself. 'Somehow I knew she would be a woman to admire.'

'Oh, she was that all right, sir. There weren't a single soul who had a bad word to say about her. She was a *real* lady, kind and gentle, with a heart of gold. She had no airs and graces, not like your usual gentry.' Mortified, she realised that he too was obviously gentry. 'Oh, I didn't mean . . .'

'It's all right,' he interrupted. 'I know what you mean, and I quite agree. Gentry are no different from any other human beings. There are exemplary ones, like Mrs Marshall and there are tyrants.' He laughed. 'I could name plenty of those.'

Jenny thought him to be more like Mrs Marshall than a tyrant. Unlike him, though, she could name only one, and that was Claudia, for there was a tyrant of the worst order and no mistake.

'What is she like, Mrs Marshall's daughter?'

Jenny moved closer to the door, desperately trying to think of a suitable reply. Her instincts told her to be careful because she had no idea who this young man was nor whether he was favourably disposed towards Claudia. In that moment, she glanced up and saw the object of her thoughts coming up the drive. 'Well, you can ask her yourself, sir,' she said with great relief, 'for here she is now.'

Inquisitive and a little nervous, he got out of the chair and went to the window. At once he looked out to where Claudia had stopped beside the car, examining it with curiosity. She had on her most attractive outfit, a straight grey skirt with a scalloped hem that touched her shapely calves, and a waist-fitting jacket in a matching colour. Round her neck she wore a crimson silk scarf, bought by one of her many 'admirers', and her long brown hair was partly covered with a deep cream cloche hat. Her lovely face was pleasantly flushed from her walk, and now, as she turned towards the house, her pale eyes scoured the windows. She glanced once more at the gleaming car and quickened her pace towards the house, wondering with excitement who could be calling on her who owned such a treasure.

'Why! She's beautiful.' The young man was mesmerised. 'I had no idea.'

Again, Jenny wondered about him. If he didn't know Elizabeth, and he didn't know Claudia, why was he here? 'I'd best announce you, sir,' she said in a more formal voice. 'Who shall I say comes calling?'

He turned from the window. 'Richard Hurd,' he declared. Suddenly he was extremely nervous, fidgeting with his tie and straightening his waistcoat. He coughed a little and shuffled his feet. 'And though I came to see the mother, I'm certain that my purpose for being here will just as surely interest the daughter.' He stood up straight, preparing himself as Claudia's steps came nearer.

'Wait here, sir,' Jenny told him, going from the room. She smiled to herself. It won't matter *why* you came here, because she'll welcome you all the same . . . you wear trousers and you've a deal of money by what I can see, so you'd best watch out or she'll have you for breakfast!

Jenny was still muttering when she came to the door and opened it, just as Claudia reached up to let herself in. 'Have I a visitor?' she asked, pushing her way into the hall and almost knocking Jenny over. She took off her gloves and hat and flung them on the hallstand. She was hot and flushed and breathing rapidly, as though she'd been chased.

Closing the door, Jenny told her, 'It's a young man, miss, calls himself Richard Hurd.'

'Oh?' Claudia preened herself in the mirror. 'And is that his motor vehicle outside?'

'I believe so.'

'Is he handsome?'

Jenny thought about that for a moment before replying in a sharp voice, 'I don't know what you call "handsome", miss.' Claudia only ever had two things on her mind, men and money, in that order.

Claudia never lost an opportunity to drive the knife home. With a sly expression on her face, she answered, 'Of course you know, Jenny, because like you I found Frank to be a very handsome man, otherwise he wouldn't have caught my eye, would he?'

Tight-lipped and fuming inside, Jenny kept her composure. She wouldn't give the other woman the satisfaction of seeing how she was cut deep by those spiteful words. 'I'll bring your shoes,' she said calmly, seeing Claudia's boots were splattered with mud.

'Where's the brat?' Infuriated by Jenny's dignified response, she meant to hurt her more.

'If you mean Katie, miss, she's in the kitchen.'

'Then fetch her to my room.' When Jenny hesitated she raised her voice, but not so much that her visitor would be disturbed. 'You heard me . . . I said fetch her!' She started up the stairs. 'Mr Hurd can wait. It never hurts to keep a man waiting. Tell him I'll be along shortly, that I need to wash and freshen myself after that long walk.' She followed Jenny's departure with a look of loathing, despising the close relationship which Jenny and the girl enjoyed. 'Bastards, the pair of you,' she hissed. Yet though she despised the woman and the child, she got enormous pleasure out of making them suffer.

Coming into her room, Claudia went straight to the mirror, her face set hard as she stared at her reflection. Her greatest pleasure was herself so it was only a moment before her expression gave way to a smile. 'There isn't a man alive who can resist you,' she boasted, turning this way and that and thinking that she grew even more beautiful as the years went by.

Her devious mind turned to the wealthy visitor downstairs. 'So who is he, I wonder . . . this young man who travels in such style?' She made a sweeping gesture with her arms, as though bowing to royalty. 'Rich or not, it won't hurt to keep him dangling,' she laughed. 'It can only whet his appetite. After all, they say if a thing's worth having, it's worth waiting for, and there's many a man doesn't mind waiting for Claudia Marshall.' She laughed and twirled, delighting in herself.

After Jenny advised the visitor as to Claudia's intent, she went on to the kitchen. '"Wash and freshen" after your walk, indeed. And what else did you get up to, I wonder?' she muttered with disgust.

In the kitchen, Jenny washed Katie's hands and face then dressed her in the white pinafore which Claudia insisted she wore whenever she was about her duties. 'The mistress wants you,' she explained.

Katie didn't argue. She never did. Instead, she dutifully followed Jenny through the hall and up the stairs, trotting alongside and merrily chattering. Her chattering stopped when she saw Claudia waiting for them.

'Come here.' Claudia was seated on the dressing-table stool. Her jacket was draped over the bed and her hair was unkempt round her face. She had unbuttoned her blouse and was leaning backwards on the chest of drawers, her elbows supporting her weight. For one awful minute, the child thought she had been summoned by a witch. She hid behind Jenny and Claudia was incensed. 'I SAID, COME HERE!' she yelled. She knew that from the higher reaches of the old house, there was no danger of the visitor overhearing her.

'Go on, Katie,' Jenny urged, drawing the child out. She could feel her trembling, and it was all she could do not to take her and run from that place. Only her commonsense and the knowledge that Claudia was Katie's mother stopped her.

Claudia was delighted to see Jenny stiff with apprehension. Satisfied, she watched the child approach, and her satisfaction turned to a strange kind of fear. The resemblance between her own mother and Katie was unnerving.

Katie stood before her, and though she was extremely nervous, made herself brave for Jenny's sake.

It was a while before Claudia could speak. With Katie's innocent green eyes staring up at her, she was put in mind of another pair of eyes of the same hue, accusing eyes, sad and regretful eyes, eyes which by her own dreadful actions were put to sleep forever. Now, when she spoke, it was in a small trembling voice. 'Do you earn your keep?'

Katie knew what this meant because Jenny had explained. 'Yes, miss,' she said, her little chest puffed out.

'What do you do?'

'I polish the kitchen range, and I help Jenny.'

Claudia considered this, and still she wasn't satisfied. Addressing Jenny she said, 'I want her duties written down. That way, I know exactly what she's doing at any given time.'

Jenny gave the slightest nod. Up until now she had let the child off with the lightest of duties, but she was afraid that Claudia would want to work Katie into the ground. Somehow she must not let that happen.

Claudia's shrill voice cut the air. 'Take off my boots.' She was actually smiling at Katie, and Katie was smiling back. It was a sight to make Jenny's heart go cold.

At once, she stepped forward. 'Let me do that,' she said.

One baleful glance from Claudia stopped her in her tracks. '*You* were not asked,' she snapped. 'But you can watch and see that she does it properly.' She stared down at the child, and the green eyes stared back. In that moment Claudia's fear was almost more than her enjoyment. 'You do realise that you'll be punished if you don't do it properly?' Her whole manner had changed, and sensing it, Katie cringed. 'I said . . . you know you will be punished if you can't do it?' she insisted in a harder voice.

'Yes, miss.' Katie turned to Jenny for reassurance, and she smiled encouragement. It was enough. 'I can do it,' she told Claudia proudly. 'Jenny showed me how to tie my laces, and I can untie them as well.'

Without answering, Claudia stuck out her left foot and the child knelt before her, tiny fingers fumbling with the knot. When it didn't come undone immediately, Claudia began to fidget, and the more she fidgeted, the more the knot tightened. She stared down at the small figure with its head bent, and was oddly captivated by that mass of auburn hair. It might have been Elizabeth there. She began to panic. 'Get on with it, damn you!' she cried, and in that moment the child looked up. There were tears in her eyes. It was more than Claudia could bear. 'GET AWAY!' she yelled, kicking out at the child and sending her sprawling. 'Useless, that's what you are. Bloody useless, the pair of you.'

Horrified, Jenny rushed to pluck Katie away. As she did so, Claudia stormed across the room and snatched the girl to her. Screaming at Jenny she told her, 'You've taught her *nothing*. Make a good servant of her, that's what I said and that's what I'll have. Oh, I know your little game, but it won't work.' Beside herself with rage, she gripped the terrified child by the shoulders and made herself look into those stricken eyes. 'Have you ever tasted a strap across your bare legs,' she asked in the softest voice, 'when the leather bites into your skin and cuts deep?' She stretched her neck upwards and closed her eyes, groaning as though in agony. 'I have,' she confessed. 'When I was small and did naughty things, my own father punished me in that way.' She glared at the terrified child. 'If you don't do as you're told, I might have to take a strap to *you*.'

Katie began sobbing. 'Jenny won't let you,' she cried.

Claudia glanced at Jenny and smiled. 'She would have no say in it.' Realising that Claudia was deliberately goading her, Jenny forced herself to stay calm.

Frustrated, Claudia returned her attention to the child. 'There are good children and there are bad,' she told her slyly. 'I think *you're* a bad one in the making, and perhaps I should take a strap to you anyway,' she suggested callously.

'I DON'T LIKE YOU!' Katie cried, struggling and fighting to escape.

Something snapped in Claudia then. Making a noise like a wild animal, she raised her arm and brought the flat of her hand crashing down against Katie's face. Everything happened at once. There was the crack of flesh against flesh, then a shocked silence as Katie's head went back and her nose spurted blood. Jenny was across the room in two strides. Gathering the child in her arms, she stared at Claudia who had fallen backwards against the chest of drawers. 'She may be yours,' she said in a low shocked voice. 'But I'm warning you . . . *don't ever hurt her again.*'

Claudia made no reply. Instead, she began trembling violently, staring at Jenny as though she had never seen her before.

As Jenny helped Katie down the stairs, the door to the drawing room opened and the young man appeared. 'I wondered if I'd been forgotten . . .' he began, and then he saw Katie, obviously in distress and clinging tight to Jenny. She was pressing a handkerchief to her nose, but the blood was already seeping through. 'How did this happen?' he asked with concern, lifting

Katie into his arms, oblivious to the crimson stains that dripped over his jacket.

Afraid that Katie might say what had happened, Jenny gave her a knowing look. 'She fell and banged her face.' Katie realised she must say nothing and so she didn't. Instead she began crying again because the whole of her face was hurting.

When the worst was over and Katie was quieter, Jenny wanted the young man out of her kitchen. But he seemed to have a need to talk, and so she listened with interest.

'Charles Marshall and my late father fought together during the war. Marshall was the senior officer, a man of immense courage,' he told her. 'At great risk to his own safety, he saved my father's life.'

Jenny recalled all the proud things Elizabeth had said about her husband, and was compelled to remark, 'He was a good man and well respected hereabouts.'

He nodded and seemed lost in thought for a moment until Jenny said kindly, 'Thank you for your help, sir, but I can manage fine now.' She continued to dab gently at the child's face with a cold flannel; Katie was seated on the drainer, her eyes red from bawling and her little fists holding on to Jenny as though she would never let her go. Now and then she would look at the man and cling all the more. In her fright Jenny was everything to her.

'If you're sure?'

Jenny nodded. Collecting his jacket from the airing horse, she gave it back to him; it was still damp from where she had swabbed it. 'The stains won't go altogether,' she warned. 'You'd do well to have it done professionally.'

'You have a delightful daughter,' he said, chucking Katie under the chin and making her giggle through her tears.

Before Jenny could put him right, he was gone. Bemused and a little sad, she realised he had made a natural mistake because Katie was still wearing her little work pinnie and her shoes had seen better days. Besides, it was obvious that she was at home and content in the kitchen with Jenny.

'I like him,' Katie declared, drying her eyes.

'So do I. He seems a good kind man,' she replied, at the same time wondering whether he could possibly know what he had got himself into. It was obvious that the first sight of Claudia had enchanted him. 'I hope you don't forget that beauty's only skin deep,' Jenny whispered after him. 'For your sake, I hope you'll see the ugliness underneath.'

Less than ten minutes later, Claudia breezed into the drawing room, smiling sweetly and looking unusually lovely in an emerald green dress that showed her curves to advantage. 'I'm so sorry to have kept you waiting,' she lied, going to the fireplace where she tugged on the bell-pull. Looking at the tray she said, 'We'll have that taken away. I for one would like a fresh pot of tea.' Gesturing to a nearby chair, she invited him to make himself comfortable.

He seemed unsure, not wanting to sit before she did. Claudia sensed this, and cursed herself for having forgotten how a lady should behave. She smiled to herself as she realised she had spent too much time with the coarser elements of society. Fixing him with her most dazzling smile, she seated herself in the armchair opposite, deliberately crossing her slender legs to catch his attention, and feigning embarrassment when she 'caught' him admiring her. 'So what can I do to help you?' she asked with an air of innocence, cunningly plucking at the hem of her dress as though trying to stretch it over her knee, being well aware that she was attracting even more attention in the process.

At that moment there was a tap on the door and Jenny showed her face. 'Oh, Jenny,' Claudia said in a shockingly friendly voice which she hoped might make a suitable impression on her visitor, 'take this tray away. Tea, please, and some of your splendid ham sandwiches.' She bestowed a wonderful smile on Jenny, who not for the first time wondered whether Claudia was quite mad.

Glancing at Jenny, the young man asked, 'Is the child all right?'

'Yes, thank you, sir. She's fine now,' Jenny replied, coming into the room.

'Of course she is,' Claudia interrupted. Deliberately ignoring Jenny, she turned to Richard, urging, 'You were about to tell me the reason for your visit here?'

'Of course.' Leaning forward in his chair, he began, 'My family and I have lived in India for many years. Even after my mother was killed in a riding accident, my father couldn't bring himself to leave the country he had come to love. Unfortunately, he died last month, and it was only then that we learned the facts. You see, along with everything else, I inherited a batch of letters and my father's war diary, which described how your own father, Charles Marshall, saved his life in the trenches.'

'My father was a man of immense courage,' said Claudia, and her hatred for him intensified, but already her devious mind was thinking ahead of itself. '*Inherited* . . . Along with everything else,' he'd said. She was elated. Here was the opportunity she'd been waiting for. Richard Hurd was wealthy, and he was indebted to her father. It was perfect!

Suddenly she was aware that Jenny was still in the room, busily replacing the crockery on to the tray and able to hear what was being said. 'One moment, please,' she told the young man. Addressing Jenny, her tone sharpened. 'As quick as you can,' she remarked. 'I'm thirsty after my walk in the fresh air.'

After Jenny had gone out of the room and closed the door, Claudia returned her attention to the young man. 'Please, go on,' she encouraged, her pale eyes fixed on him.

'I made efforts to contact your father immediately on my return to this country last month, and it was with regret that I learned of his death . . . and now of your mother's too. I'm so sorry, Miss Marshall.'

She cast her eyes downwards as though the sorrow was too much to bear. 'Thank you,' she said. 'It was a bad time.'

'I'll get straight to the point of my visit here,' he said, and for a moment he wondered whether she might throw him out once he had explained. 'Forgive me but . . . it's common knowledge in the City how your father's fortune was lost. I had to come and see for myself that his family was not suffering the consequences.' He was unsure as to whether she would be offended, but then he didn't know Claudia. 'The plain truth is this. I have a debt to repay.'

She looked suitably shocked. 'What are you saying? Do you imagine that I'm in need of your charity, is that what you mean?'

Mortified, he assured her that he had not imagined any such thing, but that he felt he was under a moral obligation to satisfy himself that the family of Charles Marshall was well taken care of. 'Please, I meant no insult,' he finished.

She smiled then. He would be easy to ensnare. 'I have a suggestion to make,' she said warmly.

'If it means that you've forgiven me, I'd like to hear it.'

'Stay awhile. Join me for dinner, and you can tell me all about India and your family.' It was important she should learn as much as possible about him.

He visibly relaxed. 'Thank you, I accept.'

Jenny returned then, carrying a tray set out with the best bone-china, a pot of tea, dainty pastries, and a plate of her best ham sandwiches. 'Thank you. You may go,' Claudia said, obviously impatient to see the back of her.

As Jenny quickly left, she heard Claudia ask of the young man. 'Do you have any other family, a wife perhaps and children?'

'No other family, apart from a younger brother and an old

spinster aunt who lives in the North of England.' Already he was beginning to feel at home here. 'And you?'

'No,' she lied. 'I have no family at all.'

It was late when the young man drove away. After a frantic evening, during which she was backwards and forwards to the dining room, and afterwards up to her armpits in washing-up, Jenny went to her bed exhausted.

During the course of the evening she had seen how Claudia wove her spell over Richard. Later, she heard them talking in the hallway, whispering and laughing, enjoying each other's company. She heard him drive away, and then heard Claudia laughing to herself. 'God help him,' Jenny murmured. 'He'll be back, and he'll live to rue the day.'

At five the following morning, after a fitful sleep, Jenny went downstairs and was astonished to see Claudia helping herself to a glass of milk in the kitchen. 'I couldn't sleep,' she explained. She stood with her back to the dresser, sipping her milk, her pale eyes following Jenny's every move.

She was acutely aware that she was being watched, but made no comment until she could bear it no longer. 'Is there something you want, miss?' she said cuttingly.

'Why no, not at all,' Claudia replied with a smile. Jenny was shocked to her roots. Claudia was actually being *pleasant*! 'Is Katie all right?' she wanted to know.

'She's sleeping.' Jenny suspected she was about to be sent for the child.

'Let her sleep then.' She regarded Jenny for a moment, then in a penitent voice said, 'I shouldn't have lost my temper like that.' When Jenny made no reply, Claudia placed her empty glass on the dresser and departed, leaving Jenny with a look of astonishment on her face. 'What's she up to?' she asked herself. 'She *is*

227

up to something, I'm sure of it, or she wouldn't be in my kitchen at five of a morning . . . and being *pleasant* into the bargain.'

Claudia was pleasant all that day, and she was pleasant well into the evening. And the more pleasant Claudia was, the more deeply suspicious Jenny became. 'We'll have to watch ourselves, Katie gal,' she told the sleeping child. 'There's something nasty brewing, and for the life of me I can't make it out.' With that, she got into her own bed and said a little prayer. 'Whatever it is that she's up to, Lord, please don't let the child get hurt.' And she left the door open so that she might hear even the slightest sound outside Katie's room.

# *Chapter Eleven*

Mr Taylor leaned on his spade and wiped his brow. 'It wouldn't surprise me if the two of 'em didn't soon get wed. I mean, he's already taken to staying over the odd night, and with him being a respectable sort, it can only be a matter of time afore they make it legal.'

Jenny put her shopping basket to the ground and sat on the bench. 'I hope not for his sake,' she remarked, taking off her headscarf. It was the warmest April she could ever recall, and she was hot and tired after that long trek to the shops. 'Are they back yet?' she wanted to know. It would suit her if Claudia and Richard Hurd stayed out to lunch, as they had done yesterday.

He shook his head. 'Nope. There's been no sign of 'em since they left just afore you and Katie.' He wiped the back of his hand across the sweat on his forehead. 'The young fella, Richard Hurd's brother – well, he wanted to stay behind, but they were having none of it,' he said thoughtfully. 'He's a pleasant little chap an' no mistake, though he seems a bit old-fashioned for a lad of only ten years old. He strolled down here early on and I'm telling you, talk about an old head on young shoulders! We had a very serious conversation.'

'What about?'

'Oh, this and that. He talked about India, and how much he

missed it. He went on at length about his late mammy, and how his daddy fought in the war. But mostly he spoke about his brother Richard. Idolises him, it seems. He was most curious about the mistress . . . trying to ferret information out of me he was, but I know better than to get involved so I told him she paid me wages and that were that.' Leaning forward, he touched the tip of his finger against his nose. 'If you ask me, he don't care much for Claudia Marshall, an' that's a fact.' Sniffing a dewdrop up his nostril, he chuckled and said, 'Still an' all, he's a nice young fella, and he's tekken a real shine to our Katie.'

At the mention of her name, Katie looked up. Taking off her coat, she gave it to Jenny. 'When will Alan be back?'

'Soon, I expect.'

'He won't be going home straightaway, will he?'

'I don't know, sweetheart.' She ran her hand over the child's unruly auburn locks. 'Why? Is it so important?'

'He wanted me to show him the brook where all the fish are.' She blushed a little. 'I hope he doesn't go home yet.'

Jenny slid her arms round the girl's neck and pulled her close. She was a little afraid and it showed in her voice when she told Katie, 'You don't really know him.'

She bit her lip. 'Well, I like him, and he likes me too,' she declared, bending to poke at the bag of flour in Jenny's basket. 'Do you think he'll stay for his tea?'

'He might.'

Katie poked again at the bag of flour. 'Can I help you bake a cake?' She thought Alan might taste it and be impressed when he knew she had helped in its making.

Jenny laughed aloud. 'I don't see why not.' She could read Katie's mind like an open book.

'Can I carry the basket in?'

'No, sweetheart. It's too heavy.'

'Can I play on the swing then?'

230

''Course you can.' Jenny smiled as Katie ran off. 'She's growing up so fast.'

'She's a credit to you,' Mr Taylor declared. 'Katie's making a lovely girl, and it's no thanks to her mother, that's for sure.'

Jenny had to speak her fears. 'I don't know if it's good for her and the boy to be together.'

'Whyever not? The poor little thing don't get many friends up here, and he seems a nice young man.'

'Oh, I don't know. It's just that I was watching them through the kitchen window yesterday morning. They were in the orchard, enjoying a little picnic I'd made for them. They hadn't been there above a few minutes when Claudia marched down and took the boy in. I could see from her face that she didn't like their being together.'

'I can't see how she could object to it. After all, when she and Richard Hurd get wed, the boy will be related in marriage to Katie, and they'll be thrown together anyhow.'

'I'm telling you, she didn't want them together.'

He scratched his head and thought on Jenny's words, and didn't doubt them for a minute. 'It beats me,' he commented. 'When all's said and done, Katie's her own flesh and blood.' He scowled. 'Though you wouldn't think so, the way she keeps her at a distance.'

Jenny watched Katie for a while as she climbed on to the swing which Mr Taylor had hung from the apple tree. 'I think you're right about them getting wed.' She glanced up at him, her pretty blue eyes squinting in the sunlight. 'It's been six months since he first showed his face here, and he's hardly been away since. The last three times he's brought his younger brother with him, and I don't think he'd do that unless he sees them becoming a family, like you said.'

'Plain as the nose on your face. She's got her hooks into him good and proper, and now he can't bear to be parted from her.'

He sniffed and coughed and drove the spade into the ground. 'She's bewitched the poor bugger, that's why.'

Jenny thought on that for a while, and she knew he was right. 'You'd think he'd have enough sense to see through her.'

Mr Taylor laughed at that. 'There ain't a man alive who can see past a woman's cunning, and they don't come no more cunning than Claudia Marshall.' He paused in his labours to tell her in a serious voice, 'It's my job I'm worried about . . . and happen you should be worried about yours an' all.'

'How's that?'

'Think on it,' he urged. 'Miss High and Mighty won't be content to stop round these parts once she gets Richard Hurd to the altar. Oh no! She's got her sights set much higher than this poor old house which has seen better days. No! It's a *fancy* house she'll be wanting . . . with lots of servants at her beck and call, and carriages to run her here, there and everywhere.' He hesitated, wondering whether he should say what else was on his mind, but he was talking to Jenny and there was nothing she didn't already know. 'I don't have to remind you how the villagers know her bad side. So far she's managed to keep it from him, but she'll not be able to do that for much longer because tittle tattle will always out.' He came and sat beside her. 'Tell me, what's she up to where young Katie's concerned, eh?'

'What do you mean?' Jenny knew well enough what he meant.

'I've been given orders that I'm not to speak about Katie to anyone, especially not to Richard Hurd.' He regarded her curiously. 'I reckon she wants him to believe that Katie's yourn.' When Jenny made no response, he insisted, 'I'm right, aren't I?'

'Who can tell what goes on in her devious mind?' Jenny replied evasively. Collecting her basket, she got up from the bench. 'I'd best be going,' she said. 'If they decide to come back for their lunch, I'll be caught on the hop.' She began walking away, but turned when he called her name. 'Yes?'

'Be careful, gal. Lately she's too smarmy by half. I know she's playing a game o' some sort, and I can't help but feel that you and the young 'un might come off worst.' He took up his spade again but kept his eyes on her. 'You do know what I mean, don't you?'

She knew all right. 'Yes,' she admitted. 'And don't worry, I *will* be careful.' As she hurried away, Jenny told herself aloud, 'He's right though. The sly cat's up to summat, I know, but I ain't quite figured it out yet.' Until she had, she meant to keep a close eye on young Katie because she felt instinctively that her young charge was at the bottom of it all.

It was two o'clock when the motorcar pulled up outside. Impatient and excited to be back, young Alan was the first to clamber out. He was a handsome little fellow, with brown eyes, fair hair and long sturdy limbs, and his first thought was for his newfound friend. 'Can I go and see Katie?' he asked hopefully, staring up at his brother with a bright smile.

At once, Claudia protested. 'Don't you think he should go to his room and get his things together?' she suggested sweetly. 'After all, you'll be leaving soon for the journey North, and though I haven't yet met your aunt, I'm sure she wouldn't thank you if you turned up with a grubby child.'

'The boy will be fine,' Richard told her. Wagging a finger at his brother he said, 'Miss Marshall's right though. You know how particular your Aunt Helen is, so keep yourself tidy. And be back in half an hour to get your things together. You've had a wonderful two days, and it won't be too long before we're back again.' He sighed aloud as Alan went quickly out of sight. His voice could soon be heard calling, 'Katie! Where are you, Katie?' She hid it very well but Claudia was furious at having been over-ruled.

Sweeping into the house, she was full of her own importance

as she addressed Jenny. 'You needn't concern yourself about lunch,' she said. 'We've already eaten.'

'I wouldn't say no to a cup of tea though,' Richard Hurd added, smiling at Jenny with kind eyes. He admired her immensely and made no secret of it to Claudia. 'How that young lady manages to keep this house going all on her own, I will never know,' he'd told her. He had even offered to pay for extra staff, but Claudia had seemed suitably offended. 'I will not take charity,' she told him. What she thought was: But I'll take every penny you have, once you've put that ring on my finger. She was incensed that he should admire Jenny so openly, but knew better than to show him her worst side. She was so close. Too close to risk it all now.

Richard was curious as to Jenny's background. 'Why has she a child and no husband?' he wanted to know.

Claudia knew he believed the child to be Jenny's, and it suited her to let him go on believing that. 'Jenny Dickens was never married,' she explained. Wickedly, she left the rest to his imagination.

When Jenny brought the tea in, the two of them were standing by the window, deep in murmured conversation. When she returned later to collect the tray, they were seated on the settee: he was holding Claudia's hand and she was gazing up at him. On seeing Jenny, Claudia became uneasy. 'Leave that for now,' she ordered with a hint of her old self, and Jenny gratefully departed.

At four Richard came into Jenny's kitchen. 'As Miss Marshall is upstairs, I thought I would choose this minute to have a quiet word with you.'

'Yes, sir?' Jenny was covered in flour and her hair was squashed beneath a white mob-cap. Though she liked him well enough, she resented his coming into her kitchen.

'From the fond way in which you spoke of the late Mrs Marshall, and seeing your present dedication to her daughter, I suspect you have been much more than a servant to this family,' he told her. 'I want you to be the first to know that Miss Marshall and I have been viewing property. I'm surprised she wants to move from this lovely area, but she does, and so we've been searching far and wide for a suitable house.' He paused, allowing the news to sink in, and not realising that Jenny had suspected it for some time now. 'At last we've found a house to her liking . . . a large and beautiful place where I know we'll be happy. It was important that we find the right house for Miss Marshall's sake, especially as my business will take me away from time to time. So there you are. We'll be married within the year.'

'Thank you for telling me, sir.' Jenny thought him a fool, but didn't altogether blame him. After all, it was right what Mr Taylor had said: men couldn't see further than their noses where someone like Claudia Marshall was concerned. And who should know that better than me? Jenny thought. For hadn't her own life been shattered when Frank fell hook, line and sinker for what was on offer? The memory threatened to overwhelm her so she pushed it from her mind.

He was amused. 'Is that all you have to say?' he asked. 'Aren't you even going to congratulate me?'

'Congratulations, sir.' And God help you, she thought.

As he left, he remarked, 'I hope you won't be disappointed at the changes that are bound to take place?'

Recalling Mr Taylor's warning, Jenny dared to ask, 'Will you and Miss Marshall be getting rid of me, sir?'

'Whatever put that idea into your head?' He sounded horrified, but Jenny was not reassured.

'I was just wondering, sir.'

He regarded her for a moment, thinking what a pretty little thing she was, and wondering why Katie's father wasn't around. 'You're a real treasure,' he told her. 'I'm sure Miss Marshall would never want to get rid of you.' He smiled again. 'In fact I would positively forbid it,' he said light-heartedly. With that he left and Jenny sat in a chair, her eyes closed and her thoughts racing ahead. Things seemed to be happening too fast and she wondered what her future would be. She thought about Katie, and realised that there was no future if she wasn't with that darling child.

'Jenny, will you please tell Alan that I'm going to help when you bake a cake for tea?' Katie's voice cut the air.

When Jenny swung round to see the two children standing there, Katie took hold of the boy's hand and brought him into the kitchen. 'He doesn't believe me,' she said indignantly. 'Because I can't catch fish, he thinks I can't do nothing at all!'

Composing herself, Jenny looked from one to the other. There was something about the way in which they stood, close to each other, Katie's small hand in his, that touched her heart. '*I* can't catch a fish either,' she told the boy. 'But I reckon I can bake the best chocolate cake in the whole of Bedfordshire. What's more, I don't think I could manage it without Katie's help.'

'Told you,' Katie said proudly, tugging at his hand and looking up at him with shining eyes.

He turned his head and gazed down at her. 'Sorry,' he murmured. When her green eyes smiled back at him, his face broke into a sheepish grin. 'When we're married, you can bake the cakes and I'll catch the fish,' he announced boldly. With that, Katie giggled and ran out. 'You'd best go after her,' Jenny said, hiding her amusement. 'Tell her she's to be in shortly for her tea.'

'Are you having chocolate cake?'

'Happen.'

'And will there be some for me?'

'I shouldn't be at all surprised.' He blurted his thanks and ran out of the door. Jenny burst out laughing. 'Well, I never!' she said. 'Love's young dream, and the pair of 'em little more than bairns!' The way things were, she didn't know whether she should laugh or cry.

As it was, the boy didn't get his chocolate cake because in no time at all he was bundled into the motorcar and driven away. Katie stood at the side of the house, her soulful eyes following the car as it went out of the drive. The boy stared at her from the back window. He waved once and then was gone, leaving her with a sad face.

Jenny had seen the exchange between the two, and was uneasy. 'He'll forget me, won't he?' Katie asked forlornly.

'No, sweetheart, he won't forget you,' Jenny promised. If she knew anything at all, she knew that.

A little happier, but still feeling lonely, Katie set about shelling the peas. It was a job she loved, because first she helped Mr Taylor to pick them, then she shelled them, next she put them into the pan, and finally, when they were cooked to perfection and drained off, Jenny let her help in spooning them into the serving dish.

A few moments after the brothers had departed, the bell above the door rang to tell Jenny that she was wanted in the drawing room. Taking off her mob-cap and wiping her hands, she hurried there.

'Close the door,' Claudia told her. She was standing with her back to the fireplace, a serious expression on her face. 'I understand that Mr Hurd came to tell you the news?'

'Yes, miss.'

Claudia bristled. 'I don't approve of his going into the kitchen and talking to the staff,' she said sharply. 'I'll make certain it doesn't happen again.' She met Jenny's forthright stare with a look of cunning. 'Still, you would have known soon enough. We're to be married, and if I have my way it will be sooner rather than later.'

Jenny smiled. 'Of course.'

'But then again, it's none of your business what I do,' she snapped. 'It isn't *anyone's* business!' She waited for a response from Jenny but her face remained impassive. After a while, Claudia went on, 'I have a proposition to put to you.'

'What sort of proposition?' Fear crept into Jenny's heart.

'I don't have to tell you that it would give me a great deal of pleasure to get rid of you, but for some ridiculous reason, Mr Hurd has got it into his head that you have devoted yourself to me, and to my mother before me.' This wasn't the real reason why she meant to keep Jenny under this roof where she could keep an eye on her, and she hated her all the more. Jenny's next words only made her more wary.

'I loved your mother.'

'And you loathe me?' In her terrible guilt, Claudia detected an accusation in Jenny's quiet voice.

'I didn't say that, miss.'

'You didn't have to.' Claudia swung away and rested her hands on the mantelpiece. 'Mr Hurd believes that Katie belongs to you,' she said in a quiet voice.

'I know.'

Claudia was staring at her now, her eyes wide with disbelief. 'You knew? And you said nothing?'

'I only wish she *was* mine.'

'That is why I sent for you. I want you to go on letting him believe she's yours . . . in fact, I want you to encourage it, and to let Katie believe the same. She's a quick-witted child and I'm surprised she hasn't already started asking questions.'

'I won't lie to her.'

Claudia grew angry. 'Mr Hurd must not discover that Katie's mine!'

Jenny was secretly enjoying herself. 'I can understand that, miss. I don't suppose he'd be too pleased if he knew how you seduced my fella and then cast the child aside.'

'Don't overstep the mark,' Claudia warned. 'If you won't do as I ask, there are other alternatives.' Suddenly she had to test the extent of Jenny's knowledge. 'I could send you packing and ship her off to boarding school.'

Jenny's heart froze. 'I don't think that would be very wise, miss,' she warned. 'If that happened, Mr Hurd would be certain to find out.'

Now it was Claudia's turn to be afraid. 'Find out what?'

'I'm surprised you need to ask, miss.' Jenny was innocently referring to Claudia's unsavoury relationships. 'Though *you* may believe your past behaviour is without stain, I doubt whether a gentleman like Mr Hurd would see it in the same light.'

Always uncertain and a little afraid, Claudia braved it out. 'What you're saying is that you would make it your business to tell him?' More than ever, she was convinced that Jenny knew how Elizabeth had died, and was using it to her own advantage. Yet even now, she was afraid to bring it out into the open. 'You're a spiteful woman. Here am I trying to mend my ways and marry a decent man, and you mean to make me suffer for things that are long gone. Is it because I took your man? Is that what's at the root of your hatred? Oh, I know I shouldn't have done it, but he was to blame as well. He could have said no. He could have walked away.'

When she realised that she was only making things worse, she changed tack. 'I can't understand you at all. You love the child, and she loves you. All I'm asking is that you let her believe she's yours. I wouldn't interfere. You must know I would never risk everything by laying claim to her.'

'I don't trust you.'

'For God's sake!' Claudia took a step forward, but Jenny kept her ground. 'I never wanted her. I don't want her now, so why should I want her at any time in the future?'

'Would I be free to leave with her?'

Claudia's face became relieved. 'That might suit even better.'

'I dare say it would.'

'As long as you knew how to keep your mouth shut.'

'About what?'

'Don't play games with me!'

'It's all right. You've no need to worry, because I have no intention of leaving. It wouldn't be in Katie's interest, d'you see? Not while she needs things that I can't afford to give her. Soon she'll be of school age, and I want her to have the best. Like you say, she's quick-witted and capable of going far. With the best will in the world, I can't give her what she deserves. I'm only a servant . . . "Born to serve" as you so rightly put it, and Katie shouldn't be made to lose out because of something that was never her fault.'

'You're blackmailing me!'

'How can you say that, miss?' Jenny asked with feigned innocence.

'Mr Hurd would be curious. How could I explain money spent on a servant's child?'

'Tell him you're doing it out of the goodness of your heart. He would admire you for it, I'm sure.'

'No doubt, but it would be easier if you were to rent a small house somewhere. I could send you money.'

'Now that really would be blackmail.' Jenny squared her shoulders. 'No, miss. If it's all the same to you, Katie and I will stay.'

'I can see your little game, you bitch! You won't leave, because you want to bleed me dry . . . haunt me. That's it, isn't it?'

'No, miss,' she answered truthfully. 'I don't want any such thing. All I want is for Katie to get what she deserves, a good education and decent clothes.'

Claudia lapsed into a sullen silence before demanding, 'You'll do as I ask then? You'll keep your mouth shut about my past and tell the girl she's yours?'

'No, miss. I've already told you, I can't lie to Katie in that way. But I'll tell her she came to me when her own mother abandoned her, and that I've loved and cared for her ever since.' She stiffened. 'That would be the truth as I see it.'

'And there'll be no mention of my part in it?'

'No, but only because I believe Katie will be better off never knowing what you did to her.'

'One other thing.'

'What's that?'

'I don't want her mixing with the boy.'

'Easier said than done, miss. They've struck up a grand friendship, and Lord knows, Katie ain't got no friends of her own age.'

'You'll do as I say, and keep them apart!'

Jenny was defiant. 'I can only try.'

Knowing that she would get nothing more out of Jenny, Claudia dismissed her.

When Jenny came out of the drawing room, her heart was soaring. Going into the kitchen, she watched Katie struggling up the garden with a basket of vegetables. 'Thanks be to God, we've got what we want, sweetheart,' she murmured, her tender gaze following the child's approach. 'Your hard-hearted mammy's getting wed and wants to sweep all the mess under her new expensive carpets. Sadly, she sees you and me as so much dirt to be hidden along with it. But it don't matter, Katie luv, because we'll have each other, and I'll love and protect you for as long as I draw breath.'

She reflected on the cold exchange between herself and Claudia, and there was a murmur of regret. 'There's nothing I'd like better than to leave this place and never set eyes on her again, but I daren't take you away, sweetheart. I can't trust her. So we'll stay for your sake, and I give you my word . . . though you've been deprived of a loving mammy, you'll not be robbed altogether. Sadly you've got Claudia Marshall's blood in your veins, but you've been blessed with your grandmother's goodness. And though it breaks my heart every time I see him in you, you've also got the strong, kind heart of your daddy.' She thought awhile on Frank, and sadness overwhelmed her. 'He was a good man,' she whispered. 'And, God help me, in spite of everything, I'll always love him.'

On 2 May 1924 Richard Hurd bought the house which Claudia had chosen. It was a beautiful old place with several splendid bedrooms, three bathrooms, and two acres of landscaped gardens. By the end of the month, it had been completely redecorated to Claudia's taste.

The house was situated in the lovely old village of Ickwell, in Bedfordshire, some thirty miles from Woburn Sands; far enough away from those who knew of Katie's background and her mother's sordid past. The front of the house overlooked the village green; the back of the house had wonderful views across the fields, and through the grounds ran a meandering brook which attracted all manner of wildlife. Claudia was satisfied that here her past would never catch up with her.

Encouraged by Richard, she spent a fortune on furnishings and decor. Every room was filled with the most expensive artefacts; walnut dressers and silk-covered settees, grand beds with fine covers, fringed lamps and fine ornaments, carpets so deep that your feet sank into them as you walked. 'Happy are you, darling?' Richard asked, sliding his arm round her tiny waist as they watched the last delivery man drive away.

Like a child, she ran from room to room, crying with joy,

making him adore her all the more. 'I love it all,' she told him, her eyes gleaming with excitement.

'And do you love *me*?' he asked softly, sweeping her to him.

'Of course I do,' she replied eagerly. But when the kiss was over and she turned away, her face told a different story.

Two months later, on the first Saturday in July, Richard Hurd and Claudia Marshall travelled North. 'I'm nervous,' Claudia told him as they neared Darwen and his aged aunt. 'What if she doesn't like me?' Until she had him at the altar, with the wedding ring on her finger, Claudia saw everything as a threat.

Edging the car into the kerb and drawing it to a halt, Richard took her hand in his and kissed it tenderly. 'How could she not like you?' he asked. 'Anyway, it's me you're marrying, not my Aunt Helen.'

'Is she a dragon?' Claudia asked with a flutter of her eyelashes and a nervous expression.

He laughed at that. 'Yes,' he admitted, 'I think she is.' When her face fell, he quickly assured her, 'But, like me, she'll adore you. So stop worrying. Everything will be fine, I promise.'

As he got out of the car and walked round to open her door, Claudia smiled. 'What's the matter with you?' she asked herself. 'Helen Hurd is just an old woman. What can she do that will stop you now?' By the time Richard opened the door and she graciously stepped out, her confidence had returned. She linked her arm with his and together they crossed the pavement and walked on towards the house. The nearer she came, the bolder she felt, and when he pointed out the house, her confidence was restored tenfold.

It was not a grand place, merely a large terraced dwelling with long windows and a small flight of steps leading to the front door. The wood was peeling from the window-frames, and the brass knocker in the centre of the blue-painted door was dim and discoloured. 'There are so many things I could do for her but she's infuriatingly stubborn and independent.' Richard reached up and took hold of the chain to the side of the door. When he gave it a sharp tug, the bell could be heard sounding somewhere inside the house. A moment's silence, then he tugged it again. 'It wouldn't surprise me if she hasn't dismissed the housekeeper again,' he said with a chuckle.

'*Again?*' Claudia was intrigued.

'Oh, yes,' he said. 'Poor old Edna is sent packing at least once a month, but thankfully she's as stubborn as my aunt. She goes away for a couple of days, and then she comes back and carries on as normal. It's as if nothing has happened and neither of them mention it. Things go as normal until Edna gets on the wrong side of Aunt Helen once more, and the little farce is played out all over again.' He laughed. 'It's been like that since as far back as I can remember.'

'How long has your aunt lived here?'

'Forever, I think,' he said with a smile. He was pensive then, going back over the years and feeling the loss of his parents. 'My family wasn't born rich, you know. We come from right here in Lancashire, of ordinary stock. My father had a way with figures and soon found his fortune through buying and selling . . . knowing a good buy when everyone else thought it was too risky. He made his money from the quickness of his brain, while his father made his living from delivering coal hereabouts.'

Claudia was horrified. 'A *coalman*?'

'Oh, a little more than that, I think. Grandfather Hurd was a clever businessman in his own right. He soon built up a sound business, until he owned six wagons in all. He raised his family in this very house. When my father married and moved away from Darwen, Aunt Helen stayed. She and Grandfather lived in this house together until his death many years ago. Aunt Helen inherited the business, and rightly so. She never married.'

'Is she wealthy?'

'I'm not sure. She won't discuss things like that with me. But she's not without money, I do know that. She's shrewd and careful where money's concerned. I keep a close eye on her, and I'd know if she was in need.' He shook his head, 'I can't say whether she's wealthy, but I'm sure she has more than enough for her needs. Certainly she kept the business going for a while after Grandfather's death, and even made it more profitable.'

Claudia wasn't pleased to hear these things. 'She sounds like a hard woman.'

He tugged the chain again, and this time footsteps could be heard approaching along the hallway. 'She's nobody's fool,' he warned, 'but she's an old softie at heart. When the business was sold, the horses that had worked the rounds since Grandfather's time were old and decrepit. The new owner was planning to have them put down, but she wouldn't hear of it. Instead, she bought a parcel of land between here and Blackburn where they roam the fields to their hearts' content. There were six at one time, and now there are only two. She goes out to see them every Sunday afternoon without fail. Only the very best will do for her old nags. She pays a nearby farmer to feed and fend for them, and the vet checks them over every now and then, whether they're ill or not.'

'Who's that?' The voice startled them.

'It's only me, Aunt,' Richard replied, pressing his face nearer to the door.

It was flung open and there stood a small elderly woman. She was stiff and upright, with bright squirrel eyes and thin white hair which was scraped tight into a bun at the nape of her scrawny neck. On seeing Richard, she stared disapprovingly at him. 'You're a bad 'un!' she told him. 'You stayed away too long this time, and I've a good mind to close the door on you.'

'Oh, well then, I'd best go and never come back.' When he turned away, he winked at Claudia, but she remained stiff-faced.

She sensed the affection between these two, and took an instant dislike to the other woman. 'Don't you dare, you scoundrel!' the old lady cried, plucking at his jacket. When he turned round she opened her arms and he gathered her to him. 'I'm sorry it's been so long,' he told her, 'but I've been kept busy in the City.'

She thrust him away. 'Stocks and shares . . . bonds and money. That's all you men ever think about. Your father was the same. Just the very same! Even as a young man, he could never lower himself to carry a sack of good honest coal.' Her keen eyes caught sight of Claudia. 'And are you going to keep the little lady standing on the doorstep for goodness' sake? Fetch her in. Fetch her in this very minute!'

When they were all seated inside the parlour, Helen informed them, 'I can give you a sherry or a drop of the good stuff, but if you want tea or a bite to eat you'll have to get it yourself because *I'm* certainly not waiting on you.' She chuckled then, telling Richard, 'She's gone again. Up and went without so much as a by your leave. And this time she can stay away.'

'Oh, Aunt Helen! You've dismissed her again, haven't you?'

'And what if I have?'

'You're like a pair of children. The older you get, the worse you get.'

'Huh! I'll thank you to mind your own business, young man.' She turned her attention to Claudia. 'You're much too pretty by far.' There was a certain arrogance about Claudia that put her on her guard.

'Oh, and who would you have me marry, Aunt?' Richard interrupted. 'A plain and uninteresting young woman who might bore me to tears?'

Helen made no immediate answer. Instead she continued to stare at Claudia with the frankness given to old folk. Presently, she asked Richard, 'Bring us some tea, there's a dear.'

'You want to get rid of me, is that it?' he asked with some amusement.

'Something like that.' When he was gone, she spoke to Claudia. 'Do you love him, my dear?'

'Yes, I love him.'

'And would you love him as much if he was poor?'

Claudia knew then she had an enemy in this woman. 'But he isn't poor.'

'If he *was*, would you still want him?'

'Are you implying that I'm marrying Richard for his money?'

'I'm old, my dear, and old folk don't have much time to waste on niceties. I've always spoken my mind and I'm speaking it now. My nephew is a very wealthy man. He's also kind and generous, and easily taken in by a pretty face. I wouldn't like it if you were marrying my nephew for his money. Are you?'

'No. And I resent your questions.'

At that moment, Richard returned with a tray of refreshments which he placed on the low table before his aunt. 'Edna left you well provided for,' he teased. 'If she doesn't come back, it'll serve you right.'

Helen smiled and poured the tea. 'We'll see,' she said. When tea was finished and the small talk was exhausted, the conversation moved on to the wedding arrangements. Helen was all in favour of Richard's marrying from her house. 'Your father and his father before him grew up in this house. They attended the local church. Don't you think it would be fitting if you were wed there?'

It was Claudia who answered. 'Oh, surely not? Richard and I ought to be married in the South.' Turning her large eyes to Richard, she appealed, 'Perhaps in that delightful little church in Ickwell. After all, we mean to make our future there, isn't that so?'

Torn between the two women he loved, Richard was moment-

247

arily flustered until, smiling at Claudia, he said, 'It's your wedding as well, my darling, and if that's what you want?'

She couldn't hide her triumph. 'Oh, it is!' she declared, looking directly at Helen.

She was inwardly seething when Helen sweetly remarked, 'Very well. You win on this occasion, but I do hope you're not going to be the sort of wife who comes between a man and his family.' She looked at Richard. 'You and Alan are the only family I have. I wouldn't want to lose that.'

'And you won't. I'm getting married, not moving to the other side of the world.'

'Sometimes it can be the same.' Her meaningful gaze met Claudia's hard round eyes as she addressed Richard. 'But I won't let your being wed shut me out of your life. I'm not so old and decrepit that I can't travel to Ickwell and see you now and then.' She handed round the biscuits, quietly smiling to herself and knowing that she had successfully ruffled Claudia's fine feathers.

Claudia knew she had met her match. For the remainder of the visit, she smiled and she laughed; she joined in the talk and she appeared to be thoroughly enjoying herself – when in truth she was incensed by this old woman's open hostility towards her. Like all men Richard had not seen it, but it was there all the same.

Like Claudia, Helen Hurd was both cunning and devious. But while one was driven by cruelty and greed, the other was motivated by love of her family. Claudia played her part well. When she and Richard left, the two women embraced each other. 'It's been lovely meeting you,' Claudia lied.

'Look after him,' Helen quietly remarked. 'Or you'll answer to me.' Then she smiled and waved them away.

As the car went slowly up the cobbled street, Claudia glanced back. Helen was standing on the step. The look on her face said it all. I don't like you, and I'll be watching every move you make.

# Chapter Twelve

'Oh, Jenny, I wish I could be bridesmaid.' Katie was seated on the bench beneath the apple tree. Jenny sat beside her, thankful to be out of the house for a while. All morning there had been a steady stream of people going in and out; first the removal men taking the good furniture to the new house, then the men from the warehouse in Olney, collecting the worn furniture Claudia was discarding and which they would sell on at a handsome profit. Now the carpets were being removed and the whole place was in chaos. It was the first Saturday in July, and this was the day when the entire household would move to Ickwell. The wedding was planned and all the arrangements were made. Two weeks from today, Claudia Marshall would become the wife of Richard Hurd, and already she was playing the part, strutting about giving orders and belittling everyone who dared to question her instructions.

'You can't be bridesmaid, sweetheart,' Jenny told the girl. 'But I shouldn't worry about it if I were you, because there'll come a day when you will walk down the aisle in all your finery, with bridesmaids of your very own.'

'And will I have lots of flowers?'

'What! There'll be wagon-loads of 'em!' Jenny put her arm round Katie's shoulders and the two of them imagined the day. 'There'll be flowers everywhere, magnificent garlands draped from the rooftops and posies lining the streets as you pass. They'll be in every corner of the church, and you'll have the biggest, most beautiful bouquet you've ever seen.'

'Bigger than Miss Claudia's?'

'Oh, much bigger.'

'And will I be as beautiful as she is?'

Jenny held the girl away, her soft loving gaze dwelling on Katie's splendid green eyes as she told her softly, 'Real beauty comes from within, and you're already far more beautiful than she could ever be.'

Jenny's words were too profound for the girl to understand, but she sensed the truth in them, and so she was content to snuggle into Jenny's arms and be still for a while.

Here, in the shade of the branches beneath a cornflower blue sky, with the girl in her arms, Jenny cherished the moment. She had much to be thankful for and so she counted her blessings. Today was a mixture of excitement and regret. Soon they would be gone from this house, and Jenny found herself reliving her life here. Before the bad times, there had been contentment and happiness that she would not easily forget. Frank was with her then, and life was wonderful. Now there was Katie, and *she* was Jenny's reason for living.

'Can't say I blame you for hiding out here.' Mr Taylor's voice disturbed them both. 'They've even been in my shed and carted off all my best tools.' He took off his cap and wiped his brow with it. 'You'd 'a thought the buggers would have waited 'til I'd cut the long grass in the orchard. It won't get done now and that's a fact, 'cause I'm not breaking my back to cut it with the shears, I can tell you that!'

'I don't suppose they care about the long grass,' Jenny pointed out. 'Not now we're leaving.' She sat up straight and Katie wandered away. 'Did you go after that job at Nettles Farm?'

His face crumpled into a grin. 'I did!' he said, his chest

rounding with pride. 'And what's more I got it . . . start a week on Monday, that's what they said. It's more pay an' all. Though it needn't be much to better what I get now.'

'That's wonderful.' Jenny was delighted. Suddenly she was overwhelmed by sadness. 'I'll miss you,' she muttered. 'And this house too.'

He was surprised at that. 'Shouldn't have thought you'd miss the house. Especially when you tell me there'll be more servants tekken on at the new place. By! You've had your work cut out here an' no mistake.'

'Oh, I'm not denying that. But I have fond memories all the same.' In her mind's eye she could see the kind face of Elizabeth Marshall. Times were good when she was alive. Then there was Frank. In this house, in that very kitchen, he had courted her. They'd made their plans for the future; a future filled with hopes and dreams, when they would be man and wife and she would raise his children. Though her love for him was as strong as ever, he was gone now, and she had come to accept that.

'I never thought you'd go with *her*.' Mr Taylor sat his cumbersome frame onto the bench and sighed. 'I don't like this heat. It saps a body's strength.' Glancing at her out of the corner of his eye, he went on, 'I know why you're going with her, though.'

'Oh?' Jenny was curious and a little concerned. Had he somehow overheard her and Claudia's conversation with regard to Katie?

'It's 'cause of the girl, ain't it? You can't bear to part company with her, can you, eh? Oh, I don't blame you. I understand, I do. But, well, you should be thinking of yourself and your own future. You're young and pretty, and there's time enough for you to find a husband and have young 'uns of your own.' He chuckled. 'Lord knows the missus was far older than you when she had our last 'un.'

'I've no thoughts of marriage or anything like that, Mr Taylor,'

Jenny was quick to remind him. Even the idea of another man after Frank stabbed at her heart like the point of a knife. She had long ago decided that if she couldn't have him, she wouldn't have anyone.

Mr Taylor was instantly mortified. 'I didn't mean . . . I'm sorry. I completely forgot. Meg told me about your fella, Frank Winfield weren't it?' When she didn't answer, he hung his head. 'You must think me a heartless bugger, but I didn't mean nothing. I can understand how it would take a long time to get over being deserted like that. Though how a man could turn his back on a lovely woman like you, I'll never know.' Realising he was only making things worse, he stood up. 'I'd best get on,' he said sheepishly. 'Or they'll have everything away an' I'll not be able to dig the vegetable patch over.'

With that he ambled away, leaving Jenny with her thoughts. She lay back against the seat and closed her eyes, her mind filling with the image of Frank's handsome laughing face. These days she could let him into her heart and not feel too much pain.

'JENNY! JENNY!' Katie's excited voice caused her to sit up. 'They're here! Mr Hurd's here, and he's got Alan with him.' With that she turned round and ran off again. Jenny followed. Sure enough, the motorcar was already at the house and the boy was scrambling out. Katie caught hold of his hand and the two of them ran off towards the orchard. Jenny called out, but they were gone. 'Little rascals,' she muttered, shaking her head and hoping Claudia hadn't seen them. 'They'll get me hung, drawn and quartered.'

Seeing her approach, Richard Hurd waited for her. He was smiling as he looked towards the spot where the children had disappeared. 'Can't keep them apart, can we, eh?' he said, smiling.

'Miss Claudia wouldn't approve.' Somehow it pleased her to let him know that.

He wasn't surprised though. 'If *you* don't tell her, I won't,' he answered.

Just then two men came out, carrying a large chest between them. As they loaded it on to the horse-drawn wagon, Richard commented light-heartedly, 'Looks like they're removing the family silver.'

'Oh, I should think that went long ago.' In fact Jenny could recall the very day Elizabeth sold it all. That was one of the bad memories.

'Are you looking forward to your new home, you and the child?'

Jenny nodded. 'Very much, thank you, sir.' She was always wary whenever he spoke to her, always fearful that he would see the truth in her eyes – that Katie was really Claudia's child.

'No doubt the domestic arrangements will give you a little more leisure time.' He shook his head slowly as he stared at her in amazement. 'Goodness knows how you kept this old house in shape.'

'It was a labour of love, sir.'

'Hmh.' He glanced towards it. 'Somehow I find that hard to believe. Having seen my future wife in full flow, I think she may have given you a few frantic moments.' The comment was made with a smile, but Jenny got the feeling that he had glimpsed the other side of Claudia.

As though summoned, she came rushing from the house. Her first instructions were to Jenny. 'See that the china from the dining room is properly packed. There are only the best pieces coming with us, but the men are a little ham-fisted and I don't want any breakages.'

'I saw to it earlier, miss. All the china is packed and safe.'

Claudia appeared to be exasperated at this. 'Then go and keep an eye on things! I can't be everywhere.' As Jenny turned away, she pulled her up sharp with another instruction. 'As I'm to be

253

married shortly, you had better get used to addressing me as ma'am.'

Jenny stared at her for a moment, when only the two of them knew what the other was thinking: Jenny silently accusing Claudia of abandoning her child while raising her own status, and Claudia wondering what had been said between Jenny and Richard before she arrived on the scene. 'Come, Richard,' she said, taking him by the arm and propelling him towards the house. 'It's almost all done, and we can soon be on our way.'

He was visibly shocked as he walked through the door. The stairs were haphazardly draped with tapestry curtains and floral cushions. The hallway was scattered from end to end with boxes and bags, bits of furniture and lamp standards, and there was hardly room to walk between. 'Really, Claudia, I still think it would have been better if we'd moved house *after* we were married. It would have been much easier all round. We could have married from here and gone on honeymoon while all of this was taking place.' He waved his arms to indicate the mess all around. 'On our return we could have gone straight into our new home, without any of this.'

'Oh, now, Richard.' She began to pout. 'We've already been through all of this. I didn't want to be married from here, you know that. I want to be married from my new home. Oh, I'm so excited. Please don't spoil it for me.' Linking her arm with his, she nuzzled her face against his neck and he couldn't help but love her.

An hour later, at twelve-thirty, the house was empty. Half an hour after that, Richard and Claudia departed with the boy. While Richard went to collect his brother, Claudia gave Jenny the keys. 'Lock up and take the keys to the agent. He has his instructions and will be discreet. Tell him I'll be in touch, then make your way to Ickwell on the bus. Please be very careful not to tell anyone our new address.' She gave Jenny a knowing look. 'Of course, if you change your mind about coming to Ickwell, I will understand. Send me an address, and I'll make certain you receive payments with regard to our little arrangement,' she said hopefully. Jenny assured her she had not changed her mind and would be along just as soon as her duties were done here.

'I wanted to go with Alan,' Katie said, emerging from the trees where she had stayed until the car was out of sight. Already she was missing her friend. 'Why couldn't we go in the car with them?'

'Because folks like them travel in motorcars, and folks like us go on the bus,' Jenny told her firmly. She was angry and it showed. Katie had every right to go in the car, but she would never know it.

'Are we going soon?'

'There are things to do first.' Jenny wandered round the house with Katie following. 'It's strange to see the place so empty,' she murmured.

Katie took hold of her hand. 'Are you sad?' she asked, gazing up at Jenny's solemn face as they came into what had been Elizabeth's room.

'A little.' Going to the window-seat, Jenny sat down on the bench. All the cushions were gone now, and it was hard and bare. Turning her face to the window she stared out across the gardens. 'Elizabeth Marshall used to sit here,' she explained. 'Oh, she loved to look out of the window, especially on a day like today.'

'Was she pretty?' Katie scrambled up on to the bench where she nestled into Jenny's arms.

She looked at the child and her heart turned over, for she was looking at Elizabeth. It was on the tip of her tongue to say, 'She was your grandmother, and you're the image of her.' Instead, she told the child, 'Do you remember what I said earlier? About beauty coming from inside?' Katie nodded, her green eyes intent on Jenny's face. 'Well, she was beautiful like that.'

Suddenly the memories were too much. Wanting to put as much distance between herself and the house as was humanly possible, Jenny led the girl across the room. Once outside Katie went down the stairs two at a time while Jenny remained by the bedroom door, her eyes roving the room and seeing it the way it was before. The sunlight poured in through the window and picked out a small object lying on the floorboards beside the fireplace. Jenny thought it strange that she hadn't noticed it before.

Going back into the room she picked up the object and was pained to see that it was a picture of Elizabeth; the kind green eyes and the rich auburn hair, the familiar face that was so often lined with worry in the later years. Jenny's fingers traced the contours of those handsome features. 'I never knew my mother, but I would have wanted her to be something like you,' she said softly. 'I've a feeling that Claudia wanted to leave you behind. I can't let her do that.' With a look of determination on her face, she slid the small framed picture into her pocket. That photograph had stood on the mantelpiece in Elizabeth's room for many a year, and whether Claudia liked it or not, Jenny had no intention of letting it be thrown out with the rubbish.

The agent was in a rush. 'Leave the keys with my secretary,' he said, pushing past Jenny at the door. 'You can tell Miss Marshall I believe I've already found a buyer for the lease, and that she should get in touch with me within the week.' With that he hurried away, donning his hat and angrily tapping the pavement with his cane as he quickened his steps towards the bank. 'Never a minute to spare!' he muttered aloud. 'It's one thing after another.'

The young lady behind the desk took the keys and gave Jenny a receipt. 'He's in a bad mood,' she explained. 'He's *always* in a bad mood.' With her bright red lipstick and thick dark lashes, black hair piled high on her head with a scarlet ribbon to hold it in place, it wasn't surprising that Katie should tell Jenny afterwards, 'She looked just like a doll.'

Jenny had already said her goodbyes to the various shopkeepers and could see no point in arousing their curiosity again. 'Are we going on the bus now?' Katie wanted to know, and Jenny lost no time in making her way to the bus-stop, where they boarded the two o'clock bus into Bedford. From there they would catch another, which, if Jenny had planned it right, would take them straight into the village of Ickwell. 'Are you excited?' Katie asked as the bus moved out of Woburn Sands and along the lanes.

'I suppose I am.' With a little shock, Jenny realised that she really was looking forward to making a fresh start, and as far as Katie was concerned, it could only be for the best.

It was four-thirty when Katie and Jenny arrived at the new house. After they had trudged along the lanes from the nearest bus-stop, the two of them stood at the gate, momentarily lost for words. Katie was the first to speak. 'It's like a fairytale castle!' she cried. And Jenny had to agree.

The kitchen was splendid, a large square room with strong wide cupboards that reached from floor to ceiling. It had a huge cooking range which looked as if it had never been used, row upon row of pans and skillets lined the shelves and hung from the walls, and right in the centre of the flag-stoned floor stood a wonderful pine table, spanking new and surrounded by eight ladder-back chairs. The windows were tall and wide and dressed with pretty frilled curtains. The whole room was bathed in soft sunlight. 'Well, do you like your new kitchen?' Richard Hurd had already spoken to Katie out in the garden, and now he stood in the doorway, watching with amusement while Jenny looked around with amazement.

'I've never seen anything like it,' she gasped. 'The kitchen in

Josephine Cox

the old house was nothing like this. It's so *big*, and everything's so new. And it's the right way round to catch the afternoon sun, which is good because if the sun shines in of a morning when you're baking, it can get too hot. And there are no damp patches anywhere to be seen! Twice a year Frank would paint the walls, but the damp always peeled the paint off in no time.' She had been taken aback by this shining kitchen which would be her place of work, and her tongue had run away with her. Now, though, talking of Frank had made her self-conscious and she felt foolish. 'It's lovely, thank you, sir,' she finished lamely.

He remained at the door. 'Frank? Was he before Mr Taylor?'

She quickly nodded and changed the subject. 'Did you see Katie outside, sir?' When he told her that Katie was exploring the grounds with his younger brother, Jenny excused herself. 'I'd best go and fetch her,' she said politely. 'We ain't seen our rooms yet. Matter of fact, I don't even know where they are.'

'I'm sure Miss Marshall will soon put you right,' he assured her. Then he swung away and went off in the direction of the drive where his car was parked. Claudia had sent him on an errand to find her silk scarf, and already he had wasted enough time.

Claudia was not happy at being disturbed. 'What is it now?' she asked, when Jenny was admitted to the drawing room.

'I was wondering where me and Katie would be sleeping, miss?' Claudia's expression stiffened and Jenny remembered. '*ma'am*,' she corrected herself.

'Outside.' Claudia's expression became a cunning smile.

'Beg pardon?'

'You and the girl have been allocated the outhouse. It's quite habitable.'

'I see.'

'There was nothing in our little agreement that said you should be given the best accommodation, and of course it would never do. Besides, what with the new housekeeper and two maids

258

starting on Monday morning, all the rooms in the servants' quarters will be taken.'

Jenny would not be riled. She knew how Claudia was enjoying this, so now when she spoke, she forced herself to sound gracious. 'Thank you . . . ma'am.'

'If that's all, you may go.'

'There is one other thing, ma'am.'

'Yes?'

'The girl needs new shoes.'

For a long moment, Claudia said nothing. She walked to the window and back to the fireplace, seeming deeply agitated. Presently she said through tight lips, 'Don't bother me with such trivialities. I have been giving all of this some thought and I believe the best way by far is to give you a modest increase in wages. No doubt that would settle the problem, and I could leave such matters to you?'

'I understand, ma'am.' In fact Jenny preferred it that way. Although if the 'increase' wasn't enough to pay for Katie's education when the time came, she would not let the matter rest there.

'Then see to it.'

'Am I to have the increase straight away, ma'am? Only Katie has need of a new Sunday best outfit as well.'

'I suppose so.' With her fists clenched tight by her sides and her pale eyes glaring at Jenny, she was visibly trembling. 'Now . . . get out!'

'Can I ask what my specific duties will be here?'

'You will be cook, and as such there will be no need for you to wander the house.'

'And Katie will not be called on to carry out menial duties?'

'I thought we had already agreed on that?' Claudia said peevishly.

'Just making certain, ma'am.' It was Jenny who was enjoying

herself now, and she was determined to wring every last ounce of satisfaction out of Claudia's dilemma. 'I'm sorry if you find my requests trivial and irritating, ma'am, but it was your decision to make your daughter my responsibility, and I wouldn't be doing right by her if I didn't insist on the very best.'

Claudia sprang forward. Gripping Jenny by the shoulders, she said in a low hate-filled whisper, 'Never, *ever* refer to that girl as my daughter.' Her long sharp fingers dug into Jenny's soft flesh, and her pale eyes bulged with anger.

The pain was intense, but Jenny stood firm, 'A slip of the tongue, ma'am,' she calmly lied.

Thrusting Jenny away, Claudia hissed, 'You've got what you came for. Now leave me.'

Undeterred, Jenny asked, 'Will you be wanting dinner?'

'OUT!'

'Very well, ma'am,' Satisfied, Jenny quickly departed. Only when she was outside the room did her smile slip away. Rubbing her shoulders and wincing, she muttered, 'Do what you like, you bugger, but you'll not get the better of me. Not in a month of Sundays, you won't.'

'I don't like it in here.' Katie stood in the centre of the outhouse, her anxious eyes staring round the bare stone walls. The main room was L-shaped, with only two tiny windows and a huge open fireplace where the wind echoed and whistled, singing a sorry lament. The floor was paved with cold grey slabs that resembled gravestones, and the only furniture to be seen was a monstrous wardrobe with bulbous feet, a wide ugly chest of drawers, and two narrow iron beds. The heavy oak door was warped with age and daylight could be seen through the cracks. 'Why can't we live upstairs with the other servants?' Katie wanted to know.

Sitting down on the bed, which was covered with a flimsy floral eiderdown, Jenny shivered. 'Because there's no room,' she explained. '*That*'s why not.' She also had been shocked by the condition of the outhouse, though she tried not to show her disappointment in front of Katie.

'Well, I won't live here. It's awful!' Katie swung away in tears.

'Katie.' Jenny got off the bed and waylaid her. 'We *have* to live here, in this place,' she said firmly. 'And the sooner we get used to it the better.'

'But it's *awful*!' She was sobbing now, angrily resisting Jenny's restraining hand.

'Come here, sweetheart.' She drew the girl towards the bed and sat her down. 'If I made a real fuss, I expect I could get Miss Marshall to find you a little room upstairs somewhere.' When Katie looked up with a brighter face, she went on, 'Only I won't be close by.'

The brightness dimmed. 'Why not?'

'Because I'm going to stay here. I intend to make this place really cosy.' Besides, she didn't want to give Claudia the satisfaction of knowing she'd succeeded in upsetting the two of them.

Katie wiped her eyes. 'How can you make it cosy?'

'You'll see.'

'Can we have rugs on the floor?'

'You and I can make some pretty peg rugs, if you like.'

'And flowery cushions, and frilly curtains?' Katie was smiling now, beginning to see the outhouse through Jenny's eyes.

'We'll make them as well.'

'Can we make some new eiderdowns, and have a fire in the grate when it's cold?'

''Course we can, sweetheart. By the time we've finished, the other servants will wish *they* could live here.'

Katie's green eyes grew wide with concern. 'We won't let them though, will we?'

Jenny laughed and hugged the small figure to her breast. 'I thought you wanted to move upstairs?' she teased.

'I never!' Katie was horrified.

'Does that mean you want to stay here with me?'

'I always want to stay with you, Jenny.'

'That's settled then.'

'When can we start making all the things?'

'We'll go to Bedford market next Saturday . . . that's when I get my next wages, and we'll make for the draper's stall. They're bound to have all manner of odd squares for the eiderdown and different coloured rag pieces for the rugs.'

'Can I help to choose the colours?'

'I don't see why not.'

'What if the market doesn't have a rag stall?'

'*All* markets have a rag stall.'

'Oh, but, Jenny, we won't have time to make everything because we have to work in the house like before, and this house is bigger.'

Jenny told her then how the other servants would relieve them of so many of their old duties. 'I'm to cook, and you're free to be just a little girl.'

'I can still help you though, can't I?'

'If you really want to.' Anticipating Katie's next question, and not wanting the girl to know how this change of circumstance had come about, she quickly added, 'When we go to the market, we'll get you some new shoes and a best frock. And we'll get you some books off the bookstall. It would be grand if you could read a little by the time you go to school.'

'It's not my birthday.'

'It doesn't have to be your birthday for you to have nice things. It's just time that you did, that's all.'

'I love you, Jenny.' Katie gazed up adoringly into her pretty face.

'I know,' she whispered, holding her close. 'I love you too, sweetheart.' Gently shaking her, she said firmly, 'Now then, which do you want to do first . . . wash the windows or sweep the floor?' Though she was delighted that Katie didn't have to do these things by order any more, it was true that a little hard work never hurt anyone.

Jenny brought a bucket of water and Katie carried the broom. In no time at all, the dust was flying. The chest of drawers was polished and proud, then the eiderdowns were shaken and fluffed up. With Elizabeth's picture taking pride of place on the mantelpiece, it didn't look so grim any more. Next, the windows were washed and buffed to a shine. Jenny 'borrowed' the curtains from the kitchen and hung them up. 'When we get our own, we'll put them back and nobody will ever know,' she said. Katie laughed. Already the cold outhouse was beginning to look like home.

The days flew by. On Saturday, the two of them went into Bedford on the bus. The market was large and colourful, with vendors drowning each other's shouts, and everything they wanted was there.

Afterwards they fed the ducks on the river and began their way home, weary and contented. Jenny had a book for Katie in her pocket, and a bag full of rags tucked securely under her arm. Katie proudly carried her new frock and smart black shoes. When they got home, Jenny put the clothes in the big wardrobe. 'We'll keep them for the wedding,' she told the girl. Katie didn't mind, because she was too enthralled with her new picture book. It had wonderful drawings of animals and rows of big red words beneath each picture. 'Teach me what they say,' she entreated, and Jenny promised she would.

The following Friday, the household staff was assembled and lined up in the hallway. 'The mistress wants to address us,' the housekeeper said in a crisp authoritative voice that put the fear of God in some of them.

They made an odd assembly. There was Miss Clayton the housekeeper, a small scrag of a woman with hook nose and high forehead but the voice of a sergeant major. Alice Taddle was the scullery maid and general runabout, a long thin soul with big droopy eyes and a lost look. She was a total contrast to Margaret Pearce the parlour maid who was a smart little thing with an upright figure and highly polished black patent shoes. Next came Ted Chivers, a portly brown-haired man of middle age who would serve as chauffeur and handyman. There was talk of more servants joining the ranks as soon as the mistress had organised herself properly, and Jenny for one was not surprised. Claudia Marshall, soon to be Mrs Richard Hurd, was made for pampering.

Jenny and Katie stood at the end of the line. They were each well scrubbed and properly presented, though Jenny had not allowed Katie to wear her new clothes. 'You're not a skivvy like the rest of us,' she told the girl. 'By rights you shouldn't even be in the line up at all.' But Katie had argued that she wanted to be there. 'With you,' she declared, and Jenny didn't see the harm in that. Besides, it wouldn't hurt to remind 'Her Majesty' of the fact that she had a daughter, and with it a responsibility that wasn't that easy to shed.

So there they all were, six people of lesser means, born to serve others more fortunate. The air bristled with anticipation as they waited, stiff-backed and straightfaced, dreading the experience to come.

When Claudia arrived some moments later, it was with a flourish and an arrogance that made them tremble. Slowly and deliberately she walked along the line, her pale eyes scouring their appearance, coolly examining each and every one, searching for the smallest reason to whip these willing workers with her spiteful tongue. But Miss Clayton knew her job, and she had already examined her staff with even sharper eyes for she knew that any shortcoming would fall on her shoulders first.

Claudia walked along the line twice more. She never went as far as her own daughter. Instead, each time she quickly glanced at Jenny's impassive face and sharply turned away. Finally she addressed the housekeeper. 'Very good. You may set them about their work,' she ordered. 'Mr Hurd should be back from town shortly. Arrange dinner for eight-thirty, I think.' Without a backward glance she hurried away, leaving a wave of relief in her wake.

Soon the house was bustling with activity. Now that the awful preliminaries were over, everyone settled into their own routine. Though it was late afternoon, the day had been taken up with arranging the house to Claudia's liking. Precious time had been lost, and there was still a great deal to be done. Jenny took to the kitchen and began her day's baking. She was Cook now, holding an immense responsibility, and with more mouths than ever to feed.

'There's eight folks to cook for now,' she groaned anxiously to Katie. 'I've never looked after that many before.'

Katie wasn't a bit concerned. 'Don't worry,' she said grandly, climbing on to the chair where she reached across the table and picked up a long wooden spoon. 'Everybody will love your cooking.'

Tipping the currants into the flour, Jenny pushed the bowl towards the girl. 'If you say so,' she chuckled.

'Well, *I* like it, and so does Alan!' she declared. After vigorously stirring the currants until they were half buried beneath the flour, she paused a moment, counting the fingers on her hand and looking up at Jenny with a puzzled frown. 'You counted wrong, Jenny.'

'Oh?'

'You said there were *eight* people, and there are nine. See.'

She held up her hands, slowly counting the fingers and saying in a firm voice, 'You and me. Miss Marshall and Mr Hurd, the housekeeper woman and Alice Twaddle . . .'

'*Taddle*,' Jenny corrected. 'Alice *Taddle*.'

Katie went on, 'Alice Traddle. Then the other lady, and the man who's going to do all the jobs like Mr Taylor. Nine,' she affirmed, holding up her hands, with one small thumb bent down. 'That's *nine*, Jenny.' Her face broke into an impish grin, ' 'Cause you forgot Alan.'

'I didn't forget.' Since she had learned that young Master Hurd would be away at boarding school for most of the year, Jenny had been waiting for the right moment to tell Katie. 'He won't be here very often after the wedding, sweetheart. He's going away to school. A boarding school somewhere near London.'

'What's a boarding school?'

'Well, it's a place where young men are educated, but for most of the year it's their home as well.' Seeing Katie's downcast face, she added brightly, 'He'll probably be allowed home on holidays and some weekends.'

Katie's green eyes softened with tears. 'Why can't he go to the same school as me?'

'Because he's the son of a wealthy man, and wealthy families always send their children away to be educated.'

'What if he doesn't want to go?'

Jenny collected the milk from the pantry, using the moments to calculate her answer. 'I don't reckon it would make any difference.'

'But that's not fair.'

Jenny smiled wistfully. 'Not much in life *is* fair. You'll find that out as you grow up.'

Climbing down from the table, Katie said quietly, 'Can I go out to play? Happen Alan's back.'

'If you like, sweetheart.' It was plain to see that the news was a great disappointment to the girl.

'Jenny?'

'Yes?'

'I will see him sometimes, won't I?'

She nodded, her smile reaching out to the child, ''Course you will.'

'Alan said his Aunt Helen's coming to the wedding. He said she's very funny and he loves her a lot. When's she coming, Jenny?'

She tutted and sighed, then shook her head and told Katie, 'That's *ten* mouths to feed. I'd forgotten all about the aunt, and she's supposed to be arriving any day now. Honest to God, I won't be sorry when this wedding's over and we can get back to a proper routine.'

'Have I got an aunt?'

'Not that I know of, sweetheart.'

'Will Alan's aunt tell Mr Hurd not to send him away to school?'

'I wouldn't count on it.'

One question led to another, but this time Jenny was not prepared. 'Jenny?'

'What now, sweetheart?'

'Has Alan got a daddy?'

'No. He died.'

'Have *I* got a "daddy"?'

She felt the colour drain from her face. 'Of course you have, sweetheart.' The words found their way out past the painful lump that blocked her throat. She was actually trembling as she waited for the next inevitable question.

'Where is he then?' The girl threw her arms out in a gesture of frustration. 'Why hasn't my daddy come to see me?'

Lost for a moment, Jenny gazed at that small familiar face, a face that looked up at her with such trust. What could she say? How in God's name could she explain that Katie's daddy had gone away, and she had no idea where he was? Worse, how was she to tell of the circumstances that had given the child to her? The fleeting thought that she might lose Katie was overpowering.

Knowing that she would have to give some sort of answer, Jenny took a deep breath, wiped her hands on her pinnie and went reluctantly to the child. 'Katie . . .' she began. Her heart leapt within her when another child's voice sailed into the kitchen from the outer yard. 'KATIE! WHERE ARE YOU, KATIE?'

Her face lit up. 'It's him!' she cried. 'It's Alan.' And she ran out to meet him.

'Thank you, Lord,' Jenny murmured on a great sigh of gratitude. She watched the children laughing together, and her emotions were a mixture of fear and relief. For the moment anyhow Katie's questions were stilled. 'But she'll not forget now. She'll want to know, and I'd best be ready with the right answers.' The problem of Katie would not easily be settled. But she had no option. She must take her courage in her hands and talk to the girl. Somehow, she had to deal with those questions that as yet had gone unanswered, 'Well, Jenny girl,' she told herself, 'you knew the day would come, and here it is, God help you!'

The new maids were quick and efficient, making Jenny's job so much easier. Dinner was served and eaten by nine. The boy was sent to wash and go to his bed, while Claudia and Richard retired to the drawing room where they discussed the forthcoming wedding. When the dining table was cleared and the room left in an orderly fashion, the servants gathered in the kitchen to sit around the table and enjoy the last meal of the day. 'Can't say I think much of *her*,' Margaret Pearce remarked. 'She's got a real sour face on her an' no mistake.'

'Don't make quick decisions,' Miss Clayton warned. 'And

don't be so free with your opinions or you'll soon find yourself in hot water.'

'She's right though, ain't she?' Alice Taddle said. 'I were trembling all over when she stared at me like that. If there'd been a hole in the floor I'd 'a gladly dropped through it to get away from her.' She dipped a chunk of crusty bread into her soup and sucked at it noisily until Miss Clayton glared at her, when she quickly took up her spoon and daintily scooped it into the bowl. 'Anyroad, I don't reckon it'll be easy working for that one,' she insisted sullenly. 'She's a right madam.'

Margaret Pearce gave Jenny a curious look. 'You've been with the family a long time, haven't you?'

'Yes.' Not wanting to be drawn into a revealing conversation, Jenny added quietly, 'Like Miss Clayton, I don't think it's wise to tittle-tattle.'

Margaret Pearce was not so easily dissuaded. 'You don't like her either, do you?' she insisted.

Miss Clayton intervened. 'Whether we like her or not makes no difference. We're all here to do a job, and as long as we're paid for it, that's really all that matters.' Noticing that everyone had finished their soup, she addressed Alice. 'Take the bowls away.' At once the young woman scurried about doing as she was bid.

Jenny sliced the pork on to each plate, which was then passed round the table. Next came the peas and carrots, and the small round baked potatoes. 'My, that looks delicious,' remarked Miss Clayton, carefully tipping the gravy boat over her plate, until the smooth brown liquid coated the thinly sliced pork and dripped over the mounds of vegetables. 'You're certainly a good cook, I'll give you that.'

In between enjoying the splendid meal and a smattering of conversation, it wasn't long before the wedding itself was discussed. When the housekeeper confirmed that the newly weds planned to leave straight after the reception for a long honeymoon in Europe, Margaret Pearce commented with a sigh, 'Well, at least we'll be left alone for a while, thank goodness.'

Miss Clayton was the first to excuse herself. 'I'll just pop in and make sure the boy is comfortable.'

'Now, *he's* a nice little soul,' Alice said.

'Friendly and polite,' agreed Margaret. 'Not like *her* at all.'

Jenny said nothing. Instead, she recruited Alice to help with the clearing away. Throughout the meal, Katie had been very quiet and thoughtful, and Jenny wondered whether she was thinking about her 'daddy'. She knew what had to be done, and she dreaded it. 'Do you want to put the plates away?' she asked her.

But Katie was in a world of her own. 'Can I do it tomorrow instead?' she asked with a sad little face.

''Course you can, sweetheart.' Jenny was concerned about her. 'You're all right, aren't you? I mean . . . you don't feel poorly?' It was so unusual for Katie not to want to help.

'No, I'm not poorly.'

'All right then. Off you go, and I'll be in shortly.'

In fact it was ten-thirty by the time Jenny came into the outhouse. She was bone tired and ready to drop straight into her bed. Katie was curled up on the settee, waiting. 'I don't want him to go away,' she murmured, and her eyes were red from crying.

Jenny took the pathetic little figure into her arms. 'Oh, Katie, what are we going to do with you, eh? Like I say, no doubt the boy will be home from time to time. You'll see him then, I expect.'

'But I'll miss him, Jenny.' Soulful green eyes shone in the lamplight. She was so unhappy.

Jenny recalled Claudia's warning about Katie staying away from the boy, and knew she must be cruel to be kind. 'Katie, you must listen to me. It's not good for you to get so attached to Alan.'

'Why not?'

'Because the two of you are always destined to go your separate ways, him to a posh boarding school, and afterwards maybe to work in the City, or even to go abroad. As for you, well, you'll go to the local school, and then who knows? Happen you'll work in an office, or God willing maybe even become a teacher yourself. Whatever you do, you've the brains and looks to make a better life than I have.' All the old regrets came creeping back, and she thought of Frank and what might have been. Mentally shaking herself, she went on, 'You mustn't think too much of the boy, Katie. When you get to school, you'll make lots of new friends. Girls and boys of your own kind. And you'll have so much to occupy your mind. Oh, Katie, it'll be so exciting.'

Like the child she was, Katie quickly brightened. 'They'll have all kinds of books there, won't they, Jenny?'

'You'll be that busy you won't know which way to turn. You'll be reading and writing and drawing. Learning all manner of things. Before you know it, the teacher will be telling me how well you're getting on. And, oh, I'll be that proud!' Now that the girl seemed less unhappy, Jenny got the bowl and water ready, and Katie was soon washed and ready for bed. 'Tired are you?' she asked when Katie gave a big yawn. The girl's answer was a weary little nod. 'Right. Into bed with you.' Jenny had prepared herself to broach the subject of Katie's 'daddy'. Instead, she was immensely thankful that the whole episode appeared to have gone from Katie's mind. It was obvious the child had been more concerned with losing the boy's precious friendship, and somehow Jenny found that equally disturbing because, one way or another, Claudia Marshall's little outcast seemed to be heading for a deal of heartache.

Satisfied that Katie was sleeping at last, Jenny took off her own clothes and washed from top to bottom. The feel of the cold water splashing against her skin was refreshing, 'Well, at least I passed the test today,' she told herself. 'It's the first time I've cooked for so many folk, and they polished their plates, every one.' She felt very pleased with herself.

Someone else not too far away also felt very pleased with herself. 'Don't be silly, Richard, the boy can't hear you. I was careful to put him at the far end of the house, close to the servants, where Miss Clayton can keep an eye on him.' Taking off her silken robe, Claudia threw it on to the chair where it slithered to the floor. 'And anyway, would it matter if he *did* hear us?'

He watched her saunter to the bed where she lay down, with legs slightly apart and her mouth open in an enticing half-smile. 'You're very beautiful,' he murmured, coming closer.

'Do you want me?'

'What do you think?' His voice was hoarse. His passion was roused. But still he made no attempt to discard his clothing.

'Take me then.' Her lips parted wider as she slid her legs further apart. Her long slender fingers reached down to stroke the fuzz of dark hair between her thighs. 'Don't tease me,' she whispered. 'I don't like it when you tease me.'

He smiled. 'Would I tease you?' His hands moved in the shadows. First his waistcoat fell, then his trousers. As he knelt on the bed, Claudia tore at his shirt. There was no tenderness, no romance or soft endearments as she stripped his clothes away. Her appetite was insatiable. She was hungry for him, impatient to feel his swollen member inside her, probing, thrilling. Compared to her other lovers, she thought Richard Hurd poorly endowed. Angrily she drew him to her, curving her slim form until it was one with his. Aching with her desperate need of him, she clung to him, digging her fists into his back, scoring his bare flesh with her long nails as he fought to fulfil her. How was he to know that one man had never been enough to satisfy her? As he drove into her, frantic with passion and incensed by her wildness, she secretly longed for the days when she hunted her lovers at will. But that day would return, she promised herself that. And looked forward to it with great excitement.

As she lay beneath him, her naked body striving to meet his every move, there crept into her heart a feeling of hatred. He was too caring, too gentle with her, much too considerate. Richard Hurd could never satisfy this deep longing in her. She thought of all the men she had coupled with, and one in particular rose in her warped and evil mind. Frank Winfield had been all kinds of man. Only now did she curse herself for having let him go.

It was the day before the wedding. Claudia had been up since the early hours and now she was ensconced in her room with the dresser. Her abuse could be heard all over the house. 'STUPID WOMAN! How can you possibly expect me to hold a bouquet against my gown? Can't you see it's bound to stain?'

The servants had been run off their feet since early light, and the atmosphere was fraught with anxiety. Only Jenny was calm and collected. 'That's because I don't give a fig whether she walks down the aisle or whether she don't,' she told Miss Clayton, who herself was worn to a frazzle by Claudia's constant demands.

'To tell you the truth, I'm beginning to feel that way myself,' the housekeeper admitted. 'I can honestly say I've never worked for such a sour-tempered and selfish little madam in the whole of my career.' She gratefully accepted the cup of tea which Jenny offered. 'Though of course it wouldn't do if the other servants were to hear how I feel,' she warned, seating herself at the table. 'I am the housekeeper after all, and as such I'm expected to set an example.' She was red in the face and upset at the way she had been treated. 'She's rude and arrogant, and there's no graciousness about her at all,' she moaned. 'I can't think why such a nice gentleman as Mr Hurd would want to marry a woman like that.'

Jenny smiled at that remark. 'He loves her, that's why,' she

Josephine Cox

said, seating herself opposite and sipping at her tea. 'Love makes fools of us all.'

Miss Clayton raised her eyebrows. 'It sounds as though you're speaking from experience?'

'You could say that.' There was a sadness in Jenny's heart, and it showed in her voice.

'Do you want to talk about it?'

'Better not,' Jenny replied. She was not ungrateful but: 'Some things are best left alone. And anyway, it happened a long time ago.' She couldn't believe what she was saying. 'Do you know?' she remarked with astonishment. 'You're the very first person I've ever admitted it to.'

'I had a bad experience too . . . left waiting in the church I was. Later I heard he'd gone off and joined up as a sailor on some merchant ship. Of course I never married after that.' Miss Clayton drained the last of her tea and put the cup down gently. 'Anyway, none of it matters now because he's been dead these many years.'

'I'm sorry.' Jenny didn't know what else to say. In the weeks they had known each other, she had taken a shine to this woman and was genuinely concerned for her.

Miss Clayton shook her head decisively. 'Don't be.' She looked at Jenny and her voice was softer as she asked, 'This young man?' She paused. 'Do you still love him?'

At first Jenny shrank from answering such a question. But before she could stop them, the words fell from her lips. 'Yes. I still love him very much.' Shocked by her own revelation, and before the other woman could ask anything else, she scraped the chair back and stood up. 'Hear that? It's the motor vehicle. Mr Hurd must be back with his aunt.' She hurried to the window. 'Good heavens, it's them!'

Miss Clayton joined her there, and the two of them peered out of the window. Richard Hurd opened the door for his aunt and she stepped out of the car, a small elegant figure with bent

274

shoulders and snow white hair rolled into a fluffy halo about her head. She smiled at her nephew and said something. He appeared to argue, but when she shook her silver-handled stick at him, he bent to kiss her and afterwards reached inside the car for her portmanteau. He appealed to her once more, but she made a grim face and so he left her.

'Hmh!' Jenny laughed aloud. 'Looks like she's a feisty old bugger. Seems to me he wanted to take her straight inside, and she was having none of it.'

'You're right, and look, she's off exploring already. Well, I'll be blowed! She's come a long way, and she's bound to be weary, but by the look of it, she'll not be ordered about.'

Jenny watched as the small bent figure headed towards the orchard. 'I think she's wonderful,' she said with a rush of admiration. 'I hope *I'm* as sprightly as her when I'm a great age.'

Miss Clayton clicked her tongue and moved away from the window. 'No doubt I'll be needed, so I'd best be on my way.' She went quickly from the room and Jenny returned to her baking. 'I hope Helen Hurd doesn't come bothering *me*,' she muttered, rolling up her sleeves and kneading the dough with the point of her knuckles. 'I've enough to cope with, and that one looks to be a right old tartar.'

'So *this* is the famous Katie, is it?' Helen Hurd was hardly out of the car before Alan ran to meet her, and holding fast to his hand was Katie.

'She's my very best friend,' he said proudly.

The old lady gazed long at the child, and was strangely astonished at her beauty; at the perfectly chiselled features and rich auburn tresses that sprang from her head in deep waves, culminating about her face in a multitude of wispy ringlets. Large green eyes stared up at her, shining with a brightness that came from within. 'My! She's certainly pretty.'

275

The boy was delighted. 'I told you, didn't I, Aunt Helen?' he chuckled, shaking Katie's hand and reassuring her with a special look. 'I *said* she was pretty.'

Katie took an instant shine to the old lady. 'Do you want to see where I live?' she asked.

'Well now, that's very kind, my dear, but I'm sure your mammy won't want an old biddy like me poking about.'

Alan reminded her. 'No, Aunt. Don't you remember? Katie hasn't got a mammy.'

'But I've got Jenny, and I've got a daddy too,' Katie interrupted brightly. Her mood changed suddenly. 'Only I don't know where my daddy is.'

Realising she had touched on a delicate matter, Helen Hurd was quick to make amends. 'From what Alan tells me, your Jenny is both mammy *and* daddy to you?'

'I love her,' came the simple reply.

'Well, of course you do.' The old lady's curiosity was re-kindled. She had heard about Jenny from Richard, and he had nothing but good things to say about her. 'If you're sure she won't mind, then yes, I would love to see where you live,' she told Katie.

When the children led her towards the outhouse she was surprised but said nothing. If she found anything to complain about, she would take it up later with Richard and his intended. It seemed to her, though, that it was hardly correct to put a child in an outhouse.

'See?' Katie flung open the door and Helen stepped inside. 'This is our own little house . . . mine and Jenny's.' She was very proud.

Alan followed his aunt in and closed the door behind them. 'It was horrid at first,' he interrupted. 'Cold and horrid. The walls were wet and the wind blew in through the cracks in the door.'

Katie continued, 'There weren't no curtains and the bedclothes were all scruffy.' She chuckled and put her hand over her mouth as though to stifle the secret she was bursting to tell. But it popped out anyway. 'We borrowed the kitchen curtains . . . but we put them back when Jenny made ours. She made the cushions too, and new eiderdowns . . . and I helped to make that peg rug.' Excitedly, she pointed to the colourful rug on the floor. 'Isn't it pretty? Oh, Aunt Helen, don't you think our little house is wonderful?'

Amused at being addressed by the girl as 'Aunt Helen', the old lady felt no need to correct her. 'I must say, you and your Jenny have done a wonderful job. What? I wouldn't mind living here myself.'

Katie was thrilled. 'You can if you want. But you'll have to fetch your own bed, 'cause we've only got one each.'

The old lady laughed aloud. 'Bless your heart, child,' she said, 'I'd only be a cuckoo in the nest. And besides, I have my own little house in the North. I have a friend too . . . just like you have your Jenny.'

Alan was astonished. 'But you keep throwing her out!'

Helen winked cheekily. 'Only when she deserves it. It pays to let her know who's boss, and she always comes back, so there's no harm done.' She passed her hand over her eyes for a moment.

'Are you all right, Aunt?' Alan slid his hand into hers.

'I'm fine,' she assured him. 'Just a little tired, I think. Perhaps you had better take me to the house.'

The three of them went towards the house together. The children walked either side of the old lady, Katie holding her left hand and Alan holding her right. He carried her silver-topped walking stick under his arm. 'I won't fall over if you let go of me,' she said fondly. 'I'm quite capable, you know, although Richard might be right, I do tend to forget how old I am.'

'Are you *very* old?' Katie wanted to know.

'Older than Methuselah.'

'Who's Methuselah?' This time it was Alan's curiosity that was aroused.

The three of them continued chatting and laughing and enjoying each other's company. But the enjoyment was cruelly curtailed as they approached the house and Claudia appeared at the door. Instantly her frosty gaze fell on Katie, and her meaning was unmistakable.

The girl slowed her pace, causing the other two to do the same. 'What's the matter, child?' The old lady had seen the frightened look on Katie's face and she was intrigued. She tugged at Katie's hand, urging her to continue, but was even more curious when the girl stiffened and began backing away. In a moment she had taken to her heels and was running away towards the outhouse. 'Whatever's the matter with the child?' The old lady had sensed Katie's fear and was deeply troubled.

It was Claudia who answered. 'The girl is a born troublemaker,' she said haughtily. 'I've had occasion to punish her in the past, and like all children she doesn't easily forget.' Knowing that Richard was watching from the drawing-room window, she reluctantly linked her arm with that of the old lady, but was inwardly fuming when her offer was quickly rejected. 'I'm quite able to walk without assistance, thank you,' she was sharply reminded. The incident was another wedge between Helen and the woman who was about to marry her nephew; a woman whom she disliked immensely.

Richard was full of plans. Over a cup of tea and some of Jenny's best ham sandwiches, he outlined them to his aunt. 'Before Alan comes in from the garden, I should tell you . . . Claudia thinks it might be a good idea if he went back with you after the wedding,' he revealed. 'Although I'm not so sure. He loves it here, and because it won't be too long before he leaves for school, I thought perhaps he could stay here . . . but only of course, if you're not in a great hurry to return home?'

'What? You want me to remain here, to take care of Alan, until you return from your honeymoon? Is that what you're saying?'

'That's the idea.'

'Then why don't you come right out and say so?' She tutted. 'You should know by now that I have no time for people who beat about the bush. Say what you mean, that's the way!' She frowned at him, but her deepest scowl was for Claudia. 'Whose idea was it to pack the boy off to boarding school anyhow?'

'It's the best place for him,' Claudia snapped. 'There's nothing here to keep him occupied, and already he's struck up a friendship with a servant's child. You saw that for yourself. In fact, you seemed to be actively encouraging it.'

'They're just children. What does it matter whether they're servants or masters?'

'I'm shocked to hear you say such a thing.'

'When you get to my age, you'll find that you are not so easily shocked. As far as I can see, the children enjoy each other's company. What possible harm can there be in that?'

Claudia was trembling with anger. 'A great deal of harm as I see it. The boy comes of good stock, he's well mannered and cultivated, a different class altogether. The girl, on the other hand, is from the servants' hall. She's common and ill-spoken. You can't imagine the trouble I have keeping them apart. No! I will not allow it.'

'If you feel that strongly, why don't you dismiss the woman? If the woman goes, the child goes too, isn't that so?' Helen was testing her. There was something very odd here, she thought.

Flustered, Claudia was momentarily lost for an answer, then she said quietly, 'The woman would be hard to replace. In spite of her personal shortcomings, she's a good worker and easily satisfied. Servants of that ilk are hard to come by.'

'What is the girl to her?'

279

'I don't pry into such matters.'

'All the same, you strongly object to her?'

'Of course I object, though I do believe she is beginning to know her place. As long as she stays clear of her betters, I suppose I can tolerate her presence here.'

'Isn't that rather harsh, my dear?' Richard had remained silent throughout this exchange, but he was compelled to remark on Claudia's last words. 'As far as I can see, the girl has caused no trouble.'

'You don't know her. She's a born troublemaker, and I have to watch her all the while. As I say, the sooner your brother goes to boarding school, the better.'

Helen asserted herself. 'To my mind, it's unnatural to send a child away to school.' She addressed herself to Richard, 'Your grandfather would never have dreamed of such a thing.'

'Times change, Aunt, and I don't have to remind you that as soon as I was old enough, our father did not hesitate to send me away to boarding school. I know he would have wanted the same for Alan.'

'More's the pity!' she remarked harshly. Something about the girl and her fear of Claudia had stirred her interest. 'I *will* remain here and look after Alan, if that's what you want, Richard. Though I can't pretend I will be as vigilant as Claudia with regard to the children.' She smiled sweetly. 'Now, what about this wedding? What part am I to play in it?'

Conversation quickened as they talked about the forthcoming event. Richard eagerly outlined the details, and Helen listened attentively. Claudia quietly brooded and spoke only when she was spoken to, bitterly resenting the old lady's remarkable influence over her nephew. Once she was married, Claudia meant to weaken their alliance and rid herself of the old biddy once and for all.

* * *

280

The wedding of Claudia Marshall and Richard Hurd was a splendid affair. People lined the streets to get a glimpse of them, he in his tails and top hat and she resplendent in a shimmering white gown with a coronet of orchids and a satin train that fanned out behind her like a peacock's tail. Some said they looked like the couple on top of a wedding cake, and others tearfully remarked that they were: 'Just like royalty.'

From the back of the church, Helen Hurd dutifully followed the proceedings. She was proud of young Alan, attentive and handsome in his best bib and tucker, and she saw how incredibly happy her elder nephew seemed as he stood beside Claudia, reverently taking his vows and quietly smiling at his future wife. The occasion was solemn and magnificent, and it should have been so right. Yet there was something about the union of this man and woman that was deeply wrong. As she watched, Helen's instincts told her that while the man adored the woman, she had little feeling for him. She was a cold and calculating creature, seeing only the money and power which she had long craved and which were now within her reach.

Suppressing her suspicions, the old lady attended the service smilingly. No one would ever have guessed her apprehension.

Seated in the back row with the other servants, Jenny followed the ceremony with great interest. Her thoughts were much akin to the old lady's, yet, in spite of her misgivings, she hoped for Richard Hurd's sake that Claudia would be the wife he wanted her to be. Certainly, she looked very beautiful, with her slim figure and gracious manner, and those pale eyes that now looked up at him with a measure of affection. Oh, yes, she *looked* the part, Jenny thought bitterly. The wrapping was perfect, but the person beneath was shamefully soiled.

'Look, they're coming down the aisle!' Katie had been in a state of excitement since first light. Now, as Claudia and her new husband passed the pew where Jenny and the girl stood, Claudia's hard glance sought her small daughter's face. She gave a half smile, but it was not the loving smile of a mother for her child. Instead it was a sly, forbidding grimace that made the girl shrink from her. 'I'm glad I wasn't bridesmaid,' Katie whispered, clinging to Jenny's hand. 'She frightens me.'

'Shh.' Jenny warned. The organ was playing and people were beginning to file out behind the bride and groom. 'You're not to say things like that, sweetheart.'

Jenny led the girl out into the sunshine where the two of them waited side by side until the newly weds had driven away in the car. Jenny was lost in her own troubled thoughts when Katie's voice spoke up. 'It's true, Jenny, I'm really glad I wasn't the bridesmaid because she takes Alan away from me when we're out in the garden.' When she looked up at Jenny now, her green eyes glinted with defiance. 'I don't like her,' she said harshly. 'She's a very bad person!'

Before Jenny could chide her another voice spoke. It was Helen Hurd. Addressing Katie, she said kindly, 'Well, she won't be here for a while, will she, my dear? So how would you like to walk in front with Alan while I talk to Jenny here?'

The children didn't need any encouragement. Soon they were running ahead, laughing and chattering. Much to the astonishment of the other servants who were already climbing into the horse-drawn cart, the old lady and Jenny walked slowly behind. 'I'm of the same mind as the girl,' Helen confided. 'I don't like her either.'

Embarrassed and uncertain about this grand old lady, Jenny merely answered, 'Katie didn't really mean what she said. She blurts things out without thinking, I'm afraid.'

'You mean she speaks her mind.' Helen smiled at Jenny, and there was friendship in her smile. 'You know what they say, don't you?'

'What's that, ma'am?'

'Out of the mouths of babes . . . the truth. The girl was only telling the truth. It seems she has seen what I saw from the first, and she's right. Claudia Marshall, sadly now Claudia Hurd, really *is* a very bad person.' She came to a halt. Regarding Jenny with inquisitive eyes, she remarked, 'I'm given to understand that you have been with the family a long time?'

'Yes, ma'am.'

'You knew her parents?'

'I knew her mother. The master was away for long periods of time.'

'I know of him. My own brother served with Mr Marshall in the forces.' A look of sorrow dimmed her eyes. 'War is a terrible thing, my dear,' she said softly. 'Like your late master, my brother was deeply affected by the shocking things he witnessed. Fortunately he found some sort of order in his life afterwards, while it seems Mr Marshall did not?' She waited for Jenny to confirm this, but was not surprised when she lowered her gaze and remained silent. Walking on, Helen waited for Jenny to do the same before continuing, 'The mother. What was she like?'

'A lady,' Jenny answered simply. 'Mrs Marshall was a real lady . . . fair and kind. Dignified too. When news came of the master's death, she just knuckled down and got on with looking after everything. It wasn't easy.' Jenny thought of how Claudia had made Elizabeth's life unbearable, and could hardly contain herself. 'Yes, ma'am, she was a real lady, that's what she was.'

'Not like her daughter then?'

At once Jenny was on her guard. 'If you say so, ma'am,' she answered.

'Do *you* say so?'

Jenny's breathing quickened. She knew little of this woman, and so she must be very careful what she said. 'It doesn't matter what I think, ma'am,' she said. 'All I know is that I was very fond of Mrs Marshall, and I miss her. And, yes, I won't deny that she was different in nature from her daughter.' Different as day from night, she thought bitterly.

Helen Hurd glanced sideways at Jenny, and realising she was putting her in an awkward situation, told her gently, 'Don't think I'm prying, my dear. The truth is, I've taken a strong dislike to Claudia Marshall. I don't trust her motive for marrying my nephew. Do you know what I'm saying?'

'I think so, ma'am.' Jenny knew exactly what the old lady was saying, and she agreed wholeheartedly though she would not admit it to this woman who was little more than a stranger to her. Claudia Marshall was marrying for money and that was the ugly truth.

'Oh, it's plain as the nose on his face that Richard is besotted with her, but – well, to be honest, I suspect she's only interested in what she can get out of him. My brother left the boys very well off, and of course she must know that by now.' Putting her hand on Jenny's arm, she gently drew her to a halt. 'I don't know anyone here, my dear,' she said with a little smile. 'And I have no right to put you through an inquisition, but you must see how anxious I am?'

'I understand, but please don't worry. I'm sure things will work out all right.' Jenny's intention was to put the old lady at ease.

'No, my dear.' Helen saw through her well-meaning comment. 'I may be old, but I'm no fool. As far as I'm concerned, Claudia Marshall has her hooks in my nephew, and I know she won't be satisfied until she's lord and master over everything he owns. She'll find a way, I'm certain of it, because women like her don't usually settle for a part of something. They want it all.'

'She may come to love him?' Jenny hoped so, but like this dear soul she doubted it.

'She'll *use* him, and like the fool he is . . . like the fools all men are . . . he won't see it happening. Until one day he'll wake up and she'll be gone, and with her his fortune.' She shook her head. 'No, my dear. However much I wish it could happen, she won't come to love him. Though I've known her for only a short time, I've seen what lies beneath that dazzling smile.'

'I'm sorry.' Jenny was out of her depth. Everything the old lady said was true, but there was little either of them could do about it. Wanting now to move away, Jenny beckoned Katie to her. When she had the girl's little hand firmly in hers, she told the old one, 'We'd best get in the carriage or we'll be left behind.'

'Nonsense!' Helen Hurd waved the servants' carriage away. 'You must travel back with me and my nephew,' she said. And when Katie whooped with delight, Jenny merely shrugged her shoulders and muttered her thanks.

Inside the carriage, Katie and the boy took pleasure in hanging their head out of the window and counting the cows in the fields. Jenny had thought she would feel uncomfortable and embarrassed riding in this grand carriage. Instead, she was at ease in the old lady's company; especially as it seemed she was becoming resigned to her nephew's marriage.

Jenny was wrong. As they approached the house, Helen Hurd told her in a whisper, 'Just as I know she is bad, I know that you are good. Katie has already told me how she has no mother, and from what she says I assume that her father has abandoned her?'

'Then you assume wrong, ma'am.' Jenny could have explained how Frank didn't even know of Katie's existence, so had not abandoned her. That was the very last thing he would have done. Her heart turned over, though, when she reminded herself of how he had abandoned *her*. 'Katie was wrong to give that impression.'

'No. It was wrong of me to interpret her innocent remarks in such a way. But from what I do understand, you have brought the girl up, and to me that's a fine thing to do. What's more, she's a real credit to you.' Helen Hurd was more curious than ever, but

285

was too much of a lady to probe any further. Instead she went on, 'I like you. I feel I can trust you.'

'Thank you, ma'am.' Jenny got the feeling that the old lady was leading up to something, and it made her nervous.

'Will you help me, Jenny?'

'In what way?'

The old lady seemed suddenly weary. 'I know you won't betray my confidence, and I realise I have no right to ask anything of you, but there is no one else I can turn to.' She looked into Jenny's face, an honest face, a good face, and her courage was restored. 'I'm an old woman and given to imaginings, but there's something about her, something in her pale eyes that frightens me. I can feel it in my bones . . . she'll destroy him. Of course I could come here to live, where I could keep an eye on her, but even though Richard has made it clear I would be welcome, it's impossible. I could never leave my own home, and of course there's my dear friend Edna to be considered.' She chuckled. 'We have our little rows, but we've been together a long time now and are inseparable.'

She sighed and her smile faded. 'But I'm worried, and I do need to know how things are faring here.' Digging into her handbag she drew out a small piece of paper. 'No doubt you think I'm an old fool, and I probably am, but indulge me, will you, my dear? This is my address. Keep it safe and don't let them know you have it.' Her old eyes were beseeching, 'My nephew would never forgive me.' She laid her hand over Jenny's and she was trembling. 'Please, my dear. Will you write to me? Let me know of anything untoward?'

Jenny was astonished. Like Katie, and now Helen Hurd, she had no liking for Claudia. But to have this old lady confiding in her, a mere servant! She really must be deeply anxious to do such a thing. In many ways Helen Hurd put Jenny in mind of Elizabeth, and in spite of her misgivings, she was drawn to her. 'You mustn't worry,' she coaxed. 'Things will probably work out fine.' She accepted the piece of paper and pushed it into her pocket. 'But I promise I'll write if anything worries me. Does that put your mind at rest?'

The old lady's smile was almost beautiful. 'Thank you, my dear,' she murmured. 'It's a great pity he didn't marry a young woman of your quality.' When Jenny looked away, she added, 'I've caused you a deal of embarrassment, and I'm sorry. But you see, like yourself I come from ordinary stock, and to tell you the truth, I feel more at home talking to you than ever I do talking to her. Though you won't say it, and I respect you for your loyalty, I *know* you dislike her almost as much as I do.' She settled back in her seat and turned her gaze to the lane outside. Now she could go home with a lighter heart, because she had found a friend in Jenny Dickens.

Jenny closed her eyes. She could feel the piece of paper brushing against her thigh, and wondered if she would ever have cause to write to Richard Hurd's aunt. She thought not. But then she couldn't possibly know the dangers that lay ahead.

# *Chapter Thirteen*

'When you've shoed the mare, happen you'd be so kind as to look at another horse for me?' The ruddy-faced man stood by the door, with his large work-worn hands pushed deep into his breeches' pockets as he watched Frank at work.

'Which horse?' Frank squeezed the fidgeting mare's fetlock between his knees as he looked up. 'One o' your own is it?' He knew most of the horses in this stable; some belonged to Tad Lockett himself, but almost half he kept for others, charging a sizeable fee but earning every penny. He was a rare breed, a horse-dealer who cared for the animals and always placed them well.

'It's the cob,' he replied. 'The one as belongs to Miss Hurd.' Coming into the barn, he took out a pipe and tobacco wad from his pocket. 'I've sent for the vet'rinary and, according to the housekeeper, he's out on an urgent call.' With great clumsy fingers he proceeded to stuff long strands of dark tobacco into the bowl of his pipe. 'So I can't wait on him. The cob's hoof seems infected to me, and I'd be more than grateful if you'd give it the once over.' He lit his pipe and drew hard on it, letting the smoke curl away between his narrow lips. 'By! If owt happened to that horse, I wouldn't dare face her. Oh, Miss Hurd is a kind enough soul, but I wouldn't want to get on the wrong side of her and that's a fact!' He shook his head and frowned at the thought. 'You've never met her, have you?'

Frank prised the iron shoe from the horse's hoof and, letting the mare stand on all fours again, pressed his fists into the small of his back and straightened up. 'Nope. I've never had the opportunity, seeing as she won't have her horse shod so has no call for my services.'

'She won't have the cob shod because she reckons he's spent too many years plodding the roads with his hooves clad in irons.'

'He'd know it if he'd plodded the roads *without* irons to protect him.'

'Oh, she accepts that, but like she says, he's done his work and now it's time he had the shoes off and spent the rest of his days striding the meadows.'

'She sounds a decent sort to me or she would have sold the beast along with her father's business. Thank God there are still others like her who value these magnificent creatures for what they are. Sadly, though, there's too many folks who see the horse as a work object and nothing more.'

'Aye, that's right. It's the young lads mostly . . . no soul some of 'em. It's on with the harness of a morning, strap the horse to the wagon and drive it on hard all day, then off with the harness of an evening, toss the animal a bag of hay and turn out the light without so much as a thank you. They don't take the time to get to know the beast that keeps the wheels turning, and it's their loss because they're missing out on a very special friendship.'

'If you ask me, it's them that wear the blinkers, not the horses.' Frank led the bay mare to the field gate and turned her away, smiling as she loosed herself at full pelt across the meadow, kicking her hind legs and whinnying with sheer pleasure. 'Miss Hurd? Won't she mind me interfering? Didn't you tell me she doesn't like anybody handling the cob other than yourself and the vet?'

The other man leaned on the gate beside Frank, his eyes squinting in the strong September sunlight as he stared up. 'When needs must,' he said, 'I'm sure she'd rather have you look at it than wait hours for the vet'rinary to show. After all, it's not as if you don't know what you're doing.' He patted Frank on the shoulder. 'There's not much you don't know about horses, Frank Winfield. Come to think of it, I wouldn't be surprised if you don't know as much as any vet'rinary.'

Frank brushed the comment aside but his face betrayed the pleasure he felt. 'Away with you. I'm no vet'rinary. All I know is their hooves, that's all.'

'You know a great deal more than that!'

'Because you've asked me, I'll take a look,' Frank agreed. 'But I'll not cross the vet'rinary's path, same as I wouldn't want him to cross mine. Each man to his own job, that's what I say.'

The other man laughed at this. 'Can you see old Tompkins bent at the middle, with a row of tacks between his teeth?'

'Happen not now, but when he was younger, I dare say he might have shod a horse or two.'

'Aye, well, I wouldn't count on it. There are two kinds of vet'rinary . . . one who'll roll about in the mud with his animals and stuff his arm up to the elbow in its insides when a foal's caught up; then there's the other kind, who'll let the farmhands do the dirty work while he keeps well back. Happen old Tompkins didn't mind getting his hands soiled when he were younger, I don't know. What I do know is that he should have retired years back. Sad though it is, the old bugger's past his best. He takes twice as long to do his round, and he's never about when he's wanted. I'm worried, Frank. The cob's limping badly, and needs looking at right away.'

'You'd best take me to him then, hadn't you?' Frank squared his shoulders and waited. When the other man began to walk towards the far stable block, he followed him.

The cob was miserable. Standing in the darkest corner of the stable, with his head hanging low and his ears laid flat, he hardly looked up as they came in. 'How long has he been like this?' Frank asked, waiting by the door until the beast became used to his presence.

'I first noticed him limping when I brought him in from the field last night. There was a stone in his hoof. I tickled it out and thought that was an end to it. This morning, though, he wouldn't touch his food, and his hoof looks badly.' He ventured forward. 'The old sod won't let me near him now. I reckon he blames *me* for it.' As though to prove the truth of this, the cob angrily pawed the ground with his good hoof and stared at them both through large pained eyes. 'See that?' Tad observed, stepping back a pace. 'He's got real tetchy.'

'Leave us.'

'Do what?'

'You've been round horses long enough to know that he's not blaming you,' Frank remarked softly. 'The fella's in pain and he's not in the mood to trust either of us, so if you still want me to take a look, it's best if you stay the other side of that door.'

Tad didn't need telling twice. In a minute he was gone, staring into the stable from the outside and remaining very still and very quiet, his concerned eyes following Frank's every move. After washing his hands in the half-filled water bucket, Frank began talking to the frightened animal. 'All right, sunshine,' he murmured, all the while moving forward, 'I'm not here to hurt you.'

And he didn't. After gaining the animal's confidence, he tenderly stroked its mane and soothed its trembling withers while looking into its big brown eyes. Then with the greatest of care he stooped to lift the offending hoof, and saw straight away that it was badly infected. The yellowing pus oozed between his fingers when he pressed, and for one frightening moment, when the

291

animal started to rear, he thought he would be tipped out of the manger. But this great and lovely creature seemed to know that he was in good hands, and patiently endured the ordeal.

While Frank continued to expel the poison, all the while murmuring encouragement to the shivering animal, the man outside marvelled at the deep trust which grew between these two kindly creatures. It was a wonderful thing to observe. As he watched, he was filled with admiration. And a little envy too.

An hour later, the animal appeared to be out of pain. The wound was thoroughly cleaned then bathed in warm salty water, and though at first he hesitated when putting the hoof to the ground, the cob soon realised that it wasn't going to hurt like before. 'You're a bloody marvel, Winfield!' Tad declared as he rubbed his two hands down the animal's withers. 'What do I owe you?'

'How about a mug of tea?'

Tad led the way to the farmhouse, saying he'd drummed up a real thirst while watching Frank at work with the beast. 'I'll tell you what though,' he said, 'you'll have Helen Hurd's thanks. Make no mistake about that! She's an old sod when it takes her, and if anything had happened to that cob, my life wouldn't be worth living.'

On the following Saturday at four o'clock, just as Frank was about to close his blacksmith's shop, his attention was drawn to a carriage which pulled up directly outside. The door opened and an elderly lady stepped down into the sunshine of a hazy autumn afternoon. Her bright old eyes sought him out. 'Mr Winfield?' She had a pleasant manner and a friendly smile as she approached him. 'Mr Frank Winfield?'

Tugging the great door to, he clicked the lock and slid the key into his pocket. 'That's me, ma'am,' he answered with a smile. 'What can I do for you?'

'It isn't what you *can* do for me,' she told him. 'It's what you've already done.'

Realising that this lady must be Helen Hurd, he silently cursed Tad for sending her here. 'The cob!' he remarked, his smile slipping away. 'You've come about the cob. Look, I'm sorry if I interfered, but he really was in a bad way. If the vet'rinary had taken just another hour to get to him, the poison would have spread from the hoof and caused all manner o' trouble. I know it weren't my place to look at him, because like I told Tad, I'm no vet'rinary and I don't pretend to be . . .' He would have gone on, desperate to justify what he did, but when she smiled and held out her hand in a gesture of friendship, he was struck dumb. 'You don't mind then?' Relief flooded through him. Helen Hurd's formidable reputation went before her.

'Mind!' Her eyes grew round with surprise. 'I'm only glad that you were there. I don't mind telling you, I've changed my veterinary. Old Tompkins won't be attending the cob again, I can promise you that!'

Frank rubbed his grubby fist against his overall, and grasping her hand, shook it gently up and down. 'I was pleased to be of service, ma'am,' he said with a grin. 'The old fella was in a deal of pain, and the wound had festered badly.' He smiled at the memory of that wily old thing. 'He's a magnificent beast, old though he is,' he admitted.

'He means a lot to me, and I must reward you for what you did.'

'I won't hear of it.'

Helen Hurd narrowed her eyes and pursed her lips then said in a frosty voice, 'You'll do as you're told, young man! I'm an old fool who doesn't get much pleasure out of life. Kindly allow me to be generous when I feel like it.'

'But, really . . . there's no need.'

Ignoring his protest, Helen asked, 'How do you make your way home?'

'On foot.'

'Not today. You'll ride with me.' When she saw that he was about to protest, she stiffened her face and told him in a hard voice, 'Help me into the carriage.' She chuckled then, a mischievous sound in one so old. 'I can't remember the last time I entertained a handsome young man. You'll indulge an old lady by allowing her to take you home,' she announced, leaning on his arm as they went to the carriage. 'We can talk on the way.'

As the carriage made its way from Peters Street, Helen Hurd unashamedly expressed her curiosity by asking all manner of personal questions, such as where he'd lived before he came to Blackburn, and what were his future business plans, and how was he finding married life? 'Tad talks about you a lot,' she revealed, 'but you mustn't mind because he greatly admires you. And you mustn't mind me either,' she remarked briskly. 'I'm an old woman, and old women have the right to ask impertinent questions.'

'It's all right.' Frank was more amused than offended, and anyway he shouldn't be surprised that she was down-right nosy, because it was well known how forthright she could be. There was even talk that she threw her housekeeper out on to the streets at regular intervals, though it was said that the two women had played the same little game for many long years. 'I really don't mind your asking questions. My future plans are simple. I mean for the business to grow and expand, until I make my fortune. As far as my marriage goes, well, I've a good woman who tends me well. What more could any man want?' His voice said one thing. His heart said another. Jenny. That was what it said.

'Oh? And what's your fortunate wife's name?'

'Doreen, and it's *me* who's the fortunate one.' He went on to explain how he had come from the South some five years since, and Doreen had offered him both home and friendship. 'To tell you the truth, I don't know what I would have done without her.'

The old lady smiled. 'You'd have managed, I'm sure. Tad tells me you've built up your own blacksmith's yard, and that your reputation has reached the ears of some of the other horse-owners hereabouts. Many send their horses to you, and others pay you a tidy sum to tend their beasts in their own fields?'

'That's right, ma'am.'

'Then you must be making a good living.'

Frank chuckled. 'I am an' all,' he confessed. 'But I'd do it for half the price. I love the animals, and consider I'm lucky to do the work I do.' He peered out of the window to see where they were, hoping they might be nearing Jubilee Street. But the carriage seemed to be going unusually slowly and he wondered whether she had ordered the driver to take his time.

'Have you always worked with horses?'

'Oh, I've done this and that in my time, ma'am . . . caretaker, handyman and general groundskeeper. A man earns a living best he can. But, yes, mostly I've worked with horses. I'm a trained blacksmith, d'you see?'

'What did you do in the South?' She was perched on the edge of her seat, her small bright eyes intent as she studied his handsome face.

He hesitated. Even with Doreen he avoided talking about his previous life. It was still too painful. After all these years, his heart was sore from memories of Jenny and of what he had done to her. 'This and that,' he said lamely.

She was at once mortified. 'Oh, my dear! I'm so sorry. I've pried too deeply, haven't I?' She clapped her hand to her mouth as though to hold it shut. 'Edna always says that my mouth is far too big for my own good.'

Frank assumed 'Edna' to be the housekeeper. 'It's all right, ma'am,' he said, turning the blame on to himself. 'I'm not much company at the minute. That's because I've a lot on my mind, y'see? What with the wedding and everything.'

His friendly manner reassured her. 'All the same, I'm a nosy old bugger,' she said, making Frank smile. 'One of these days I'll dig my own grave with this tongue of mine.'

There was a moment then when the two of them were lost in their own thoughts, and they were troubled. 'A wedding can be an ordeal,' she said presently. 'Although of course you sound as though you've found the right person to share your life with?' She peeked at him, and was surprised at the shadow which flitted across his face. 'I've recently come from a wedding in the South,' she said, anxious to redeem herself. 'Oh, it was a grand affair. The bride was very beautiful, and my nephew obviously adores her.' Her voice fell almost to a whisper. 'Oh, I do hope she'll be good to him.'

Something in her manner caused Frank to turn and look at her. In that instant, before she composed herself, he saw the sorrow in her face, and it made him wonder. He knew from Tad that Helen Hurd was a spinster, and that she had recently attended the wedding of her eldest nephew; though he hadn't realised that she had been South. 'I don't suppose for a minute my wedding was ever as grand as your nephew's,' he remarked candidly, 'but it was a memorable affair all the same.' Certainly *he* would remember it all his life, just as he would regret that it wasn't his beloved Jenny standing beside him at the altar.

'Mr Winfield?' They were coming into the top of Jubilee Street and Helen was anxious to change the subject.

'Yes, ma'am?'

'Tad Lockett tells me that you're looking for larger premises . . . apparently you've outgrown your blacksmith's yard on Peters Street?'

'Aye, that's right. The yard I'm in now was only ever a temporary measure. Business is swamping me of late, and I'll soon have to move. The way things are going, I'll have to keep an eye out for a young lad to train as well.'

'Well, I can't help you with the latter, but I can certainly do something about the premises. I don't know if Tad Lockett told you, but I own four acres and a string of outbuildings adjacent to his own land. You're very welcome to set up there.'

'That's very kind of you, ma'am, but there's no need.' This was obviously her 'reward' for tending the cob, and he could see she was disappointed at his refusal. 'Like I said, I'm glad I was able to help. Besides, I've no intention of moving from Peters Street. It would be a bad decision for the business. You see, the yard is central, and if I was to move out of town, I'd likely lose a lot of my customers. No, I've a few ideas brewing over in my mind. I've got my eye on the unused bakeries next door to the yard. It would be perfect . . . knock down the adjoining wall and put a second forge in there. I've already started enquiries about the owner, with a mind to making them an offer. Rent or buy, either would do.'

The carriage jolted to a stop. 'Thank you kindly for the ride home, ma'am,' he said, preparing to open the door. 'You've saved a weary pair of feet from a lengthy trudge.' For some reason, he felt heavy of heart. He wondered whether it was because, with her talk of weddings and the South, she had unwittingly opened that private corner of his heart where Jenny was kept safe.

'Good day, young man,' she called from the carriage window as he stepped down. 'I shan't forget what you did.' Suddenly impatient, she struck the roof of the carriage with her stick, at the same time calling out sharply to the driver to, 'Get on!' Equally impatient, the poor man in turn struck the horses with the edge of his long whip and, startled, they reared forward and took the carriage with them.

Frank stood on the pavement, his brown eyes stricken and his mind alive with thoughts of Jenny. 'I miss you, sweetheart,' he murmured. 'You'll never know how much.'

Having heard the carriage stop outside, Doreen had peeked through the window. She was astonished to see the door of the carriage open and Frank stepping down to the pavement. Her curiosity was roused, and she would have rushed down the passage to ask him who had brought him home in such a posh vehicle but something about his demeanour stopped her. She remained at the window, waiting for him to make the first move.

Her spirits dipped when she saw how forlorn he looked, that tall handsome figure with the thick mop of fair hair and downcast eyes. So alone and lost in thought. She had seen it all before, and in those moments she felt like an outsider. It was an uncomfortable feeling, yet it seemed so natural. She didn't doubt that Frank had secrets. All men had secrets of one kind or another. Women too, and she should know that better than most because she had secrets. Things of the heart and soul which she could never discuss with anyone. So when Frank seemed a million miles away as he often did she never pried, and she never would. She accepted that he was his own person. She understood that and, if anything, respected him all the more because of it.

When he came into the house, the feeling of home and familiarity enveloped him and once again he pressed all thoughts of Jenny to the back of his mind. He had made many mistakes in his life, but he knew that the greatest was when he threw away the love of that good and lovely woman. It was a mistake he would go on paying for until the day he died.

'All right, are you?' Doreen was standing by the stove. Steam was pouring out of the kettle and the smell of baking permeated the air. 'You're early.' She was hoping he would tell her of the carriage and its owner. 'Dinner won't be above a few minutes.'

He crossed the room to kiss her gently on the forehead. 'No hurry,' he said. 'And I'm early because I got a ride home with no less a person than Helen Hurd.' Smiling at the astonishment on her face, he swung away and took off his coat. 'Don't look so surprised,' he teased, hanging the coat on the nail behind the scullery door. 'Am I not grand enough to ride with such folk?' He chuckled. 'By! She's a surprising woman, an' no mistake.'

'*Helen Hurd* brought you home?' Doreen's eyes widened as she looked at him. 'Well I never! Why would she do such a thing?'

Frank came to the sink and washed his hands. 'She came to the yard just as I was leaving,' he explained. 'Wanted to reward me for tending the cob she keeps at Tad Lockett's place. I were just locking up and she insisted on fetching me home.'

Taking the kettle off the stove, Doreen poured the boiling water over the tea leaves in the pot. 'Oh,' she remarked, frowning deeply while turning her attention to the task in hand. 'And what do you mean, she wanted to reward you?' Grabbing a thick cloth in both hands, she opened the oven door and took out the sizzling meat pie. Carefully she placed it on the top of the stove. The pastry was crisp and brown and the aroma of meat over onions filled the scullery. 'Well?' she persisted, taking the pie and going into the parlour where the table was already laid. In the centre of the table was a thick bread-board. She laid the pie plate on this, before returning to the scullery where she strained the cabbage into the colander.

'She owns four acres and a string of outbuildings in the country. She offered me the use of 'em for a new yard.'

Doreen spooned the cabbage into a large dish. 'That was kind of her,' she said, enacting the same procedure with the peas and potatoes. 'And what did you say?'

Frank collected the pile of plates from the dresser and followed her into the parlour where he sat himself at the table. 'I said thank you, but no.' He explained how it wouldn't do to move out of town. 'I'd lose some of my customers . . . the brewery for a start, and I can't see the coalmen fetching their horses four mile out to have their horses shod.'

'You're right, of course,' she agreed. 'It does seem a shame though.'

They looked around as the door opened and in walked Rodney. 'What's a shame?' he wanted to know, staring from one to the other.

'Don't be so nosy,' his mother told him good-naturedly. 'Dinner's ready, so you'd best get washed and sat down.' While he was doing that, she served up the pie and put the ladles into the vegetable dishes.

As always, after the rush and demands of a hard day's work, dinner was an enjoyable and leisurely treat. The three of them ate heartily, then they talked a while and Frank explained about Helen Hurd's offer. Like his mother, Rodney agreed that Frank was the best judge of what was right for his business. 'I only wish I was as shrewd as you,' Rodney moaned. 'I expect I'll still be working for others even when I'm old and grey.' He excused himself from the table and sat in the armchair by the fireside, stretching his legs until his feet rested on the fender.

'You'll not live to be old and grey if you don't take your feet down from that fender!' his mother snapped, impatiently tutting as he swung his legs away from her polished brass fire-surround.

When the dishes were done and put away, the three members of that small unsettled family relaxed in comfortable chairs by the fireside, each engrossed in their own disturbing thoughts. Not wanting to indulge in the small talk that usually started about now, Frank closed his eyes and feigned sleep. But he couldn't rest. For some reason he was deeply agitated. When he sensed Doreen's curious gaze on him the urge to get out of the house was overpowering. Opening his eyes he gave a half-smile. 'I'm thinking I'll stretch my legs before bed,' he decided. 'I've eaten too much of your delicious apple pie.' Out of courtesy he asked if she wanted to accompany him. When she answered, 'No. I'll sit here awhile,' he was secretly thankful. In a few minutes he had donned his cap and coat and was gone from the house.

'Why didn't you go with him?' Rodney demanded as the front door closed. As always he was deeply anxious, acutely aware that his mother and Frank were not as happy as he had hoped.

'I didn't go because I didn't want to.'

'You're not regretting having wed him, are you, Mam?' Sitting bolt upright in the chair he stared at her with troubled eyes.

'I'm not too happy about it, you should know that.' She met his gaze with a bold expression. Each knew what the other was thinking, but neither of them would speak it out loud.

'You won't split us up though, will you?' He was frantic.

She didn't answer straight away, and his face hardened. It softened again when she murmured thoughtfully, 'No. I won't change my mind.'

'You promise, Mam?'

'I don't need to promise and I won't, but Frank's a good man and you must know I'm doing my best to make it work.'

'Do you mind if I go down to the pub?'

'Do what you like, son.'

Out of the corner of her eye she saw him rise and go towards the scullery. A moment later he passed her chair and bent to kiss her. She pulled away and though he was taken aback by her rejection of him, he made no comment. Instead he went out of the room and down the passage, his heavy boots making a hollow thump against the carpeted floor as he went.

When the front door closed behind him, she leaned back in the chair and closed her eyes. She felt cheated, and incredibly angry. 'Life's too short,' she told the pictures on the wall. 'And we should take what happiness there is while we can.'

Overwhelmed with regrets, she let her mind wander back to the day she and Frank were wed. Everyone had said she looked very fetching in a simple beige two-piece, while Frank looked incredibly handsome in his best dark suit, with his black shoes polished to a brilliant shine and his thick hair unruly as ever. Tall and straight, he was a fine figure of a man, and she couldn't deny how proud she had felt.

Only once during the service she had noticed a fleeting regret wash over his features, causing her to wonder whether he too was already questioning the wisdom of their decision; one effectively foisted on them by Rodney's desire to have a 'proper family'.

As they walked towards the hired motor vehicle, arm in arm and he smiling down on her, Frank had uttered a promise. 'I'll make you happy, Doreen,' he'd said, and he had meant it. This woman had entrusted herself to his care, and he would not let her down.

Now, reliving those memories, she recalled the moment before they were driven away, when the familiar figure had stepped out from the shrubbery where she had been hiding. Sensing her presence, Doreen turned and saw her there. For one inexplicable moment their eyes met. The moment was held, and then the vehicle pulled away.

Unbeknown to Doreen, the woman would have stayed a while but Rodney had also seen. Incensed, he had confronted her. 'Haven't you done enough harm?' he demanded, fists clenched to his chest and a look of murder in his eyes. 'I could kill you, do you know that?' he asked, his face crumpled into an expression of loathing.

For a long time, the woman had stared at him defiantly, her face grim and dark as his, until without a word she turned away and left him there.

Thinking on the woman now, Doreen shed tears. 'I'm so sorry,' she murmured. 'I'd give anything to turn the clock back.' Drying her eyes, she sighed deeply and got out of the chair. 'But I expect it's all too late now.'

Some time later, she was lying in her bed when she heard Frank's familiar footsteps coming up the stairs. Wanting to make amends for cheating him, she welcomed him with open arms.

Sensing her anxiety, yet not fully understanding it, he drew her close. That night, as on many nights before, they made love.

With gentle fingers, he removed her nightgown and caressed her body. All day long he had been tormented by thoughts of Jenny. He was tormented now. Like a rising tide the passion overwhelmed him. When he pushed into Doreen, it was Jenny he saw in his mind's eye. Jenny whose soft lips he kissed. Jenny who took him to the heights of fulfilment.

Encouraged by his ardent lovemaking, Doreen shivered in his arms, giving herself up to him, caught in a frenzy of passion, her nakedness merging with his until the frenzy became a rage that carried them along. Soon the rage was gone and in its place was a strange unsettled peace.

Afterwards they lay together, fulfilled but not content, she with her head in the crook of his shoulder, and he with his face pressed to the top of her head. Soon she fell asleep. Restless, he laid her against the pillow. There was no sleep in him. No desire to lie beside this woman who was his wife. Instead, his thoughts were alive with images of Jenny and he felt ashamed. Deeply troubled, he got out of bed and quietly dressed. He needed to think, and couldn't do that with Doreen so close.

On tiptoe, he crept downstairs to the scullery. Here he put on his coat and shoes and walked into the yard. 'What kind of man am I?' he asked himself angrily. 'God Almighty, will I never stop wanting her?'

The night air struck cold to his face. Shivering aloud, he reached into his coat pocket for his pipe and matches. For a long lonely while he leaned on the back wall, lazily puffing on his pipe, his mind going back over the years and bringing a smile to his face.

As the memories deepened, the smile became a sad expression. 'Oh, Jenny,' he whispered to the moon, 'I'm a married man, and for the sake of my sanity I should put you behind me.' He smiled a bitter-sweet smile as he added, 'God help me but I can't. And I never will.'

From the bedroom window Doreen watched him, and she knew he was in that secret place where she was never allowed to enter. 'I know I've done wrong by you,' she said softly. 'I never wanted to hurt you, Frank, but sometimes we're driven a certain way, and whether it's right or whether it's wrong, there's little we can do about it.'

Returning to her bed, she slithered thankfully beneath the warm sheets. 'Sometimes I wonder whether I should tell you the truth,' she muttered. 'One day I might have to.' The thought frightened her. 'Time alone will tell,' she mused aloud.

With that she closed her eyes and fell asleep. But it was a shallow sleep, fraught with fear, and suspicion, and a deep crippling sense of guilt.

# Part Three

## *1930*

## FEARS

# *Chapter Fourteen*

'I don't want you to go away, Alan.' Katie's emerald green eyes were swamped with tears. 'But I know it's something you've always wanted to do, so I wish you well.' This summer had been wonderful. For three unforgettable months after Alan had finished school and was contemplating his future, he had remained here at Ickwell. Though Claudia had watched him like a hawk and had employed every conceivable means to keep him away from his dear friend Katie, they had somehow found a way to see each other.

During the long lonely months when Alan was away at boarding school, Katie had spent many an hour wandering the beautiful countryside hereabouts. It was on one of her meanderings that she'd come across this lovely valley. Her precious discovery was now lovingly shared with Alan; this quiet paradise, with its cool running stream and wide ancient willow whose branches dipped into the rippling water, silently drinking, keeping secrets and sheltering the young ones from the sharp eyes of Claudia.

Here, on the mossy grass inside the encircling veil of branches, the lonely Katie had found total seclusion where she could sit unseen to dream her girlish dreams. Now they were shattered by the news that Alan had decided to follow a tradition set by his grandfather. He was going into the armed forces. That was *his* dream, and Katie had to abide by it.

'You've grown so tall and handsome, and I'm proud of you,' she told him now. 'You'll make a fine soldier, I know.' Alan had returned home in early June, almost three months ago. He had been away almost a year, and when he stepped out of the car on that wonderful day, Katie barely recognised him. His Christmas holiday had been spent with his Aunt Helen in Lancashire while Claudia had persuaded Richard that she desperately needed the sunshine of Switzerland. 'Just the two of us, darling,' she'd pleaded, and loving her as he did, how could he refuse?

Alan was kept away on one pretence or another until at seventeen years of age he sat and passed all his exams, and was ready to embark on a new future. 'I'll miss you,' Katie said brokenly. 'Promise you'll write to me, won't you?'

He gazed on her, thinking what a splendid face she had; so proud and beautiful with its high cheekbones, wild abundance of auburn hair and large round green eyes. Katie was not yet twelve, but she had grown into a willowy beauty. She was wise and knowing for her young age.

'You know I'll write to you,' he promised softly. Clutching her hand in his, he stood up, taking her with him. For a moment they looked at each other, two children with the same heartbeat, sharing a dangerous, forbidden yearning. Tenderly, he brushed the tears from her long lashes. 'Don't cry,' he pleaded. 'Eyes like yours were never made for tears.'

Together they walked away from that lovely valley. Hand in hand they came nearer to the house until, more afraid for him than for herself, Katie pulled away. 'I'll see you before you go, won't I?' she asked anxiously. When he merely nodded, her face melted into the most beautiful smile, and then, with a small wave, she was gone; running along the beaten unmade track towards the back of the house until the shrubbery lost her to his sight.

Dejected, he set himself on the other path, the wide, meticulously paved path which would take him to the front door. Not for the first time, he questioned a Fate which let him walk through the front of the house, while Katie was confined to the servants' quarters. 'It won't always be that way,' he assured himself. Wisely, he realised that he and Katie were still too young, and that it wasn't only the years between which kept them apart.

As he came into the drawing room, two pairs of accusing eyes turned on him. With a little rush of horror, he remembered he was to have gone into Bedford with his brother. 'You should have been here an hour ago.' Richard was angry, but as always his anger was controlled. 'Where have you been until now?' He was standing in front of the fireplace, hands behind his back and his foot tapping impatiently against the carpet.

Before he could answer, Claudia rose from the armchair, her pale eyes riveted on Alan's face as she accused in a shrill voice, 'It's *her*, isn't it? Don't deny it! You've been with that little slut from the kitchen, haven't you? HAVEN'T YOU?'

'What if I have?' He stood proud before her. 'And Katie is no slut.'

Claudia stiffened. 'Can't you see she means to get you into trouble?' Realising her fury would only alienate him, she changed tack. 'You must know what a catch you are,' she continued in a sweeter voice. 'Your father divided his fortune between you and your brother. In four years' time you will come into your inheritance. Any fool can see she has her sights set on it.' She regarded him slyly. 'She does know about the money, doesn't she?' The mere possibility of her own shameful offspring living the life of a lady was more than she could bear.

'You've got her wrong. Katie doesn't care about money the way you do.' He meant to antagonise her, but instead he made her smile.

'Ah! So you don't deny she *knows* about your inheritance?'

309

This time it was Richard who spoke. He was shocked. 'Surely you haven't discussed such a thing with that child?'

'Katie isn't a child. She's almost twelve.'

He couldn't hide his anger. 'Of course she's a child!' He took a pace forward. 'Up until now, I haven't forbidden you to talk to the girl. I have nothing against her. Like her mother, she seems decent enough . . . polite and hard-working. Even ambitious in her own small way. But now, I don't know. Perhaps Claudia is right after all. Maybe the girl really *is* having an adverse influence on you.'

'That's nonsense and you know it.' Alan's brown eyes flashed fire.

Momentarily silenced, Richard quietly studied his younger brother. He was still astonished at how grown up he had become in the space of a year. One minute he had been a boy, now he was almost a man. 'Whether you agree or not, she *is* just a child, and if as you say she is not an adverse influence on you . . . would you consider that you may well be an adverse influence on *her*?'

'What exactly are you saying?' The very thought was shocking to him.

Aware that he had touched a sore point, Richard carefully continued, 'All I'm saying is, you ought to remember that her mother is a servant in this house, and their lifestyle is very far removed from ours. You are a very good-looking young man, well educated and with prospects that a young girl like that could only dream of. Worlds apart, that's what you are. And if you lead her to think otherwise, you are doing her a very grave injustice.' When he saw how his younger brother appeared to be thinking deeply about this, he visibly relaxed. 'Enough said about that,' he remarked brightly. Just as he had intended, the point had struck home. To labour it now would only reduce its impact. 'Sit down, please,' he instructed. 'There are other, more important matters to discuss.'

'I hope you're not going to try and dissuade me from going into the Army, because my mind is made up.'

'Yes, yes, I know.' He sat down and waited for Alan to do the same, 'I just want to satisfy myself that you really do know what you're getting into.'

Claudia had sat through this argument before and she didn't relish the thought of doing so again. Besides, she had a stern warning to impart to Jenny Dickens, and it wouldn't wait. 'Will you please excuse me?' she said, going quickly to the door and out of the room. The men barely raised their heads to witness her departure.

'Look, Richard, the papers are signed. It's no use hoping it can be undone now.'

'I wouldn't want that. In fact, I'm proud of you.' And he was.

'So why don't you leave it be?'

'It's just that – well, I wouldn't be doing my duty if I didn't point out all the possibilities. The world is in a state of unrest . . . rioting in India; Soviet troops opening fire on strikers; rebels taking power in Peking; and the Nazis winning seats from the moderates in Germany. Anarchy and a greed for power. It's like a slow-burning wick to a powder keg. There's talk of war, and God only knows it could come from any of a dozen directions.'

'I'm aware of all that.'

'And are you aware that you could get caught up in it?'

'I would be disappointed if I was left out. A soldier is a soldier after all, wouldn't you say?'

The other man sighed deeply, then cast his eyes to the ceiling and sighed again. Now he clasped his brother's hand in his own and told him quietly, 'I've never said this, but I love you.'

Alan looked into his brother's eyes. 'I know that,' he said simply. 'But I don't want you to worry about me.'

'I'll try not to.' Disguising his apprehension, Richard stood up and slapped his hands on his brother's shoulders. 'Now that

311

we've said all there is to say on the subject of your becoming a soldier, are you ready to accompany me and my good wife into Bedford? As you're leaving tomorrow, we thought we might take you out for a special treat . . . lunch in that delightful restaurant along the river, then a seat along the bank to watch the boat race.' He rubbed his hands with glee, 'I'm quite looking forward to it.'

Firmly propelling the younger man towards the door, he told him, 'Off you go and freshen up. No longer than ten minutes, mind. The table's booked for one-thirty, and it's five minutes past twelve already.' Once the door was closed, he sank back into his chair, 'Keep him safe, Lord,' he said forlornly. 'And find him a woman of his own station.' Because however much he admired Jenny and the girl, they had no place in Alan's life.

That night, Jenny was woken by strange sounds. Putting on her dressing gown, she went softly to see who it was. She was not surprised to see that it was Katie. 'Whatever are you doing up at this hour?' she asked, glancing at the clock on the mantelpiece. 'It's two in the morning. You should be fast asleep.' Yawning, she went to the stove, collected the kettle and filled it at the tap. 'How long have you been wandering about?' she called from the scullery.

Lighting the gas ring with a match from the shelf, she turned to stare through the door at Katie, who was looking out of the window, her face doleful as she gazed at the big house. Jenny's heart fell like a stone inside her. For once in her life she knew Claudia was right; Katie's deepening friendship with Alan Hurd would only heap trouble on their heads.

'Tomorrow he'll be gone,' Katie sighed. 'And I don't know when I'll see him again.'

Heavy of heart, Jenny padded across the room and drew the girl away. With her arm round her shoulders, she led her to the settee where the two of them sat side by side. 'Mrs Hurd came to see me today,' Jenny said softly. It had been a bad confrontation.

Katie looked up. In the lamplight her eyes were bright with tears. 'She's a monster. I've never liked her, and I never will.' She had not forgotten how Claudia laid into her all those years ago. Even now the memory caused her nightmares.

Jenny forced herself to be firm. 'Whether you like her or not makes no difference. Claudia is mistress of this house, and we're here to do as we're told.'

'I expect she told you to keep me away from Alan . . . or else?'

Jenny had to smile at that. What Claudia had actually said was, 'Don't tempt me to do something I might regret. And don't forget we have an agreement with regard to the brat. An agreement that was wrenched out of me by means of blackmail, which I'm sure I don't have to remind you is a criminal offence. I'm warning you – keep her away from me and mine. She's giving herself airs and graces, deluding herself that she's a creature of some value. I won't have it! Do you hear?'

In threatening mood, she argued, 'It's true what they say: "Educate the workers and you'll soon have trouble on your hands."' When Jenny quietly reminded her that Katie was not a 'worker' but her own flesh and blood, she bristled with rage, saying in a low guttural voice, 'I advise you to watch what you say or suffer the consequences. Circumstances have a habit of changing, and agreements can be made invalid.' With that she swept out, leaving Jenny alone and afraid.

She was in no doubt that Claudia Marshall was capable of anything, and once again was racked with feelings of insecurity with regard to Katie. As far as she could see, there were two things Claudia could do. Firstly, she could confess all to her husband, but that would be the act of an honest and repentant woman – Claudia was neither. Alternatively, she could scheme to separate Jenny and Katie, to be rid of them once and for all, and in some way still protect her shameful secret. 'You'll separate us only over my dead body!' Jenny had murmured aloud. Even as the words touched her lips, she realised the implication of what she had said. Her blood ran cold. Once again she was forced to remind herself that Claudia would stop at nothing if she sensed a threat to her security.

'I'm sorry, Jenny.' Katie's voice permeated her frightening thoughts, 'I've caused you so much trouble, haven't I?'

Instinctively, she clasped the girl close. 'It isn't your fault,' she replied, forcing herself to smile down into that sad uplifted face. 'I can understand the affection you have for Alan. When you were small and had no other playmate, he befriended you. But that was a long time ago, Katie. You're much older now.' She hugged her closer. 'That innocent friendship between two little children belongs to another age. Do you understand what I'm saying?'

'No. *Why* can't we still be friends, me and Alan?'

'Oh, Katie! You must see the impossibility of it all. There are certain unspoken rules by which we must abide. Alan Hurd comes of a wealthy background. You and I are servants in his brother's house. It isn't right that you should have such affection for each other. Can't you see, Katie? It will only lead to trouble.'

'You're saying you and I could be dismissed, sent packing?'

'That and more.'

Katie sat up, her face set like stone, 'She can do her worst. I'm not afraid of her.'

'Then you *should* be!' In that moment when Katie stared at her with such defiance Jenny's fears were increased tenfold. 'She can be a bad enemy, and you would do well to remember that.'

'But I know *you're* not afraid of her.' Katie's face was a study in pride as she looked at Jenny.

Realising that her response was vital, she told the truth, 'You're wrong, sweetheart,' she said bravely. 'I *am* afraid. People like the

Hurds hold a great deal of power over the likes of us. If we step out of line, you can be sure we'll be made to pay the price.'

'Alan said he would write.'

'Then you must ask him not to.'

'No. I *want* him to.'

'Please, Katie. Be sensible.'

'He's my friend, and I love him.'

Katie's answer froze Jenny's troubled heart. 'And am *I* not your friend?'

Katie was horrified, 'Oh, Jenny! You're my very best friend in the whole world.' Flinging herself into Jenny's arms she broke down crying, 'I know what you're asking, but, it's so unfair.'

'Life *is* unfair, sweetheart, and sometimes we have to make sacrifices.' Holding Katie at arm's length, she looked her in the eyes and in a loving voice told her, 'I won't order you not to communicate with him, because I have no right to do such a thing. But I'm asking you to think very carefully about what I've said. Will you do that? Will you consider the price we may both have to pay if your friendship with Richard Hurd's brother continues?'

Katie wiped her eyes and reluctantly nodded her head. Just as Jenny was feeling reassured, she made a remark that turned Jenny's heart over. 'I wish you were my *real* mother.'

'Good Heavens, child! Whatever made you say a thing like that?' She felt the blood drain from her face.

'I don't know,' Katie confessed a little sadly. 'It's just that, well, I do love you so, and you know I wouldn't willingly do anything to hurt you. I've only ever known you as my mother. Now I don't ever want anyone else.'

Taking in a great gulp of air, Jenny sat back in the chair and sighed long and heavily. After regarding Katie for a little while, she said wonderingly, 'Does it play on your mind, sweetheart? The fact that you've never known your real mother?' In her mind's eye she relived the day when Claudia disowned her newborn girl-child, and secretly thanked the good Lord that Katie couldn't read her mind in that moment.

'I would like to know.'

'There's nothing I can tell you about your mother,' Jenny lied. 'You already know that. As for your father, he could be anywhere.'

'Tell me again how I came to you.'

Deeply troubled by her own lies and by Katie's longing for reassurance, Jenny told the same story she had told a dozen times before, 'When you were no more than a few days old, you came to me by way of a stranger. She said your mother had abandoned you and your father had gone away.'

'And you didn't know who this stranger was?'

'She wouldn't give her name. But she was old and withered. She could not have been your mother.'

'And my father?'

Jenny smiled, a great wave of nostalgia engulfing her. Now, when she spoke of Frank, all the old feelings came to the fore. 'By all accounts your father was a good, if misguided, man. From what I was given to understand, he didn't know of your existence. The woman spoke more harshly of your mother than she did of the man who fathered you. It isn't much, but it's all I can tell you.'

'I don't think I want to know *her*. But one day, when I'm old enough, I think I would like to find my father.' She observed Jenny through curious eyes. 'I'm not really sure, because I'm happy with just the two of us, but if I did want to find him, would you mind very much?'

'That will be your choice, sweetheart,' Jenny said warmly. 'No one can take that right away from you.' In her heart, she feared the day, yet somehow she truly believed it would never come.

After a time, when they had talked a while longer about school and Katie's love of learning, Jenny asked, 'Are you ready for your bed now?' When Katie replied that she was, Jenny accompanied the girl to her own little room, 'Good night, God bless,' she said, quickly leaving before Katie could ask her any more questions.

Outside, she leaned against the wall, eyes shut and weariness enveloping her. 'What's going to become of us?' she whispered ruefully.

Three months later a ghost from the past appeared: someone who could tell Katie of her mother; someone who could tear apart the safe little world which Jenny had so painstakingly created for the child she had come to love as her very own.

It was ten in the morning on 12 December 1930. Jenny was polishing the furniture in the dining room when she heard someone going out of the front door. Curious, she wandered to the window and looked out. It was the master. ''Course, you're off to the City for a few days, ain't you? Lucky thing,' she mused aloud, dreamily rubbing the polishing cloth over the window-ledge, and wondering what it would be like to stay at one of the posh hotels in London.

When Claudia came on to the scene, Jenny quickly stepped back a pace. 'Wouldn't do for *her* to see me gawping,' she muttered. 'Like as not she'd make a meal of it, and ruin a good day.' When Richard kissed his wife before climbing into his motorcar, Claudia fussed and fretted over him, convincingly feigning upset and disappointment. With delicious disrespect, Jenny made faces and mimicked her every gesture.

Suddenly, Claudia seemed to sense her there and, swinging round, glared at the dining-room window. But Jenny, chuckling and full of mischief, had wisely withdrawn into the shadows. 'You might have wrapped that poor bugger round your little finger,' she told the unwitting Claudia, 'but you can't fool *me*, you sly bitch! As good and trusting as he is, you're glad to see the back of him, and that's the truth.'

As Richard Hurd drove out on to the lane, the coal lorry drove in. It was a beautiful morning and the driver had his window down. As he drew alongside Claudia, he turned his head to greet her and his face paled with astonishment.

Claudia was still waving her handkerchief when suddenly she caught sight of the driver in his cab. Her hand froze in mid-air and her pale eyes widened until they were like full moons. For one split second she stumbled, as though she might faint. In a minute the vehicle had come to a halt and out stepped the driver, a big man with a ruddy face and a common manner. With an odd smile on his uncouth features, he sauntered across to where Claudia was standing. She, trembling still, could not take her eyes off him.

Jenny too was shocked. At first she wasn't certain, but when the driver stood before Claudia and boldly put his hands on her shoulders, the truth hit Jenny like a ton weight. 'Good God almighty!' She pressed her face to the window, staring from the man to Claudia, then back again. 'If it ain't the postman from Woburn Sands!'

All manner of emotions tore through her; shock on seeing him after all this time, alarm in case the master should suddenly double back for some reason or other, and finally, as her thoughts began to settle, she realised that this man, this ghost from the past, knew everything there was to know about Katie's mother.

'Dear God, what am I to do?' she uttered, falling into the nearby chair and trying desperately to calm herself. 'Be sensible, Jenny!' she chided firmly. 'There's nothing he can do . . . nothing he can say to harm your Katie.'

Oh, but there was! There was! This man knew that Katie was Claudia Marshall's daughter, and if he had the slightest idea of what was happening here, he was bound to see something in it for himself. 'He'll not stay, don't worry. *She'll* have him away from here before his feet can touch the ground. It's in her own interests as well as mine and Katie's.' But Jenny couldn't imagine how Claudia was already seeing this unexpected visitor as a blessing in disguise.

Once the shock of seeing him had passed, she was thrilled by the memories of his coarse and brutal lovemaking. Moreover, she was secretly excited by the devious schemes which were already taking shape in her warped and evil mind. 'It's so good to see you again,' she told him sweetly.

'That the truth, is it?' The big man eyed her coolly. 'You wouldn't be leading an old admirer up the garden path now, would you?'

Claudia's smile was enchanting, 'Why would I want to do that?' she asked coyly. 'I've thought about you often. Married life isn't everything I imagined it would be.'

'Rich though, ain't yer?' He glanced about him, at the lush expanse of landscaped grounds and the house of a kind that he could never afford. 'You always were a cunning bitch.'

She touched him suggestively on the bare flesh of his arm. 'Luxury isn't everything, you know. I've missed . . . being with you,' she whispered meaningfully.

He laughed hoarsely, 'Yer a strange bitch!' Suddenly a thought occurred to him, 'I don't know if I can altogether trust anything you say. You've already shown yourself to be deceitful. You cheat on yer husband and you left me without so much as a cheerio, kiss me arse!' He studied her lovely face and wondered whether she really did have some feeling for him. 'Funny thing, though, I reckon you're telling the truth when you say you missed me.'

Her eyes darkened. 'I didn't know how much until now,' she confessed.

'Got kids, have yer? I mean, apart from that bastard you brought with yer.'

Her smile slowly melted. 'Thankfully, no.' Though if it hadn't been for her own cunning, things might have been very different.

'Hate him that much, do yer?'

She didn't answer. 'Hmh. So the bastard will inherit it all one day, eh?' He laughed and the sound sickened her. 'Makes you wonder, don't it, eh?'

'What do you mean?'

'I mean, it pays to be born on the wrong side of the blanket, that's all.' He nodded his head as though affirming the wisdom of what he had just said. 'The bastard would be what . . . twelve? What about your old man, eh? Can't have been a pleasant thing, taking on somebody else's brat.'

Luring him away from that delicate subject, she remarked, 'The years have been kind to you, Bill. You're every bit as handsome as ever.'

'And so are you, darling, so are you.'

'We have a great deal to talk about. This evening . . . late?'

'I'll be here.' He smiled. 'Keep the bed warm, my lovely.' With that he made an odd little gesture from the neck and climbed back into his cab. Claudia made her way into the house, but not before she exchanged a secret little smile with him.

Jenny saw the two of them deep in conversation. It puzzled and frightened her. When they parted, it was with a smile and an intimate touch of the hand. She knew then that Claudia was up to something, and her heart sank like lead inside her.

Aware that the coal lorry was coming round to the rear of the house, she ran to the cellar and down into the blackness there. Frantically, she swept clean an area for the coal, and then waited nervously, going over and over in her mind what she would say to him.

Soon the trapdoor above was swung open and his face appeared at the opening. 'All right down there?' he called. 'Stay clear.' When Jenny stepped forward, he laughed out loud, 'Well, I'm buggered! You an' all, eh? It's like happy families again, ain't it?' His face darkened and his voice fell to a harsh whisper. 'Ran away, didn't yer, eh? The lot of yer . . . took off to where you thought you'd never be found.' He laughed, a fearful rumbling sound that might have frightened away a less spirited soul.

But Jenny stood her ground, her gaze never wavering as she told him sharply, 'Be off, why don't you? Stay away from us, Bill Saxon. We none of us want you here.'

'Well, I'm buggered!' he chuckled, leaning further into the cellar. When he spoke again, his face was grim, 'You never did like me, did you, eh? Miss Prim and Proper never did like me cheating on the wife, did yer? Well, it don't matter now, 'cause she's long gone. I'm foot loose and fancy free, an' what I fancy is the old days back again . . . me and *her*.' He hooked a thumb in the direction of the big house, then hammered his fist on the trapdoor.

'I've found her again, just like I knew I would. What's more, I don't intend to let her run away so easy this time.' He rubbed his hands. 'Matter o' fact, from what I can tell, she's over the moon to have me back again.' He licked his lips like a dog with a juicy bone. 'Can't say I'm surprised though. I expect her old man don't know which way to start pleasing her, eh? That's the brunt of it, I dare say . . . these posh gents don't have much idea when it comes to satisfying a woman of her sort.'

'How do you know I won't tell him?'

'Because I'd wring your bloody neck, that's why.' He was sure of himself, and as far as Jenny was concerned, he and Claudia deserved each other. She did feel for Richard, but more importantly she was deeply troubled as to how this man's return might affect her and Katie.

'Get out the way or I'll do for you now!' No sooner had he

shouted than a black mountain of coal spilled from the sack on his shoulder, pouring down into the cellar and falling all around Jenny. She moved quickly, but not quickly enough; as the sound of his laughter echoed into that dark place, one large and jagged lump of coal tore the delicate skin of her ankle, splitting it wide open.

Somehow, Jenny knew this was only the beginning. There was trouble brewing, and in her heart she knew that she and Katie would be caught right in the middle of it.

322

# Chapter Fifteen

'How dare you question me!' Claudia sprang out of her chair, glaring at Jenny with naked loathing. 'What I decide to tell anyone is no business of yours. I've warned you often enough . . . one of these days you'll overstep the mark and face the consequences!'

'I'm sorry, ma'am, but I need to know if me and Katie will be left alone. I *know* it's none of my business what you do or say, but it's been almost a week since he turned up and I can't rest. That man knows Katie is your daughter and, to be honest, ma'am, I don't trust him. He could stir up trouble if he has a mind. He could decide to tell the master, and well – where would that leave me and Katie, that's what I need to find out? I'm sorry if you thought I was meddling in your private affairs, but years ago you charged Katie to me and now I don't want to lose her.' This past week she had lived on her nerves. Now, when the chance to say something presented itself, the words poured out in a torrent. In spite of her determination not to let Claudia see how anxious she was, Jenny was close to tears.

Claudia stood with her back to the fireplace, her pale eyes surveying Jenny's distraught face. To see her that way was a source of immense pleasure. 'My, my! You have worked yourself into a state,' she commented with a sly smile. Now, when the firelight caught Jenny's blue eyes, she could see the tears glinting there. 'I do believe it would be the end of your world if the girl was taken from you now.' The thought bred another thought more cruel, and Claudia was feverish with delight. 'Perhaps I'll find a way to settle our dilemma once and for all,' she mused aloud.

At once Jenny realised how foolish she had been to reveal her anxiety. 'What do you mean?'

'The girl.'

'What about her?'

'All these years she's been a thorn in my side!' Claudia's arms went rigid and her fists clenched into tight little balls. 'You can't possibly imagine how unbearable it's been, having to endure her presence here . . . with her likeness to my mother, haunting my every waking moment. And you. OH, YOU!' She seemed to choke on the words, clenching her teeth and stretching her neck upwards as though trying to wrench the very head from her shoulders. 'Your demands on her behalf are tantamount to blackmail. You've *both* been a thorn in my side, and it's time to end it!' Her eyes rolled in her head and the strangest smile came over her features. In that moment Jenny was more afraid than she had ever been. She had seen a glimpse of madness.

'If you're threatening to part us, I would think again,' she replied. The calmness in her voice belied the awful churning inside her. 'It's true my world would end if Katie was taken from me, but *you* have more reason to be afraid than me.' Something in Claudia's manner warned her to change tack. To attack was the best form of defence. 'If your gentleman friend was to reveal that you had a child, there would be awkward questions to answer.' She smiled when Claudia appeared to ponder on this. 'If you ask me, ma'am, you ought to make certain he knows how to keep a secret . . . for *both* our sakes.'

324

No sooner had the last word left her lips than Claudia rushed across the room. 'BITCH!' she screamed, at the same time fetching her fist hard against Jenny's head and knocking her down on to the settee. Breathless and white with rage, she viciously kicked out at Jenny with the sole of her shoe. 'Get out of my sight,' she hissed. 'And don't ever again assume to advise your betters.' When, dazed from the first blow, Jenny was slow to move, she kicked her again, laughing insanely when the blood seeped through the stocking over Jenny's ankle.

As Jenny went quietly from the room, Claudia's voice followed her. 'I'll be rid of you yet! You're nothing, do you hear? You and that bastard are only so much dirt beneath my feet.'

That night, deeply troubled and too restless to sleep, Jenny paced her room until the early hours. On soft footsteps she went to Katie's bed, where she gazed down on that beautiful sleeping face. 'She's right, you know. You *are* the living image of your grandmother.' She tenderly touched the auburn tresses and imagined those large green eyes beneath the sleeping lids. 'You're so much like her in other ways too, my lovely. You have the same strong and loving nature, the same compassion for others, and when you love, you love with all your heart . . . though you're too young to think of *him* in that way.

'Alan Hurd is not for you and never will be. Even your fragile friendship is wrong. I'm sorry, sweetheart, but like me you're destined to learn the hard way. Oh, but you're young yet, with your whole life in front of you.'

Gently she sat on the bed, and her blue eyes softened as she regarded that beloved face. 'I don't know what will happen to us, but I do know she means to hurt us. I saw it in her eyes today. She's eaten up with malice, more dangerous than ever, and I can't deny it, I'm afraid. Afraid of what she's planning. And she *is* planning something, I can feel it in my bones.' Carefully rising from the bed, she added softly, 'We're in God's hands now, sweetheart.'

With that, she returned to her own room where she quietly dressed and went out into the night. At the kitchen door, she drew her long shawl over her head and shoulders. The wind was icy cold, slicing through the trees with a shrill lament that curdled her blood. 'Sounds like the devils are out in force tonight,' she murmured, shielding her face against the wind and casting her eyes to the savage sky.

As she lowered her gaze to the perimeter of the shrubbery, her attention was drawn to where the moonlight picked out a sudden movement. She was astonished to see that the 'devils' were indeed out tonight for there, pressed up against the thick trunk of a tree, was Claudia – legs wide open and arms raised high, a low guttural sound issuing from her open mouth. Frantically pushing against her was the form of a man, and from his build and colouring Jenny believed him to be the 'gentleman friend' who had returned from the past to turn their lives upside down. Wedged hard between her thighs, with his great arms locked round her slim waist and his mouth bent to her nipple, he was half laughing, half crying as he pushed himself into her again and again. The two of them were in a frenzy, stark naked and going at each other like two wild animals.

At first Jenny was mesmerised by the sight of these two, brazenly copulating out here in the hostile night. But then she realised with a distasteful shudder: what crazed and sorry creatures you are. Fearful that she might be seen observing them, she quickly returned to her room and sat in the chair where she eventually fell asleep.

Panting and laughing, Claudia and her love ran hand in hand through the shrubbery. They were fully dressed now, and for the moment their lust was satisfied. 'You're completely mad, do you know that?' Tugging at her arm, he sat down on a tree stump and laughingly pulled her on to his knees. 'But that's why you excite me. You're different.'

Reaching down, she opened the buttons on his trousers and, fumbling inside, she shamelessly played with him until the member in her hands grew large and erect. 'If I'm mad, so are you,' she argued sullenly, but her eyes met his with dark temptation. When he raised his face and kissed her long and hard, she curled her fingers round his hand and pushed it beneath her skirt. 'Touch me there,' she whispered against his mouth. 'I like that.'

'You're insatiable.' He leaned forward, easing his arm upwards and forcing her legs wider apart. With practised skill he pushed his fingers up and down, in and out, exciting her beyond endurance. When she moaned, his movements grew frantic. Probing her mouth with his tongue, he asked, 'Want some more, do you?' Her answer was to wrap herself round him, grab his hair with both hands, and kiss him with such passion that he could hardly breathe. But when he would have stripped her there and then, she giggled and pulled away. 'No more. Not tonight.'

'Teasing cow!' He spat the words out. Enraged, he thrust her from him and sprang to his feet. 'I ought to smother the life out of you.' Standing over her now, he calmly took out his pipe and wad from the pocket of his jacket. His hands were trembling. Once the pipe was lit and jammed between his lips, he glared down at her. 'I'm fed up playing games,' he said angrily.

Dragging herself up, she feigned innocence. 'I don't know what you mean? What games?'

'Don't gimme that. You know all right.' He raised his hand to strike her but thought better of it. 'You and me . . . hiding out here on a night like this, snatching too little time together and always afraid we might be seen.' His face grew hard.

'Don't you think *I* hate the arrangement too?' she asked

327

sweetly. Secretly she was delighted. At long last he had grown impatient with what little she offered him; always enough to tempt him, to drive him mad with desire, but never enough to satisfy completely. Whenever she sent him away, it was with a feeling of frustration. It was a deliberate ploy, one which she had honed to perfection, and now it was about to pay dividends. 'I'd like nothing better than to take you to my bed,' she lied, 'and to hell with everyone. But I must be careful, you know that. My husband is a jealous man. If he ever found out.' She grimaced, as though the consequences were too awful to contemplate.

'That's easily settled. If you're telling the truth and you really want *me*, all you have to do is leave him. Like I said, I'm foot loose and fancy free. Things aren't the way they were before. There's no "little wife" counting on me for every damned thing. I'm my own man. I've saved a fair bank balance, and I've got a decent little place in Bedford. We can be comfortable there, the two of us.' He recoiled when she laughed out loud. 'What! Not good enough, eh?' he demanded sourly. 'Too used to the high life, are we?'

'Oh, it isn't that,' she said demurely. 'He wouldn't let me go, don't you see? He would hunt me down. There would be no peace for us.'

'Tell him you love me. Surely he'd give you your freedom then?'

'He would *never* let me go.'

That made him chuckle. 'What? You mean he hasn't seen the wicked side of you yet?'

'Unlike you, he sees only what he wants to see.' A look of evil came over her features. 'He's so pathetically boring, I can't tell you how much I hate him. If I wasn't the clever thing I am, he would have me mothering a dozen brats.'

'There must be a way to make him see you don't want him any more?'

'There is one way.'

'Oh? He tapped his pipe out on the bark of the tree and turned to face her. 'And what would that be?'

'Be rid of him.'

His scowl deepened. 'I hope I'm wrong, but you're not suggesting *murder*, are you?' He laughed nervously.

Now the suggestion was out, she grew bolder. 'Yes. That's exactly what I'm suggesting.'

He stared at her in disbelief. 'You're out of your mind!' he snarled. 'Whatever ideas you've got, you can count me out. I've heard of men being persuaded to commit murder on the promise of a woman. Well, I ain't so easily bamboozled. Oh, I haven't forgotten how you involved me in that business with your own mother, but it weren't *me* that did for her.'

'As good as.'

He laughed then. 'You're a bad 'un! A man must be out of his mind to get involved with a woman like you.'

'I'm worth it though, don't you think, Bill?'

He laughed again. 'You must be, or I wouldn't be standing here now.' He shook his head and thought hard. 'All the same, you're talking cold blooded murder. I'm not sure I could do it. I'm not even sure I want to.'

'Not even for me?'

He gazed at her in the shadows, and knew he would live or die for her. 'There must be some other way?' he said lamely. 'It seems too harsh to take a man's life.'

Afraid of his reluctance, she insisted, 'What if I said we'd both be wealthy afterwards? Imagine it, Bill, you and me together living in the lap of luxury. We could go anywhere you wanted. Just the two of us.'

With a coarse laugh he demanded, 'Just the two of us, eh? And what about your bastard daughter? Do you intend to kill her as well?'

'The girl's away at boarding school,' Claudia lied. 'She won't come between us.'

In the moonlight his eyes sought her out. 'On good terms with her, are you?'

'Of course.'

Shaking his head, he said ruefully, 'Somehow I didn't think you'd keep her.' Staring at her hard, he asked again, 'Does yer old man get on with her?'

'From the start.'

'Hmh! He must be soft in the head. You wouldn't catch *me* taking on some other man's bastard.' He looked up at the sky, stretched and said without looking at her, 'Thank Christ it weren't mine, or you'd 'a' soon been after me paying money for its keep. God knows you've wrung enough money out of me in your time.'

In her heart she thought of Frank. 'It was a better man than you,' she murmured.

'All water under the bridge,' he said casually. 'An upset like that would have mattered then. It don't matter now.' He studied her a while longer, musing on the interesting, if shocking suggestion she had made. He remembered what had taken place between her mother and them, and somehow the knowledge that she could coldly murder made her all the more attractive to him. 'Though it does mean we wouldn't be alone like you said . . . the two of us.'

'I've told you. The girl's at boarding school.'

'Huh! Won't be there forever though, will she? There'll come a time when she'd be under our feet . . . asking questions an' all, I shouldn't wonder.'

'I promise you, she won't be a problem.' Claudia snuggled up to him. 'But we have to get *him* out of the way.'

'And what exactly have you got in mind for the poor unfortunate bugger?'

'Leave the details to me,' she insisted softly.

'Gladly,' he agreed. Then closing her in his arms, he asked with genuine curiosity, 'What made you take up with me again? Was it really because I threatened to tell all, or do you find me irresistible?'

She peered at his face, a handsome if coarse face whose roguish smile often charmed her, and she was moved to confess, 'The blackmail was only a part of it. You appeal to my baser nature, and yes, you do hold a certain attraction, I suppose. Certainly you make love better than any other man I've ever encountered.' Nuzzling close, she shocked herself by being even more truthful, 'Besides, I knew I would have *another* use for you sooner or later.' Her blood was fired by his nearness, and the urge was on her again. 'Do you intend to keep me waiting?' she asked meaningfully.

Slipping out of her clothes, she stood before him in all her nakedness. And she could tell by the look in his avaricious eyes as he gazed at her that however much he might protest, he was putty in her hands. He was already halfway to killing. All she had to do was confuse and excite him, and he would do whatever she wanted him to. While he frantically threw off his clothes, she turned away to tell the dark side of the moon, 'It's time I was rid of them *all*.' The thought filled her with immense joy.

It was a week before Christmas. On this Friday afternoon everything seemed the same, with little indication of the tragedy that was to follow. The master had returned home the day before and wasn't due back in the City until the New Year. As usual, afternoon tea and sandwiches had been served to him and Claudia in the drawing room, and now, with everything left spick and span, Jenny was preparing to meet Katie from school. 'I shan't be too long,' she told the scullery maid who was sitting at the table polishing the best silver cutlery.

'Well, there ain't nothing else to do a while yet, so take yer time if you've a mind,' came the chirpy answer.

'Well, thank you kindly.' Jenny went away chuckling to herself. The scullery maid lived in a world of her own. Most of the time, she had little idea of what went on around her, and it was the devil's own work to get her into conversation. Still, she was a hard-working soul, and she sang a lot. 'I'd give a fortune to be content like that,' Jenny muttered aloud as she followed the path along the moors and towards the school.

Katie was standing at the entrance to the grand stone-built institution. Katie was not alone. 'Miss Treet wanted to have a word with you,' she informed Jenny.

Miss Treet was tall and thin as a pencil, and grey as a cloudy day. She was also a fine woman and a conscientious teacher who took a great pride in her pupils' achievements. She stood beside Katie until Jenny came near, and then took a step forward. 'I hope you don't mind my waiting here with Katie?' she asked anxiously. 'Only I did want a quick word with you. I won't keep you a minute.'

'Of course.' Jenny wondered why the other woman hadn't asked her to go to the office, until she realised that Miss Treet was dressed for leaving.

'I'm going away for the weekend, and I did so want to see you before I went.' Without waiting for the others, she began walking forward. Jenny and Katie quickly fell into step with her. 'Katie works hard at school, so it isn't surprising that she's striding ahead,' she informed the delighted Jenny. 'She shows the most amazing ability in art.'

'At home she sketches all the time,' Jenny enlightened her. 'She has any number of drawings in her bedside cupboard.'

Miss Treet stopped then, and looking directly into Jenny's thrilled blue eyes, told her, 'With your permission, Miss Dickens, I would like to enter Katie for a certain scholarship that has come to my attention. I'm not saying she would be successful, but if she was it would mean her going away to London, perhaps for a number of years.' Before Jenny could recover from the news, she swung away. 'I must go or I'll miss my train. Katie knows the details. Think it over and let me know on Monday.' With that she was gone, leaving Jenny staring at Katie and wondering what it was all about.

As they walked home, Katie explained. 'It seems an old gentleman, a painter by all accounts, has bequeathed a sum of money to the school. This money is to be used for sending promising pupils to art college, and Miss Treet has put my name forward. I'll have to pass the exams into college and there are more pupils chasing them than there are places, so it's no good getting excited yet.'

Jenny's heart sank at the thought of losing Katie to the big city, but she was determined not to dampen the girl's spirit and spoil what was the opportunity of a lifetime. Besides, wasn't this what she had worked towards all these years? 'A posh school in London, eh?' She hugged her warmly. 'Do you want to go?'

Katie shrugged, surprising Jenny with her answer. 'I'm not really sure. I know I don't want to leave *you*.'

They talked and talked, Jenny arguing that a chance like this might never come again, and Katie saying how she realised that, but it would be so lonely in London without her. It was a long meandering walk to the house and because they had so much to discuss they were in no hurry. They cherished this time of an afternoon when there was nothing around them but peace and solitude and the cry of birds wheeling overhead.

As they came out of the spinney at the top of the brow, the silence was broken by a thundering of hooves. At first they took little notice. This path was close to the bridleway, and it was a common thing for riders to exercise their horses along here. Only when the sound came closer and the horses appeared to be travelling at great speed did Jenny put up her hand to still Katie's chatter. 'I expect it's the young grooms from the top stable racing each other,' she said with exasperation. 'Some of 'em have no sense at all.'

When the two riders came into view, both Jenny and Katie were surprised to see that they were none other than Claudia and Richard. Claudia was racing away while her frantic husband, obviously under the impression that her mount was out of control, was yelling and shouting, and desperately trying to catch up with her. The look of horror on his face intensified when he saw Jenny and Katie standing on the path. When he roared for them to get out of the way, Jenny pushed Katie to one side and together they stumbled into the undergrowth.

Everything happened at once, and later, when Jenny was bound to recall it, she could remember only a great confusion while the two beasts bore down on them, with Claudia hanging on for dear life and Richard reaching out time and again to catch hold of her reins. Yet there was something else, something which she *imagined* she saw. In that mind-splitting instant before Richard was plucked from his horse as though by a mighty fist, and flicked through the air like a rag doll to land broken and torn on the ground, Jenny thought she saw something glint in the afternoon sun, something akin to a spider's web when the light plays on it. As she ran towards the carnage, a movement in the spinney caught her eye. Perhaps a figure fleeing through the undergrowth? But she could not swear to it.

Richard Hurd was killed instantly. 'A shocking thing,' they said. 'The narrow branch whipped into his chest and lifted him clear off the horse with one vicious swipe. Near cut the poor bugger in half.' The coroner decreed it 'a tragic accident', and the book was closed on the incident. His distraught wife could now bury her beloved husband and afterwards be left in peace to mourn.

* * *

The funeral took place on Christmas Eve. Old Helen Hurd travelled from Blackburn, and young Alan was granted compassionate leave. He looked tall and splendid in his khaki uniform, but in spite of his dignified bearing, there was an air of grief about him that touched everyone there. His stricken brown eyes stared with disbelief at the coffin and the name written there. This was his brother! A kind and good man who had been everything to him. Now he was gone, and the loneliness was unbearable.

Helen stood close by, constantly dabbing at her face with a prettily embroidered handkerchief and adjusting her cloche hat to hide the puffiness of her eyes. Like her young nephew, she could not altogether come to terms with what had happened.

Claudia was bedecked in black from head to toe, with a veil that covered her face so well that not a feature could be seen. It was impossible to know what was going on under that thickly scrolled lace, but from her intermittent bouts of uncontrollable trembling an impression of inconsolable grief was conveyed. They could not see the smile on her lips, nor the glint of satisfaction in her pale eyes.

Along with the other household servants, Jenny stood with Katie at the back of the church. Her eyes were dry, but in her heart she was weeping. If it hadn't been for the fact that she had witnessed what happened with her own eyes, Jenny would have sworn that Claudia had somehow caused his death. But it was an accident. Everyone said so. 'Her horse was wildly out of control, and in truth she was fortunate to have escaped the same cruel fate as her poor husband.' The official conclusion was feasible, and everyone poured out their sympathies for the 'heart-broken' widow. But not Jenny, because in her heart she was not altogether convinced. Yet it was only an instinct.

Later, when the few guests were gone and the high tea was cleared away, Claudia feigned illness and went to her bedroom. Helen sat in the drawing room and softly cried. 'Don't make yourself ill, Aunt,' Alan pleaded, and they clung together, bound by their grief, and deeply shaken by the awful realisation that Richard was never coming home.

'I'll be fine,' the old lady said, though she was pale and visibly trembling. 'Will you leave me awhile, please?'

'Are you sure you don't want me to stay with you?' He was concerned. His aunt was old and very precious to him.

She smiled a whimsical smile, and in that moment he realised that she was stronger than he. 'I dare say you'll want to see Katie?' she murmured, squeezing his hand. 'And I'm sure she'll want to see *you*.'

He bent his head to kiss her and she cupped his face in her hands. 'We still have each other,' she said. 'Never forget that.'

'I won't,' he promised. He ran his hand over her grey hair in a gesture of affection, then, without another word, he left her there while he searched out his beloved Katie.

'She's in her room,' Jenny told him. 'I'm afraid she's not good company though. She was fond of the master, as you know.' Like her, Katie was still reeling from having seen the incident that took Richard Hurd's life. For Jenny, though, it had raised a spectre more disturbing than she could admit.

She watched Alan's tall upright figure going towards the outhouse, and thought how quickly he had grown. 'A fine young man,' she murmured. Somehow she felt afraid for him. Yet she didn't know why.

'Will you want me to do anything else, miss?' The scullery maid put away the last plate and closed the cupboard door. Like all the servants, she was subdued by what had happened.

'No, you're free to do as you like,' Jenny told her. 'I've already been informed not to serve dinner tonight, so there's nothing else to be done 'til the morning.'

The maid screwed her face into an odd sort of grin then quickly departed, leaving Jenny to sit at the table and wonder what would become of them. 'God only knows what she'll do now,' she mused aloud. 'With Claudia Marshall, there's no telling.' It was with a little shock that she realised she had used Claudia's maiden and not her married name. 'Oh, but she's not married now, is she?' she asked herself. 'Her Majesty is foot loose and fancy free, and I can't imagine her being sorry about that!' A great anger rose up in her. Something was wrong about the master's death, but for the life of her she couldn't put her finger on it.

Katie was curled up in the window-seat, her knees tucked up under her chin and a faraway look in her lovely green eyes. When the knock came on the door she turned her face towards it. Almost immediately the door opened and there stood an upright figure in a dark uniform. Their eyes met and with a cry of joy she ran towards him, throwing herself into his arms. 'I prayed you'd come and see me before you went back,' she said. 'You looked so lonely at the church. I wanted to talk with you then, but it didn't seem right. And anyway, Claudia watched my every move.'

'*I* watched you too,' he admitted. 'Didn't you notice?' His brown eyes melted. 'Even when they lowered him into the ground, it gave me strength to know you were never far away from me.' Taking her hands, he clutched them and raised them to his lips. 'You must know I love you,' he said, kissing her clenched fists.

She couldn't speak then. Her eyes filled with unspilt tears and she had to lower her gaze or let them tumble. 'Jenny says I'm too young to know what real love is,' she confessed. 'But I know I miss you every minute when you're away, and I want to be with you all the time. Isn't that love?'

He stroked her face and wondered at its silkiness. 'I have to go back tomorrow.' His voice was filled with regret.

'I know.' She looked at him longingly. 'I'm so sorry about your brother. When others looked down on me and Jenny, *he* always made us feel important.'

Alan nodded, his face grim as he remembered. 'He made everyone feel important. Richard had that way about him.'

'Thank you for coming to see me. I know Claudia would make life difficult for you if she knew.'

'It doesn't matter to me what she thinks,' he remarked firmly. 'It never has.' He placed her hands in her lap and put his long fingers around her face. 'She won't keep us apart,' he promised. Then he shocked her by adding, 'Jenny's right though . . . you *are* too young, and perhaps I am too.'

'What are you saying . . . that you don't want to see me any more?'

'I'm saying that time passes quickly, and soon you'll be old enough to know for sure. Now that Richard's gone, I won't come back here. I want us to give it four years, Katie. By then, I'll be over twenty-one, and you'll be almost sixteen. I know I'll feel the same way about you, but I want *you* to be certain.'

'I am certain.'

'Four years, Katie. It isn't that long, not if at the end of it we'll have each other for the rest of our lives.'

'Suppose Jenny and I aren't here when you come back?' The tears were tumbling now and she felt ashamed.

'I'll find you wherever you are.' She dropped her head. With his fingertips he touched her jawbone and raised her face to his. After kissing her long and softly, he murmured his goodbye and went out into the cold grey light of evening.

That night, the girl sobbed in Jenny's arms. 'I'll never see him again,' she told her. 'And I *do* love him. I do!'

'I know you do,' Jenny confessed. 'But I wish you didn't.'

Katie was angry then. 'You're wrong. Alan and I don't care

about the difference in our backgrounds. If two people love each other, they shouldn't let anything or anyone come between them.' Her pain blinded her to Jenny's real motive, her desire to protect Katie from too much hurt. 'Anyway, what do *you* know?' She snatched herself away. 'You're as bad as *her*, only in a different way.'

'In spite of what you think, I do know about love, and the pain that can be caused by it.' She wasn't offended by Katie's remark because she realised it wasn't meant to be spiteful. Like all things we come to regret, it was said on the spur of the moment and in the wake of all that had happened.

At once Katie was repentant. 'Oh, Jenny, I'm sorry. I didn't mean it.' She threw her arms round Jenny's neck and clung to her. 'Forgive me?' she begged.

Disentangling herself, Jenny gave a broad smile. 'There's nothing to forgive,' she said.

'Jenny?' Katie sat back, regarding her with a degree of curiosity.

'Yes, sweetheart?'

'You've never spoken about having loved before.'

'Oh?'

'Who was he?'

'Someone I knew many years ago.'

'Did he love you?'

'Yes.'

'And you never married?'

'No.'

'Why not?'

Katie's questions were cutting too deep. 'It just didn't work out, that's all. It was a long time ago.' Frank's face was etched into her soul. It came to haunt her, bringing with it a sea of pain and anger. 'There's no point talking about it now,' she said a little too sharply.

'I'm sorry.' Katie was silent for a second, and then she asked impatiently, 'Do you still love him?'

The question took Jenny by surprise, and it showed in her face as she stared at Katie. It was an age before she answered, and then it was a simple truth, straight from the heart. 'Yes. I love him still.'

She was thankful there were no more questions. Instead, Katie fell asleep. For a long time Jenny lay in her bed, listening to the snow falling on the rooftop. She was all churned up inside. First she was thinking of Richard Hurd and the way he had met his death. Then she was thinking of Frank and the depth of her own feelings. 'In spite of everything, I miss you,' she whispered. 'You have a fine daughter, Frank Winfield.' Suddenly she was bitter. 'It's a pity you're not here when she needs you, you bugger!' Sighing, she wiped the angry tears from her eyes. 'When we *both* need you!'

With that, she turned over and went to sleep. But her sleep was not a restful one. They wouldn't let her sleep. Frank. And Claudia. And then there was the thing that glistened in the sunlight. And the shadow of a man. She had to know. Somehow, she had to find out what really happened. Even if it meant putting herself in danger.

For the next few days, Jenny wrestled with her conscience. Was she wrong in thinking there was more to Richard Hurd's death than had been revealed? Did she dislike Claudia so much that she was allowing her feelings to cloud her judgement? She suffered a turmoil of emotions. One minute she was certain there was something sinister about his accident, and the next minute she was reproaching herself for being so vindictive. 'If you're not careful, Jenny gal,' she mused aloud as she watched Katie going off to school, 'you'll end up as twisted as her upstairs.' The thought shocked her so much that she vowed then and there to keep an open mind about the whole business; although, when the time was right, she would carefully broach the subject with Claudia, and gauge her reactions.

A few weeks later, something unexpected happened. Something so disturbing that Jenny was forced into committing a drastic act.

In public, Claudia was still grieving, while in the privacy of her own home she was revelling in being the merry widow. Not a day went by when she wasn't either rolling drunk or rolling round the bedroom floor with her gullible lover. All the old wicked traits returned with a vengeance, putting Jenny in mind of what poor Elizabeth had been made to put up with.

'She's an absolute disgrace!' Sickened by what she had seen, the housekeeper broke her vow of discretion and made the fatal remark to the sad-eyed parlour maid who had just got on the wrong side of Claudia and was dismissed on the spot.

'She's a bad 'un an' no mistake,' sobbed the distraught girl. 'Men in her room, and booze in her belly. I thought she were supposed to be a lady.'

'Unfortunately she doesn't know the meaning of the word,' replied that fine upstanding woman. She choked on her words when Claudia marched into the dining room, having heard everything. For what seemed an age she glared at the two women before addressing the housekeeper with contempt. 'Obviously you don't enjoy your work either so you have my permission to leave this house at once. Of course you realise there will be no references? The very idea!' With that she swept out, leaving the two women consoling each other as they went off to pack their cases.

Jenny was not surprised by the turn of events. In fact, she had seen it coming, and was forced to consider her own position once again. 'Surely she won't expect *you* to do all the work?' Katie declared. 'Because if she does, you can tell her what to do.' Gone was the small frightened creature who had suffered nightmares after Claudia had viciously attacked her. 'Perhaps we should leave too,' she suggested recklessly until she remembered there was a chance that Alan might come back, so she tempered her words with, 'You know I'll help you all I can, Jenny, but you must stand up to her. Don't let her use you like she did before.'

Jenny's answer was a knowing smile and the heartfelt promise, 'Don't worry, sweetheart. She won't use me ever again.' And she meant every word.

The following morning, Bill Saxon returned. When Jenny opened the door to him, he strode through the house and up the stairs as though he had every right, and Jenny's suspicions returned to haunt her. 'Don't worry, *I'll* wake the sleeping beauty,' he told her with a brassy wink. 'And don't disturb us, there's a good 'un.' His laugh was coarse. 'She'll be too busy to eat any breakfast, I can promise you that.'

All day long lewd noises and laughter emanated from Claudia's room. Deliberately ignoring the images that assailed her mind, Jenny firmly shut the kitchen door and set about her own business. When Katie returned from school a warm aroma still lingered in the kitchen, the mingled smells of baked crusty bread, lardy cake and steamed fish. Unusually for this time of day, when the other servants would gather round for a light snack, the table was laid for only two.

As usual, Jenny had prepared a wonderful meal; there was fish pie with succulent vegetables, and to follow a choice between fresh currant scones and homemade preserve, and a huge fluffy chocolate gateau with cream on top.

Throughout the meal, Jenny directed questions at Katie as to how she was getting on at school. 'Have you heard anything about a place at art college yet?' she wanted to know. Katie laughingly told her she must be patient because it would be weeks before the results came through, and Jenny said she was certain that when the announcement came it would be in Katie's favour. At that Katie lapsed into silent reflection, and Jenny feared the danger of her refusing what could be the greatest opportunity of her life. Yet she would not persuade the girl one way or another, because after all in the end it had to be Katie's choice.

'Is that awful man still here?' Katie asked, rolling her eyes towards the ceiling. 'I saw him coming up the path when I left for school.'

'Yes, he's still here,' Jenny replied, beginning to clear the table. 'And that's all I want to hear about it.' The last thing she needed was for Katie to become preoccupied with the way Claudia conducted her life.

Springing from her chair to help with the clearing away, Katie shrugged her shoulders. 'I know she's free to do what she likes, but honestly, Jenny, I daren't think what Alan would have to say about it all. I've a good mind to write and tell him.'

Jenny spun round. 'You'll do no such thing, my girl!' she reprimanded. With a little shock she wondered whether Katie had kept certain information from her. 'Besides, how could you write to him when you don't know his address?' she asked suspiciously.

'I could write to Army headquarters or something. I'm sure they would forward the letter on.'

Jenny's relief showed. 'I thought you and Alan had agreed not to see each other for four years?'

Katie sighed and collected a clean dish-cloth from the cupboard. 'I know,' she said dreamily. 'But don't you think he should know about the way Claudia's behaving? When all's said and done, she is his sister-in-law.'

'As it happens, no. I do *not* think he should know. That young man has a career to carve out, and I'm sure he could do nothing at all about her behaviour, even if he wanted to. What's more, since he's made the difficult decision not to contact you until you're sixteen, I believe you must respect that decision even if you don't much care for it.' In fact, when Katie told her what Alan had said, her respect for him grew tenfold.

Katie was penitent. 'You're right, Jenny. I'm sorry.'

'Good. So you won't write?' With a rueful expression on her face, Katie shook her head. 'Fine!' Jenny declared. 'That's settled then.' She studied the girl hard before saying, 'I don't have to tell you that the sorry creature upstairs and I go back a long way. The plain truth is, I've come to know her like the lines on my own face, and regardless of what you might think, Katie, I am always one step ahead of her.' When Katie continued looking at her in puzzlement she said with frustration, 'Oh, look. What I'm trying to say is this . . . I would be grateful if you could put that woman and her doings out of your mind and leave her to me.' She handed her a plate. 'Will you do that for me, Katie?' Katie nodded and Jenny said softly, 'Thank you. Now then, young lady, I've got nothing else, so if you want to go, I can manage quite well on my own.'

'Well, there's some artwork I have to do.' Katie considered for a moment before declaring soundly. 'No. It isn't fair. I'll stay and help you finish.'

'I'm not tired, you know,' Jenny protested. 'In fact I'm bursting with energy.' And anger, she thought. I'm bursting with anger too.

'You didn't do any other work today then?'

'I didn't lift a duster nor poke one dead cinder through a grate. The bell from her room rang twice this afternoon, but I stuffed a bit of rag in it so I couldn't hear the blessed thing.' They glanced up at the old sock that was jutting out from the bell cage, and the two of them giggled. 'My days of being chief cook and bottle washer are over,' she said confidently. 'Besides, I expect she'll soon take on more servants, because she does like to be waited on when all's said and done.'

Katie hugged her. 'Good for you.'

By this time the dishes were dried. 'Off you go. I'll stack them away,' Jenny said. 'I'm sure you have better things to do?' She took the cloth out of Katie's hands and ushered her out of the door. 'I'll be a while yet,' she added.

No sooner had she closed the door behind Katie than the bell above her head made a muffled sound and the sock fell to the ground. 'Ring all you like, you bugger,' she muttered, going to the table and clattering about amongst the dishes. When the bell continued to ring, she began singing at the top of her voice: 'I'll take you home again, Kathleen, to where the fields are fresh and green . . . To where your heart has ever been, I'll take you home again, Kathleen.' But the sound of her voice could not shut out the clanging of the bell. 'I'm damned if I'll come up there!' she yelled, flinging the dish-cloth at it and holding the palms of her hands over her ears.

As suddenly as it had started, it stopped. 'Thank God for that,' she said. 'Happen I can get on with what I'm paid for.' She wiped down the sink and draining board and carefully stacked away all the crockery. When she turned from the cupboard, her heart nearly leapt out of her mouth for there in the doorway stood Claudia's fancy piece, dishevelled and unsteady on his feet, and eyeing her bare ankles as though he'd never seen one before.

The smell of booze went before him, and as he stepped further into the kitchen, Jenny stepped back a pace. 'Been leadin' her a right dance, ain't yer, eh? Yer a bold bugger and that's a fact,' he chuckled. 'But then, I've allus known it.' Flicking the end of his thumb towards the stairway, he went on gruffly, 'I shouldn't try her patience too much if I were you, though. She can be a bad 'un. Who should know that better than me, eh?' He came further into the kitchen, swaying as he walked, and Jenny thought he would fall on top of her. But this time, intrigued by his words, she stood her ground. 'What yer done to upset her, eh? Tell me that. She hates yer guts fer summat, there's no mistake about it.

345

By! I'd rather she were *your* enemy than mine, any day.'

'Are you trying to tell me something?' Jenny suggested irritably. 'Because if you are, I think you should know I'm quite capable of looking after myself.'

He laughed and the rush of his breath sent a sickening stench of booze to her nostrils. 'I'm just trying to warn yer, that's all, me beauty,' he said, coming ever nearer. 'She's got it in for you, an' – well, I reckon that's a right pity, 'cause yer a sweet-looking little thing an' all.' Reaching out to touch her, he made a sour face when she pulled away. 'Please yerself,' he said sullenly. 'It'll be yer own funeral, I reckon.' As he went towards the door, he rounded on her, furious at having been repelled. 'Think I'm lying, don't yer?'

'I don't think anything,' Jenny said proudly. 'Except that you and her are disgraceful.'

'Proud bitch.' He stared at her a moment longer, as though trying to decide whether he would be wise to say any more. In the end he decided he could say what the hell he liked. 'I bet yer wouldn't believe me if I said she was capable o' *murder*, would yer, eh? Not once, but twice. That's right, lady . . . TWICE!' His expression was smug when Jenny was obviously staggered by his words. 'Ah ha! That's made yer sit up, ain't it, eh?'

'You're mad.' In the back of her mind she had always known that Claudia was capable of the most heinous deeds. But what was he saying? That she had committed murder twice over? Dear God above!

He cocked his head to one side as though examining the statement she had just made. 'Happen I am mad,' he said at length. 'Happen she didn't get rid of the two of 'em after all. And happen if she knew I'd been talking to you, I'd be next on the list.' He roared with laughter at the sight of her stiff little body and her wide shocked eyes. 'Then again, it might be *you* who's next on the list . . . you and that brat o' yourn.'

Summoning up all the courage she could muster, Jenny demanded, 'Are you threatening me?'

He tutted and shook his head, then he tutted again. 'Whatever d'yer mean, lady?' he asked innocently. 'I come into the kitchen to get meself a glass of water, and here you are . . . accusing me o' saying things I never uttered at all.' He laughed again. 'I swear I never said a word. What's more, I'll swear the very same to anyone you put afront o' me.' Still laughing, he stumbled out of the door and out of the house. And Jenny was left reeling from the awful things he had said.

Sinking into a nearby chair, she asked herself out loud, 'What did he mean? He as good as said that Claudia had killed twice.' As though to stem the sound of her own voice repeating such terrible things she clapped her hands over her mouth, with her stricken blue eyes peeping over the top. '"Capable of murder", he said,' she muttered. '"Not once but twice," he said . . . "GOT RID OF 'EM!" That's what he said.'

The words tumbled over and over in her mind until in a frenzy she rushed to the dresser and from the drawer took out a writing pad and pen which she carried to the table. As though the devil was sitting on her back, she wrote fast and furiously.

'She'll know what to do,' she muttered as she wrote. 'Katie mustn't write to Alan, but his aunt has to know what's going on here. It's something far worse than ever I imagined, that's for sure.'

Suddenly a thought sprang into her mind and she sat bolt upright in the chair. 'Elizabeth!' She could hardly believe what she was thinking but it was there and it would not go away. In hushed tones the thought spilled into the open. 'Surely to God she didn't kill her own mother?' Even as she said it, her head was shaking from side to side in disbelief. She already had her suspicions about Richard's death but not this. Never this. It was too horrific to contemplate. But he said 'Twice' . . . 'Got rid of 'em.' They were his exact words. What else could it all mean?

With trembling hands she sealed the envelope, and after finding Helen Hurd's address in her handbag, wrote it down. Then she stuck a stamp on the corner, and with the letter clutched in her hand put on her shawl and hurried out, going by way of the house so Katie wouldn't see her. 'Got to post this right away,' she murmured. It was a long walk to the postbox on the corner of the lane, but she felt the compulsion to get the letter away out of the house before anyone could clap eyes on it.

She half walked, half ran to the postbox, furtively looking about as she went, thankful that there was no one in sight. She nearly died of fear when his arm reached out and snatched the letter from her. 'What's this then, eh?' Bill Saxon had been relieving himself behind a tree when he spied her there. 'Got a lover, have yer?' he taunted, hurriedly reading the address on the envelope. 'Oh, it's a *woman*!' His laughter was crude. 'So that's why yer don't fancy me, is it?' He stopped laughing when she snatched the letter back.

'What woman in her right mind would fancy a common oaf like you?' she cried indignantly, at the same time thrusting her two hands into his broad chest and sending him backwards into the ditch. 'That's where you belong,' she told him. 'Keeping the rats company.'

More angry than afraid, she dropped the letter through the mouth of the postbox and ran all the way back to the house where she collapsed over the table in fits of laughter. But then she recalled the reason for sending the letter to Helen Hurd, and her mood became deeply sober again. 'You'll get what's coming to you now, Miss High and Mighty,' she said, raising her blue eyes to the door and beyond to the stairs in the hallway. 'If there's any justice at all in the world, you'll get what's coming to you.' With that she finished her duties and went to her own quarters where she locked the door and drew the curtains. 'It's not dark yet, Jenny,' Katie reminded her.

'Dark enough,' she replied softly. 'In her mind's eye she could see Claudia, spreadeagled on the bed, blind drunk and senseless. Going to Katie, she hugged her close. 'It's dark enough, sweetheart,' she murmured. 'For some of us anyway.' She thought of the letter she had just written, and in her deepest heart knew she had done the right thing. She only hoped that Helen Hurd was half the woman she appeared to be.

349

# *Chapter Sixteen*

Helen Hurd sat at one end of the fireplace and her companion sat
at the other. Edna was the same age as Helen, but her hair was
not as grey nor her face as attractive. She had striking features, a
long nose and jutting eyebrows and a soft-lipped mouth that
seemed to spread from ear to ear. She was a fine strapping woman
who loved her friend with fierce protectiveness. Occasionally she
glanced up from her sewing, anxious at the other woman's
obvious restlessness. But all she got for her trouble was the curt
remark, 'What the devil are you staring at, you old fool?'

Ever patient, and knowing how, even after two months, Helen
was still in despair about what happened to Richard, she answered
with warm affection, 'I didn't mean to stare. I just wondered
whether you might feel the need to talk?'

Helen sighed, throwing up her hands and looking ashamed.
'Oh, take no notice, Edna. It's me who should be sorry,' she
apologised. 'I know what a cantankerous old biddy I've been
these past two months, but for the life of me I can't accept that
he was killed while out riding. There was no better horseman than
Richard. His mother used to write from foreign parts, describing
how the lad almost stopped her heart with his daring antics on
horseback. He would out-race anyone, and there wasn't a single
rider who could better him.' She shook her head. 'The more I

think about it, the more I'm convinced that there was something very suspicious about his death. I should have said so at the time, but of course I was swept along by the verdict and too swamped with grief to think straight.'

'Oh, my dear, I do wish you would stop fretting.'

Sitting forward in her chair, the old lady brought a softer gaze to her friend's homely face. 'I can't,' she told her. 'All right. I know what they said, about the branch whipping into him, and I know it can happen that way. But – well, I'm not sure. There are too many questions. For instance, why was *Claudia* able to avoid that branch? And why was her horse out of control? Like Richard, she's an accomplished rider and she's ridden that same mount across that same bridleway many times before.'

'It was an accident, Helen,' Edna urged. 'You told me yourself that everything was brought out in the coroner's court. How Claudia's mount took fright at something in the undergrowth, how it bolted with Claudia in fear for her life and Richard pursuing her to grab the reins. In the moment before Richard was struck down. Claudia's mount veered her away from the trees. The plain truth is, Richard was travelling at such speed that he didn't see the overhanging branch. You have to accept it, Helen. Richard's death was an accident and there's an end to it. You'll only make yourself ill believing otherwise. Please, Helen, you must put it out of your mind.'

'I'll try, of course I will, and you're right – I'm a foolish old woman.' It was true she couldn't stand the sight of poor Richard's widow, and there was nothing she'd like better than to see her shown up for the greedy creature she was, but being greedy and awful by nature wouldn't necessarily make her a murderess.

The two women drank their cocoa and with the heat from the fire and the constant rocking of her chair, Helen was soon lulled into memories of Richard as a boy. These days memories were all she had left, apart from Alan who was her pride and joy. From all accounts he was already making his mark in the Army, and enjoying every minute.

Thankful that at last her old friend appeared to be more restful, Edna folded up her sewing, lay back in the chair and watched her awhile. For a long time all that could be heard in that cosy parlour was the ticking of the clock and the click of the rockers as Helen gently pushed her chair backwards and forwards.

After a while the old lady was vaguely aware of coals being poked through the fire and the guard being hooked into place on the hearth. Then the sound of a drawer opening and shutting, and she knew that Edna had put away her sewing box. 'I'm off to bed now,' came that familiar voice. 'Is there anything you want before I go?'

Without opening her eyes, Helen shook her head from side to side. 'Goodnight,' she said. And soon the parlour was quiet again.

It was an hour later when Helen made her way up to her own bedroom. All day long, she had suffered the feeling that something was about to happen. And it did. The very next morning. Two things, one after the other, and both unpleasant.

On a Saturday morning, Helen and Edna would normally spend a happy hour or two wandering about Blackburn market where Helen would choose the juiciest shell-fish from the shrimp-woman's heavily laden basket. 'These 'ere shrimps were freshly caught when you were still abed and dreamin',' she would say with a cheeky wink. Afterwards the two elderly women would saunter between the stalls, with Edna buying sewing threads and Helen admiring the latest fashion in hats.

'For goodness' sake, hurry up, do!' Helen called out from the hallway. 'Anyone would think you were going to meet your sweetheart.' When Edna came into view wearing her best fur-collared coat and long boots, and clutching an umbrella, she chuckled, saying wryly, 'Or the Arctic.' But she was in good spirits for she had decided to take Edna's advice and try to put the matter of Richard out of her mind.

'You might laugh,' Edna chided, 'but the skies are full of snow and I for one don't intend to get caught out.'

But Helen did laugh. Until there came a knock on the door, and on opening it she found a young man there, the young groom at the farm where she kept the old cob. 'Farmer says you're to come quick as yer can,' he said breathlessly. 'Yer cob took a kick from a new mare in the field. Vet's on his way, an' I've been sent to fetch yer.'

'Is it bad?' Helen was shocked.

'Bad enough, Missus.'

Edna pushed her way past and was already hailing a cab. 'I'm sure it'll be all right,' she told Helen from the pavement. 'Do you want me to come with you?'

The idea that she wasn't capable of attending to a matter like this on her own put the old lady's hackles up. 'Of course I don't want you to come with me!' she snapped. 'Whatever next?' The cab drew into the kerbside. A man with a toothless grin and a flat cap peered out of his window at them. 'Cabbie?'

'Get a move on, boy,' Helen told the flustered groom. 'We haven't got all day.' And she gave him a sharp jolt with her cane, sending him at a frantic run down the steps.

Edna did a quick sidestep or she might have been sent hurtling into the road. 'I won't go to market without you,' she promised. 'You'll be back in no time. The old fella's been in fights before and given a good account of himself. I'm certain he'll be all right,' she said, ever optimistic.

'Don't be so bloody patronising!' Helen shouted as she climbed into the cab. 'And take yourself off to the market. I want *fresh* shrimps for my tea, not the day's leftovers. And if *that's* too much trouble for you, pack your bags and don't be here when I get back.'

Turning away, she didn't see the patient little grin on Edna's face, nor the muttered protest, 'Not again! You've been through too much for us to play games, old lady. I'll be here when you get back, with your fresh shrimps and all.'

Reaching out to close the door, Helen caught sight of the postman rushing towards her and so kept the door ajar. 'Hurry up, hurry up,' she said sharply. 'Can't you see I'm in a rush?'

Tommy Lassiter had been on this round for three years now, and he knew all about the old lady's temper. Handing her the letter, he said chirpily, 'Mornin', Miss Hurd. There's only the one today so I thought you might as well save me the trouble of droppin' it through the letter box.' Having delivered the envelope into her hands, he went on his way whistling.

The old lady gave the address to the driver, and he straight away scrunched the gear-handle into place. The motorcar went forward and the wheels turned to a tune on the cobbles. 'That old horse is a grand 'un, if yer don't mind me saying,' offered the young groom. He was seated opposite the old lady, his short fat legs tucked under the seat and his cap set at a jaunty angle on his flyaway red hair. 'Likes a fight, he does, but he picked on this new mare just brought in yesterday an' this time he got as good as he gave.' He shook his head forlornly. 'It's a bad kick, Missus. A real bad kick.'

Helen wasn't listening. Her sharp eyes were already scanning the contents of the letter, and as she read she grew more disturbed. Finally she folded the letter precisely and deliberately before placing it in her handbag. 'Must be that awful woman up to her tricks,' she muttered. 'Or Jenny Dickens would never have put pen to paper like this.'

'What's that you say, Missus?' The groom had been chattering away to her when he was pulled up short by her inaudible comment.

She waved her hand in a gesture of impatience. 'Nothing. I

said nothing. Now kindly keep quiet and let a body think.' He sat back and looked out of the window. Judging by the look on her face and the sting in her voice, the letter had put her in a foul mood. He knew enough to keep his mouth shut for the remainder of the journey.

The vet was adamant. 'I'm sorry. The beast will have to be put down.'

What with one thing and another, Helen was distraught. 'Surely there's *something* you can do to save him?'

He was not unsympathetic. 'Look, Miss Hurd . . . he's old. The cuts on his legs are deep and the bone itself is badly infected.' He stared at the animal as it writhed on the straw. 'I could treat him, I suppose, but it would only be a waste of time and money. Believe me, the kindest thing is to put him to sleep.'

'Get out of here!'

'I beg your pardon?' He was so shocked he fell against the stable wall.

Unleashing all her fury she told him, 'You're not fit to be a vet. You'd be more suited in a slaughter house. NOW GET OUT!'

His nostrils flared and he stamped his foot on the ground, and the groom thought he looked every bit like the bad-tempered mare in the field. With an arrogant toss of his head, he gathered his bag and strode out. 'I've given him a painkiller, but it won't last. When he's half mad in agony, don't call me back. Get someone else,' he called over his shoulder.

'That's exactly what I'll do,' she retorted.

The farmer took off his cap and wiped it over his brow. 'I'm not sure that was wise,' he said worriedly.

'Fetch Mr Winfield,' she said impatiently. 'He'll know what to do.

'*Frank Winfield?*'

She smiled for the first time since arriving at the stable. 'I'm sure that young man wouldn't dream of putting the old cob down because of a few cuts and bruises.'

'He's no vet, Miss Hurd,' the farmer protested. 'Good man that he is, there's nothing Frank can do here.'

'Fetch him, I tell you.'

He sighed and groaned, and realised that she would not be satisfied until Frank himself told her how hopeless it was. 'All right,' he reluctantly agreed. 'But it won't do no good.' With a crook of his finger he told the groom to see to it while he stared down at the uncomfortable beast and cursed himself for not letting the vet put him out of his misery before the old lady arrived.

It was less than an hour before Frank came rushing into the stables. But to those who waited it seemed like a lifetime. 'It was quiet for a Saturday morning,' he told them, immediately rolling up his sleeves and falling to his knees beside the cob. 'I understand he took a bad kick?' He glanced up at the farmer who discreetly shook his head as though to signify that there was nothing anyone could do for the beast.

Frank understood, and he was saddened. 'If the vet's seen him, I can't imagine that I can do any better, but let's see the damage.' He cast his anxious gaze over the cob's sweating face. Huge brown eyes stared back at him, pleading just as Helen was silently pleading.

She spoke then. 'Please, Mr Winfield, do what you can. I don't want to lose the silly old bugger.' She was not unaware that all eyes turned to her when she swore aloud. Nor was she sorry, because that was what he was, a silly old bugger who had let himself get badly kicked.

While roving his hands over the shivering creature, Frank told her gently, 'I can't promise anything but you know I'll do my best.' Bending over the animal, he spoke in softer tones. 'What's to do, old fella? Been chasing a mare who wanted nothing to do with you, is that it?' His thoughts jolted back over the years to Claudia. Now *there* was a mare if ever there was one!

For the next fifteen minutes, while Frank took his time examining the extent of the damage, the silence in that stable was like a tangible presence. Presently, he sighed deeply and stretched his aching back. With a look of consternation he addressed Helen. 'He's in a fever and going downhill fast. The bone's badly infected and there's no easy way of telling how serious the internal injuries are.' His voice hardened. 'I'm a blacksmith, Miss Hurd, not a vet.'

The old lady's eyes swam with tears. 'Are you saying that fool of a veterinary was right? He really can't be saved?' Lately she was beginning to feel her age and it was deeply disconcerting. She came nearer to him, her voice broken as she asked, '*Please! I have such faith in you, and you have a way with animals. I've seen it with my own eyes. Won't you help him?' She brought her gaze to bear on that once handsome horse who for many years had faithfully drawn her father's coal wagon through the streets. 'Please don't let him die,' she pleaded.

Frank bristled at the idea. 'Who said I was going to let him die?' he demanded. When her face brightened, he added, 'Like I said, I'll do my best, but it may not be enough.'

The farmer intervened then. 'Think what you're saying, Frank! Even I can see there's little hope.'

'But there *is* hope. He's a fighter, and I've got to give it my best.' Squaring his shoulders, he snapped, 'But I can't do it alone. I need your help.'

The farmer felt Helen's silent wrath, and shrugging his shoulders said, 'All right. I know what you need.' Striding across the stable he propelled the groom out of the door with him, listing the essentials as he went. 'A razor, sharp knife, and buckets of hot water. Plenty of clean cloths and carbolic.' He groaned aloud

357

when Frank called after him, 'Spirits, too, don't forget.' Breaking into a run, he told the groom, 'There goes my last bottle of best whisky.' But he didn't begrudge it. Not if there was the remotest chance the cob could be brought back.

There were back in a matter of minutes, by which time the cob was deeply unconscious. But that was just as well, considering what had to be done. 'You'd best go into the house, Miss Hurd,' Frank advised. 'You won't want to see any of this.' He also reminded her that the cob would probably not recover consciousness.

The old lady was adamant, 'I'm staying,' she told him. So the groom was ordered to fetch her a decent chair, and she sat against the wall, following the procedure without a word and never wavering, not even when the cob's whisky-soaked coat was scraped away and the skin sliced apart with the tip of the blade. The smell when the wound was laid open was nauseating, but still the old lady remained. Her faith in Frank was absolute.

Helen was old, though, and as the day wore on she slept and woke intermittently, wincing only once when Frank chipped away at the infected bone and the blood splashed up his arm. At one stage the smell was so powerful that she was forced to take out her handkerchief and cover her nose with it. Yet she would not leave. Not until Frank gave her the word that the old cob was safely out of the woods.

It was four o'clock in the afternoon when he washed his hands in the bucket and rolled down his sleeves. 'All we can do is wait now,' he said. Turning to the groom, who was filled with admiration and astounded by his natural skills and courage, Frank told him, 'Make a strong brew of herb tea and rainwater.' No sooner was it said than done, and for the next few hours Frank gently persuaded the old cob to swallow a teaspoon every now and then. 'They don't like this,' he told the others. 'But it's nature's own remedy.' While he knelt by the cob's head, the groom knelt by its great back, regularly swabbing its fevered body with cold water in an effort to stem the rising fever.

By now it was almost dark. 'If he doesn't give us a sign before long, I'm afraid it's all been for nothing,' Frank warned.

As though in answer the old cob shifted and coughed. 'That's it, old fella,' Frank cried. 'Let's see what you're made of, eh?' The huge brown eyes opened just a little, staring at him for what seemed an age, then they closed again, and all in a minute the old cob's breathing fell into a more natural rhythm.

Frank was ecstatic. 'He's done it!' he cried, choking back the emotion. 'I'm blessed if he won't pull through.'

'No, Mr Winfield.' Helen was on her feet and standing over him. 'It's *you* who's done it,' she said thankfully. 'And I'll never be able to thank you enough.'

Now she could go home and get a good night's sleep, knowing the old horse was on the mend. Tomorrow she would arrange for her journey South, because according to that letter Jenny Dickens had something very urgent on her mind. Something she was loath to put in writing.

# Chapter Seventeen

It was late Monday afternoon when the cab drew up outside the big house. After a long train journey and the cab ride along the narrow bumpy lanes from Bedford, Helen Hurd was bone weary. As she stepped from the cab, the first snowflakes began to fall. 'Wait here, young man,' she told the driver. Slamming the door shut and pulling her fur collar tight about her neck, she hurried across the driveway, cursing beneath her breath and angrily tapping her stick on the ground as she went. There had been a slight breeze when she came out of the railway station in Bedford, but now the wind was cutting and icy cold. The thought of her own cosy parlour and mug of steaming cocoa made her feel homesick and miserable.

Coming nearer to the front door, the old lady paused to look around. 'There's something very strange here,' she said aloud, her brows knit in a frown as she searched for a sign that her arrival had not gone unseen. However, all was in darkness. There was not a soul to be seen. 'Even if "Madam" was out, the servants would have a light of some sort on,' she told herself. But there was none. 'Strange,' she muttered. 'Very strange indeed.'

She rang the door bell, and when there was no answer she knocked at the door panel with her clenched knuckles, but still no one came. In the growing twilight the silence was ominous.

Glancing at the driver, she called out, 'You wait now. I'm going round the back.' The idea of being left stranded here was disconcerting.

With careful footsteps she followed the path round to the old outhouse where Jenny and the girl lived. That too was in total darkness. 'Whatever's going on?' she said crossly, tapping politely at the door. It was far too early for anyone to be in bed, and even if they had gone out for the evening, it was inconceivable that every single person, staff and employer alike, had left the premises.

'It's like the bleedin' *Marie Celeste*!' Suddenly the cab driver's voice pierced the awful silence, making the old lady scream out.

'Good God above!' she cried, whirling round and fearfully clutching at her throat. 'You very nearly frightened the life out of me!' Her fear gave way to anger and she actually hit out at him with the tip of her cane. 'What do you think you're doing, creeping up on me like that?'

'I don't like the look of this place, Missus.' He cast a nervous look towards the big house. 'There's summat ain't right about it. Makes my flesh creep, it does.' He shivered and hugged himself. 'I had to make sure you were all right though.' He chuckled then. 'Should'a known better, 'cause all I got for me trouble was a belt round the legs with a walking stick.' He rubbed the side of his ankle where she'd struck out with her cane.

'Huh!' she snorted. 'Creep up on me like that again and it'll be your *head* next time.' As he gave an apology and went to turn away, she grabbed his arm. 'Now that you're here, you might as well stay,' she said. Like him she felt there was something very odd going on. When he pressed nearer, she knocked on the door of the outhouse again. And again there was only silence. 'I can't understand it,' she said worriedly. 'The big house is empty, and now this.'

'Who lives here?' he enquired curiously, all the while glancing about.

'This place belonged to my late nephew, Richard Hurd. Now it belongs to his widow, heaven forbid.'

In the growing darkness he stared at her. 'Richard Hurd,' he repeated softly. 'If I'm not mistaken, that's the fellow who was killed in a tragic riding accident?' When he saw her look of surprise, he informed her, 'They did a big spread in all the papers. I only live about twelve mile away and it seemed I didn't pick up a fare without they were full of it.' Suddenly realising how painful this must be for her, he apologised. 'Your nephew, eh? I am sorry.'

'Not half as sorry as I am,' she said pensively. An instinct made her push at the door. When it fell open, she and the cab-driver stared at each other in astonishment.

He was even more astonished when Helen started forward. 'You're never going in?' he asked incredulously. 'What if they're in bed. By! You'll put the fear of God in 'em.' She put up her hand and silenced him. Deeply inquisitive in spite of his forebodings, he followed her.

'Katie?' The old lady's anxious voice pierced the darkness. 'Jenny Dickens, are you there?' Just as before only silence greeted her. A deep unnerving silence.

Growing ever more concerned, the two figures went forward cautiously, lighting the lamps as they went. It soon became obvious that there was no one home. 'We'd better go,' suggested the nervous cab driver. 'I hope you know we're trespassing, and if we're caught it won't matter a fig whether this little lot once belonged to your late nephew. The fact of the matter is it doesn't belong to him *now*, and it's time we left.' Retracing his steps from the delightful little sitting room that Jenny had made home, he doused the lights one by one, until only the one remained lit, and that was the one in the sitting room.

'Something's happened,' the old lady murmured. 'Something awful has happened here.'

He was scared then. 'Give over, lady!' he laughed nervously. 'You're giving me the goose bumps. Anyway, what do you *think* might have happened?'

'I don't know, but put your mind to it, man!' she snapped. 'It's right in front of your eyes. The big house is empty too, I shouldn't wonder . . . certainly there's no one there to answer a knock on the door, and that makes me very curious to begin with. All right, I can accept that Mrs Hurd may be out gallivanting . . .' She made a sour little face. 'In fact, it wouldn't surprise me in the least. *But where are the servants?* My nephew's widow had an army of servants. It's inconceivable that they're all out on the same evening.'

She paused and stared about her, at the cosy little room with its home-made curtains and colourful rugs, at the dresser with its cherished ornaments and the window-seat with its plump frilled cushions. 'Jenny Dickens and her girl live here. Where are they?' She pointed to the door. 'I've no doubt she might leave the door open during the daytime, because she's never further than the big house, but I honestly can't imagine a sensible young woman like her going out of a night and leaving her home open for any passing vagabond or rogue.'

'What, like us, you mean?' he asked impudently.

Deliberately ignoring his quip, or perhaps not having really heard it, she went on, 'Jenny Dickens is the cook at the big house. As I recall, neither the woman nor the girl ever goes far away.' She turned to look at him, her face grim and confused. 'Don't you think it's strange that they too should be out?'

'I think *we* should be out, that's what I think!' he grumbled. All the same, he was puzzled. Crossing slowly to the mantelpiece, he looked up at the array of paraphernalia there. Elizabeth Marshall's picture smiled down at him. 'She's a good-looker, this

363

Jenny of yours.' He grinned mischievously. 'From what you say there isn't a man in her life. Well, happen she's found one and they're out enjoying themselves.'

'It's a thought, of course,' the old lady admitted. 'But I doubt whether they would take the girl along of an evening, and anyway that still wouldn't explain everyone else being out at the same time, now would it?' She came to stand beside him. When her eyes followed his gaze upwards to the picture her eyes alighted on Elizabeth's face with a little shock. 'This isn't Jenny,' she corrected him.

'Who is it then? Like I say, she's a real looker.'

'I have no idea,' the old lady replied. She gazed at the picture in astonishment. When first her eyes looked on that strong handsome face, she was taken aback. Now she was bemused. 'But it certainly isn't Jenny Dickens . . . although she's very attractive in her own way.' Taking down the picture, she studied it curiously. 'In fact, if anything, it's *the girl* who bears a striking resemblance to this handsome lady.' Her inquisitive eyes followed the contours of Elizabeth's face, the refined yet strong features, the rich dark hair and those splendid smiling eyes. 'Yes,' she said resolutely. 'I see young Katie in this woman's face.'

'Then the girl's destined to be a beauty,' the man declared. 'It's a pity the picture couldn't be in colour, because I reckon it would be a sight to see.'

Without thinking, the old lady was prompted to remark, 'I wouldn't be surprised if this woman's hair is the deepest auburn and her eyes green as the sea.'

He whistled with admiration, and as he did so she replaced the picture and ordered him in a clipped voice, 'Take me to the nearest police station.'

Before he could reply, she was already hurrying out of the door and down the path. Quickly, he doused the light and firmly closed the door behind him. 'Women!' he pronounced in a loud whisper then ran after her, amazed at how swiftly she went on ahead of him. 'Bedford's the main one,' he called out. 'Though I expect there'll be a policeman resident in nearby Haynes village.'

The police house was situated on the main road. Its resident didn't take kindly to being summoned from his soft squashy armchair on such a night as this. 'Yes? What is it?' He edged open the door and poked his face through the mean gap he had made. 'I hope it's an urgent matter.' Directing his gaze to the road he saw how the cab had mounted the pavement, and was deeply peeved.

'We won't know that until we find out, will we?' the old lady said wisely. 'Perhaps I could come in?' She thrust her cane in the open doorway, her sharp eyes regarding him with disappointment. To her way of thinking a policeman should never be seen with slippers on his feet or his sleeves rolled up. To make it worse, this person was enormously plump. 'You're not what I expected,' she said frankly, 'but as there's no one else between here and Bedford town, and the cab driver is impatient to return home before the weather worsens, I'm afraid you will have to do.'

He was incredulous. 'Well now, I'm sorry about that, but I am off duty, you know!' Smartly straightening up, he quickly fastened the top button of his shirt.

'Off duty nothing!' snapped the old lady. 'A policeman is *never* off duty.' Undeterred, she pushed herself forward and he was forced to make way. 'We'll talk inside,' she called out as she marched into his front parlour. 'I've just come from the village of Ickwell and have a very disturbing matter to report.'

'Indeed?' he queried, closing the door with his foot while he frantically rolled down his sleeves. 'What might that be then?' His temper was not improved when he caught sight of the cab driver sitting behind his wheel and broadly grinning at him. 'I'll have you for mounting that pavement, you bugger!' he muttered under his breath, though when he came into the parlour he was all sweetness and smiles. 'Now then, Mrs . . . ? What's troubling you?'

The glare she gave him would have shrivelled a rose in full bloom. 'Miss!' she told him proudly. 'The name is Miss Hurd, aunt of the late Mr Richard Hurd. I've had a long and tiresome journey so I'll come straight to the point. I was summoned here by a Miss Jenny Dickens, who is cook at the big house in Ickwell.' Delving into her coat pocket she withdrew the letter which Jenny had sent her. 'The letter itself disturbed me, and now I'm made even more anxious by the fact that she appears to have gone missing . . . or that something untoward has happened at the house.'

He nodded his head in the slow methodical way all policeman do, then kindly bade her sit. 'I'm sorry you've been distressed,' he said gently. His sudden thoughtful and generous mood made her nervous.

'There *is* something going on, isn't there?' she asked. 'I need to know.'

'You're quite right, ma'am,' he began earnestly. 'There has been trouble in the village of Ickwell. And yes, I'm afraid it does involve one or two members of the household you mention.' In complete contrast to the man who had opened the door, he now positively bristled with authority. 'Well then,' he remarked sombrely, sitting opposite her, 'I'll tell you as much as I can.'

As he went on, the old lady reeled from one shock after another. It seemed that not only had Jenny and the girl been viciously attacked while walking home from school that afternoon, but once the girl had come out of shock, she had been able to describe the attacker as Claudia Hurd's 'fancy man'. 'When the facts began to emerge, I myself was summoned straight away to the hospital. I gently questioned the girl about the incident, and because of the seriousness of it all, it was duly reported. The case has been taken over by a higher authority than me.'

The old lady was stunned. 'A "higher authority"? What are you saying . . . attempted *murder*?'

'To be honest I shouldn't be saying anything at all, but as you're familiar with the family, you might be able to shed a little light on the suspect. He's said to be a Mr Bill Saxon?'

'Surely you've questioned the pair of them?' Helen was on her feet now and preparing to leave.

As was his habit when flustered, he drew in a long breath and held it until his face went red and the words burst out in a rush of air. 'We've questioned the woman, but so far the man's eluded us.'

'When did you question her?'

'Not two hours since.' He frowned. 'I must say I was surprised when she answered the door herself.' In his mind's eye he could see Claudia in that moment when she flung open the door, a strikingly handsome woman, merry from too much port by the look of it, but when he told her what had happened she was visibly shocked, falling over herself to be helpful. 'She denied knowing this particular fellow. In fact, even the neighbours knew nothing of this "fancy man".' He shrugged his shoulders. 'Of course the girl had been knocked unconscious. She can be forgiven for imagining things. The attacker could have been anybody . . . a tramp, a vicious poacher afraid he'd been seen.'

'If the girl said it was Claudia's fancy man, then that's who it was,' Helen told him abruptly. 'Katie is a level-headed young woman, and not given to imaginings.'

'We shall see.'

She brushed this aside. 'If you ask me, Claudia Hurd herself is mixed up in this somewhere, but you won't get the chance to question her again because from what I can see she's taken to her heels. Like as not she's made off with this "fancy man" Katie speaks of.'

Before he could comment, she enquired, 'Which hospital are they in?' And when she learned it was the Bedford General she hurried away, leaving him wondering about what she had said with regard to the mistress of the big house. A short time later he too departed, but in a different direction. He was making for Ickwell and the big house. The old lady had implied that the woman had fled and his suspicions were fired.

Katie had a deep wound to the right of her forehead. It had needed six stitches, but apart from that she was unharmed. Seeing the old lady she threw herself into Helen's arms. 'Aunt Helen!' For a minute she couldn't believe her eyes. 'Who told you? How did you get here so quickly?' The questions poured out and the tears fell down her face as she clung to that familiar soul.

'It was that man . . . the one who goes with Claudia. We were walking home when he came at us from out of the spinney. I was a short way behind and I didn't see him at first, but I heard Jenny cry out and ran to her. He had a piece of branch in his hand and he was like a madman . . . Oh, Aunt Helen, he kept hitting her over and over. When he saw me he tried to run off, but I chased him a short way, yelling and shouting for someone to come and help us. But he turned on me and – oh, Aunt Helen . . . I . . . It's Jenny! See what he's done to her!' She began sobbing and the nurse took her away, at the same time pointing to the bed in a side ward where Jenny lay swathed in bandages.

The old lady sat by her bedside until morning broke. Katie returned, her soulful gaze directed to her beloved Jenny's face and her sorry heart praying that she would be well again. Outside a policeman kept guard at the door, and soon after midnight a man in a suit came to question Katie gently. She told him what she had told the uniformed officer, 'It was Claudia's fancy man', and they believed her. Especially as they had located the house-keeper who had worked at the big house and was now employed at a nearby hotel. With what she had told them, together with the fact that Claudia Hurd and her 'fancy man' had in fact disappeared, the case against them looked black.

The hours stretched by, long and arduous. The old lady and the girl slept and then woke but they would not leave the patient's side. Later that day, Jenny showed her strength, opening her pretty blue eyes and smiling at them. Her fingers reached out to touch Katie's outstretched palm, and the nurse whispered that the worst was over. Later the doctor said the same. Apparently she had taken the heavier blows on her shoulders, although there was a deep jagged cut to her face. 'She will need to wear a sling for some weeks because of that damaged collar bone, but I don't think any of the wounds will scar,' he said. 'Time alone will tell.'

Katie cried with relief and the old lady comforted her. 'You're coming home with me,' she said. 'The minute Jenny can travel, you're both coming back to Blackburn with your Aunt Helen.' She cradled the girl in her arms. 'You're family now,' she said softly, and Katie cried again, but this time the tears were tears of joy.

'For God's sake, have you gone mad?' Claudia peered out of the car window at the dilapidated house, and she was mortally afraid. In the moonlight it was bathed in a ghostly hue. Its broken window shutters swung from their hinges, gently swaying in the night breeze. The guttering hung loose down the walls, and there were many gaps in the roof where the tiles had once been. The front door was wide open and all around there were signs that the place had been neglected for many years. Never in the whole of her miserable life had she been so frightened.

Turning to the man, she complained with a show of bravado, 'You've no right to bring me here against my will.'

369

Bill Saxon viciously turned on her. 'Are yer threatening me? If so, I wouldn't advise it, my beauty.'

She appealed to the greed in him. 'If you take me back right this minute, I promise I won't tell them what you've done, and I'll see you don't go short of money.'

He looked at her as though considering her words. Mistaking his hesitation for weakness, she pressed home the empty promise. 'I really *won't* tell anyone, you have my word.' Waiting for his answer, she hoped against hope that her lies sounded convincing and he would listen to reason. So far all her efforts to escape had been in vain. It wasn't the first time during the long hours of the night that she'd felt she was fighting for her very life.

Swinging round, he pinned her against the seat with one mighty arm. 'So you won't tell them what I've done, eh?' he sneered. 'You won't tell them how I finished off your husband? Or how you persuaded me to lie in wait for the Dickens woman and the girl?'

'I won't tell,' she said desperately. 'You have my word. They won't find out from me.'

He leaned closer, his narrowed eyes scrutinising her lovely face. 'Hmh! You might open yer pretty mouth, and yer might not. Makes no difference now. But happen *I* might have a thing or two to say, though. Don't you think they might be interested to know it was *you* who decided how and when your husband should be murdered? And wouldn't they be curious to know whose idea it was to kill the Dickens woman and the young 'un?' He chuckled and she shrank back in her seat. 'That's not all either, is it?' he said slyly.

Claudia knew he was referring to her mother. In her hatred of him, she grew too bold. 'I didn't murder Richard though, did I?' she demanded angrily. '*You* did that. What's more, it's your word against mine about the incident near the spinney.' She almost spat the accusation. 'You were supposed to finish those two, but you messed it up, like the fool you are! I told you that letter you saw would bring trouble down on our heads, and it's all your fault! If you hadn't got drunk and blabbed, none of this would have happened!' Her loathing for Jenny boiled over. 'That Dickens woman has always known too much for her own good. I wanted rid of her. Why couldn't you have done the job properly, damn you?'

His face hardened, but his voice held a semblance of amusement. 'I do believe you're wild enough to send me to the gallows if the opportunity came up.'

'You *are* mad!' Her voice shook with astonishment. He was too near the truth for comfort, because after that visit from the police she had already decided to save her own skin, and to hell with anyone else.

Her remark made him laugh. 'Oh, I'm mad all right. Mad enough to commit murder for you, and to do the same over again if that's what it takes to keep you.' He tickled her under the chin, grinning cruelly when she pulled away. 'But I don't think I'd want to swing from the gibbet for you . . . some time in the future maybe. But not yet.'

'You're talking nonsense. Nobody's going to swing from any gibbet,' she lied. 'Take me back, and later, when everything's died down, I'll arrange my finances so that we can go away wherever you want, do whatever you fancy. What do you say?' The ropes were cutting into her flesh and she was frantic.

He gave no reply. Instead he got out of the car and walked round to her side, where he first checked the ropes at her wrists and ankles before roughly dragging her out and throwing her across his shoulder. 'Save yer breath,' he told her. 'There's nothing you can say now that will change my mind.'

In the dark he stumbled many times before they were safely inside the old building. Once there, he carried her down the dark narrow steps to the cellar. 'Like a cat I am,' he boasted with a sinister chuckle. 'I know this place inside out. You see, I've been coming here for some time now, getting it ready, yer might say.'

When she pleaded with him, scheming and lying, repeating her promise not to implicate him and to give him all the money he wanted, his answer brought a chill to her soul.

'It's *you* I want, my lovely Claudia. I never wanted the money, only you. I know if I take you back now we'll never be together again. So I won't be taking you back. Not now. Not ever.'

# Part Four

## 1931

## TRUE LOVE

# *Chapter Eighteen*

On 14 February 1931 Jenny and Katie left Ickwell for good.

After spending a restless night, when the events of the past threatened to overwhelm her, Jenny gave a sigh of relief as dawn broke through a shifting sky, sending a spiral of light into the outhouse. 'Another day,' she murmured, rising from her chair and going to the window. 'And who knows what it will bring?' When there came a sound from the door, she turned to see Katie standing there. 'Come here, sweetheart,' she said, holding out her arms in greeting.

Katie came to her then, and embracing each other the two of them stared out of the window at the lightening sky. The night clouds began to evaporate and the bright February sunlight sparkled through. 'It looks like it'll be a fine day at least,' Jenny told her with a reassuring smile. Though she didn't want the girl to worry, she herself was deeply anxious about the decision which was already made.

'Are we really leaving?' Katie's deepest emotions were betrayed by the slight tremor in her voice.

'It's for the best,' Jenny replied. She too was afraid. Leaving here was hard, but it would be harder, impossible now, for them to stay.

Katie reflected for a moment before voicing the doubt which

375

had been in her mind ever since the old lady's letter had arrived over a week ago. 'I know it isn't for me to question your judgement, Jenny,' she began hesitantly, 'but I don't understand why we can't accept Aunt Helen's offer. She said we could stay with her until we found a place of our own.'

Jenny smiled at Katie's words. Wasn't it amazing how the very young saw everything in black and white? 'It isn't as simple as that, sweetheart,' she protested.

'But why not?'

'For oh so many reasons,' Jenny reminded her. 'Though she's very kind and has befriended us through troubled times, Helen Hurd isn't *our* relative, and we're certainly not her responsibility.'

'But she *wants* to help!'

'I know that, and you mustn't think I'm not grateful because I am. Helen Hurd is a kind and wonderful old lady, and she has a heart of gold. And that's the very reason why I will not take advantage of her offer.' Jenny paused, recalling every word of the old lady's letter:

> Dear Jenny,
>     My offer is still open. There is room in my house for you and Katie, and I would dearly love to have you both here with me.
>     Besides, I still have many business contacts, so I'm quite certain it would be only a matter of time before we found you a suitable position.
>     Please consider my offer and let me know what you decide. Meanwhile stay well, and love to Katie.
>                                         Yours affectionately,
>                                             Helen Hurd.

'I've already written back to thank her, but I've explained we will be all right. I do have a few plans, and we're both strong and healthy so we'll manage well enough.' Her heart sank when she saw the downcast look in Katie's eyes. 'You have to trust me,' she entreated. 'You know I won't let any harm come to you.'

Katie's face brightened as she looked up into Jenny's calm features. 'And I won't let any harm come to *you*!' she fervently promised.

'There you are then. It isn't fair to lean on that dear old lady when we're quite capable of looking after each other.'

'It's your pride that's talking, isn't it?' teased Katie. 'You've always stood on your own two feet and now it frightens you to be beholden.'

Jenny was thrilled and shocked at the same time. Katie had read her like an open book. 'And I thought you were still a child!' she admitted softly. 'When all the time you've a wise old head on young shoulders.' She gazed on that lovely familiar face, and as so many times before saw Elizabeth in Katie's every feature. 'As long as I have you,' she murmured, 'I can face any obstacle that life sends me.'

Katie's answer was to show absolute trust in this woman she adored. 'I expect you're right not to accept Aunt Helen's offer,' she confirmed. 'And won't she be proud of us when we've found a home and both of us are working?'

Jenny corrected her at once. 'When *I'm* working . . . and you are attending Art School, young lady!' When she saw that Katie was about to protest, she interrupted. 'No arguments.'

'We'll see then.' Katie was secretly hoping that one day an opportunity would arise and she could go to Art School, but if it wasn't to be, that was all right too. She could see that Jenny had made up her mind on the subject so wisely chose not to pursue it for now. 'Well, if we're not going to Aunt Helen's, where *are* we going?'

'Like I told you last night, we'll make our way into Bedford where I'm certain to find work of a kind. We'll make a start along the river. There are some fine big houses there, and I wouldn't be surprised if I wasn't fixed up right away.' She laughed a little. 'After all, I can turn my hand to anything now . . . parlour maid, housekeeper, cook . . . even charlady if I have to.'

Katie looked up with tearful eyes. 'I don't want you to be a charlady.'

Jenny gently shook her. 'There's nothing wrong with being a charlady,' she reminded her. 'It's good honest work, and it should put a roof over our heads. Besides, we must get settled in order for you to get back to your studies. I won't have you losing sight of that Art School, my girl,' she reprimanded lightly. 'All right, it's too late for the scholarship, but you'll get there, Katie, I just know you will.'

'I don't think I want to. Not if it means you have to be a charlady.'

'And I don't want you to become a snob, my girl!'

Katie drew away from her. 'You know it isn't that, Jenny,' she insisted. 'It's just that you've always had to work so hard, and I know I'm a burden to you.'

Jenny could hardly believe her ears. With firm hands she guided the girl to a chair and sat her down. 'You . . . a burden?' she asked incredulously. 'I've never heard such nonsense!' Sitting herself in the chair opposite, she took hold of the girl's hands, telling her sincerely, 'Whatever happens on the road, or however hard we have to work, I want you to know something and you must never forget it.' Lifting the girl's downcast face with the tips of her fingers, she told her sincerely, 'You are everything to me, Katie. Without you, my life wouldn't be worth a fig. Since the day you came to me as a wee bairn, I've loved you like you were my own. Everything I've ever done has been for you, and I wouldn't trade one single minute of it . . . not for *anything*.'

Jenny looked into those strong green eyes and her heart was

filled with so much of the past that the memories were like a physical presence: Elizabeth, Claudia and Frank. It all began to crowd in on her until the images merged with each other.

Katie's eyes filled with tears. Suddenly she was more afraid than she would ever admit. 'I'm sorry,' she whispered. 'It's just that everything's changing so fast.'

'I know. But you and me, we'll be just fine, you'll see.' Jenny shook her gently by the shoulders. 'We're made of good stuff . . . a pair of old troopers, eh?'

Katie couldn't help but chuckle. 'I expect so.'

'And you won't ever again think you're a burden on me?'

'No. I shouldn't have said that. And, oh, I do love you so.'

Jenny was heartened. 'I know all of this must be harder for you than it is for me.' She realised that the sooner they were gone from here, the sooner it would all be behind them for good.

'Now shape yourself, my girl,' she declared firmly. 'There's been enough said. We'll have a good breakfast and then you can pack your things.' She pointed to the small portmanteau standing beside the back door. 'I've already packed mine, except for the clothes I've put out to wear and the things on my back.' She smiled wryly. 'When all's said and done, it's amazing how little a body owns.' She thought of the scanty items of clothing and her one pair of best shoes. To tell the truth, the most treasured item in that portmanteau was the picture of Elizabeth.

As though reading Jenny's thoughts, Katie looked across at the mantelpiece and saw that the picture was gone. 'Aren't you taking any of the other ornaments?'

'Not a one. As long as we have a stout pair of shoes to our feet and a change or two of clothes, that's all that matters.' She clambered to her feet and began bustling about making the breakfast, while Katie soon had the table laid and the toast thickly buttered.

With the bacon and eggs sizzling in the frying pan, and the tea freshly brewed, the tiny scullery quickly smelled warm and inviting, and as they sat down to eat a hearty breakfast Jenny's fears turned to optimism. 'We've a lot to be thankful for,' she told Katie. 'We've both got our health and strength, and because I've always had the good sense to put a shilling or two by when times were good, we've a little money to tide us over any rough patches ahead.'

'Oh, Jenny, that little nest egg was put by for your old age. I hope we don't have to dip into that.'

'Don't you worry, sweetheart,' she laughed. 'I'm not in my dotage yet, and before you know it we'll have a roof over our heads and I'll have some good honest work. I'll not be settled until you've picked up on your schooling, but it'll all come right in the end, I feel it in my bones.'

Katie laughed at that. 'You and your bones!' she said. 'Funny thing is, they're always right.'

'That's because they're getting old and canny, like me.'

Katie was disgusted. 'You're not old!'

'I'll be thirty-six next birthday,' Jenny declared with a little shock, and wondered at how quickly the years had sped away. When Frank left and Katie was born soon after, she had been a young woman. Now her youth had gone forever. 'The old saying is "Time and tide wait for no man", and it's right, sweetheart. Your teacher told me that you have it in you to be a fine artist. Make it your goal, Katie, because I would be so proud to know that you've done more with your life than I ever did.'

Suddenly, and for no reason she could think of, she felt as though her heart would break. Perhaps it was the thought of her lost youth, or memories of a long ago love, or maybe it was just the way things had been and now were no more.

Katie had heard the regrets in Jenny's voice and went to her. Draping an arm round Jenny's shoulders, she pressed her face close to hers. She couldn't put right what had gone wrong with

Jenny's life, because she suspected there were things that Jenny had never divulged. But two things she could promise, and she did. 'If I have it in me to make a fine artist, then I'll work hard, I promise. And I'll always be on hand when you need me.'

An hour later, they emerged from the outhouse which had been their home for so long. At the bottom of the drive, Jenny turned and took a last look at the house. 'Funny thing,' she said to Katie. 'I thought when the time came I would be sorry to leave, but I'm not. Not really.' Katie didn't answer. She had her own thoughts, and they were of Alan.

'Off then, are you?' The policeman on watch at the gate reached out and took the key from Jenny's outstretched hand. 'Think on,' he reminded her. 'If you hear anything with regard to Mrs Hurd and the fellow who attacked you . . .'

'Don't worry,' Jenny interrupted, 'I haven't forgotten what the inspector said. But to be honest, I'm hoping I never clap eyes on the pair of 'em again. But I will keep in touch.'

'That's the thing.' He slipped the key into his pocket. 'If you ask me, they're miles away from these parts. I dare say it won't be long before we give up watch on this house, and I for one shan't be sorry.' He shivered. 'It's a lonely occupation this, and if it hadn't been for popping into your kitchen now and again and enjoying your wholesome cooking, I dare say I'd 'a gone right out of my mind.'

He wished them well and waved them away, and when they turned the bend in the lane, he shivered again and felt more lonely than ever.

# Chapter Nineteen

'By! It's a fine day for February.' The passer-by paused as he watched Frank lock the big old doors to his premises.

'You're right there,' he agreed. 'That's why I thought I'd leave early. There's not much joy in standing about waiting for work to come in. Saturdays are always quiet after the first rush, so I sent the lad away early and now I'm off home myself.'

'That's it. Take the missus out on the town, eh?' the man chuckled as he went on his way.

'The missus is half the reason I'm going home early,' Frank muttered after him. As he climbed into his car and began the journey to Jubilee Street, his face darkened.

Things had been going so well. His business was successful to bursting, and he had a healthy sum of hard-earned money sitting in the bank. With those considerable achievements, he should have been a contented man at heart. So what was wrong? Him and Doreen, that's what. They ought to have been the most contented couple in the town of Blackburn, but they weren't. 'And why not?' he asked himself now. 'What's gone wrong between me and Doreen?' He didn't know. All he did know was that they were growing apart, and there seemed nothing he could do about it.

Frank had looked into himself for the blame. God only knew

he still ached for Jenny, but apart from that he couldn't for the life of him think what he had done that could turn Doreen from him. 'I work hard, but I try not to let it take over my life,' he reminded himself. 'I don't keep my wife short of money, and we go out on a regular basis. We make love, we talk things through. I *believe* I'm a good husband, but at the same time I have to admit that, like any man, I'm far from perfect. If I was a better husband I might realise what was bothering her.'

He prayed Doreen had not sensed his love for another woman, though he was certain he had managed to keep all that from her. 'And if it isn't Jenny, *who* has come between us?' he asked himself loudly. Realising that he was talking to himself, he smiled ruefully. 'She's got you thinking out loud now. You'll have to watch it or they'll be coming to cart you off to the funny farm.'

Yet, try as he might, he couldn't fathom it. But there *was* something, and it was destroying the good relationship he and Doreen had built up over the years.

He knew what he had to do. He had to confront her. It stood to reason. If he could find no rational explanation for this growing uneasiness between them, he would have to ask her outright and hope she might confide in him.

At the back of his mind was the awful prospect that she really had sensed his longing for Jenny. Some women had an uncanny perception of such things.

Fifteen minutes later he edged the car into the kerbside on Jubilee Street. He got out and stretched himself to his full height, feeling as though he was about to face an inquisition. 'It's no good, Frank,' he told himself, 'things can't go on the same way or it'll drive you crazy. Get it all out in the open, that's the thing to do.' Oh, but how would he broach it? And what would she reply? He daren't even think about it, and he certainly mustn't let Jenny's image cloud his thoughts.

As he went towards the front door, he heard the raised voices and was unsure whether he should wait a moment before going in. The argument was between mother and son, and there were still times when he felt like an outsider with them. Doreen's getting the better of him in this one, that's for sure, he smiled. Though Rodney was still a big influence in his mother's life, lately he'd been made to know his place.

That was another curious thing, thought Frank. There was a time when that young man had all his own way but lately Doreen was asserting herself more and more where her son was concerned.

He wasn't sure whether to enter then or to wait until the voices died away. After all, he had always made a point of never coming between mother and son. Moreover, he had been hoping that Doreen would be on her own, because what he had to say was better said in private. There were things the two of them had to thrash out. 'Though now might not be a suitable time,' he wisely calculated.

Unsure, he half turned away, but then he remembered once before when he had turned his back at an important time in his life. The memory shamed him, yet at the same time strengthened his resolve.

Squaring his shoulders, he opened the door. Once a coward is once too often! he decided. And look what it had cost him. Determined now, he strode into the parlour and straight into the most unholy row.

Doreen was shocked to see him walk in on the argument. 'Frank!' she cried out, clapping her hand to her mouth. All eyes turned to stare at him. Suddenly the silence was deafening and Frank received the uneasy impression that *he* had been the subject of the row.

He looked from one to the other. His anxious gaze sought out the third person in the room. She was seated in the chair by the fireside, and though she was bent forward with her hands over her face, he recognised her as the town hall clerk, the lodger who had lived here before him.

Suddenly he knew that whatever had happened here had something to do with her. Little incidents came to mind. How ever since he first came to this house, the woman had somehow flitted in and out of their lives. A word here, a look there, her uninvited presence at the wedding, a certain undercurrent. Above all Rodney's intense dislike of her. And yet she remained an enigma, a shadow without substance.

He stared at the woman. She was obviously distressed. 'What's going on here?' His face was set like stone. He didn't understand. How could he? For no apparent reason, he believed that all of this had something to do with *him*.

Rodney glared at the woman in the chair. 'Ask her,' he snapped sullenly.

In that moment, Doreen went to the woman. 'She has nothing to answer for,' she told Frank, at the same time placing her hand protectively on the back of the other woman's chair.

'Oh?' Again he looked from one to the other. Rodney's face was downcast, his eyes bright with anger. He glared at his mother but she met his stare with dignity. The other woman was looking up at Doreen. Her eyes were red and sore from crying, and there was a certain vulnerability about her that touched Frank's heart.

At the sight of his mother clasping the other woman's hand in a comforting gesture, Rodney stormed out of the house, slamming the door behind him. 'And don't be surprised if I never come back!' he yelled.

In fact, Doreen was visibly relieved. 'I'm sorry about that, Frank,' she said. 'It was something and nothing.' All the same, she looked harassed and nervous.

The woman spoke then. 'I'd better go.' She rose from her seat and went slowly to the door.

'You will come back though?' Doreen asked anxiously. The

woman nodded, then turned away and was quickly gone.

Frank was puzzled. 'What in God's name has been going on here?'

Doreen smiled bravely. 'Like I said . . . something and nothing.' She knew the time must surely come when he would have to be told the truth. She might have told him then, but as so many times before her courage failed her. She would tell him tomorrow, or maybe the next day. Certainly before Rodney decided to take matters out of her hands.

Frank sensed her fear and it fired his curiosity. He had been shut out again. But this time it only made him all the more determined to bring matters to a head. 'Doreen?'

'Yes?' Believing that she had allayed his suspicions, she had been on her way into the kitchen to fill the kettle.

'Please . . . will you come and sit down?' He stood with his back to the fireplace, but when she returned to sit in the armchair, he began pacing up and down. 'I *know* there's something going on here . . . I've known for a long time, but I've never been able to put my finger on it.'

'No. You're imagining things. It was just Rodney and his temper, that's all. Nothing for you to concern yourself about.'

He stood before her a moment, then with a weary sigh sat down in the chair and looked directly into her face. 'Don't fob me off again, please,' he said wearily. 'I don't know what happened here, and maybe it's none of my business after all. But I do need to know whether it has anything to do with you and me.'

The colour drained from her face. 'What are you saying?'

'I'm saying that things haven't been right between us for some long time now. Why is that, Doreen? Is it something I've done? . . . Something I *haven't* done?' When her lips tightened and she turned away, he became angry. 'Damn and bugger it, Doreen! We have to talk. Can't you see, there's no point going on like this?' Still, she remained silent. '*Is* it my fault?' he insisted. 'Have I been such a bad husband?'

She peered up at him. 'No. I couldn't have wished for a better man.'

'Then what is it?'

There was a long agonising minute before she stood up, her gaze softer now as she looked at him. 'It isn't you,' she confessed. 'There are things I should have told you right from the start, but I'm a coward, you see. I let Rodney persuade me against my own instincts.' She paused, obviously in some distress. 'I don't know how to start,' she admitted.

'Go on, Doreen. I'm listening.' He thought she might have secret financial troubles, or maybe that woman was a distant relative who had shamed the family. Whatever it was, it couldn't be so terrible that the two of them wouldn't be able to deal with it.

He watched her pace up and down, agitatedly wringing her hands and slowly gathering the courage to tell him. Suddenly she stopped and looked into his anxious face. 'I should never have married you, Frank,' she said. 'I was the worst kind of fool.' Her voice was quiet, somehow accusing. It startled him.

'Go on,' he urged grimly.

'I should never have let you put this ring on my finger.' As she spoke, she twisted it until it slid off into the palm of her hand. Placing it on the arm of his chair, she went on quietly, 'I've tried so hard, Frank. I really wanted it to work, you have to believe that.' She turned away as though she couldn't bear his brown eyes looking at her guilty face. 'The woman who was here . . .'

'Yes?' He prepared himself for the telling of a dark family secret. But nothing could have prepared him for what came next.

'She's my lover.' Once the words were out, she felt as though a great weight had been lifted from her, yet she knew from the ensuing silence that it had been a terrible shock to him.

Filled with remorse but lighter of heart now, she waited for his reaction. When she turned round Frank was leaning forward in his chair, legs wide apart and fists clenched.

'Can you forgive me?' She couldn't find words to explain how sorry she really was.

He looked up then, an expression of utter disbelief and astonishment on his face. 'Your *lover*?' he asked. 'That woman is your *lover*?' He laughed, but it was a hollow sound. 'You mean to tell me that all the time you and I were . . . together, you . . . she . . . ?' He shook his head. His meaning was unmistakable.

'I'm sorry,' she murmured. 'We were lovers long before you came on the scene. But then Rodney found out. Like you he was shocked, but he was also mortified with shame. He bullied me beyond endurance, begging me to end it, so I sent her away.' As though to apologise, she went on, 'Rodney is my son, you see, and I love him. I'm all he's got in the world. When you came along, it made everything easy for him. It was his perfect opportunity to have a "proper" family again. And, to my discredit, I went along with it. Oh, it was easy. You were good and kind, a strong shoulder for both of us to lean on, and I grew to love you in a different kind of way, more than I thought I ever could.' She bowed her head to avoid his gaze. 'It was never real love though. It never could be. I foolishly believed I owed it to Rodney, to try and make a go of it, but I only succeeded in making myself increasingly unhappy. I knew in my heart it wouldn't work, and now I can only ask you to forgive me.'

Frank walked to the fireplace where he stared into the grate. He was shocked rigid at what he had just heard. Oh, he wasn't stupid. He knew how some people, men and women alike, sought affection from their own kind. It was as natural to them as it was unnatural to him. But Doreen! How could he not have known? But then, how was he supposed to know?

'Frank?' She could only imagine the thoughts running through his head.

It was a moment before he answered, and it was with a small laugh. 'What fools we all are,' he said cynically. 'We let others rule our lives against our better judgement, then we suffer all kinds of hell because of it.' He intimated that it was Rodney in his mind, when all the time he was thinking of Claudia. Drawing himself to his full height, he told her truthfully, 'I don't really know what to say to you.'

'You're shocked, aren't you?'

'Oh, I'm that all right.'

'Disgusted?'

'No.'

'Thank you for that. Do you forgive me?'

He thought of Jenny, and of his constant longing for her. 'There is nothing to forgive.'

'What now?'

'You tell me.'

She hesitated, but now the truth was out at last she had found a new kind of courage. 'Divorce.'

'If that's what you want.'

'Isn't it what *you* want?'

He didn't have to think. 'Yes. We can see a solicitor right away if you like.' Suddenly he wanted it over and done with. 'There's a tidy sum of money sitting in the bank, and of course I'll sell the business.' Strange how it didn't hurt him to say that. 'It should fetch a pretty penny, so I'll see you're well cared for.'

It was her turn to be shocked now. 'Surely you don't intend to sell your business? Oh, Frank, you've worked so hard to build it up.'

'Then I'll work hard again . . . somewhere else.'

'Will you leave the North?'

'Maybe.'

She remembered how at times he had seemed sad and lonely wandering the night, so deep in thought that he didn't even hear her when she spoke to him. 'Will you go to her?' she said tentatively. When he looked surprised, she went on, 'Find her Frank. Find the happiness you deserve. And let's hope we'll both be given a second chance.'

The initial shock had subsided now. He was composed once again. Reaching down, he kissed her tenderly on the forehead. 'You're a good woman, Doreen, and I won't forget you. Don't worry about Rodney,' he told her softly. 'He loves you too much to walk away.'

She didn't answer. Instead she put on her coat. 'Life is so short, Frank,' she said. 'And we all have to find true love where we can.' With that she went in search of her own happiness.

The following Monday they attended the solicitor's office. All he needed to know was that the marriage had irretrievably broken down, and that they each wished it terminated. 'It will take time,' he warned. But they were prepared for that.

Once the legalities were underway, Frank set about disposing of his business. The difficulty was in fighting off the many determined buyers. But he was favourably inclined towards the young man he had taken on as apprentice. 'I know you have it in you to make a fine blacksmith,' he told him. And as the young man's father was prepared to go in as a partner, the ongoing business and goodwill was eventually sold to them, lock, stock and barrel, for a handsome price.

Frank's next mission was to persuade Rodney to make it up with his mother. 'I'm not living in that house if *she's* going to be there!' he said sulkily, referring to the other woman.

'Then stay in lodgings,' Frank pointed out. 'You seem comfortable enough here in Richmond Street, but don't turn your back on your mam. She's been a good mother to you, and she thinks the world of you, son. It's not fair you should want to dictate what she should do with her life . . . any more than if she tried to dictate what you should do with yours.' He explained that he was leaving the area. They said their goodbyes, and then he left Rodney thinking on the wisdom of his words.

The following morning, Frank received a reply to his enquiries. The letter was from an estate agent in Woburn Sands. It told him that there *was* a house for sale in the area, but it was sadly neglected and in need of money spent on it. With the letter was a photograph, and when he saw it his heart soared with joy. 'Doreen was right after all,' he murmured, looking through misty eyes at the picture of that once grand old house. 'Happen I'm to be given a second chance after all.'

Soon he was packed and on his way. 'Take care of yourself,' Doreen told him. Beside her stood the friend she had almost lost for ever. 'I only wish Rodney would forgive me,' she said forlornly.

'Give it time,' Frank told her. 'He'll be back.'

And he was. As Frank turned the corner of the road, he glanced back to see Rodney coming in from the other end. He waited long enough to see mother and son reunited on the doorstep, and then he went on his way. Somewhere his Jenny was waiting, and he meant to find her. His footsteps instinctively turned Southwards, and he knew he was going home.

# Chapter Twenty

Katie was frustrated. 'We've been on the road for a year now . . . always moving from one place to another. Why won't they ever give us permanent work? We're clean, aren't we? We're strong and healthy. Surely they can't think we're scoundrels or thieves, so why won't anyone give us work?'

Coming off the footpath, she leaned against the wall which separated the lane from a field. 'It's just not fair,' she moaned, stooping to snatch a blade of grass that was peeping through a hole in the wall. 'All we want is some good honest work, and a place to call our own.' Catching the blade of grass between her strong white teeth, she absent-mindedly sucked at it, her tired eyes pleading with Jenny to explain.

'It's difficult right now,' she offered with a sigh. They had been walking all morning and now she was bone tired. 'It isn't because they think we're gonna steal the family silver, or run a knife through their hearts in the middle of the night.' Seeing Katie was determined not to go another step until she had been reassured, Jenny trudged back down the road. Leaning against the wall alongside her, she took a deep satisfying breath. 'By! It's beautiful here, ain't it, Katie?' she said, shaking her head at the wonder of it all.

Her bright blue eyes gazed down the tree-lined lane. Some

way off, two birds were either sparring or mating, and just now the sun was creating a speckled haze through the branches above them. Across the field two hares eyed them with blatant curiosity, leaping away on powerful legs when Jenny made a clicking noise at them.

Katie too loved nature in all its glory, but at that particular moment in time she had other, more urgent matters on her mind. 'If they can see we're not rogues, why do they always turn us away?'

'Because folks are having to count their pennies, that's why,' Jenny remarked impatiently. 'There's a depression creeping up on us, and there ain't the work to be had. We should just be thankful that we've had a run of four months in Hulcote House.'

'*They* didn't seem to be short of money,' argued Katie, 'but they still sent us on our way. I really liked it there. I thought we might get taken on permanently.'

'It isn't for us to question other folks' motives, and don't you ever forget that, my girl,' Jenny reminded her. 'I agree, it *was* a pleasant place, and it would have been nice to have stayed on a while longer, but it wasn't to be.'

'I don't think we'll ever get a place of our own, Jenny.' Katie's voice had dropped so low that Jenny could hardly hear. But Katie's face told the story, and it was a sad one.

'Aw, don't let it get you down,' Jenny coaxed. 'Houses come and houses go, and I dare say we'll trudge many a long mile before we're settled again, but it'll come right, you'll see. I promise you . . . it'll come right.'

It was Katie's turn to sigh. 'You *always* say that,' she protested, throwing away the mangled blade of grass and plucking another from the wall.

'But it *will* come right!' Jenny persisted. 'I can feel it in . . .'

'In your bones,' finished Katie. She smiled then, and Jenny smiled with her, and soon they were laughing out loud. 'I know

Josephine Cox

we'll find the right place,' spluttered Jenny, relieved that Katie's melancholy had subsided for the while. 'Just think, in a few weeks, maybe even days, there'll be you and me, sitting by our own fireside of an evening, and talking about the times we were a couple of tramps.'

'What am I going to do with you, eh?' Katie scolded. She never ceased to be amazed by Jenny's resilience. As always when she was in a sorry mood, Jenny had managed to coax her out of it.

Katie's words amused Jenny. 'Good God!' she exclaimed. 'You've started talking to me in the same way I used to talk to you when you were small. The tables have turned good and proper, eh? Now it's *you* talking to me as though *I* were the child.' She didn't know whether to be cross or pleased. It seemed that life on the road had made Katie grow up before her time.

There was a brief span of silence when the two of them lay against the wall, face turned to the sky, content to be lost for a while.

Presently Katie spoiled it all when she said, 'I do wish we could have stayed there longer, though.'

'Next time happen it'll be different,' Jenny encouraged. The moment was gone now, and she was ready to move on. 'Next time we might come lucky and get taken on permanent. We shall just have to see.' She pursed her lips in consternation before confessing worriedly, 'It's your schooling I'm concerned about, Katie. You just get settled before we have to move on again. It's a shame, that's what it is. But we'll make it up, don't you worry, my girl. Soon as ever we're settled permanent, we'll make it up.'

'*Why* don't you do what the lady suggested? She says the government have brought out a new law to help people who can't find work or a place to live.'

Jenny was adamant. 'That "lady" at Hulcote House lives in luxury. What would she know about such as you and me? Oh, she

394

were nice enough, but – well, folks like her live in a different world.' She snorted aloud. 'Anyway, I don't believe it,' she said coldly.

Determined to make her point, Katie opened the newspaper she was carrying. It was dated July 1932, and carried a long article on slum clearance and assistance for the needy. 'There! See?' She thrust the paper under Jenny's face. 'Read for yourself. It's just like that lady told us.'

Jenny took hold of the paper and glanced through it. 'Where did you get this?' she wanted to know.

'The children's governess gave it to me. She said we might find it useful.'

'And is it?'

'I don't know. She only gave it to me just before we left this morning, and I haven't had a chance to look at it yet.' Pressing the paper into Jenny's hands, she pointed again to the article. 'She did show me that especially, though.'

'Well, it won't do *us* no good,' Jenny declared, 'so you can put it out of your mind.' After folding the paper she squashed it into the top of her portmanteau; not knowing that if only she had looked at the very next page, she would have seen an advert placed by Frank Winfield for the purpose of discovering her whereabouts.

Jenny was eager to be on the move. 'Come on, we've a way to go before we come across civilisation,' she urged, taking up her bag and setting foot on the road once more.

Katie was soon walking alongside. 'How do you know it won't do us any good, if you don't try?'

'I know!' Jenny told her sharply. 'Because, so long as I've lived, there ain't never been a government to help the needy and there never will be, no matter what the papers tell us. As far back as I can recall, if you didn't have work nor no place to stay, you were thrown in the workhouse. Well, *we* ain't going to no workhouse, I can promise you that! Not while our backs are strong and we can turn our hands to a good day's work, and not while there's breath in my body.' Clutching her battered portmanteau, she quickened her steps until Katie was running to keep up.

'Wait then!' Katie couldn't see any reason to hurry.

'Come on,' Jenny replied. 'If we're to reach Woburn Sands before dark, we'd best get a move on.'

Shaking her head, but smiling all the same, Katie ran to catch up. 'Do you really think we'll find work in Woburn Sands?' she asked, exasperated.

'I wouldn't be taking us there if I didn't think it were worth a try.'

'But there aren't many big houses.'

'There's work at every turn if a body's prepared to look for it,' Jenny reminded her. 'There are smallholdings, and shops, there's a baker's, and if I remember rightly there was talk of building a school at the bottom of Weathercock Lane. Who knows, happen it's built. And schools need cleaning, don't they? Bakers make a mess and often a shopkeeper might have a room above his premises in exchange for a bit of cooking and cleaning. And God only knows how much muck and glory needs clearing up on a smallholding.'

'But why Woburn Sands?' Katie had been surprised when Jenny expressed a wish to visit the village.

'Because the chimney sweep at the big house told me about the school. He reckons they're looking for cleaners, and he also reckons there's a little house that goes with the job.' Jenny paused to gaze on Katie with a look of resignation. 'There! You've got it out of me, and I didn't want to say anything until I knew for sure. Now I expect you'll go and get your hopes up, only to have them dashed to the ground again.'

Katie wasn't listening. She was too full of what Jenny had just told her. 'Oh, Jenny! Won't it be lovely if we can have that little house, and work, and everything? Oh, Jenny!' Her eyes were big and round, and her smile was from ear to ear.

'Hey! I've just said, don't go getting your hopes up. The sweep might have got his facts all wrong, and he was merry on the port when I came across him in the cellar. As far as we know, the school may not even be built yet.'

'But what if he's right?' Katie wouldn't be satisfied until she had seen for herself. 'Hurry up. Oh, Jenny hurry up!' she called, going along the road and leaving Jenny trailing behind.

'Well, I'm glad to see you can shift when you've a mind to,' Jenny chuckled, pushing along until she caught up. 'All the same, don't get too excited, my girl, or you'll come down with a harder bump for your trouble.'

When they came up the hill from Aspley Guise and followed it down the other side into the village of Woburn Sands, Jenny was beset with all manner of emotions. 'By! It's a long time since we were here,' she muttered, pausing halfway down the hill to gaze at Katie. 'You were only a little thing then, and I were young and pretty.' She glanced down at her ragged shawl above boots that were covered in a film of dust, and she was mortally ashamed.

Katie looked at this woman whom she loved above all else, and her heart went out to her. It was true that this past year had taken its toll, but Jenny was still as lovely. Her pretty eyes were blue as ever, and her fair hair just as thick and bouncy. She still had that same trim figure, and in spite of everything she had never lost her sense of humour. She felt Jenny's reluctance and told her sincerely, 'We can always go to Ampthill if you've changed your mind.'

Jenny cast her a derisory glance. 'What! After coming all this way? So what if there are still folk here who used to know me?' she declared defiantly. 'The years have come up on them, same

397

as they've come up on me. And who knows? Happen I've weathered 'em better than most.'

'You're stubborn.'

'I'll not deny that. But I'm only stubborn when I'm in the right,' she announced grandly. 'And if there's work to be had here, then it's us who'll have it or my name's not Jenny Dickens!' With that she pressed on and Katie stepped out alongside her. The idea of a little house to live in and a place to work was enough to cheer both their weary hearts.

But there was no work to be had, and no 'little house' to live in. 'There *was* work here, but you're too late. I'm sorry, luv.' The caretaker leaned on his broom and cast a dismissive glance over their dusty clothes and tired faces.

'Are you sure?'

'The authorities looked at over a dozen folk, and the lucky ones have already been signed up.' He pointed down the road to a terraced house, where two men were taking articles off a horse-drawn wagon and carting them into the premises. 'Mrs Burton's been given the job of cleaning the school, and her old man's been made caretaker. I'm a stand-in here, and only this very morning, I was given orders to get back to my duties at Bletchley where I belong. So you see, there's no doubt about it. The jobs have already been given out.'

Jenny's heart sank to her boots, but she tried not to show her despair. 'Thank you very much,' she said, preparing to turn away. Katie's disappointment was written all over her face.

'Hold on a minute, luv!' The man stepped forward. 'Have you tried the big house?'

'Which big house?'

'The one on the road to Woburn,' he replied. The news had reached his ears only yesterday. 'Up 'til a month or so ago, the house was derelict . . . left empty and almost falling down, they said. But there's a new owner and, according to the postmistress, he's put an advert in the paper . . . wants domestics, he does.' He lifted his broom and showed her the way. 'Straight along that main road, luv. You can't miss it. Used to be a grand old house it did, when the Marshalls first had it.' He had heard the history concerning that place, and he had been curious enough to take a peep at it. 'Straight on,' he reminded her. 'Place by the name of Tall Gables, it is.'

Jenny thought her heart would stop. 'Tall Gables, you said?' She had to be sure.

He nodded. 'New owner . . . wants domestics,' he repeated confidently.

'Thank you.' Jenny turned away then. But to Katie's amazement, she set off in the opposite direction to that which the man had shown her.

When Katie asked her why, she was told, 'We don't need work at Tall Gables. We'll make our way to Ampthill, like you wanted.'

Katie followed her for a short way, until they were out of the man's hearing, and then she stopped. 'I think I can understand why you don't want to go there. But, please, Jenny. I'm so tired and my feet hurt. If there's work to be had here . . .'

Jenny stopped in her tracks, but she kept her face turned from Katie. 'I can't go there,' she said softly.

'I thought you said as long as we're together, we can do anything?'

Jenny swung round, about to argue. But the sight of Katie's worn boots, and one look from that beloved face that was silently pleading, and she was lost. 'All right, sweetheart,' she reluctantly conceded. 'Though we might be too late again, and even if we're not, I can't be sure how long we'll stay.' No longer than it would take to find another position, she promised herself.

She pushed the memories away and concentrated on other things: the work they might find, and a tub of hot water, and a wage at the end of the week. Most of all, she concentrated on Katie, and how there might still be an opportunity to send her to Art School.

Anything and everything filled her mind as she walked towards that house which had been so much a part of her past. But she wouldn't let herself be drawn down memory lane because even now there were things she dared not think about.

The house looked the same. A chimney was smoking and Jenny knew from experience that it was the chimney from the range in the big old kitchen. The two of them were standing at the bottom of the drive. Suddenly Jenny felt her courage falter and her legs go weak underneath her. 'Now that I'm here, I really don't know whether to turn tail and run,' she chuckled. 'Just look at me.' She began brushing herself down and the dust flew in all directions. 'They'll think it's a scarecrow turned up at the door, or a couple of beggars looking for a crust.'

Katie too seemed unsure now, and Jenny realised that she would have to be the strong one. 'But we're here now, and we'll do what we came for,' she declared, going at a quickened pace down the drive and round to the back of the house. Encouraged, Katie followed. In truth it was an ordeal for them both.

While Jenny knocked on the door, Katie wandered towards the big barn. Deep inside a man was bent over his work, sawing wood at a trestle. He didn't notice her at first, but when she politely coughed, he turned his head and saw her there. 'Is there something you want, young lady?' he enquired, coming forward out of the gloom. Frank Winfield had seen so many people since he put the advert in the paper, but none of them was Jenny and he had made all manner of excuses to send them on their way.

'We were told you needed domestics,' Katie explained as he approached.

Frank's big frame filled the doorway. His smile was bright as he looked at her, but then he was taken aback by what he saw. His stricken gaze went from her thick auburn hair to those vivid green eyes, and he thought he was looking at a ghost. '*Elizabeth Marshall!*' The name was out of his mouth before he could check it.

He raised his eyes at a sudden movement beyond, and was dealt another blow. This time he appeared to stumble as he stared disbelievingly at the small figure coming towards him. Even as Katie regarded him with growing curiosity, the tears ran unheeded down his face. 'God Almighty, it's Jenny!' he cried.

Suddenly he was running. 'JENNY! DEAR GOD . . . IT'S REALLY YOU!' At the sound of his voice, and seeing this man whom she had believed to be a stranger running towards her, Jenny was struck dumb to recognise Frank. She dropped her portmanteau and stared at him, so deeply shocked that she couldn't move.

In the space of a heartbeat she was swept off her feet and he was burying his head in her neck, his tears wet against her face. Then she was crying with him. Now they were laughing, hysterical with joy at having found each other at last. 'I knew you'd come,' he cried. 'I knew if I put that advert in the paper, it would draw you here. This house is mine now . . . yours and mine. Oh, Jenny, my lovely Jenny.'

Katie watched in disbelief. Yet in her heart she knew that here was the man Jenny had spoken of. The man who had stolen her heart many years before. And now they were together, and so moving was the reunion that she cried with them. How could she know that this man was her own father, and that the reunion would be joyous twice over?

Breathless and caught up in a whirl of emotion, Jenny was finally put to her feet. 'What did you mean . . . when you said the advert would draw me here?' she asked. There was oh so much more she wanted to ask, but her joy was spilling over so that she could hardly think.

He was surprised. 'You mean, you didn't see it?'

She shook her head and he laughed aloud. 'Then it was destiny that brought you here,' he told her softly. 'Don't you see, Jenny? After all these years, we were meant to be together.'

'I've missed you,' she whispered. She and her man looked at each other, and their hearts said it all. 'There's someone I want you to meet,' Jenny said softly, holding out her arms to the girl who ran to her. 'Katie,' she murmured, 'you remember I told you about your father . . . that he was a good man who didn't know of your existence?' She joined Katie's hand with Frank's and it was the most natural thing in the world. 'This is Frank Winfield,' she said softly. '*Your father*.' And the wonder in both their faces was the greatest joy to her.

Together they went into the house, three people whose lives were inextricably entwined. Three loving souls separated for so long by the cruel hand of Fate. There were so many questions to be asked. So much to know. But for now it didn't matter too much because they were together. And life was worth living.

Jenny had never been so happy. One year to the day since she and Katie had returned to the house in Woburn Sands, here she was, seated on the bench in the orchard, with Frank beside her. Open on her lap was the letter she had just read, and now her joy was complete. 'How long will it take before it's all finalised?' she wanted to know.

'The solicitor reckons I'll be a free man before the month is out. Divorce is not an easy thing. It's been a hard task, but now it's all over bar the shouting.' He kissed her on the mouth and reached into his pocket. Taking out a small white envelope, he teased, 'Thought I'd save this 'til last. It looks like our Katie's writing.'

Dear Jenny and Dad,

I love it here, although I do miss you both. Everything is just as I hoped it would be, and I'm working very hard towards my exams.

If I pass these early ones, I've been assured of a place next year. Miss Laing says I'm very talented, and that I have a promising future to look forward to.

There's something else too. I'll be home on Friday and tell you all about it.

Lots of love,
Katie.

'Hmh!' Jenny carefully folded the letter. 'What's this "something else",' she wondered aloud.

'We'll soon find out. Today's Wednesday and she'll be home before you know it.' He studied Jenny's lovely face, always captivated by its girlish beauty. 'I still can't believe we found each other again. I wake up in the morning and I'm terrified that you won't be there. When I came back and found this house derelict, I knew it was waiting for you and me. Thank God I'd saved a handsome wad of cash. The business brought a pretty penny, and even after seeing Doreen all right, and making the down payment on this place, there's still enough to tide us over until I set up in business again.'

Bad dreams die hard, he thought, sliding his arms round her. He pressed her to him. 'I know this much, sweetheart, I won't ever let you go again.'

Jenny too had not forgotten how it was without him. 'We shouldn't dwell on the past,' she chided lovingly. 'We've been given a second chance and that's all that matters now.'

As they returned to the house, she remarked thoughtfully, 'Strange, isn't it . . . that Claudia and her accomplice were never found?'

'Huh! Gone to the devil the pair of 'em, I shouldn't wonder.' And he didn't know how right he was.

Jenny chose not to comment. Even the mention of Claudia's name had sent shivers down her spine. 'Can't wait for Friday to come,' she said. 'And Katie.'

'Now don't you start worrying about what she's up to. The girl has a sensible head on her shoulders.' He gave the same handsome winning smile that she had always adored. 'Takes after her dad, she does.' His smile became a frown when he added quietly, 'All the same, she has summat to tell us and, like you, I can't help but wonder what it is.' He gazed down at her as she passed him at the doorway. 'Never did like secrets,' he said. When Jenny merely smiled coyly, he thought she had never looked more beautiful.

Friday came soon enough, and with it came Katie. Frank had just finished shoeing the milkman's horse when she came running up the drive. 'Come in,' she called. 'Hurry up! I want to show you something.'

When all the embracing and greeting was over, and all the urgent questions answered, she told them, 'My results should be here in Monday's post.' And then she told them something else. 'I've heard from Alan.'

'What . . . Alan Hurd?' Jenny's blue eyes lit up. 'Oh, Katie, I'm glad. I really am.'

Frank recalled what Jenny had told him about these two young people, and a promise once made. 'I thought he wasn't going to contact you until you were sixteen?' he asked with just a glimmer of mischief.

Katie was unrepentant. 'Well, he's changed his mind. At long last, Aunt Helen thought he should know all about what's been going on. She wrote to him and he wrote to me.'

'Oh?' Frank counted himself the luckiest man on God's earth

to have two such lovely creatures about him. 'And what's he say?'

'I'm not telling you. It's private,' she teased. With that she went up to her room, leaving Frank and Jenny with a warm glow and the feeling that Katie was a little woman now.

Monday morning brought the results, and it was as Katie's teacher had forecast. 'I'VE PASSED!' She had ripped open the letter and was dancing round the room.

Frank told them to: 'Put on your best bib and tucker because we're going out tonight to celebrate.'

That evening Jenny looked lovelier than she had ever done. 'Blooming gorgeous!' Frank told her with pride. They climbed into the car and drove to the Swan Inn in the nearby village of Salford, where Frank had booked a table.

'Heard the news, have yer?' asked the portly landlord. His eyes popped with horror and astonishment as he relayed what he had just read in the evening paper. 'Fair shook me, I can tell you,' he muttered, putting a menu before each one. 'And to think he used to come into this very pub . . . bit of a drinker he was.'

'Who's this we're talking about?' Frank perused the menu, occasionally smiling at Jenny and loving her the more with every minute.

'The coalman as used to deliver up and down these parts, you remember . . . a fella by the name o' Bill Saxon?' He winked. 'Friendly with that Claudia Marshall, he was, the same lady as used to own the very house you live in.' His face lengthened as he went on in more sombre tones, 'Hanged himself out Cambridge way . . . found him in an old barn, they did. An' if that weren't bad enough, they discovered a letter in his pocket, and from what it told the authorities, they were sent searching in a cellar not far away from where he was.'

Now that he had the attention of all three, he went on in an awed whisper, 'Been there some time by all accounts, she had.

Josephine Cox

Decomposed, she were, but there must have been enough left for them to identify her as none other than Claudia Marshall.' He made the sign of the cross on himself. 'God help us all.'

Jenny found herself murmuring her name. 'Claudia? Both dead?' It was too horrific to contemplate and yet didn't they deserve such a fate? After all, hadn't they taken the lives of others without even the slightest compassion? All the same, it was a terrible end.

'All right, are you, sweetheart?' Frank had seen the colour drain from her face, and cursed the fellow for being so unfeeling.

'I'm fine,' she said, composing herself. She looked at Frank, and then she looked at Katie, and she vowed that the girl would never know from her who her mother was. Thankfully, no one in the village had linked Katie with Claudia, mainly because the older inhabitants had either moved away or passed on, and over the years there had been a new influx of residents. Added to which, Katie had not been at the big house long, before she had gone away to Art School.

'Katie's told us her secret,' she said. 'Now I'll tell you mine.' Putting out both her hands, she touched one against Frank's and the other against Katie's. 'I've been waiting for the news that me and Frank are free to wed, and it will have to be as soon as possible.' She smiled and her beauty was radiant. 'Because now there's someone else to consider.'

'Someone else?' Frank and Katie didn't fully understand at first. But then they saw how Jenny's pretty blue eyes twinkled, and they knew at once. Ecstatic, Frank rounded the table and clasped her in his arms. 'I promise you our baby won't be born without a proper name,' he whispered in her ear, and she knew it would be so.

Jubilant, he summoned the waiter. 'Your best wine!' he called out. 'We've a baby's head to wet!' Then they were all laughing at once, and other guests were calling out their congratulations, and when Frank took Jenny in his arms and swept her to him, a cheer went up and the landlord got carried away and declared that the wine was: 'On the house!'

Later that night Jenny stood by her window, looking out at the stars and thanking the good Lord for what he had brought her. 'I'm content now,' she said. 'And I know in my heart that in the precious time they have, Katie and Alan will grow together because young though they are, like me and Frank they have something very special to see them through the coming years. Thank you, Lord, for bringing us all safely home.'

For the first time, the child moved inside her. Gently spreading her palms over that tiny mound, she turned to look at Frank's sleeping form. 'What more could any woman ask for?' she murmured. And back came her own answer. Nothing at all, because she had everything she had ever wanted. The suffering was behind them now, and only the good things lay ahead. Her mind fled back over the years and she recalled something Claudia had said to her and the girl. Then, it had made her sad. Now, it only made her smile.

Turning her face once more to the skies she asked humbly, 'In one way or another, aren't we *all* born to serve?' Then she climbed back into bed and snuggled up to her man.

Life was good after all.